The Morrow Secrets

Trilogy

Book Two

Published by Sweet Cherry Publishing Limited
Unit 36, Vulcan House,
Vulcan Road,
Leicester, LE5 3EF
United Kingdom

First published in the UK in 2014
2019 edition

2 4 6 8 10 9 7 5 3

ISBN: 978-1-78226-292-3

© Susan McNally

The Shadow of The Swarm

Illustrations by Luke Spooner, Carrion House

www.sweetcherrypublishing.com

Printed and bound in India
I.TP002

*'They who dream by day are cognizant of many things
which escape those who dream only by night.'*

Edgar Allan Poe - *Eleonora*

The Shadow of The Swarm

One

Deep down, way beneath the criss-cross of murky passageways, through the stone-cold depths of the monstrous castle, past the ancient slices of jet-black rock and jagged fortifications, past the hallowed halls and sumptuous palaces, the wily Shroves slumber on, dreaming of trickery, plots and intrigue, buried in their Shrove holes, huddled in their heaving mounds against the grinding cold, waiting for the morning to arrive. High up above them, enthroned in their dark towers, locked in their sinister pact, the Morrow Swarm work their evil magic, their sinister deeds dripping like poison through the enormous castle, swirling snake-like into the core of Hellstone Tors, ensnaring all who tarry in the evil clutches of the old curse, entangled into the darkest spell of them all.

*

Embellsed rubbed his sleep-filled eyes, yawned nosily and smacked his slimy lips in the chilliness of the mouse-grey dawn. His narrow home was an unkempt Shrove hole buried deep into the dark stone bowels of Hellstone Tors, littered with the remnants of half-eaten kitchen scraps, crammed high with piles of old clothes and broken, unwanted paraphernalia. The dingy hole stored all the Shrove's treasures, hidden into the cracks and crevasses at the back of his lair, stolen from the castle and secreted away over the years. For Embellsed was a bit of a thief and an inveterate hoarder.

Hunched in the corner of his messy home, the Shrove stretched his stiff limbs and unwrapped his body from the heap of tattered blankets. His beady eyes, now accustomed to the seeping gloom, alighted on last night's pickings and he munched on a brown spotted apple, musing about the doings of the day ahead. Embellsed hurriedly dressed himself in an assortment of washed-out garments that he fastened against the deadening cold, fumbling awkwardly with the broken buttons with his spindly fingers. Cursing under his breath, he plastered down his wiry hair with a dollop of kitchen grease and rubbed his face with a stinking rag. Now the Shrove was ready to face the day.

As the early morning stirrings trickled from the adjacent Shrove holes, Embellsed cocked his ears and inched towards the edge of his burrow, listening intently. It was at this time of day that he overheard the latest gossip as the Shroves gobbled their breakfast in the central eating parlour and tittle-tattled about the goings-on in the enormous castle. That morning their incessant prattle focussed on the arrival of the girl in the high tower and the rumours that were circulating in Hellstone Tors about her forthcoming initiation ceremony into the Morrow Swarm.

'But who is she?' asked a silver-haired Shrove, licking his jammy fingers. 'Where does she come from?'

They clustered round a fresh-faced Shrove who beckoned eagerly to them.

'I 'eard she's from Winderling Spires and she's going to become one o' them,' he answered darkly.

Embellsed rubbed his hands together and his twisted lips smiled wickedly as he listened to their inane chatter. He was privy to more than their idle gossip. He had been appointed as Tallitha's Shrove-Marker: her guard and her jailor, the one who would accompany the girl whenever she was allowed out into the labyrinthine castle. His job was to ensure that she kept to the well-trodden corridors and staircases, never letting her stray into the darker, more remote corners of the towering castle. For Hellstone Tors was a house of treachery where the wickedness of the past had leeched into the fabric of the building and had soaked, bloodstained, into its steely core.

To the villagers and Grovellers, the castle was legendary and likened in local folklore to a voracious beast with a devilish appetite for preying on lost souls, leading them into the darkest, most secluded places, never to return. So it wouldn't do for Tallitha to go missing or to stray too close to the where the ancient secrets of the Morrow Swarm were stored at the top of the Darkling Stairs. The girl was a great prize and Embellsed's reputation, as well as his advancement to the highest echelons of Shrovedom, depended on keeping her close and the rest of the Shroves at bay.

The horde of breakfasting Shroves stopped babbling as the Shrove-Marker shuffled to the edge of his burrow and swung his spindly legs over the side, slyly observing the goings-on in the noisy feeding parlour. Embellsed relished the envious attention of the other Shroves and played up to his audience, munching on the last stringy bits of the apple core and spitting the pips in a spraying arc out of his Shrove hole. They landed on the earthy floor of the main burrow with a revolting yellow splat.

'Mornin', Master Embellsed. 'Any news about the new arrival upstairs?' asked the fresh-faced Shrove, winking at the others. He jerked his head in the direction of the castle. 'About that strange girl from Wycham Elva?'

Embellsed fixed his beady eyes on the errant youngster.

'You mind your business, feller-me-lad, and I'll mind mine. You best not be mentionin' *that girl* if you know what's good for ye,' he snarled, 'the Swarm will have your guts for garters if they hear you speaking that way.'

The cheek of the whippersnapper! He'd not get far in Hellstone Tors with that forward manner. Grovelling, snitching and the painstaking art of eavesdropping were the proper methods to be used by any self-respecting Shrove on the hunt for gossip.

Embellsed climbed out of his Shrove hole, inched down the rickety ladder and mumbled a half-hearted greeting to

10

the assembled party as he skittled past them. He would not be bothered with the likes of them and would tell them nothing. Shroves were secretive by nature and unless they were bonded through kinship, the older Shroves turned into lonesome creatures and, like cats, much preferred their own company. So he snuck past their eager shrovish faces and slipped out of the main burrow to commence his morning duties.

The Shroves at Hellstone Tors were corralled into a tangled maze of tunnels and burrows sunk into the darkest depths of the castle bedrock, way beneath the rat-infested fruit stores and the expanse of chilly wine cellars. Each day, Embellsed's arduous journey up to the castle required a series of intricate manoeuvres and a certain amount of wriggling through the web of winding tunnels that nestled way beneath the Tors, coming out at the back of the warm, busy kitchens. That morning the Shrove crawled through the chilly tunnels illuminated by flickering candles until he reached the warmer runs that came out behind the huge smouldering ovens. The yeasty aroma of freshly baked bread and fried bacon greeted his nostrils as he snatched a warm steaming loaf from the hob. He munched on the delicious golden crust and buried his nose in the soft, warm dough as he scurried from the kitchen and darted out into the noisy, heaving thoroughfare.

The servants' dungeonesque passageways were throbbing with the smell of unwashed Shroves and scabby serfs, all scuttling madly across the stone-flagged floors as the dull clang of the morning bells heralded the beginning of their daily

11

toil in Hellstone Tors. Embellsed hurried through the dismal passageways and presented himself at the servants' noticeboard, jostling with the crush of worn-out serfs who were scrabbling for position in order to locate their daily orders. The Shrove-Marker picked up his list of tasks that had been posted by Bludroot, the Thane's High Shrove, the evening before, scratched his head and grumbled.

'I'll be blithered,' he muttered. 'Too many jobs for me to do – poor me! Do this for t'girl, do that for t'girl, and take her … where? Damn and blast it,' he cursed, his miserable face frowning. 'I'll be jiggered by end of t'day.'

He swallowed hard and his eyes flickered nervously at the towering expanse of castle that wound its way ominously above him and at the precarious climb that would inevitably exhaust him. Sighing bitterly, he made his way to join the queue of babbling Shroves standing in line to clamber up the insubstantial servants' staircases that spanned the castle walls. Muttering seething oaths under his breath, Embellsed began the long, hard climb up the narrow flight of '*late*' stairs, the servants' dangerous thoroughfare through the castle. He clambered up flight after precarious flight chiselled from the bones of the castle and winding up through the endless floors like brittle spines until at last he reached his destination, one of the highest of the servant's platforms in a remote northern tower.

He wiped his sweaty brow, his chest heaving with the strain and looked back down the tricky ascent he had just made. A million dust motes floated in the air as the morning sunlight filtered down the heartless shaft revealing a plethora of floors as far as his tired eyes could see. He hated this part of his job the most, dangerously traversing the castle in secret so as not to be a bother to his masters and mistresses. The late stairs were a deathtrap and over the years many unsure-footed Shroves had stumbled to their deaths, slipping from the lath-wood steps, howling in vain and falling into a grisly heap at the bottom. But Shroves were ten a penny in Hellstone Tors. Embellsed had no alternative but to swallow his fear and to do the Swarm's bidding.

He felt for the key in his pocket and began shuffling along the dark corridor that twisted to the top of the northern tower and up to the grand entrance of Tallitha's apartment. The Shrove-Marker turned the key in the lock and the heavy oak door, carved with an intricate motif of flapping ravens, opened with the softest of clicks.

Tallitha's apartment was located in one of the highest and most secluded of the northern towers and adjoined her brother's suite of rooms. The children slept soundly as the Shrove sneaked about in the dull morning light, picking up Tallitha's possessions, rubbing them against his nose and smelling all the fresh scents in the darkened room. Embellsed was swift to notice any change – any unknown presence or unwanted whiff of danger. He was renowned for his acute olfactory abilities, smelling in an instant any scent of trouble and reporting it to Bludroot at the earliest opportunity. Perhaps that's why they had made him the Shrove-Marker, because of his loyalty to Bludroot and because he was an expert sniffer-out of danger and intrigue.

That morning, everything remained as he had left it when he had locked the children up the previous night. The Shrove scuttled up to the four-poster bed, roughly parted the velvet curtains and shook the girl awake. Tallitha moaned and blinked sleepily at the Shrove's weaselly face looming over her in the grey morning light, his open mouth bearing a set of stained, yellow teeth. It took her a second or two to remember where she was and then her stomach lurched with painful recognition at the gloomy surroundings that confronted her.

'Time you shaped yerself,' Embellsed growled, wiping the saliva from his lips. 'That lazy boy an' all. I'll be back presently, so get dressed.'

Tallitha stirred, peered out from underneath the quilt, and watched as the gangly creature ambled stiffly from her room and began ordering her sleepy brother out of bed.

'Mean old toad,' she whispered under her breath. 'Just like the infernal Marlin.'

She slipped from under the sheets, dressed quickly and stood by the bay of arched windows, fastening her shirt and gazing down at the sheer expanse of dark unwelcoming castle that tumbled away beneath her. Block upon block of dark grey granite intermingled with clusters of pointed pewter turrets, and a myriad of burnished copper towers erupted out of the Tors like sharp teeth in a jagged hungry mouth.

'You know it's hopeless, Sis,' said Tyaas softly, coming up and standing next to her. 'There's no way out.'

Tallitha turned quickly, her eyes darting towards the doorway.

'Where's that Shrove?' she asked.

'He's gone to get breakfast,' Tyaas replied, gazing down at the impossibly high view.

Tallitha had spent hours scanning the castle walls for any means of escape. She had noted all the grikes and crevasses as far as her eyes could see, but the most northern tower was much too high to abseil down, and in any event the windows were securely barred with heavy iron grills.

'But we have to get out of here,' she whispered desperately.

'Not that way,' he replied.

She sighed and wrapped her arm around her brother for comfort.

'There are far too many Groats down there and there's no means of escape from up here,' said Tyaas. 'Besides, Mother has that Shrove watching us at all times.'

Far below, stationed along the high battlements, an army of Groats stood to attention, guarding every exit from the castle. But Tallitha's determination to flee their captors remained undaunted.

'We must get out of this grim castle,' she whispered. 'I know we'll find a way, but first we must discover where they've taken Essie.'

Since that dreadful day in the gallery when they had been separated from Esmerelda, Tallitha's preoccupation had been focussed on finding their cousin and escaping from Hellstone Tors. The thought of what had happened to Essie after the Groats had dragged her away struck a chill in Tallitha's heart, but each night, try as she might to make contact with Esmerelda, her telepathic powers evaded her. She was nervous, fearful of every shadow in the sinister castle, and without her magic touchstone Essie, the one who enabled her to access the shadow-flight, it seemed that Tallitha's powers had grown cold.

Behind them, the floorboards creaked and they turned to see Embellsed wringing his hands and worming his way towards them. His eyes glinted with wicked pleasure as he made his announcement.

'After you've supped I'm takin' you to meet your new governess, the Mistress Flight, in the Withered Tower,' he barked.

'Governess! I don't need one of them,' Tallitha snapped, flashing her eyes at Embellsed.

'Yes you do, missy – she'll be takin' you through The Black Pages,' he chuckled. 'You've important tests to do.'

'Tests?' she asked hesitantly. 'What tests?'

'She's preparin' you to be sworn,' he answered menacingly.

A look of anguish flitted over Tallitha's face. She had already been warned about the governess – the evil Caedryl had seen to that. Sedentia Flight had been summoned to instruct Tallitha in the history and arcane ways of the Morrow Swarm, but Tallitha was desperate to avoid the meeting. It was one step closer to her initiation ceremony with the Swarm.

The children exchanged stolen glances while Croop, a young Shrove, arrived with their breakfast, presenting them with poached eggs and toast from a silver platter. Tallitha had been dreading the dawning of the day, waking fitfully during the night from torrid dreams where the Black Hounds were chasing her through the forest once more. She cried out for Ruker to rescue her and for dear Cissie to comfort her, but it was only a dream and no one came to her aid as she fled through Ragging Brows Forest with the Black Hounds snapping at her heels. Tallitha shivered momentarily as though someone had just walked over her grave.

'I had a bad dream, a hideous nightmare,' she whispered miserably to Tyaas. 'I dreamt that I was fleeing down endless dark passageways. I dreamt of the Skinks and of dear Cissie.'

The Shrove cut her dead.

'Hush your chatter,' he grizzled, standing much too close to her, chivvying her on. 'Hurry up, girl – the Mistress will not be kept waiting!'

The odious toad needled away at her all through breakfast.

'Where are we going?' she asked, imperiously dabbing her mouth.

'I've told thee all tha' needs to know – now stop your noise!'

He passed the dirty dishes to Croop.

'You stay put,' grumbled Embellsed, throwing a sidelong glance at Tyaas.

His shrovish face broke into a sinister smile as he turned on Tallitha.

'You, missy, must follow me,' he said sharply, mincing towards the door. 'And be warned, keep to the middle of the corridors where I can see thee and never mind sneaking off into the shadows.'

At that moment, the door to Tallitha's apartment burst open and three unwelcome visitors barged inside, accompanied by a sheep-faced, bug-eyed Shrove who skittled in behind them. All three Shroves stood their ground, their beady eyes darting suspiciously from one to another, fiercely protecting their space.

'We've come to see Tallitha off,' Caedryl announced, flouncing into the room as though she owned the place. 'I do hope you're ready to face the Mistress Flight,' she added sarcastically.

Caedryl was dressed in her stiff funereal clothes with the bloodstone – earth-green and deep blood-red – fastened at her throat. She seemed to rejoice in her sombre attire, wearing the clothes as a warning to anyone who dared get too close to her.

'B-But I don't want to go,' Tallitha replied, desperate at her plight.

The visitors sniggered at her naivety.

'Oh diddums,' the three chorused nastily.

Since Tallitha's arrival in Hellstone Tors, Caedryl had taken every opportunity to poke fun at her newly found cousins and encouraged other family members to take a peek at the strange new additions to the Morrow family. To Tallitha, it was like being in a curiosity show at the circus.

Caedryl was accompanied by the Morrow twins, Lapis and Muprid. In stark contrast to the darkly clad Caedryl, the vain daughters of Lord Edweard, the Thane's brother, were resplendently dressed. The three horrors stared at Tallitha, smirking and whispering nasty comments behind their hands.

Caedryl flicked her bright green eyes at the twins. She pursed her lips in a nasty sneer.

'Now you've seen her, do you think she's pretty? I've never been able to quite make up my mind,' she mused.

The twins ran their cold eyes over Tallitha, assessing her demeanour and deciding whether she would pose any threat to their position at court.

'She looks untidy,' pouted Muprid, 'and she's a little pale. Her skin could do with some attention.'

Lapis joined in the general prodding and poking of their cousin. She ran her nasty little fingers all over Tallitha's hair as though it was infested with lice.

'Her hair is a mess,' added Lapis viciously, 'and her nails are bitten.'

'Stop that!' shouted Tallitha, pulling away from their invasive hands. 'Leave me alone!'

The flaxen-haired twins were like two rotten peas in a bright pea-pod: pretty on the outside and horribly nasty in the centre. They had powdered pink cheeks, arched black eyebrows and impossibly ruby-red lips. Muprid's hair was braided in thick golden plaits that sat in a twisted crown across the top of her head. She wore a blueberry-coloured riding habit that reflected her ice-blue eyes. Lapis had waist length blonde corkscrew curls, and was dressed in a sumptuous beetroot-coloured robe. They were accompanied by their sheep-faced Shrove, Wince, whose eyes were disconcertingly off-centre. He stared at Tallitha and mouthed unkind words about her appearance behind his twitching fingers. Muprid giggled thoughtlessly while Lapis gave Wince a sharp kick for him to be silent.

'Mind your place, boggle-eyes,' she spat in the Shrove's face. 'She's to be sworn, after all.'

The twins floated about Tallitha's apartment, making disparaging comments.

'You can't possibly wear this old thing,' exclaimed Lapis, inspecting one of Tallitha's dresses.

'What about these ghastly, baggy trousers?' added Muprid, giggling.

Meanwhile Caedryl took delight in unsettling Tallitha with stories about Sedentia Flight's formidable reputation.

'The Mistress Flight has exacting expectations of her students,' she persisted, her emerald eyes flashing with spite. 'The tests from The Black Pages are difficult, especially for someone who isn't practiced in the ways of the Swarm – a little bit like you, Tallitha,' she teased. 'Of course, I was her favourite.'

'That's a lie!' Lapis squeaked, sticking her tongue out at Caedryl. 'Isn't it, Muprid?'

'She liked us too!' replied Muprid petulantly.

Caedryl threw the twins a spiteful glance that would have turned milk sour. Tallitha was appalled at her vain, self-centred cousins, battling it out with each other for superiority. There was not a scintilla of kindness amongst them. Caedryl was a sneak, and although she spoke as though butter would not melt in her not-so-sweet little mouth, her words were always barbed with animosity, whereas the twins were as bitter as bark and as thick as thieves.

'Stop daydreamin' and shape yersen,' Embellsed shouted at Tallitha, who was agog at the haughty trio.

The twins flashed their annoyance at Embellsed. He had interrupted their sport with Tallitha and they were put out.

'Remember Tallitha, if you don't concentrate, the Mistress Flight will be cross with you and will be sure to tell the Thane,' simpered Caedryl.

'While you're away we've a mind to keep your little brother company,' added Muprid, stroking Tyaas's untidy mop of hair.

At this curious turn of events, Tyaas looked as though he might burst a blood vessel and pulled away from the clawing hands of his cousin.

'I have things to do … with M-Mother,' he stammered, desperate to avoid the twins' unwanted attention.

Tyaas was upset at being left behind to endure the advances of these dreadful creatures while Tallitha went off to meet new and fascinating people, even if it was a weird old governess. The spiteful twins fluttered their eyelashes at Tyaas and made coo-cooing noises. Tyaas thought they looked like two sickly calves, mooning and making doleful eyes at him.

'Now don't be so prickly, cousin,' said Lapis, slipping her arm round his waist. 'We only want to get to know you better – don't we, Muprid?'

'You can tell us all your little secrets when your sister has gone,' added Muprid.

Tallitha pulled Tyaas to one side, kissed him on the cheek and whispered: 'They're just teasing you, ignore them.'

But he wasn't convinced.

'Touchingly sweet,' crooned Caedryl, observing the twins' antics. 'But I haven't time to waste on sullen little boys,' she sneered, 'I have important matters that I must attend to.'

The haughty threesome turned on their heels, their heads locked together in conspiratorial wickedness and muttering cruel comments to one another under their breath. Caedryl turned one last time and her green eyes darted towards her cousin.

'I'll be watching you,' she called mysteriously, mincing down the landing with her head held high in the air.

What does she mean by that? thought Tallitha.

She squeezed Tyaas's hand to comfort the sulky boy, but he pulled away in a fug of resentment. He would get over it. So she blew him a kiss farewell and reluctantly followed the grousing Shrove out of her apartment, across the grand chilly landings, down the dark winding staircases and along the unwelcoming corridors, knowing that with each step she was being taken further and deeper into the heart of the dark, old castle.

Two

The vast shadowy landings and gloomy corridors of Hellstone Tors made Tallitha's heart sink. She felt quite small, dwarfed by the castle's ominous presence and hopelessly lost. On and on she went, trailing after the grumbling Shrove and trying her best to keep up with him as he scuttled down the twisting passageways, barking commands over his shoulder. There was so much to learn about her unwelcoming home that Tallitha kept stopping to peer over the ornate balustrades at the many floors disappearing way beneath her, at once fascinated and repelled by the labyrinthine castle. Embellsed hopped about, changing direction, leading her this way and that, but Tallitha was used to the wily ways of a Shrove. She suspected that Embellsed was taking her on an unnecessarily complicated route, doubling back on himself in order to confuse her.

Tallitha's tiny footsteps echoed down the cavernous hallways as she stared upwards at the vaulted ceilings, decorated in the royal colours of gold, purple and crimson, and festooned with tattered battle flags and grand heraldic crests. High up on the panelled walls, gloomy portraits of her long dead ancestors hung side by side, their sorrowful dark-eyed Morrow features and pale white faces captured for eternity in the dismal art. Tallitha stared in awe at their sinister faces, the haunting relics of a time gone by, and read their names out loud as she dawdled past each painting.

'This strange fellow, Tollister Morrow, has extremely bushy eyebrows and a particularly glum face. He's standing with his hatchet-faced wife called Brimwell,' she announced, hoping to attract Embellsed's attention and prise as much information as possible from him. But the old weasel remained as tight as a clam. 'Here's another portrait of an odd bod called Gravelock Morrow,' she laughed, 'he has a black patch over one eye and is sitting next to his wife, Arcadia Morrow, with her long nose and pinched expression. She has the look of a poisonous rattlesnake. Do tell me about them, please?' she begged the bad-tempered Shrove.

But Embellsed was cross at the tardy girl and was having none of her chatter. He turned and hissed, his miserable face twisting into a sneer.

'They be your ancestors from the Morrow Swarm,' he replied, scurrying past the gallery of portraits. 'Now keep up girl, and remember to stay away from the darkest patches,' shouted the sullen creature over his shoulder.

Tallitha sighed and stuck her tongue out at the old toad. She was determined to find out about her family history and the hateful Swarm. They trudged down staircase after staircase until Embellsed led Tallitha into the huge gallery where her nightmare in Hellstone Tors had first begun. The magnificent throne room was draped in grand Morrow family artefacts and memorabilia: enormous swords, shields and glinting suits of battle armour were positioned beneath a series of majestic arched windows and dark wooden canopies. In the centre of the gallery stood a dais where three thrones, encrusted with precious bloodstones and upholstered in crimson velvet, were being assiduously polished by a group of nervous servants. When they noticed the girl approach, they averted their eyes and cowered behind the thrones.

'Who sits on these beautiful thrones?' she asked, stepping towards the burnished gold and running her hand over the bloodstones.

'Morrow Swarm,' was all he replied in his crusty old voice.

Tallitha's fingers tingled as she touched the earthy green and deep blood-red of the stones. The residual smear of the Morrow stain was still upon her. She rubbed the palm of her hand down her dress to eradicate the invisible blemish. But her hand still tingled. It hadn't worked.

'But who else sits here apart from the Thane?' she asked.

'Questions! Questions!' he moaned, his eyes darting about the throne room to make sure no one was spying on them. He hopped towards Tallitha. 'Sometimes the Lord Edweard, sometimes the Lady Caedryl, and when the Thane wants to annoy them both, he lets his daughters sit there instead.'

'Don't they get on together?' she asked.

'Not them! They be Swarm!' he replied sharply. 'Always vying for the best position at court. It'll all come to grief, you mark my words. Now stop blathering and go through 'ere,' he barked, leading her out into a marble corridor.

Tallitha did her best to keep up with the cunning creature as he tripped along the hallways, but he knew the passageways well, scurrying here and flitting there, and she was often left behind.

'Come on, hurry up,' he called bad-temperedly.

The castle was vast, with many deceptive twists and turns, dark nooks and dismal crannies, snaking corridors with mirrored walls that seemed to go on and on forever. Its tremendous size was quite unimaginable, hideously complex and with an unfathomable number of turrets and towers – more than a match for Winderling Spires. Try as she might, Tallitha had completely lost track of where she was. She had no way of marking her route or remembering her way back to the northern tower. The wily Shrove had led her this way and that, and had finally outwitted her. But Tallitha was determined to glean as much information as she could from the wizened creature, keeping up an endless stream of questions about the castle and its peculiar inhabitants.

'Where does that corridor lead to? What's behind that door? What's down those stairs? Do tell me, Embellsed, who lives in these grand palaces?' she asked, staring wide-eyed at the sumptuous entranceways that led up into the grand towers of Hellstone Tors.

But Embellsed just grumbled at her incessant chattering and ignored all her questions.

'Stop mithering,' was his stock response.

The interior of Hellstone Tors was a treasure trove of beautiful palaces, each one located through a grand archway leading up into one of the great towers. Each palace had its own unique style with an elegant, majestic stairway and an enormous entrance guarded by a detail of Groat guards. But Tallitha Mouldson was a curious girl by nature, and she couldn't stop herself from poking her head into one of the vast palatial suites.

'It's amazing!' she cried, peering into an entranceway carved like the roots of twisted trees. 'Let's go inside and take a look, please?'

Embellsed mewed like a terrified cat and dragged her away.

'Tha's being a nosey besom!' shouted the Shrove, grabbing her arm. 'Someone will see thee and will batter me for lettin' you stray.'

'But I want to know who lives here,' she demanded, her face turning sulky.

She pulled away from the Shrove's grasp and tried to peek through the half-open doorway.

At that moment, the Groat guards stood to attention and a tall, haughty man dressed in emerald-green brocade passed down the staircase. He eyed Tallitha menacingly down his chiselled nose and waved the desperate, obsequious Shrove to one side. Embellsed bowed and scraped, terrified that the Groat guards would apprehend him and that he would be relieved of his duties as Shrove-Marker.

'So this must be Tallitha,' said the haughty man, running his glassy eyes over the girl.

'T-The Lord Edweard,' the Shrove stuttered, cowering to the floor like a worm.

Lord Edweard's hair was raven-black and braided. His eyes

were shockingly blue and piercing, as though he could see right through to the depths of Tallitha's soul.

'Where's that cousin of yours?' he sneered.

Tallitha shook her head and looked puzzled.

'Caedryl, the one who wears black all the time,' he added.

'I saw her earlier,' she replied dismissively, her face assuming a sour look. She didn't consider the wicked girl as her cousin.

'Caedryl doesn't like you, does she?' he persisted.

His eyes glinted and an evil smile flitted across his face.

'The feeling is mutual,' snapped Tallitha. 'She's the one who deceived us all and brought us to this dreadful place.'

Edweard laughed. 'But you're stuck here now, so you'd better make the best of it.'

He turned on his heel and strode across the hallway. Tallitha gazed after him.

'What did he mean by that?' she asked.

'They hate one another somethin' wicked,' the Shrove explained. 'Caedryl thinks she's the heir to Hellstone Tors now Lord Arden is dead, but Lord Edweard has other ideas. They pretend to get on but there's no love lost between 'em.'

'So who will be the heir?' she asked, lost in thought.

'The Thane will name his successor, but what happens after his death is anyone's guess. Come on, you're bein' a nuisance with all these questions,' bleated the Shrove, 'and you'll get me into terrible trouble.'

'I want to know about the Swarm,' she whispered.

'Nay!' he cried, hopping about like someone had set fire to

his trouser bottoms. 'I know nowt about them!'

'Don't lie to me! You know everything about their evil ways. That's what Shroves like best, knowing what others don't.' She thrust her chin in the air. 'Besides, it's only fair that I should know. I'm related to them after all – and I won't move a muscle until you tell me.'

Tallitha folded her arms and refused to budge.

The Shrove's jaw dropped at Tallitha's outburst and he hopped about frantically. What was he to do? The girl was a right madam, and if he couldn't control her then the other Shroves would say he couldn't do his job properly – then the Swarm would take away his privileges as Shrove-Marker! He rubbed his whiskery chin and weighed up the pros and cons of the situation. If he told her some of what she wanted to know then she would owe him something, and as far as Embellsed was concerned, that may further his position in the Shrove hierarchy. He poked his wrinkly face right next to her.

'If I tells thee owt, then you will owe me summat,' he said calculatingly, rubbing his hands together. 'I will demand a favour from thee, or perhaps a pretty whennymeg, or both.'

Embellsed's eyes glinted and his wet slimy mouth salivated in anticipation. Tallitha could smell his musty clothes and a whiff of stale, rotten food that sat on his rancid breath. She put her hand over her mouth and reeled back from the odious being.

'I a-agree,' she spluttered, 'but you must tell me everything about the Swarm and what powers they have. Do you promise?' she said, turning to one side and taking a gulp of fresh air.

Embellsed grunted and cocked his head to one side. He would tell her a little of what she wanted to keep her satisfied.

'Very well, missy, but you've made a bargain with me now, and a Shrove will always keep you to your word.'

Embellsed was oddly suited to his new role and ambled along the grand landings, proud of his knowledge about the castle, stopping to point out each palace and describing their curious owners.

'Each member of the Swarm has a grand palace in one of the towers of Hellstone Tors, designed to their own particular fancy.'

He looked warily over his shoulder. He didn't want to be seen being too friendly with the girl, for that would get the other Shroves gossiping and would get him into bother.

'But they're a secretive lot and I can only tell thee what I know.' He shuffled onwards. 'The Thane is the master of 'em all and has many dark powers. He can gaze at mirrors and see things,' he said quietly, 'he lives in the eastern tower – the one with the shiny, copper turret. Look through 'ere,' he said, pointing through the casement window.

The tower was one of the largest in Hellstone Tors. It had a number of smaller turrets that circled the main tower like a crown.

'What's it like inside?' she asked, reaching up on her tiptoes to get a better view.

''Tis a marvel,' he replied. 'The Thane has a collection of jewels which are kept in one of the turret rooms but I've never seen it, only 'eard about its splendour from Bludroot.'

'Who's he?' she asked, turning quickly.

'He's the Thane's High Shrove and my Shrove-Master,' he bleated.

He scurried out on to the blustery ramparts.

'See there?' he gesticulated. 'That's where your mother, the Lady Snowdroppe, and her sister, Queen Asphodel, live. Their palaces are next to each other in those large southern towers.'

He pointed to an archway crowned with a monument of exotic, mythical birds. The birds were frightening specimens: eagles and vultures that almost sprang to life out of the stonework, their beaks and talons viciously slashing the air all around them.

'What's my mother's palace like?' Tallitha asked.

It occurred to her in that moment that it was most peculiar that she had never been invited to visit her mother in the Tors, but then that was Snowdroppe all over. She was cold and aloof, even with her children.

'The Lady Snowdroppe's palace has a beautiful fountain that sprays scented lavender water across her marbled terrace.' He bent towards Tallitha and whispered: 'Her special gift is being able to travel faster than anyone here, through any spell forged to keep her out.'

So that was how her mother moved so easily from Winderling Spires to Hellstone Tors!

'Her sister, Asphodel, the Queen of the Dark Reaches, has a menagerie of strange animals. That's her palace over there,' he said, pointing to an entrance where a tangle of black marble snakes lined the steps, writhing in and out of each other's bodies.

'She lives there with her son, an awkward lad called Benedict.'

At the mention of the heartless Queen and her son, a cold shiver ran through Tallitha.

'Is Benedict in the castle now?' she asked guardedly, 'and is he in the Swarm too?'

'Aye, he's a bookish sort of boy, ain't about that much,' answered Embellsed. 'Always seems to be away somewhere or other, trailing after his mother like a soppy calf.'

Tallitha knew just where Benedict had been: skulking about Winderling Spires, spying on them and pretending to be their friend. Her stomach lurched at the painful memory of his betrayal.

'And their powers?' she asked.

'The boy and Caedryl are honing their powers, so I don't know,' he replied crossly. 'I can't answer every damnable question that pops in your head. As to that Queen, she can charm animals and make them obey her.'

The Shrove led Tallitha along a grand balcony and pointed to one of the western towers.

'Now that tower has ten pink marble bathrooms, and belongs to the ladies Muprid and Lapis. Those twins can penetrate your dreams and turn them into nightmares. Some say they steal out into the dead of night to infiltrate the slumbers of unsuspecting souls.'

Tallitha wondered if that was why she'd been plagued with so many vivid dreams – dreadful hallucinations of the night, since she had arrived in Hellstone Tors.

The Shrove waved Tallitha past salons and grand sitting

rooms: huge, opulent apartments with stunning entrances.

'Caedryl lives in that burnished tower,' he said, pointing out of the window. 'She's partial to cats that meow all day long and make a right racket,' he explained. 'Lord Redlevven and his sister the Lady Yarrow live over there.' He pointed towards a silver tower. 'But you won't see much of them, they're always off huntin'. They're the Swarm's Spell-Seekers.'

Tallitha had not heard them mentioned before.

'What are they like?' she asked.

'Swarm-faced,' he grizzled, screwing up his beady eyes, 'like all of 'em – not to be messed with on any account.'

Tallitha stored every scrap of information to report back to her brother.

'But what about the Lady Asenathe, is she part of them too?'

The Shrove nodded and whispered behind his hand.

'She lives over there,' he replied, pointing at an entranceway carved with grotesque spiders. 'She's a channeller, but you know that.'

'How can she belong to the Swarm? She isn't descended from Edwyn Morrow,' asked Tallitha.

Embellsed grumbled away. 'They're a secretive lot and I'm just their hireling. I'm not party to the Thane's plans or what goes on in the Swarm.'

Tallitha noted the location of Asenathe's palace and the wrought iron balustrade running down each side of the grand spidery facade.

They continued through an armoury of weapons, pikestaffs,

swords and hammers. It was clear to Tallitha that the Swarm must have been a warring tribe in their time.

'Everyone looks so scared here,' she said warily, noting a group of servants who scurried away at their approach.

The Shrove muttered, looked over his shoulder and ignored her.

The castle was a bad, dark place. Tallitha could feel its leaden wickedness all around her: closing in, watching her.

'Embellsed, wait for me,' she called as he trotted down the next flight of stairs. 'You have to tell me about the rest of the Swarm.'

But as she spoke, something caught her eye. She stopped, her eyes fixed dead ahead of her. At the far end of the corridor, a face peered out from behind the curtains. For a second or two Tallitha saw a sun-bronzed face, the colour of a polished nut – a flash of black hair and stunning ochre eyes – then the face disappeared.

A strange youth had been watching her.

He had been staring straight at her.

Three

Tallitha noticed every detail about the stranger's face. He had the look of a wild animal – feral and untamed. His yellow ochre eyes lit up, glowing much brighter when he spied her. He had amazing black hair, smoothed and preened like a silky raven. Then, as suddenly as he had appeared, the curtains fell to one side and the youth melted back into the shadows.

Tallitha hesitated as the Shrove bumbled down the next staircase and momentarily slunk out of sight. Now was her opportunity. She ran over to the curtains and quickly drew them aside. But the space was empty. Whoever had been standing there spying on her had vanished. Yet, on the floor behind the curtains, Tallitha noticed a number of dusty footprints that disappeared right into the wall.

'There has to be a secret doorway, there just has to be,' she mumbled to herself.

She ran her hand over the wooden panelling, pressing in all the right places, but nothing happened.

'What you doin'?' asked the Shrove.

He huffed and puffed back up the stairs.

'I've never known the like,' he moaned, peering at her angrily through the banisters.

'Nothing. A bird was snagged in here and I was setting it free,' she lied. 'Just coming.'

'I telled thee not to wander off, not for any reason,' Embellsed snarled from the landing.

Tallitha took one final look before going to meet the Shrove, beaming her most engaging smile and following him as quickly as possible. She didn't want to alert him to the stranger's presence. Whoever the bronze face belonged to, it was her secret.

The Shrove bleated unhappily at her.

'I'm jiggered. Keep up and don't stray,' he snapped. 'We're comin' to a bundle of dark, snaky passages ahead of us that will gobble you up as swift as lightnin'.'

Ahead of them Hellstone Tors meandered onwards, a gloomy mess of sombre passageways and archways disappearing into the darkening distance.

'Where do they lead to?' asked Tallitha apprehensively, staring ahead into the dark cloisters of the castle.

Embellsed put his wrinkly hand over his mouth and beckoned to Tallitha to move closer.

'Deep in the 'eart of the castle there are some nasty places that no soul ever sets foot in. Mired in dark spells an' the old ways that will haunt a body or gobble 'im up.' He stared warily about him. 'Wander off and you'll get yerself lost on the Darkling Stairs and we'll never find you ever again,' he whispered. 'No, not never.' He emphatically shook his head.

'W-What are the Darkling Stairs?' she asked nervously.

'Shh! Be careful what you say!' he hissed, dragging her into a doorway. 'There may be one o' t'Swarm about.' He bent his head conspiratorially towards her. 'Those terrible stairs be the entrance to the dark place,' the Shrove whispered fearfully.

'What dark place?' she asked, biting her lip.

'Oh, I cannot say,' he grizzled, his beady eyes darting this way and that.

The Shrove's face took on a feverish, desperate look. His mouth began salivating and he hopped about, wringing his gnarled hands.

'But where do these dark passages lead to?' she asked nervously. 'You have to tell me!'

He had said far too much for one day, so he quickly changed the subject to one that would distract her.

'They lead to the Bleak Rooms, for one,' he lied nastily.

Tallitha gasped and her face clouded over. She knew all about the dank prison, sunk deep beneath the main courtyard in Hellstone Tors. Her thoughts turned to Esmerelda and she stared far away into the dark patches where the castle ebbed away into the shadowy, withering distance as far as she could see. Her heart sank at the mention of the Bleak Rooms. She was afraid that the Swarm had imprisoned her cousin in the awful dungeon.

'Is that where Esmerelda is k-kept a p-prisoner?' she faltered.

'I'm sayin' nowt,' the Shrove replied.

Her eyes widened, staring into the dead-flat darkness.

Embellsed flashed Tallitha a sidelong glance and lowered his voice.

'Some folks say that the ancient castle devours people, eats 'em up, and over t'years a few bodies 'ave gone missin'. 'Tis an enormous mountain of a place with hidden floors and secret tunnels that go way below the ground – some even say under the seabed.'

Tallitha held her breath and stared wide-eyed at the gangly creature.

'There's a deep darkness in the remotest places where a soul can lose their way,' he said ominously, rubbing his whiskery chin. 'So that's why you 'ave to keep to the middle of the corridor where I can see thee, and you 'ave to keep near to me at all times!' he snapped.

Tallitha inched closer to the Shrove, if only to be near another warm body in the sinister castle. She could smell the Shrove's fusty clothes and the faint aroma of stale bacon fat. She wanted to know all about the dark secret places and the nasty snaky passageways, but most of all she wanted to know who had lost their way on the Darkling Stairs.

'Who's gone missing?' she asked hesitantly.

'Nay, I cannot answer,' he grumbled, 'that would be more than my poor life's worth.'

'But I want to know about the Darkling Stairs,' she persisted.

The Shrove hopped about excitedly.

'Don't ask me, ask your mother or the Mistress Flight – they know all about those dreaded stairs,' he snapped bad-temperedly.

Tallitha was certain that those two miseries would never tell her anything. There were many dark secrets still to be discovered.

'You haven't finished telling me about the Swarm,' she said, trying to catch the Shrove unawares.

He hopped about feverishly and shakily pointed towards a distant tower in the west. Then his face clouded over, he changed his mind and turned away.

'Well now,' he hesitated, scratching his chin. 'You've already seen Lord Edweard's tower.' His gnarled finger gesticulated back the way they had come. 'And anyway, he's the last of 'em, and his talents are as dark as the Thane's.'

Tallitha put her hands on her hips and stared at the wily creature.

'You're not wriggling out of our agreement,' she said as she counted off the members of the Swarm on her fingers. She gave Embellsed a quizzical look. 'Because that only makes eleven.'

Embellsed grunted. 'Well, you've forgotten to count yerself, haven't you? That is, o' course, when you're admitted into the Swarm,' he sneered.

Tallitha's face burned hot. She couldn't bear the thought that she would belong to the Swarm against her will. But the Shrove had counted wrong.

'But even counting me that still only makes twelve. Who's

the thirteenth member? I won't get you a pretty whennymeg,' she said artfully, 'unless you tell me the truth.'

Embellsed seemed to shrink into himself and he hurriedly put his gnarled fingers to his lips.

'Nay, I've told thee all about 'em. 'Tis your poor countin',' he bleated. 'You've not added them up right,' he added, trying to wriggle out of the bargain.

But Tallitha knew that the crafty Shrove was lying. She wasn't going to be duped that easily.

'You promised to tell me about every last one of them!'

'Shh! I cannot say,' he moaned, hopping about in an agitated fashion. 'Don't badger poor Embellsed with your questions.'

He put his hands over his ears to block out Tallitha's questions.

'You promised,' insisted Tallitha.

He grizzled and tried to ignore her, but Tallitha persisted.

'The last one o' t'Swarm is so evil,' he said, 'I'm not mentioning owt about her, you'll find out soon enough!'

'But who is she?'

'Nay they'll cut my gizzards out and put my 'ead on a pikestaff for mentionin' her. The Swarm's always ruled us poor Shroves with a rod of iron and they can be so wicked,' he snivelled. 'They've formidable powers, and I must hold my tongue.'

'Then you can just forget about our bargain!' she snapped.

'You mun get me summat or I'll tell you nowt else,' he replied, poking his face right into hers.

There was so much she still had to discover about her

sinister family, so Tallitha nodded begrudgingly at Embellsed. The Shrove nervously looked about him and cocked his head to make sure they were not being overheard.

'I'll tell thee this, but this alone. There's dark magic that abounds in Hellstone Tors – dredged up from the olden days, from the time of the Morrow pact,' he croaked, looking warily up and down the dark corridor.

'What do you mean?' she asked nervously.

As Embellsed spoke, the old castle grew even darker, the gloomy shadows lengthening and creeping along the stairways like dark twisted fingers clawing at Tallitha's shivering body. Her frightened eyes searched the Shrove's face.

'What's happening?' she asked.

'Them's the terrible *old ways*,' he answered feebly as the heavy darkness pressed down on them.

The Shrove raised his head at the clustering shadows, and fear flickered across his eyes.

'You'll discover all about it soon enough!' he cried. 'I mustn't say more.'

Embellsed's words caught in the back of his throat and he threw Tallitha a nervous glance.

'Stop pesterin' me or we'll be late for t'Mistress Flight. Come on,' he gasped.

Embellsed was too frightened to speak about the final member of the Swarm. As the darkness bore down and over-shadowed them, the terrified Shrove grabbed Tallitha's hand and dragged her along the murky passageways, past scurrying

Shroves and servants who leapt out of their path. The girl was one of *them* after all.

Tallitha's heart was thumping. She was mesmerised by the Shrove's stories and the dark foreboding castle mired in its sinister history. She wriggled her fingers, trying to free her hand away from the Shrove's clammy grasp, but he held her fast, racing through the swirling darkness.

Eventually the Shrove stepped out on to the windy ramparts.

'We're here at last, there's the Withered Tower,' he bleated, pointing to a crooked tower that wound up against the sky, covered in ivy and creepers.

They stood in front of a huge blackened door that oozed a reddish liquid. It trickled down the surface like gore from an infected wound. Tallitha stared upwards at the dark twisting edifice that blocked out the sun. The ancient, crumbling tower was located at the outer edge of Hellstone Tors, surrounded by weeds and ivy that covered every stone of the hideous building.

Embellsed fumbled with his keys, opened the ironclad door and pushed Tallitha into the dismal tower. The entranceway smelt of mould and years of neglect. It was ice-cold and inky dark.

'Shape yersen, there's another terrible climb ahead of us,' he moaned. 'Always climbin' …'

In a blink of an eye Embellsed darted up the stairway and disappeared out of sight. The wind swept down the tower, making a ghostly wail that gathered momentum and blew scattered leaves into Tallitha's path. Her stomach lurched. It was dark and cold. The walls of the tower were covered in ivy that had forced its way through the cracks like dark clawing fingers. Clumps of sickly coloured toadstools clung to the walls and dripped pools of sticky moisture, making the floor underfoot slippery and slimy. Tallitha steeled herself and began the long gruelling ascent up the dark, wet stairway, past the small, dirty windows choked with ivy where the sunlight had failed to penetrate. It was a miserable place and the weaselly Shrove had deserted her. As she clutched at the broken wall she slipped in the slimy wetness and stumbled to her knees.

'Argh! Help me, Embellsed!' she called out.

High above, the wind whistled down the winding stairwell making an eerie, wailing moan, loud enough to wake the dead.

'Embellsed,' she called desperately again. 'Don't leave me alone! I don't like this place, it's so dark. Please wait for me.'

Then Tallitha heard the door to the tower creak open.

'Embellsed!' she shouted. 'I-I can hear someone following me!'

Behind her the swirling blackness had soaked up the stairway like spilled ink on blotting paper – creeping up the walls, swallowing her up in its grasp.

'Shut tha noise! I'm just here,' he called. ''Tis just the old wind blowing its guts out. Now keep steady girl, there's 'undreds more steps to climb,' the Shrove hollered, his shrill voice bouncing menacingly off the walls.

Tallitha began racing up the slippery staircase for all her life was worth, desperate to escape from whatever was following her, lurking behind her in the darkness. But the girl and the Shrove were not alone on the treacherous staircase. The youth with the ochre-coloured eyes and the raven hair was stalking them, slinking along just a moment out of sight. He watched the girl falter and fall on the gloomy staircase, calling out for the Shrove.

The youth was a cunning creature. He knew they were on their way to see the Mistress Flight, and that Tallitha's task was to become practiced in the art of The Black Pages. He planned to spy on the girl in the Mistress's tower: to observe her, to see what she could do, to see whether she had the special powers he desperately needed and whether she could be of any use to him.

Four

Embellsed entered the tower room and roughly pushed a reluctant Tallitha forward.

'She's 'ere, Mistress,' the Shrove barked. 'I'll be off then.' And with that he slithered out of the room like a worm and locked the door firmly behind him.

Tallitha, dishevelled and exhausted after her long and terrifying climb, stumbled, coming face to face with the pinch-faced governess.

Sedentia Flight had the sort of look that would curdle fresh cream. Her black frizzy hair was pulled into a severe bun at the nape of her neck. Her teeth protruded, her ears stuck out and she had an assortment of hairy, brown moles on her chin.

'So, Tallitha,' the governess said crossly, inspecting the messy girl. 'You're late.'

'Sorry, it was such a long climb up that dismal tower,' answered Tallitha, looking fearfully over her shoulder.

Tallitha struggled to her feet, rearranging her clothes as she surveyed her strange surroundings. The small, dark tower room was painted in a violet inky paint with silver and black symbols stencilled across the walls. It was obviously a room designed for outlandish experiments. Brightly coloured pots, phials and crystals were arranged on the table where Sedentia had been plying her trade, mixing potions and aromatic brews.

'I've been instructed by the Thane to prepare you for your initiation,' Sedentia said ominously. 'You are to become accomplished in the old ways and will study the tests from The Black Pages.' The Mistress Flight's cold gaze surveyed the crumpled girl before her. She clicked her tongue. 'I hope you're ready,' she snapped.

The girl looked anything but prepared, standing there with a face like thunder.

'I don't know anything about anything!' Tallitha snapped.

The governess turned her stern eye on Tallitha and blinked several times. The girl was trouble. She could smell it.

Suddenly a thin, slippery-bodied, cat-like creature with enormous paws and tufted hairy ears snuck out from behind Sedentia's skirts and darted across the floor. The cat's bright liquid emerald eyes flashed, and she hissed at Tallitha.

'This is my Wheen-Cat, Slynose. She is the queen of the cats and a great stalker. She loves to catch mice,' said Sedentia.

The cat sprang in one enormous leap onto the mantelpiece where she sat queen-like, swishing her tail backwards and forwards. She hissed venomously, her deep green eyes revolving and gazing straight at Tallitha in a disconcerting manner. There was something about the sleek black animal that made Tallitha's flesh crawl.

'We only have a short time until you're sworn,' said Sedentia coldly. 'You have much to learn about the Swarm and their ways.'

Sedentia turned swiftly towards the mantelpiece, pressed a lever in the wall and began chanting in the ancient Ennish tongue.

'*Tellan sam le nerva manvellus, Tellan sam le nerva manvellus,*' she repeated bewitchingly, over and over again.

With a flourish, Sedentia pointed towards an emerging gap in the wall panelling. Tallitha heard a grinding noise of scraping metal as the tower room began to turn in a circular motion, revealing a dark aperture in the wall where a trail of purple smoke appeared from the mysterious interior.

'This secret room holds the library of the old Books of Morrow: a most revered place where we will begin our lessons.'

Sedentia pursed her lips and made a series of kissing noises for the Wheen-Cat to follow. The creature leapt off the mantelpiece, slipped through the governess's legs and pranced into the Book Room with her tail held high.

Tallitha gingerly peered through the unwelcoming gap into an exceptionally high space. The room was the height of four or five rooms positioned higgledy-piggledy on top of one another like a set of toppling teacups.

'It's not very inviting,' Tallitha said with foreboding.

The light came from an array of tall violet-coloured candles, patterned with the same ominous silver and black symbols that adorned the walls in the outer room. The candles oozed a dank, sulphurous smell that pervaded the atmosphere.

'Don't stand there looking gormless, girl – enter!' her governess snapped.

Tallitha stepped inside the windowless room where the smouldering candles had left stalactites of dripping wax running down the candelabras. Before her were rows upon rows of topsy-turvy bookshelves reaching high up into a shadowy dome. There were thousands of ancient books, manuscripts and parchments towering above her, balanced on the bookshelves in a precarious, haphazard fashion.

Tallitha heard a squabbling noise coming from the highest, darkest corners of the bookshelves. Then several small black creatures with bat-like faces stared down at her. Their long bulbous fingers were busily employed keeping the books from toppling down on their visitors' heads, sifting and re-sorting the piles of books and manuscripts into their correct place whilst the irascible creatures argued vociferously with one another.

'What are they?' asked Tallitha, bewildered.

She had never seen a creature quite so strange. They had long arms, fat bodies and spindly legs, with suckers on their fat fingers and toes that they used for climbing the shelves in a crab-like motion.

'These are Nooklies,' explained her governess. 'You keep things tidy, don't you?' she shouted at the noisy creatures. 'Quieten down, we have a visitor today.'

The gaggle of Nooklies poked their heads from behind the books to take a better look at their visitor. One of their heartless brood narrowed its bulging eyes and spat venomously at Tallitha. She jumped out of the firing line as the loathsome Nooklie gave an ear-piercing scream of delight before going back to prodding the books into place, and arguing with its mates.

'Ignore them and they'll ignore you. Now let me see,' said Sedentia, perusing the lower shelves. 'No, it's not down here. Now where did I leave that book?'

The governess lifted her voluminous skirts and hauled her rotund body up the wooden library steps, proceeding to edge along the bookshelves, balancing herself by sticking her pointy black shoes into the gaps between the large volumes. She inched her way along, muttering away and peering into the cobwebby crevasses, brushing the annoying Nooklies out of her way and prodding behind the thick tomes on the dusty shelves.

'These are wonderful, magical books,' she said, turning to Tallitha. 'They include the ancient books of the Morrow family, the Book of Guises, the Seven Colourings, and ...' She pulled a heavy book wrapped in black silk from the shelves. 'Here we are,' she said at last, blowing away the cobwebs and caressing the lavish binding. 'This great book will teach you in the ways of our people. Treat it well.'

Our people, thought Tallitha angrily. She wasn't about to become one of them, if she could help it.

Sedentia wobbled as she trundled down the steps, and placed the large black leather-bound volume into Tallitha's hand. If the governess had expected Tallitha to be impressed she was disappointed. The girl looked disparagingly at the old book.

'Today we will start with one of the first tests in The Black Pages. I want you to access the shadow-flight and show me what you can do.'

Sedentia waddled over to a pair of squashy armchairs positioned beneath the bookshelves, and wriggled her large behind into the cushions, patting the other chair for Tallitha to join her. Slynose lay stretched out by the door as though guarding the exit, her liquid green eyes transfixed on Tallitha all the while.

'I-I'm having a bit of trouble with all that,' Tallitha said, twisting her hair in and out of her fingers.

'Nonsense, I need to observe you, and once I'm satisfied with the progress of your shadow-flight we will move on to the next test,' she explained in a matter-of-fact tone.

'How many tests will I have to do?' asked Tallitha.

The Wheen-Cat slunk across the floor, then leapt on Sedentia's knee to be petted. She fixed her spiralling green eyes on Tallitha and breathed in her body-perfume, absorbing it fully into her cat-memory. For a moment, Tallitha thought that she heard the Wheen-Cat whispering something into the governess's ear.

How ridiculous, she thought. *Surely cats can't talk?*

'You will do four tests in all. The first two you will complete with me,' the governess answered.

'What about the others?'

'Questions and more questions,' Sedentia snapped exasperatedly. The girl was a bothersome child. 'They will be performed later with another who has deeper, more ancient powers than I,' she answered mysteriously.

'Why do I have to do these tests?' Tallitha replied sullenly. 'I don't want to be here at all.'

Sedentia looked as though someone had slapped her face.

'Don't want to!' she exclaimed. 'Of course you want to. You just don't know it yet. This is your birthright, and you *will* be the next one to join the Swarm. The Thane of Breedoor has decreed it.'

'But no one has told me anything about being sworn in!' Tallitha snapped. 'So I'm not doing any of these tests until you tell me what to expect!'

Tallitha folded her arms and glowered at Sedentia. Snowdroppe had already warned the governess that Tallitha might prove to be a difficult student. The governess looked the girl square in the face and stroked the purring Slynose, whispering into the cat's tufted ears. The Wheen-Cat's liquid green eyes stared at Tallitha.

'You've got a mouth on you,' said Sedentia, looking vexed.

She wasn't used to her students answering back. She stared at Tallitha for some time, weighing up the situation and how to manage the girl. Eventually she spoke.

'On the other hand, I suppose this information can be described as part of your education,' she said, becoming momentarily distracted by a long hair that was attached to one of her disgusting brown moles. She pulled at it until it pinged out of her chin. She cleared her throat. 'There will be a ceremony,' she said flatly.

'I'd sort of guessed that,' Tallitha replied sarcastically. She wasn't that stupid.

The governess came much too close. She smelled of mint humbugs and tea.

'When you are ready, you will be taken to the *dark place*,' she whispered. 'There you will swear to uphold the ancient pact of the Morrow Swarm.'

'Where is this dark place?' Tallitha asked hesitantly.

'The Bone Room,' Sedentia replied ominously. 'The pact is kept in Micrentor's Cabinet. It was written by Edwyn Morrow in his own blood when he fled from the accursed Wycham Elva. It has the Morrow stain upon it,' she spoke reverently and her eyes became misty.

Tallitha tried to maintain her composure when Sedentia referred to Wycham Elva as accursed. She knew all about the Morrow stain: the dark red cobwebs that had been soaked in blood, now mouldering away in the Raven's Wing in Winderling Spires. The blood-red webs had sullied her and laid their mark upon her the day she had explored the old wing. But Tallitha was an artful girl, and had years of practice wheedling information out of Cissie. She twisted round to face Sedentia and posed her next question using the most innocent tone she could muster.

'Why should I swear to uphold this old pact when no one has told me anything about it?' Her face turned red with annoyance.

'Since I came to Hellstone Tors, Tyaas and I have been locked in our apartments!' she moaned, thumping the armchair.

The girl was persistent, headstrong and unruly. She needed to be taken in hand.

'The bloody words must be spoken,' explained Sedentia.

Tallitha looked bewildered. 'What w-words are those?' she stammered.

Sedentia shuffled in her chair and licked her protruding teeth in a most unattractive manner. Slynose sat like a petted queen and demanded attention, purring and rubbing her head against Sedentia's leg, eyeing Tallitha all the while.

'The bloody words are part of an ancient rite that must be performed when a new member joins the Morrow Swarm,' Sedentia explained.

'But what will I have to promise?' she asked.

Sedentia tutted and shook her head. This girl was exasperating.

'It's a secret oath. The bloody words can only be revealed at the time of the swearing-in ceremony,' said Sedentia mysteriously.

Sedentia's face darkened and she slithered her bottom over to Tallitha's chair. Then she listened intently for a second or two, but the only sound that could be heard was that of the chattering Nooklies high up on the bookshelves. She cupped her hand and whispered into Tallitha's ear.

'The pact is kept in Micrentor's Cabinet in the Grand Duchess's Tower.'

At the mention of a Grand Duchess, Tallitha opened her eyes wide and bent her head towards Sedentia.

'A Duchess?' she asked in hushed tones. 'Where's the tower?'

'At the top of the Darkling Stairs, but it's a wild place protected with ancient layers of sorcery,' whispered the governess.

Tallitha was intrigued. It was the second time someone had mentioned the mysterious Darkling Stairs.

'Tell me about the Duchess?'

Sedentia put her whiskery face right next to Tallitha's ear. The bristly hairs ticked the girl's cheek.

'Why, she's the Thane's Neopholytite,' said Sedentia.

'What's that?' asked Tallitha, sounding horrified.

'The charmer, the enchantress – the Thane's witch,' whispered her governess.

Tallitha gasped at the mention of a witch. She had never met a real witch before, unless Queen Asphodel counted. But perhaps they were all witches and sorcerers in Hellstone Tors.

'The Witch's Tower is protected with arcane spells – some of which you will discover for yourself, but only if work through The Black Pages,' Sedentia added, trying to entice Tallitha to attempt the first test.

But Tallitha knew quite well what the governess was up to.

Sedentia suddenly stopped and listened, holding her finger to her lips.

'Those annoying creatures have stopped chattering,' said Tallitha.

The noise of the Nooklies had ceased, and the Book Room

had become eerily quiet. A glint of fear flitted across Sedentia's face. She shuffled to the doorway and listened.

'We must be circumspect,' she whispered, 'that's all I can tell you. Now let's continue with the first test.'

Tallitha pretended to focus her attention on The Black Pages but her thoughts were full of the mysterious witch, how to get her hands on the Morrow pact and the sinister Darkling Stairs.

But way overhead, high up in the gloomy dome and far away from the chattering Nooklies, someone was listening intently and watching Tallitha's every move. The governess sensed an unwanted presence. She raised her head, sniffed the air and wrinkled her nose.

'Can you smell something?' she asked. 'It smells like ... honey.'

Sedentia's nose twitched again. Tallitha shook her head: she couldn't smell anything apart from sulphur and burning candles.

'Peculiar, I could definitely smell honey,' Sedentia replied, staring about her. 'Now, take a look at the book and tell me what you see.'

But Tallitha's thoughts were too preoccupied with images of the Grand Duchess – a Neopholytite and a witch, no less, to be able to concentrate on The Black Pages. Now she had even more questions about the mysterious Morrow family that required answers.

But high up at the very top of the Book Room, where the last shelf abutted the dusty wall, there was a gap where the books had been carefully moved to one side. The youth had climbed up inside the dusty wall cavities, wriggled his lithe body into position and poked his head out between the books. He watched, taking in every detail of the interaction that took place between Sedentia and the girl. From his vantage point he could see a violet fuzzy glow begin to surround Tallitha. That could only mean one thing. She had the special gift he was looking for.

Five

Trapped in the mysterious Book Room, Tallitha knew there was no way of avoiding the clutches of the dreadful governess or the tests that she must perform from The Black Pages. She shuffled back into the squidgy armchair and flicked the black-edged pages of the old volume in an offhand manner. At first they had no effect on her; they were just pages of boring introduction and instructions. Then, when she turned the page of the first chapter, her fingers tingled and the book transformed before her eyes. The pages sprang into life, illuminated with incredible colours: iridescent blues, smouldering reds and vivid greens metamorphosed into bees, moths and butterflies that leapt off the amazing pages. Then her whole body began to tingle.

'Tell me what you see,' her governess whispered enticingly, observing the violet fuzzy glow about the girl's head.

'The colours are so vivid,' she answered, staring in disbelief at the dancing patterns.

Her head throbbed. She couldn't take her eyes from the mesmerising pinks and hot oranges.

'It's beginning – relax and set your shadow-self free. I can see the telltale sign,' she said, gazing at the brilliance of the violet glow.

Tallitha's head was swimming. She was entranced by the strands of magical colours that spun round the room like a spinning top. In an instant she was part of the merry-go-round, going faster and faster – the reds, greens, and blues spinning before her eyes until they blurred into one strand of dazzling kaleidoscopic colour.

'*Tellan lenne nervella manvellus, tellan lenne nervelle manvellus,*' the governess chanted softly into the girl's ear.

Then the psychedelic colours separated and spun about the room, darting towards the book and delving into the pages as the illustrations sprang into life. On each page, fabulous paintings of wild extravagant butterflies, exotic flowering plants, swirling snakes and fabulous birds erupted like a volcano: a cornucopia of wonderful illustrations in vivid colours captured on each page, entwined in leafy Ennish lettering.

'Relax and let yourself drift into the spellbinding colours. Look deep into the steaming reds, the verdant greens and the shimmering pinks.'

'These are incredible!' Tallitha cried as she gripped the edges of the powerful book. 'They're – they're –' she whispered, her voice became faint. 'They're whisking me away!'

Tallitha began to slide from her body as the colours hummed

and vibrated, sucking her further into their mesmerising density, the layers upon layers of thick absorbing hues pulling her downwards. In an instant she was falling head over heels into the blues, tumbling into the pinks, reds and yellows. She was bewitched.

'Tell me, what do you see?' Sedentia murmured, her mellifluous tones sounding like the softest music. She moved closer to Tallitha, whispering hauntingly: 'You're entering the elemental level of The Black Pages.'

'I'm losing control,' Tallitha moaned, clutching her head.

'Let your mind absorb the colours – colours so deep that you become lost in the swirling blues and stinging yellows ... *tenteth shallam et lucier malam na cora,*' she whispered beguilingly into Tallitha's ear.

The amazing hues throbbed and hummed as the pages became alive in Tallitha's hands. The shapes began to jump off the page in a myriad of wild dancing patterns. First an array of multicoloured butterflies erupted from the pages and flew into the air, filling the room with their dazzling, fluttering wings. Then a tangle of swirling, wriggling snakes slithered from the pages and darted across the room, disappearing in a puff of crimson smoke. Twirling deep green tendrils, black calla lilies, red tulip heads and blossoming exotic flowers punctuated the room with their twisting stems and glorious pungent aromas.

A giant kaleidoscope of twirling colours and fabulous shapes spiralled before Tallitha's eyes like a carousel. For a fleeting moment Tallitha was back in Winderling Spires where the dazzling colours in the Jewel Room had bewitched her. She imagined the jewels sparkling like a thousand bright stars, entrancing her.

The girl shuddered uncontrollably as her dream-self began to take over. She slipped away, further and further from her body. Sedentia's voice was like oozing treacle, dripping into Tallitha's mind as the vibrant colours overpowered her.

Then, Tallitha's head slumped onto the armchair. The familiar drifting sensation sucked her dream-self away from her body. The old sensation of dragging, then *pop, pop* and *whoosh!* – she slipped, tumbling down into the swirling grey mist. The Book Room vanished in an instant and she slid into the soft grey light.

'Where are you, Tallitha?' Sedentia whispered, watching for the sign that the shadow-flight had begun. But Tallitha was motionless, lying like a deathly soul in the armchair.

'Tallitha, speak to me,' the governess commanded, shaking the girl's limp body, but Tallitha did not respond.

Sedentia listened to the girl's regular breathing and the rapid beating of her heart, but could make no contact with her beyond the Book Room. It seemed as though Tallitha had completely disappeared.

*

Down in the foggy grey light, Tallitha spun round and round, the silver cord trailing behind her, searching in vain for the tunnel. She stumbled in the mist, lost, unable to move towards the shadow-flight and unable to return to Sedentia's Book Room. A powerful force held her there. Slowly the mist began to clear and Tallitha saw the hazy outline of the silver-haired woman who had forewarned her about entering Hellstone Tors. She spoke softly:

'The governess cannot see or hear you. My power is too strong for her in the middle plane.'

Tallitha felt her icy breath touch her face like icicles. The spirit's eyes were iridescent blue and her hair curled in silver strands to her feet. But it was her face that was the most striking. It was translucent, the fine taut skin shimmering like sunlight through an insect's wing.

'What do you want of me?' asked Tallitha, mesmerised by the spirit-creature.

The spirit's cold fingers stroked Tallitha's face.

'You entered Hellstone Tors against my warning and of your own free will,' she whispered in a haunting voice. 'Why?'

Her flimsy body shuddered and she floated upwards, encircling Tallitha.

'W-We had to f-find Asenathe,' Tallitha replied, trembling. 'W-We had travelled so far and endured s-so much.'

The spirit spread her arms, engulfing the space all around them.

'But they have imprisoned you and are preparing to have you sworn,' the apparition whispered.

'I'll never be part of that hateful brood!' she answered feverishly.

The silver-haired spirit swooped down and took Tallitha's face in her icy hands.

'If you mean that, Tallitha, then there is only one course of action.' The spirit hesitated and stared at the girl before her. 'You must decipher the pact and assemble the forces needed to destroy it.'

Tallitha gasped – then there was a way out after all!

'Tell me what I must do.'

'The Morrow pact is protected by a dark spell crafted many years ago to protect the Swarm,' she replied.

'But how can I break it?' she asked.

'It is held in place with a powerful spell-seal. The pact was written in Edwyn Morrow's blood and it is a three-fold hexing spell.' The apparition looked warily about and her silvery light dimmed. 'You must take care Tallitha – I have been sent by another to warn you.'

'Am I truly the one to break the Morrow pact?' Tallitha asked nervously.

'Many have tried and failed,' the spirit replied sadly. 'Those poor creatures who were captured on the Darkling Stairs, and rewarded with eternal misery in the Neopholytite's lair. You will face a terrible ordeal in order to break the pact.'

The spirit's aura began to fade. 'I must go,' she whispered.

'Wait, please!' Tallitha cried, reaching out for the spirit's flimsy being. 'What else must I do?'

'Do the tests and find your cousin Esmerelda – you will find a way to free her.' The silver-haired spirit slipped past Tallitha like an icy cloud. 'You must find the child that was taken from Winderling Spires'

'What child was that?' Tallitha exclaimed.

'You must discover that for yourself.'

The apparition spun round, then turned to impart a final warning.

'Beware the Neopholytite, she is an old and powerful being.'

Then the silver-haired spirit shimmered and vanished.

The middle plane turned into a soaring whirlwind, buffeting Tallitha in its raw ethereal elements. She spun round, lost in the mist and cried out. She must find Esmerelda – her cousin would help her with the quest. Tallitha cried out to Sedentia to return.

'There, Tallitha, be calm,' said Sedentia gently, 'you can come back to me now.'

The governess clicked her fingers and Tallitha felt the familiar popping sensation and tumbled back into her body with a jolt.

High above them the youth observed all that had taken place. This girl had the power that he sought. He had found her at last. He squeezed himself back inside the wall cavity and slid away into the underbelly of Hellstone Tors.

When Tallitha opened her eyes, Sedentia Flight and the Wheen-Cat were staring at her.

'What did you see?' Sedentia asked excitedly. 'Tell me everything.'

Tallitha put her hand up to her head. It ached from the shadow-flight.

'I-I couldn't find the tunnel, I became lost in the mist,' she explained. 'It was thick, clawing at me like lumpy pea-soup.'

Sedentia pursed her lips. 'Did you try,' she asked disappointedly, 'or are you deliberately resisting me?'

'N-No, I couldn't move. Usually I'm whisked away by the shadow-flight but this time I stumbled around, quite lost.'

But an idea had occurred to Tallitha.

'Essie always helped me access the shadow-flight,' she added, appealing to her governess.

Tallitha would do the tests, but not until she had her way and Esmerelda was back with her.

Sedentia bit her lip. 'You must try harder. My task is to prepare you to be sworn. You must access that tunnel!'

Sedentia pulled a face and wriggled her bottom further back into the lumpy cushions. She sniffed the air once more. The aroma of honey had disappeared.

'Take a look at the next chapter, it may provoke a more satisfactory response,' she said huffily.

Sedentia painstakingly instructed Tallitha, talking about the family and softly planting ideas here and there about their influence and power. As she spoke she turned The Black Pages, pointing to the fabulous illustrations, but nothing unusual happened.

'I need Essie to help me,' Tallitha pleaded.

The book was bewitching, but Tallitha would not be drawn in by the dazzling, colourful illustrations. She pretended to be befuddled and woolly-headed. It was the only way she could think to bring Esmerelda back to her.

'You've disappointed me,' her governess said coldly.

Sedentia began chanting, and the circular tower turned once

more, enabling her to step through the aperture. Tallitha and the Wheen-Cat followed behind her.

'The Thane will employ more forceful methods if you prove to be resistant,' she said ominously.

Sedentia rang her bell, the door was unlocked from the outside and Embellsed shuffled inside from one of the Shrove lairs. He had been snoozing, his hair was ruffled and his eyes looked puffy with too much sleep.

'Take Tallitha back to her apartment and look sharp about it!' she growled at the shove. 'Return with her early in the morning'. Sedentia turned to Tallitha. 'Tomorrow you must progress through The Black Pages. There will be consequences, if you resist.'

'What about Essie?' Tallitha pleaded. 'She's the only one who can help me.'

'Not now!' shouted the governess, turning on her heel.

With that, Sedentia dismissed Tallitha and ambled back to the Wheen-Cat and her books.

Six

When Tallitha returned to her apartment, her thoughts were full of images of the silver-haired spirit and the Neopholytite in her tower. As Embellsed opened the door, Tallitha found her mother standing impatiently in the sitting room eating canapés and sweet fancies, petting her wretched fennec fox. Snowdroppe pounced on her daughter and led her over to the window seat, stroking her hair and pretending to be affectionate. She offered Tallitha a bite from her specially prepared platter, coo-cooing all the while.

'Take a caramel delight or a vanilla fudge,' insisted Snowdroppe too sweetly, her hair hanging down in rich golden-red tresses.

Tallitha regarded her mother suspiciously and popped a chocolate fondant into her mouth. It melted on her tongue as a trail of gooey chocolaty sweetness oozed from its centre.

'Ah, Embellsed,' Snowdroppe rounded on the bumbling

Shrove, 'how has Miss Tallitha progressed with The Black Pages?'

Snowdroppe continued to beam at Tallitha, stroking her hair and offering her more sweets.

'I know nowt about the learning she's done,' bleated the miserable Shrove.

He knew better than to give bad news to a member of the Swarm. A thwarted high-ranking personage in an ill humour was something to be avoided at all costs.

'Did she progress swiftly through The Black Pages?' asked Snowdroppe, her voice turning swiftly to impatience.

The Shrove hopped about and grizzled. 'I already says, m'Lady, I know nowt.'

Snowdroppe's face turned sour.

'Be off with you then, annoying creature! Bludroot wants to see you,' she said, dismissing him with a wave of her hand.

Embellsed hurried away, flattered that the High Shrove wanted to speak with him.

Snowdroppe gazed expectantly at her daughter, but Tallitha turned away to avoid her mother's attention and fiddled nervously with her hair, twisting it in and out of her fingers. Snowdroppe's beautiful face clouded over.

'Well? I haven't all day,' she demanded, drumming her perfectly manicured scarlet talons against the deep azure of her velvet dress.

Tallitha watched as her mother's fury began to make an imprint on the velvet, her nails digging viciously into the fabric.

'What do you want me to say?' asked Tallitha, squirming on

the window seat. 'I only looked at some boring old books.'

Snowdroppe became vexed.

'Did you progress through The Black Pages as you were bidden?'

'Erm, not really. Nothing much happened,' she lied, moving away from her mother's sharp nails.

'Not really!' Snowdroppe pouted. 'But you must do the tests with Sedentia, otherwise …'

'Otherwise what, Mother? I got a bit stuck and it's not my fault. Essie usually prepares me and she isn't here.'

Snowdroppe pulled Tallitha towards her by the scruff of her neck, nipping her flesh.

'Ouch, Mother, let me be! I tried my best.'

'Don't dare disappoint me!' she snapped. 'You must do this by yourself!'

'But Essie –'

'Shut up about Essie!' her mother shrieked.

Snowdroppe circled the room like a slithering viper, glaring all the while at her errant daughter. She angrily dropped the tiny fennec fox to the floor on its jewelled lead, clicking her fingers at the animal. The fox yapped annoyingly, and its little nails pit-pattered along the wooden floor as it obediently followed its mistress.

'Do better tomorrow! Do you hear me?' she shouted in Tallitha's face, her eyes flashing with venom. 'Or else you will live to regret it!'

'Yes Mother, I hear you,' replied Tallitha sullenly. 'What about Essie?'

But Snowdroppe ignored her. She gathered her skirts and swirled out of the room, flinging the huge door wide open in annoyance. It banged with such ferocity that it swung open once more on its hinges. Tallitha watched as their mother flounced down the corridor shouting for her Shrove to attend to her demands. A second or two of agonising silence passed before Tallitha heard a key clatter to the floor just outside her room. She held her breath, waiting for Embellsed to shuffle back in his usual annoying fashion and lock the door, but outside in the corridor, all was silent.

Tyaas inched into Tallitha's apartment. He wanted to make sure their mother had departed.

'What's going on?' he asked, observing Tallitha's intent face staring at the wide open door.

'Wait a moment,' Tallitha whispered, listening again for the Shrove.

But outside the apartment the corridor was ominously still. They couldn't hear any footsteps rushing to lock them in.

After a while Tallitha crept towards the door, looked furtively along the corridor to make sure no one was about, then she picked up the key and gently closed the door behind her.

Tallitha smiled gleefully at her brother and tapped her pocket. Now she had the key to the apartment in her possession.

She locked the sitting room door from the inside and waited for the snivelling Shrove to return. Tallitha told her brother all about the Neopholytite and the silver-haired spirit. Tyaas perked up when the word "witch" was mentioned.

Later Tallitha heard Embellsed scampering along the long corridor and trying the door handle several times. She could imagine the mystified creature standing in the corridor scratching his head and trying to remember what he had done with the key, wondering whether he had locked the door or whether it had been someone else. Tallitha hugged herself and smiled. For once she had outwitted the Shrove.

Embellsed scratched his head and hopped about. He was befuddled by the turn of events, but he decided to leave the children undisturbed for the night. Besides, he couldn't remember what he'd done with the blasted key! Off he scampered down the corridor, muttering away to himself and feeling in all his pockets for the missing key. It was nowhere to be found.

*

That night, as the haunting hours of midnight clanged out from the high bell tower, Tallitha awoke from yet another bad dream bathed in sweat, the nightmarish images of the hounds in Ragging Brows Forest, snarling and pounding through the wood and snapping at her heels, filling up her fetid imagination.

She sat up in bed and lit the candle, when all at once she glimpsed the shadowy figures of the Morrow twins, Lapis and Muprid, smiling eerily in the corner of her room like two ghosts. Then, in an instant, they vanished like the stuff of bad dreams.

The hateful twins had penetrated her dreams with a spell and turned her slumbers into a nightmare.

'Tyaas, Tyaas,' she whispered, but he was fast asleep.

She crept into his room and shook him.

'W-What's happening?' he mumbled.

'Those spooky twins came to me in my sleep. They made me have horrible dreams,' she murmured.

Her brother stared at her and swallowed. This castle was more sinister than Winderling Spires.

'Come on,' she said. 'It's time to do some exploring.'

She slipped from her bed, tiptoed across the sitting room floor and gently turned the key in the lock. It opened with a soft click. She snuck her nose round the edge of the door, peeped out and listened to the silence. Outside, the grand landing stretched ahead in swathes of patchy darkness with only glimmers of moonlight falling here and there, sending darting slivers of light across the polished wooden floor.

Night in the Tors was as still as the grave.

Tallitha inched furtively out of her apartment, beckoning to her brother to follow. The two small souls began creeping along the shadowy landing, gripping hold of the banister to guide them and making their way through the intermittent pattern of leaden darkness and shards of moonlight.

'Which way are we going?' asked Tyaas, roughly pulling a sweater over his head.

It was cold in the northern tower. Howling draughts blew along the corridors, whistling up the late stairs and across the platform to where Tallitha and Tyaas crouched in the darkness.

'To find the Neopholytite's tower,' answered Tallitha, whispering behind her hand. 'Embellsed pointed out the direction of the Darkling Stairs, so that's where we're headed.'

Tyaas looked completely blank.

'The witch, silly,' she uttered hastily under her breath. 'Weren't you listening at all?'

'Yeah, I heard that bit,' muttered Tyaas. 'Now we can have some fun at last.'

His sister pulled him close and spoke in a hushed voice.

'We must be careful. We have to uncover the mystery behind the pact to find out what Edwyn Morrow had to give up in return for the dark favours that saved him.'

'What's this old witch got to do with it?'

'I don't know yet – I told you about the silver-haired spirit, do you remember that bit?'

Tyaas shrugged. He'd been half-listening, but he hadn't heard anything after Tallitha had mentioned the witch.

'What's a Neopholytite?' he asked.

'The witch!' Tallitha sighed with exasperation. 'The Thane's enchantress who lives in the tower.'

Tyaas's eyes opened wide.

'Will we get to meet her?'

'I hope not, she's a sorceress and exceedingly nasty. Now, come on! It's so dark along this corridor, I can hardly see.'

The castle was sound asleep, wrapped in a haunting silence. Nothing much stirred in the chilly hours after midnight, not even the artful Shroves – they were snoozing in their Shrove holes, deep down in the depths of the shadowy Tors. But unbeknown to Tallitha, high up in the northern tower, someone was lurking and watching as they crept along the upper hallway, moving through the patches of darkness, shadows and streaks of moonlight.

Just inside a shadowy recess, standing behind the long curtains, the face with yellow ochre eyes peered out, glinting fiercely in the darkness. The youth had been hiding for several hours, biding his time and waiting for the Shrove to depart. Now, as luck would have it, the girl and boy had appeared, creeping towards him, moving in and out of the pitch-blackness and stepping briefly into the fleeting strands of moonlight. The youth had no trouble with the inky blackness of the night: his amber eyes were used to seeing in the dark.

As Tallitha and Tyaas inched along the upper landing, the curtains suddenly moved to one side and a figure emerged from the gloom.

'Psst! Over here!' he whispered, gesticulating wildly at the startled pair.

They looked like two frightened mice frozen to the spot, suddenly confronted by a prowling cat.

'Who's that? What do you want?' Tallitha cried, stumbling backwards into the shadows.

A tall slender youth slunk out from behind the curtain. He had sleek black hair and a hard, bony face like a wild animal. Tallitha gasped at the sight of him – it was the same feral face she had seen staring at her that morning. She gripped Tyaas's hand.

'How dare you jump out at us? I'll have my Shrove on you!' she whispered hoarsely, attempting to be brave.

The youth laughed in her face.

'I'm the one that will get you into trouble,' he said menacingly, moving swiftly across the landing.

Tallitha retreated, dragging Tyaas after her.

'P-Please, don't tell them, will you?' she pleaded.

The youth stared at her, his yellow-grained eyes narrowing. Tallitha could smell a distinct aroma of honey.

'Who are you talking about?' he asked, taunting her.

'Embellsed and M-Mother.'

The youth's face twisted into a smile that played across his lips, which he licked again and again with relish. His teeth shone in the single beam of moonlight that fell on his tanned face.

'That all depends,' he said playfully. 'Tell me where you're going at this time of night? It's the dangerous bewitching hour after all and you two are definitely up to something.'

Tallitha gasped. What did he know about their plans to seek out the witch?

'W-Why should I tell you?' she asked hesitantly.

His yellow eyes slanted malevolently like a cat homing in on its kill.

'I can always call for Embellsed,' he threatened, 'or you can tell me all about your little secret.'

Tallitha bristled and pulled away from him. But there was something fearless and oddly familiar about the youth. He was different from the Swarm. She sensed that he wasn't one of them.

'We're just going for a midnight stroll. We've been cooped up all day and need a breath of fresh air,' she answered, trying to sneak further down the landing.

'Liar,' he hissed, grabbing her arm. 'Now tell me or I'll begin shouting.'

He moved to open his mouth.

'No, don't!' Tallitha whispered frantically, 'I-I'll tell you.'

'Well, spit it out,' he hissed.

Tallitha swallowed hard.

'We're on our way t-to the G-Grand D-Duchess's tower,' she stuttered.

The youth's face darkened and his wolfish teeth flashed menacingly.

'What do you want with the Neopholytite?' he asked, his eyes narrowing. 'Whatever you want with her, she'll demand much more in return if she catches you.'

The youth stood poised in the hallway like an animal ready to pounce. His earth-coloured clothes fitted him like a glove. Tallitha noticed a small silver dagger at his hip.

'We don't want to actually meet her, we only want to get inside her tower,' she explained.

From far below there was a faint noise coming from the lower floors. Tallitha leaned over the banister but it was too dark to see anything.

'What do want from that dark place?' he asked, searching her face for answers.

'We're not sure,' she lied, 'but we'll know when we find it.'

'How will you get inside the tower? It's an evil place for little girls to be roaming around in,' he sneered. 'And small boys,' he added, throwing a dismissive glance in Tyaas's direction.

Tallitha bristled again. He was patronising them.

'You know who I am, don't you? You know they mean to have me in the Swarm,' she said fiercely.

The youth's eyes ran over her face, reading her desperate expression. His lips twisted once more into an unpleasant leer that bared his teeth.

'I know you,' he said flatly, giving nothing away, 'but how did you get out tonight? I thought the Shrove locked you in after nightfall.'

Tallitha took the key from her pocket and it glinted in the moonlight.

'Clever, aren't you?' said the youth. 'You know the Swarm will never let you go.'

'We don't belong here. We must escape and go home to Winderling Spires,' she said determinedly.

'You can't stop us,' added Tyaas, full of bravado.

The stranger lunged in one movement and grabbed Tyaas by the collar, spit flying into the boy's frightened face.

'No one escapes from Hellstone Tors! We're all trapped here one way or another,' uttered the youth with emotion.

He pushed Tyaas away and the boy stumbled to the floor.

'But we will escape,' replied Tallitha, going to her brother's aid. 'I'm going to break the Morrow pact. I'm going to find out about Edwyn Morrow's blood-oath. That's why we're going to the Witch's Tower.'

The youth's eyes burned brighter in his angular, skull-like face. He studied the young girl before him.

'You'll never make it alone,' he said. 'If the witch catches you or the Swarm discover you're out after dark they will lock you up somewhere much more nasty. Then you'll never escape.'

Tyaas whispered into his sister's ear: '*Who is he?*'

The youth overheard him. His hearing was as acute as his eyesight.

Tallitha voiced her brother's words.

'But who are you?'

'I'll be a better friend to you than any here,' he said mysteriously. 'Someone who can help you break the pact and escape.'

'How can we trust you?' asked Tallitha, her eyes searching his face.

There it is again, she thought – the sound of distant scratching on the wooden floors. Tallitha's heart missed a beat and she peered down into the hallway once more. But it was all shadowy and dark in the bowels of the castle.

'It's your decision whether you trust me or not. It makes no difference to me if you turn round and go back to bed where all good children should be,' he jested, toying with their vulnerability.

'Stop it!' spat Tyaas, his face turning hot with anger and a tear running down his cheek. 'You might betray us to the Shroves or to our mother!'

The youth's face softened.

'Calm down, young man. Of course I won't tell, and I'm sorry if I startled you. I can be a little gruff – I spend a lot of my time on my own ...' He hesitated. 'But you'll get used to me. So, what do you say? Do we have a deal?'

Tallitha took her brother to one side. After Benedict's betrayal she had promised to listen to what Tyaas had to say.

'Well, Tyaas, can we trust him?' she whispered in his ear.

Tyaas wasn't sure. Tallitha searched her brother's face for an answer.

'We don't have a choice. If we want to get to the bottom of the secret pact and get out of this dreadful place then we need his help,' he said cautiously.

'Okay, but what if he tells Mother?' she asked, biting her lip.

'We'll have to take that chance. Come on, it's the only exciting thing that's happened to us since we arrived in this forsaken place.'

The youth smiled. He had overheard every word they had said.

'You mustn't tell anyone you know me if we meet again. You must act as though we have never met. It's our secret,' the youth insisted. 'Is that agreed?'

Tallitha nodded.

'Yeah, sure,' said Tyaas. 'But what's your name?'

'Best not say,' he smirked. 'Now, do you have any idea how to find the Neopholytite's tower?'

Tallitha and Tyaas shook their heads.

There was that noise again and it was getting closer. She wasn't imagining it and this time it sounded ominously familiar.

'What's that awful noise?' she asked.

In the distance Tallitha could hear the faint sound of something moving quickly over the polished floors – it was the sound of scratching noises coming towards them, racing up the staircases, gaining momentum.

'It's the dogs,' said the youth, his eyes flashing. 'The Thane's vicious wolfhounds are on their nightly prowl around the castle. They must have found your scent.'

Tallitha hurriedly looked over the banister. Now she could hear them quite plainly.

'But I thought no one stirred after dark?' she exclaimed.

'No one stirs *because* of the wolfhounds,' added the youth menacingly. 'They patrol the castle to make sure that no one escapes.'

'What shall we do?' cried Tallitha, searching the landing for any sighting of the dreaded beasts.

'Follow me or stay here and face the dogs.' The youth turned on his heel and began striding back the way he had come. 'Up to you,' he called after him.

For a moment they held their breath, staring at each other on the shadowy landing as the sound of the wild dogs became louder. They could hear the beasts moving closer, pounding through the dark castle and scratching the floor with their hideous claws as they built up pace along the lower landings, springing in a ragged pack up the next staircase.

'Let's go!' Tallitha shouted.

She grabbed Tyaas's hand and they raced after the youth just as the pack of monstrous wolfhounds leapt onto their landing and slunk to the floor, growling and baring their fangs, finally locating their quarry. Their eyes burned red with bloodlust.

'Quick!' shouted Tyaas. 'Let's follow him!'

In an instant Tallitha and Tyaas sped down the corridor, darted behind the long flowing curtains and into the dark, musty recesses of the sinister castle, leaving the snarling hounds behind them on the dark landing baying for their blood.

Seven

'Hurry, get inside!' shouted the youth.

Tallitha and Tyaas scrambled through the opening just as one of the hounds forced its hideous snout through the gap, sinking its fangs into Tyaas's leg. The youth reacted like lightning, clubbing the wolfhound on the nose and slamming the wall panelling shut behind them, bolting it into place.

'Ouch, it stings,' moaned Tyaas, holding his leg, the warm blood trickling over his fingers.

'It's just a flesh wound,' Tallitha replied, dabbing her handkerchief over the punctured flesh.

They could hear the dogs snuffling on the other side of the wall, growling and pounding the floor, going round and round in circles trying to work out what had just happened and where their quarry had disappeared.

The youth struck a match and as the lantern spluttered into

light, the youth's yellow-flecked eyes glinted hungrily. He looked more like a huntsman than a castle dweller. *From out of the frying pan and into the fire*, thought Tallitha as she stared at their strange companion. But for some reason he was willing to help them and show them his secret places. They found themselves in a cramped dingy passageway within a dark maze of wall cavities.

'Here,' he said, handing her a bundle of leaves. 'Wrap these round the wound and it will draw any poison.'

Tallitha gave him a curious look.

'It's dangerous climbing in these rat-infested cavities – don't know what diseases you might pick up.'

Tallitha began to dab Tyaas's leg with the youth's remedy.

'Careful! I can do it,' Tyaas insisted, pulling away.

He rolled up his sock to keep the damp leaves in place and hobbled to his feet.

'Ready?' asked the youth, staring at their frightened faces in the gloom. 'Then follow me into the netherworld of Hellstone Tors,' he said enticingly.

The passage was narrow and dusty, smelling of vermin droppings and stale air, but as Tallitha stared about her she noticed that the walls were lined with glinting knives, sharp axes, and hanks of ropes and twine, an arsenal of weapons that the youth had gathered together to protect himself. *But against who or what?* thought Tallitha.

'You look young,' he said gruffly, running his yellow eyes over her. 'What I want to know is what's so special about you?'

Tallitha turned pink and shuffled from one foot to the other.

'Nothing much,' she replied, sounding embarrassed.

'So why have the Swarm chosen you?'

'I'm next in line, according to the Thane – but this isn't my choice and I don't want to be here!' she exclaimed.

'He could have chosen him,' he said pointing at Tyaas, 'but he didn't. So what special talents do you have you to offer them?'

Tallitha shrugged. The youth was beginning to irritate her with his silly questions.

'I don't know what you mean. I'm just a girl from Wycham Elva and Mother ...'

'Ah yes, Snowdroppe,' replied the youth, his face turning sour as he bundled ropes into his backpack.

'The *Lady* Snowdroppe to you!' said Tyaas sharply.

The youth sprang as if to grab the boy by the throat but thought better of it. He clenched his teeth and Tallitha noticed his jawbone grinding aggressively as he desperately tried to control his emotions.

'Mind your tongue,' he snarled viciously.

Tallitha pulled Tyaas to one side and stood in front of him.

'What do we do now?' she asked the youth, trying to deflect his attention away from her brother.

'While it's dark we must make haste to the Neopholytite's tower. Here,' he said, digging into his bag, 'you'll need to wear these amulets round your neck.'

He handed them a bloodstone set in a gold mesh case that emitted a pungent smell of decaying petals and ash.

'What are these for?' asked Tyaas, pulling a disgusted face and inspecting the smelly object at arm's length.

'They will protect us from the witch sniffing us out,' he replied, hanging a pendant around his throat. 'She has a keen sense of smell, and the power of this amulet will mask our scent and repel her evil.'

The amulet was similar to the bloodstone that Tallitha had seen in the Jewel Room in Winderling Spires and the one that had adorned Caedryl's neck.

'Does this have power against the Swarm?' she asked, placing the pendant around her neck.

The sickly aroma made her feel a little dizzy.

'There's a curse tablet inside to ward off the witch's power,' said the youth.

Tallitha was curious. 'Where did you get these?' she asked.

The youth sliced his eyes at her. 'Never you mind, just keep them close.'

He turned on his heel, jerking his chin towards the gloomy passageways.

'At the end of this run there's a series of deep shafts with ropes and ladders. Do you think you'll be able to climb using the ropes? It's hard at first.'

'We're used to climbing,' said Tyaas aggressively.

He hadn't forgiven the youth for being rude about his mother.

'Yes, we've climbed many times before,' answered Tallitha.

She pinched Tyaas to warn him to be quiet.

The youth nodded gruffly. 'It's easier getting around the castle through these passageways so as not to be seen by the

Swarm or the wretched Shroves,' he explained. 'Just follow me, I'll tell you what to do at each point. So pay attention.'

The youth shot them a sideways glance as he put tools and supplies in his bag.

Tallitha pulled Tyaas to her side.

'Don't annoy him,' she mumbled. 'He's a strange one and we don't know how he'll react.'

'I don't like him,' whispered Tyaas, 'but I don't think he'll harm us.'

The youth threw them a wary glance and walked to the end of the passageway, blowing out the candle. Tallitha knew that it could all be a trap. Now they were alone in the darkness with this strange, feral creature.

They felt along the walls, following stranger through the narrow spaces, easing their bodies through the tight bends and crevasses full of the dust and grime of the ancient castle. The youth was impressed with their agility as they skimmed effortlessly down the ladder and skilfully landed at the first main intersection.

'I'll go first. You can ease yourself down using the lath boards as resting points.'

At the next level he stopped and lit another candle as Tyaas nipped easily down the shaft, moving hand over hand, making the task look easy. One by one they tripped down the vertical shafts, past the ancient lath and plaster structure that lined the castle walls.

'From here we go under the floors,' he said. 'Like this.'

In a heartbeat the youth disappeared through a trapdoor.

There's something of the Skink in this youth, thought Tallitha as she jumped in after him, squirreling away under the floorboards, squeezing her body between the lintels and travelling through the warren-like arteries hidden in the castle.

'These tunnels are incredible – eurgh! – but there are way too many cobwebs,' she coughed as she breathed in the dusty underbelly of Hellstone Tors. 'How did you discover them?'

'I like to have an escape route handy,' he replied enigmatically. 'These cavities provide a whole bunch of them.'

The youth burrowed through the narrow spaces like a ferret. His taut body edged over the lintels and through the under floor spaces, avoiding the mice droppings and fusty places where a number of creatures had crawled in and died.

'It's a bit smelly,' said Tyaas, poking the maggot-eaten back of a stiff dead rat.

'Shh, nearly there,' the youth called over his shoulder. 'There are spies everywhere – we must creep about like mice.'

The youth pulled his body out from beneath the floorboards and up inside a dark hollow space. Then they were climbing up inside the walls again, pulling their tired bodies up the ladders and ropes until they came to a trapdoor. On the other side a trickle of moonlight fell to the ground from a skylight far above them.

'Where are we?' asked Tallitha, looking warily up the long gloomy shaft.

The youth held his finger to his lips. 'We're in one of the

oldest part of the castle. Most of these old service shafts have been knocked down, but this one remains and is attached to the Witch's Tower. This is the only way to avoid the Darkling Stairs.'

'That sounds exciting,' said Tyaas. 'Why can't we use them?'

'Too dangerous,' he answered, tapping the flaking plasterwork. 'Behind this wall is the witch's staircase, known as the Darkling Stairs. Not a route I'd ever like to take.'

But the youth had whetted Tyaas's appetite for adventure: he might be scared of the Darkling Stairs, but Tyaas wasn't.

'Where's the entrance?' asked Tyaas.

'Over there.' The youth pointed to a small wooden doorway recessed in the brickwork. 'There's a Groat guard at the head of the staircase, which they change at certain times,' he said, looking over his shoulder. 'But there's no one coming, we're safe for now.'

'Can we take a look?' asked Tyaas excitedly, moving towards the door.

The youth grabbed him by the collar and dragged him back.

'No! You must never go in there – it's too dangerous!'

'Why ever not?' asked Tallitha.

'The Night Slopers will catch you, for certain.'

'What are they?' asked Tyaas.

'The witch's familiars, black cat-like creatures, they live under the stairs, on the alert for any intruders.'

'But if that's the only way to get inside the tower,' persisted Tallitha, twiddling with her hair, 'then we'll have to use those stairs if we mean to destroy the pact.'

'Not tonight!' he said gruffly. The youth's eyes looked terrified. 'You must understand that entering the Witch's Tower and locating that pact will be very risky – many have tried and have met a terrible fate.'

Tallitha and her brother exchanged knowing glances. This was the route they would have to take if they wanted to find the Morrow pact. It sounded deadly dangerous.

'Come on, you can take a peek inside the Witch's Tower from up there,' the youth whispered, pointing up into the darkness. 'Then you'll have some idea of the challenges you face.'

He began climbing the open staircase that wound around the sides of a brick shaft, twisting upwards in a spiral. The stair treads were fashioned from planks of wood precariously slotted into intermittent gaps in the walls of the shaft. Glimmers of moonlight glinted from the highest point, lighting their way as they clambered up the narrow treads.

'Put your fingers into the crevasses and pull yourselves up by feeling the bumps in the stone,' he murmured. 'Balance carefully on the treads. At the top there's a platform where we can peek inside the tower.'

The youth climbed with agility, turning to help them over the more treacherous places where the treads had almost worn through.

'Take my hand – watch that step,' he called taking Tallitha's hand and guiding her up the precarious staircase.

Tallitha held her brother's hand and they clambered upwards until they reached the platform, fashioned from a number of roughly hewn planks. Through the gaps in the floorboards, Tallitha could see a distant glimmer of light seeping from one of the interconnecting floors. It was a long way down. At the top of the shaft, a colony of bats clustered in the hollow of the domed glass ceiling. They flittered and fluttered, clinging to the walls and eyeing the intruders from their lofty vantage point.

The youth removed a tiny piece of brick and peered through an aperture in the wall. He stood still for some time, peeping cautiously into the witch's lair. Then he took hold of Tallitha's shoulders and carefully positioned her in front of the spy hole. At first it was too dark to see anything, but as Tallitha's eyes became accustomed to the gloomy interior she was able to differentiate between the patterns of light and darkness inside the tower. The room was an odd shape, like an upturned boat carved out of the skeleton of an enormous dead animal. The roof had a central spine spanning it, with the bony vertebrae running down each side of the walls. There were no windows that she could see, only the light from several tall candles that cast shadows across the skeletal infrastructure. All around the room tattered reddish-brown muslin hung from the walls like trailing bloody drapes, winding across the floor like coiled snakes.

'What do you think of the Neopholytite's tower?' he whispered, coming closer to her.

His breath was warm and he smelled of honey.

Tallitha started at the sound of his voice. 'It looks like the carcass of a dead animal,' she whispered, staring at the huge ribcage that formed the walls at the top of the Witch's Tower.

'That's what it is,' he replied: 'the skeleton of an ancient beast retrieved from battle long, long ago.'

'Eurgh, let me see,' begged Tyaas, standing on his tiptoes to peer through the hole. 'How did it get up here?' he asked.

'Sorcery and magic,' the youth whispered menacingly.

Tallitha gasped.

'The skeleton was brought to Hellstone Tors by the Grand Witch Selvistra, and placed here so its potent magic could always protect the witches that lived in this castle.'

'Where is Selvistra now?' asked Tallitha.

The youth shrugged. 'No one knows the whereabouts of the Grand Witches, they come and go as they please. Maybe they're in Hegglefoot or beyond the Northern Wolds.'

Tallitha had never heard of lands beyond the Northern Wolds. She screwed up her eyes and looked through the aperture again.

'The room is full of nasty drapes stained with blood.'

'That'll be the Morrow stain. The encrusted blood was woven into the fabric to protect the Neopholytite and all the witches that have used this lair.'

'That stain is also on me,' she said gravely. 'Somehow I must get rid of it, or the Swarm will always be able to track me.'

Tallitha nervously rubbed her hands down the front of her trousers, trying to get rid of the Morrow stain, but it tingled across her palms.

'How do we get inside?' asked Tyaas, excited by the prospect of entering the witch's lair.

'There's no way in apart from the Darkling Stairs, but we could take a closer look and maybe see her too. Are you ready?'

The youth began climbing to the top of the rickety steps, to where the bat colony roosted in the dome. They fluttered angrily, agitated by the disturbance.

'Be quiet, don't frighten them,' the youth warned, unlatching a dirty glass panel in the domed skylight.

But the moonlight flooded through the window and the creatures swooped and squeaked at their trespassers, darting out of the skylight in a trail of silky blue-blackness into the cool night sky. The air was chilly, blowing in gusty bursts through the domed window, and straight into Tallitha's face.

'Quickly step out onto the ledge,' said the youth, offering his hand.

Tallitha climbed through the domed skylight and out onto a stone bridge that linked the shaft to the Grand Duchess's tower. Way below, the dark threatening outline of Hellstone Tors cascaded in all its nefarious glory, the moonlight shining along the castellated rooftops and revealing the enormity of the infernal structure. The pointed roofs of Hellstone's myriad towers pierced the night sky like sharp swords, their coppery burnished tops shining as the sound of the sea crashed again and again, lashing its heart out on the jagged black rocks. Before them, the roof of the Neopholytite's lair was bathed in an eerie fog that hung in sulphurous clouds, obscuring the extent of roof space.

'Don't look down,' the youth shouted fiercely into the wind.

'Keep your arms out like this,' he said, stretching his arms to each side to maintain his balance.

He stepped onto the plinth and began walking across the stone arch, taking deliberate steps and looking dead ahead. Like a tightrope walker he balanced carefully over the terrifying drop and moved quickly over the bridge that connected the two buildings. Tyaas went next and Tallitha followed.

She had a good head for heights and wasn't worried – besides, the excitement of seeing the Neopholytite spurred her onwards. Halfway across, Tallitha missed her footing and stumbled, tripping forward and lunging out into the terrifying drop. The night air rushed past her face as she fell. In an instant the youth moved like lightening. He grabbed her flailing arm with one hand, jerking her swiftly upwards and planted her firmly on the ground next to him. Tallitha was shaking uncontrollably. He held her close for a second. Again the smell of sweet honey filled her senses.

'Tallitha! Oh Tallitha,' moaned Tyaas, distraught by his sister's near-disaster.

She buried her head in the youth's jacket then, realising her proximity to his body, yanked her head back and stepped towards her brother.

'T-Thank you, I don't know what h-happened out there.' She gesticulated towards the arched walkway.

'You didn't follow my instructions,' the youth said gruffly, turning slightly red.

'I'm sorry I stumbled. I didn't *intend* to throw myself off the parapet,' she muttered sarcastically.

The roof space was oddly shaped. It bulged out to one side and was flat at the top. The soupy yellow fog clung to the battlements and soaked down the sides of the tower like a foaming potion, thick and bubbling.

'What next?' Tyaas asked excitedly.

'There's only one way in and it's mucky.'

The youth moved towards the chimneystack, lifted the chimney pot from the top, and began to manoeuvre himself inside.

'Is that the way in?' asked Tallitha, sounding horrified.

The youth grinned and began edging his way down the chimney shaft.

'I'm not sure I can do that,' she whispered.

'We don't have to go far. There's another chimney branch inside, and there's a gap where they connect. We can get a good vantage point from there and you'll be able to see her,' he said enticingly.

'What if the witch has a fire in the grate?'

'Don't be silly,' said the youth, 'we'd see the smoke.'

The acrid foggy-light ebbed across the roof as the youth slipped down inside the stack.

'Be quiet,' he warned. 'If she smells us or hears us we're done for.'

With that he slipped out of sight.

'Come on,' said Tyaas excitedly.

He climbed over the lip of the stack and began slithering down the chimney, holding out his hand to help his sister.

'Okay, if you're sure we won't get stuck or burned to death,' said Tallitha nervously.

She clambered in after him and slid down into the chimney's inner core and into the dead flat darkness.

Eight

'Careful where you're putting your feet,' whispered Tyaas hoarsely, struggling down the inside of the chimney, 'and watch my head!'

He roughly pushed Tallitha's foot to one side and climbed down into the black hole.

'It's so dark in here. I told you it would be horrible,' his sister replied. 'I can't see a thing!'

'Shh,' hissed the youth, his yellow eyes glaring at Tallitha up the chimney, 'or we'll be discovered.'

The chimney was much wider than Tallitha had first feared, with slippery layers of soot that clung to her fingers and pervaded her nostrils. Small footholds ran throughout the brickwork and although the chimney was grimy and stuffy, they soon reached the intersection where the main chimney branched off to the right. The youth lit a tallow candle and stood before them on a blackened ledge, his smudged face tense and wary. He put his

finger to his lips and held out his hand, guiding Tallitha and then Tyaas to the vantage point.

'Be as quiet as you can,' he whispered, standing close behind them. 'We're much closer to the witch up here – now take a look into the curious Bone Room.'

He removed a small stone and positioned Tallitha before the spy hole. She gripped the brickwork with her blackened fingers, leant forward and stared through the aperture into the nightmarish world of the Neopholytite. Slowly her eyes became accustomed to the gloomy interior, and dark blurred shapes came into focus. Black candles stood at intervals around the room, spluttering and casting pools of light that brought segments of the eerie space into view. Along the ribcage walls, glass fronted cabinets flickered in the candlelight, filled with large specimen jars containing grisly body parts.

'Eurgh,' Tallitha whispered, turning to the youth. 'There are bits of dead animals in there.'

'Let me see,' Tyaas pleaded, craning to take a peek.

'Not now, Tyaas,' she whispered.

Her brother pulled a sullen face. It wasn't fair. Tallitha always had the first go at everything.

Tallitha peered at the outline of the bone roof – at the skeleton of a long dead beast, the bloody red sinews falling from the ribcage in ominous tangled shreds. These were the remnants of the ancient Morrow stain that had marked her out too. There were stacks of jewelled caskets, and a wall of mirrors that illuminated a table covered with painted cards. All in all, the room displayed the sinister paraphernalia and artefacts of an extremely skilled sorceress. Scattered around the Bone Room and tucked into the crannies of the bone rafters were a number of blue, green and scarlet witch bottles used to protect the Neopholytite against magical attack. About the room, large birds of prey, some caged and some chained, were perched in pods of twos and threes, preening their feathers, squawking and fluttering their wings.

'Can you see her yet?' murmured the youth into the girl's ear.

Tallitha shook her head. Her eyes were drawn to the peculiar twisted trees growing out of the floor of the Bone Room and reaching high up into the rafters. Their branches were wizened from the lack of light, and different coloured papers had been attached to each twig.

'Look towards the back of the room, through the Curse Trees,' the youth urged.

Then Tallitha spied the old witch sitting with her straggling entourage: a motley band of Shroves and Groats. The Neopholytite sat hunched, curled up in her chair like a snarling animal. She had sharp bony features – her thin nose and cheekbones looked as though they could slice like a knife. Her dead eyes stared straight ahead of her like clouded glass. She sniffed the air and leaned forward.

'Have you collected all the green curses?' the witch asked a hooded figure sitting before her.

The figure clicked her fingers and one of the Shroves bustled towards the Curse Trees, and handed the Neopholytite a few flimsy pieces of green paper. The witch smelled each one in turn, sorting through the different aromas. She clutched them tightly in her stick-like fingers.

The Neopholytite's misshapen stiffened dress was the colour of dried blood, matching the drapes that hung about the Bone Room: brownish red and tattered beyond repair – a hideous warning of her wickedness. The witch's wizened face was partly obscured, covered by a dark red veil that she sat picking apart, pulling at the dark tangled threads. Her crimson fingerless gloves gave her hands the appearance of red-raw claws, as she continued picking at her garments like a vulture at a carcass. By her side stood four lumbering Groats, their grey translucent skin glistening with sweat, their ugly faces fixated on their mistress. At the foot of the Neopholytite's chair lay a group of slumbering hounds, and by their side a big raggedy beast sat alert, its vile tongue panting and drooling, revealing its pointed fangs.

'It's death-like in there,' Tallitha whispered. 'Are they in mourning?' she asked, peering at the dreary sight.

There was a strong smell of sulphur, but the lingering stench of decay lurking beneath wholly pervaded the atmosphere.

'In a way,' the youth whispered. 'The Bone Room holds the Emporium of Lost Souls.'

Tallitha swallowed hard at the grisly sight before her as two Shroves ambled out of the shadows. They poured phials of coloured liquid, scattering flowers and herbs into a whirlpool that sprang out of the floor.

'Snare! Snare!' the witch shouted to one of her Shroves.

'Make the whorl-pit sing! Add more Banewood Syrup and the purple Clamourspun Nettle Heads.' She reached into her pocket and flung a handful of green and red beads onto the table before her. 'Read the words to me,' she demanded.

The oval beads scattered across the table as the hooded figure replied to the witch in words that Tallitha could not hear.

'Then that's what we will do – add Cloudspit and Frog's Vomit, Wricken Bark and Shrockle Plants,' she instructed. 'Mix them together in the whorl-pit – bring the potion alive.'

The Shroves scuttled about the Bone Room, ferrying the phials and boxes and throwing their contents into the pit. The concoction bubbled rapidly to the surface, hissing and spitting an array of violet, silver and green starbursts that fizzed like a roman candle into the sulphurous air.

The witch sniffed the curse paper she had chosen.

'*Lilletha le durna, Lilletha le durna,*' the Neopholytite chanted. '*Lilletha le durna, Lilletha le durna.*' Now open the Emporium and set them free!' she called.

The hooded figure released a glass stopper on a large bell jar. Tendrils of yellow fog floated upwards and curled about the room, trailing and swirling, turning into a whirlwind of ghostly breath that circulated over the Neopholytite's head like a cloud. It was the same fog that hung over the top of the Witch's Tower. Then suddenly the Neopholytite disappeared into the cloud.

'*Ledanta smilla, ne sentallita, talla,*' she chanted.

Tallitha was mesmerised by the curious ways of the witch. She felt drawn to the ethereal faces that appeared in the ghostly breath: apparitions from the Emporium of Lost Souls. Tallitha's hand began to itch and, without warning, she felt the familiar sensation of the shadow-flight – as though she was about to be sucked from her body. She gripped the brickwork and gasped.

'I-I'm going into a trance,' she moaned, grabbing the youth's hand. 'Stop me, do something!' she wailed softly. 'I'm being pulled into the Bone Room.'

The youth dug his nails into Tallitha's arms, holding her tight to prevent the trance taking hold. He noticed a fuzzy purplish light begin to surround the girl. His eyes, those snaky amber orbs, glowed in the sooty blackness. This was yet another sign that she had the power he sought.

'I'm slipping,' Tallitha called out as his nails dug in deeper, drawing blood.

The floating sensation dragged at her shadow-self and she saw the faces of the lost souls moving closer, their desperate mouths crying out to her to free them from the witch's evil spell. Tallitha resisted their potency and concentrated her mind on the present, then *whoosh!* – she slipped back inside her body with a thud. Tallitha lurched forward against the parapet as the youth caught her slumped body.

'You okay?' he whispered. 'I nearly lost you.'

She looked pale but her eyes were bright. 'It's over,' she moaned. 'That's never happened like that before. Those lost souls were reaching out to me, pulling me in.'

'Perhaps you're too close to all this dark magic,' whispered the youth.

Tallitha nodded and peered once again through the spy hole as the yellow misty breath snaked down the witch's body and engulfed her like a shroud.

'*Lilletha le durna!*' she cried, lapping up the essence of the ghostly apparitions, feeding on the lost souls that wrapped her up in their ghostliness.

Tallitha steadied herself and watched as the mist evaporated and the Neopholytite reappeared, seemingly refreshed. The old witch looked rejuvenated. The whirlpool disappeared beneath the floor and the witch clicked her fingers. One of the Shroves hurried to her side, and began to place the beads into the Neopholytite's hand. The cloaked figure watched intently as the witch caressed her fingers over the surface of each bead.

'*Nempora de la sentoras, vestellier,*' she chanted.

The hooded figure clapped her hands excitedly. As the sleeves rolled down her skinny arms, Tallitha noticed the dark blood-red talons. The woman muttered something in Ennish and the Neopholytite shouted again:

'*Lilletha le durna, Lilletha le durna!*'

The hooded figure collected the beads and placed them in a small wooden cabinet.

'We can't stay too long, she may smell us,' warned the youth, urging Tallitha to come away.

'Can't I see her too?' moaned Tyaas, pulling a face.

'We must go,' said the youth, 'we've stayed too long as it is.'

They began the sooty climb back up the inside of the chimney and out onto the windswept roof.

*

In the heart of her hideous chamber, the Neopholytite raised her head, wrinkled her nose and smelt a waft of scented ash mixed with the aroma of Morrow stain, fresh and blood-scented. She breathed deeply from the sweet smell, relishing the scent, and as she wove her spells, she wondered whether some creature had somehow pierced the armour of her Bone Room and stolen into her curse-protected lair.

'Difficult to achieve,' mused the witch.

She pulled the threads on her tattered dress and worried about whether the Grand Witches were on the prowl, tricking her with the aroma of the Morrow stain.

'Snare, come here,' she called to her Shrove. 'Take me to inspect my spells.'

The Shrove, a particularly sneaky and malignant individual with spiky black hair, ambled towards the witch, his shifty eyes moving disconcertingly in his eye sockets like wobbly marbles in a jar.

The Neopholytite, aided by Snare, rose stiffly from her chair and felt her way around the edge of the Bone Room, holding onto the ribcage of the old beast as she crept to the top of the Darkling Stairs. The witch bent down on her creaky knees and whispered dark Ennish words to the host of Night Slopers, instructing her cattish-ones to be ever vigilant and guard her inner sanctuary against any strange and invading witches. She bade the Groats accompany her to inspect the rows of spirit traps, made from rowan sticks and strands of long hair caught up in spiders' webs. The traps were set to catch any witch who tried to steal into the Neopholytite's lair, but the contraptions remained taut, firm and ready to warn the witch of any magical malevolence.

The Neopholytite lifted her bony finger and pointed up into the murky roof of the Bone Room.

'Check my witch bottles!' she cried.

The Groats climbed the bloody ribcage way up into the bone rafters, feeling along the arches and stone lintels for the coloured witch bottles, shaking them to ensure that their contents were secure from any prying fingers and that the curse tablets were intact, ready to counteract any harmful invasion of the witch's lair.

But although the Neopholytite was an old sorceress, steeped in aeons of powerful magic, she feared the Grand Witches of the Larva Coven, and as she stared dead-eyed into her darkened lair she yearned to discover the true nature of her trespasser.

*

They were filthy, covered from head to toe in soot.

'You'll have to get rid of those clothes,' said the youth, balancing on the parapet.

He led the way down the rickety steps, climbing through the enclosed walls and wriggling under the floorboards until they came to a narrow wooden doorway nestled high up inside one of the smaller turrets. The room, just like the musty passageway, was full of weapons, ropes, knives and jars of sticky honey.

So that's where the smellcomes from, thought Tallitha.

'Here take this,' he said, offering them berry cordial and day-old bread that he smothered with the delicious honey.

They were starving after their strenuous climb and fell upon the food.

'How do you know your way around this castle so well?' asked Tallitha inquisitively.

'I've made it my business to get around Hellstone Tors without being seen,' the youth replied, voraciously pushing food into his ravenous mouth.

'Don't you trust the Swarm?' she asked.

He shook his head as Tallitha and Tyaas returned the bloodstones set in their metal cases. He hid them away for safekeeping.

'I have my reasons,' he replied.

'What were those scraps of paper?' she asked.

'The witch's library of curses,' the youth replied.

Tyaas's mouth dropped open and he nudged his sister to continue.

'Who were those faces in the fog?' she asked.

The youth didn't respond, so Tallitha, twisting her hair in and out of her fingers, sidled up to him and tried a different tack.

'Embellsed told me that some poor souls have been lost in the castle, never to be seen again.'

She watched his face. It twitched slightly. He thought for a moment then replied.

'They are the lost souls caught for eternity until the pact is broken,' answered the youth. 'The Neopholytite feeds on them, bathing in their youthfulness. She isn't a Grand Witch, so eternal youth is denied to her – she grows old like the rest of us. The Neopholytite uses the Emporium to try and delay the hands of time.'

'Eurgh!' she moaned. 'But how did those souls come to be there?'

'Either the Night Slopers captured them on the Darkling Stairs, or they were handed to her by the Dooerlins. Their souls were turned into the apparitions you saw today,' he replied ominously.

The Dooerlins, those dreadful creatures again, thought Tallitha. A cold shiver ran through her. 'So do the lost souls give her eternal youth?'

'You saw her rejuvenation. It only works for a short while, but it keeps her alive. She's an ancient being.'

'How old is she?'

The youth shook his head. 'For many generations she's been weaving her awful spells and casting her evil net.'

'I wanted to see the witch too,' Tyaas complained. 'What was she like?'

'Weird. Covered in bloody red drapes and extremely scary,' replied Tallitha. 'But I couldn't see her face, it was obscured.'

'What did she do?' asked the boy.

'Magic and sorcery – spells and chanting – but there was something odd about her dead eyes.'

'The Neopholytite has no sight,' explained the youth. 'She cannot see the world through her eyes – she can only see through her wickedness.'

'Was that Micrentor's Cabinet by her side?' asked Tallitha.

The youth nodded.

'Then it holds the Morrow pact. We have to get inside the Neopholytite's tower!'

'That will be extremely dangerous,' replied the youth.

'Well, there's no way to avoid it,' insisted Tallitha. 'That cabinet holds the key to our freedom.'

'What else did you see?' asked Tyaas, clearly fascinated by the witch.

'The Bone Room was dark and frightening.' Tallitha replied. 'In the ghostly breath I saw the faces of wailing women,' she shuddered. 'Their plaintive cries were blood-curdling.'

Tyaas's eyes opened wide. 'What else did you see?'

'Rowan wands and rows of coloured glass bottles.'

'They'll be the spirit traps and witch bottles laid across the room to protect the Neopholytite.'

'Why does she need protecting?' asked Tyaas.

'From any Grand Witch who must be kept at bay,' replied the youth. 'In case they try and pierce her armour of spells, and take her place in the Bone Room.'

'There was a woman with her, but I couldn't see her face,' said Tallitha. 'The witch was surrounded by those wolfhounds – they looked like the Black Hounds from Ragging Brows Forest.' She paused, twisting her hair in and out of her fingers. 'Last night I had a nightmare about the hounds and when I opened my eyes Lapis and Muprid were in my room, watching me.'

'They're playing with you, testing you out,' he said. 'Keep some Comfrey under your pillow and leave a light burning. Then they will leave you alone.'

'But those Black Hounds are terrifying,' said Tallitha. 'They nearly killed us in the forest.'

'We call them the Death-Hounds here,' said the youth.

The colour drained from Tyaas's face. 'What do you mean, Death-Hounds?' he whispered, fearing the reply.

'The Death-Hounds visit the Neopholytite whenever her granddaughter comes to stay. The hounds protect her in the forest.'

The youth lifted his eyes to observe Tallitha's reaction.

'Was she the cloaked figure sitting opposite her?' she asked.

The youth nodded.

The small candlelit space became ominously quiet as Tallitha began to recall the skinny outline of the female figure, and those blood-red nails … such a telltale sign. The bread cake suddenly dropped from her hand.

'Who is the witch's granddaughter?' Tallitha asked apprehensively.

The youth stopped eating, wiped his mouth and allowed a smile to play for a moment on his lips.

'Why, Asphodel, the Queen of the Dark Reaches,' answered the youth.

Tallitha and Tyaas stared at one another. It was yet another dark layer of their evil ancestry falling into place.

'Is the Neopholytite part of the Swarm?' she asked.

The youth continued eating and nodded at Tallitha.

Then the Neopholytite was the thirteenth member of the Morrow Swarm! She was the missing member; the one that Embellsed was too afraid to mention. Tallitha shuddered and took hold of her brother's hand.

'You know what this means?' she whispered, biting her lip.

Tyaas shook his head.

'It means that the witch, that evil Neopholytite, is related to us too.'

Tyaas stared and his mouth fell open.

'She's our great-grandmother!'

Nine

Embellsed was frantic. He ferreted about in his Shrove hole, flinging aside tattered blankets and sticking his fingers into all the grotty, smelly places in search of the missing key.

'Where is it?' he moaned desperately, scrabbling to the back of his pit and peering with one eye closed down into the gap. 'Oh, what's to be done? They'll flay me alive!' he cried, shaking with fear.

Beads of sweat appeared on his brow as he stretched his skinny arm as far as he could, pushing his fingers to the bottom of the cracks in his stinking lair.

'Damn those nasty children, makin' me get into bother!'

The sweat trickled down and dripped off the end of his beaky nose. He wiped his forehead with his coat sleeve and grizzled away to himself. He must cover his tracks at all costs. The fault mustn't be laid at his door. If the Swarm discovered

that he had misplaced the key, he would be consigned to the lower Shroveling ranks forever. He sat moodily in the corner of his lair with his spindly legs wrapped beneath him, twitching now and then as he pulled at his long ears and muttered away to himself. What was he to do? It was a terrible mess, and no mistake.

He sat hunched in a ball, scratching his long skinny legs and ruminating over the problem, going over and over in his mind the last time he had the key in his possession. Then it came to him. That tall, haughty creature, the Lady Snowdroppe, must have the key! Anyway, it was her fault for shooing him away so nastily. He would say nowt about it – that was the answer. He would just *borrow* a duplicate key from Bludroot's storeroom when no one was about.

*

The High Shrove's accommodation was set apart from the rest of the miserable Shrove holes. This lair was Bludroot's treasure trove, the special place where he kept all his snitchings: mostly missable objects and items he had stolen from the castle over the years, including a box of jewels hidden somewhere amongst the rubbish and bric-a-brac. There was an odd assortment of crockery, trinkets, bottles, and clothes discarded by the Swarm, and a huge box with an assortment of spare keys. There were ornate keys, long thin keys, latchkeys, keys to jewellery boxes, brass keys with fobs on the end and heavy iron keys. Embellsed had committed the outline of the girl's key to memory. It was a heavy iron key with a set of double teeth.

He settled on a plan. He would wait for Bludroot's order to run an errand and, whilst the High Shrove was busy attending to the Thane, he would sneak into the High Shrove's storeroom. The order came within a short while and Embellsed scuttled off to begin his plunderous deeds. Soon he found himself inside Bludroot's treasure trove with his hand in the box, searching for the girl's key.

'Which one is it?' he cried, grabbing a bunch of keys and inspecting them one by one.

Then he heard a creaking noise on the floorboards behind him. A tickly, nasty feeling ran down his spine.

'What you about then?' asked a weaselly voice.

Embellsed froze. It was that dreadful scallywag Wince, the twins' sneaky Shrove.

Wince had been watching Embellsed for many days. He was jealous of Embellsed's new status as the Shrove-Marker and wanted some of the rewards for himself.

Embellsed jumped at the sound of Wince's voice.

'None o' your business – now be on your way, you dirt-stopper!' he shouted insultingly. 'I'm on Bludroot's errand, not yours.'

Wince stood in the doorway and cocked his head to one side.

'Nay,' he announced, picking his nails with his teeth. 'Now, as I remembers it correctly, that errand didn't involve puttin' your dirty mitt in 'is box of keys and nickin' 'is stuff. 'Now then, tell me what you're doin', or I'll be 'avin a little word in the High Shrove's ear,' threatened Wince.

Embellsed boiled with loathing for the cunning Shrove as he desperately tried to invent an excuse, but unfortunately he wasn't adept at thinking on his feet. Embellsed was flummoxed and turned bright red.

'Out with it,' persisted Wince, pouncing on Embellsed's weakened state, and forcing his hand out of the key box.

Embellsed's head was pounding as he oscillated between darting out of the storeroom and punching Wince on the nose. In the end he caved in.

'If I tells thee, you 'ave to keep the secret,' bleated Embellsed desperately, rubbing his hands together.

''Course, Master Embellsed – you can trust old Wince,' murmured the crafty Shrove.

So Embellsed spilled the beans about the girl's key and that he seemed to have misplaced it.

Wince's boggle-eyes rolled with nefarious pleasure.

'Well now, that's a pretty pickle you find yourself in, Master Embellsed. I'd be scared to death meself, had I lost that key. And you being a Shrove-Marker too. That doubles the heinous crime in the eyes of the Swarm. That is, of course, if they get to hear of it.'

Embellsed brow was sweating and he looked as though he might throw up. Wince inched towards him and whispered furtively, looking over his shoulder.

'I'll not say a word, of course, if you get me a whennymeg for my trouble.'

Embellsed grizzled and groaned, but there was nothing for it. Eventually he nodded reluctantly.

'It'll have to be a pretty whennymeg, now – none of your cheap rubbish.'

'Oh dear,' moaned Embellsed, hopping feverishly about.

This pickle was not one that Embellsed could stomach for long. His insides were awash with anxiety. Now he was in cahoots with another Shrove, and a mean one at that. Embellsed shrank when the boggle-eyed Shrove put his arm around his shoulders – because now he was in the debt of the weaselly, wily Wince.

*

Embellsed hurried up the late stairs clutching the duplicate key in his sweaty hand. On the top landing he ran up to Tallitha's apartment and turned the door handle. It was securely locked. He breathed a sigh of relief, opened the door with his key and let himself in. Tallitha spied him from her desk as he muttered away to himself about "finding keys" and "forgetfulness".

The Shrove was a nervous wreck from his encounter with Wince, but at last something was going his way.

'You ready?' he barked, ambling over to where she was sitting.

'Of course,' she replied, giving the Shrove an old-fashioned look. 'Dark old night last night, wasn't it, Embellsed? This castle is a strange, haunting place after midnight.'

The Shrove froze and eyed the young madam. He took a moment to inspect the scents in the room. Then he smelt a new aroma. It was the smell of honey.

'You been eatin' honey?' he asked.

Tallitha smiled and walked towards the door.

'Maybe,' she replied, 'shouldn't we be going?'

Embellsed grizzled and hopped about. He was perplexed by the girl's manner, but he persuaded himself that all was well and that the Lady Snowdroppe must have locked the children in their apartment on the previous night. The girl was just being her usual uppity self. So he scampered off down the landing and through the labyrinthine castle, barking orders at the girl to hurry up, and presenting Tallitha to the Mistress Flight in good time.

'That will be all,' said Sedentia, dismissing Embellsed.

He scurried off for a bit of a sit and a good half-pint of reviving berry juice. His tattered nerves could take no more blistering excitement for one day.

Sedentia eyed the recalcitrant Tallitha, standing awkwardly before her, moving from one foot to another.

'I hope you're properly prepared this time to do the first two tests,' she announced.

Tallitha flicked her eyes at the governess and tried to look interested.

Sedentia began chanting in the ancient Ennish tongue:

'*Tellan sam le nerva manvellus, Tellan sam le nerva manvellus ...*' she repeated once more.

The secret tower room opened as before, smelling of smouldering candle wax and sulphur. The Nooklies chattered annoyingly and spat on Tallitha from their towering piles of manuscripts. She just managed to jump out of the way of the globules of spit that were about to land on her head.

'They don't like me,' she cried, narrowly avoiding the final missile.

'They don't trust you,' answered Sedentia. 'Now, let us turn to The Black Pages and continue.'

Slynose hurried to her mistress's side and snuggled onto her lap, but not before her green liquid eyes focussed on Tallitha. Sedentia opened the big book at the same page.

'Look Tallitha,' she whispered in her melodic tones. 'Drift into the colours and look deep into the flashing yellows, the pulsating purples and the revolving reds.'

Once more the colours leapt off the page in the shape of wild animals, butterflies, lizards and fabulous snakes, filling the Book Room with a kaleidoscopic spectacle of slithering, flapping creatures.

'*Della tenteth, lucier malamma lana centa,*' Sedentia whispered softly again and again.

Tallitha was determined to resist. From deep within her she focussed on being in the present. As the colours and shapes leapt from the pages, Tallitha made them evaporate, bursting each colourful bubble with a pinprick of negative thought.

'You're resisting!' Sedentia cried as the Wheen-Cat leapt from her knee.

Tallitha had been hatching a plan to free Esmerelda.

'I've tried my best,' she replied, 'but it doesn't work. I'm sorry.'

Sedentia screwed up her eyes. 'I don't believe you!'

'Essie always helped me with my shadow-flight, I'm no good on my own,' she said quietly.

'Well that woman can't help you now!'

'Do you know where Essie is?' Tallitha ventured at last.

The governess stiffened.

'Most likely they've put her in the Bleak Rooms,' replied Sedentia. 'Now concentrate on this illustration. Forget about that woman: let the colours talk to you and transport you on the shadow-flight.'

But Tallitha's mind was racing with images of Essie trapped in the bowels of the castle. How would she escape? Her worst fears were confirmed. Essie had joined those wretched souls, Cremola Burn and Leticia Trume, in the dank, dismal dungeon. Her thoughts flashed back to the courtyard, and the poor woman who had spoken to her from her imprisonment in the Bleak Rooms. Tallitha was distracted and twisted her hair in and out of her fingers. Sedentia was displeased with her determined lack of progress.

At noon Croop brought lunch, and a note for Sedentia.

'We are to visit your mother. She wants an update on your progress. Shall we try another illustration? So far you have been a disappointment – so unlike your cousin Caedryl,' Sedentia trilled nastily, snatching the book from Tallitha's hand and stroking Slynose.

The cat purred with delight. Tallitha ate her lunch whilst Sedentia probed her about her experiences on the shadow-flights.

'How did you make contact with the Lady Asenathe?'

'Essie put me into a trance, I've told you,' answered Tallitha, stressing once more Essie's part in the process.

'Did the Lady Asenathe always look the same?'

'No, I saw her as a girl and then as a woman on different occasions,' explained Tallitha.

'That means you can travel through time,' Sedentia replied excitedly, 'how did you learn to do that?'

Tallitha shrugged her shoulders. 'I have no idea, it just happened.'

'But you must know how you did it! Travelling through time takes practice, yet you say you did this easily.'

Tallitha answered as best she could but Sedentia was dissatisfied with her vague replies. Croop cleared away their plates, sidled up to Sedentia, and whispered furtively in her ear. The governess nodded and whispered back to him.

'They are ready for us. Come, we are to visit your mother and grandfather in the Great Tower.'

'But what will they do to me?' asked Tallitha.

'They will force you to obey their orders by whatever means,' snapped Sedentia, as she trundled down the staircase.

*

Tallitha followed her governess down the winding steps and along the battlements. The wind howled and frantic seabirds hung uncertainly in the biting wind, screeching their plaintive cries into the grey, ashen skies. Tallitha hung back. She didn't want to meet her mother or the dreadful Thane. She felt betrayed and orphaned by their wickedness.

At the foot of the Great Tower, two Groats stepped forward and accompanied Tallitha and Sedentia to the Grand Receiving Room, a large circular room with round stained glass windows. It had been set for a banquet, with a horde of Shroves running around, carrying trays of food and drink and an army of grisly Groats lining the walls. The light shone through the coloured glass and made fleeting patterns on the polished floor, occupying Tallitha's thoughts, and reminding her of the Jewel Room and home.

Eventually Snowdroppe floated into the gallery, accompanied by Caedryl and the Morrow twins. The Thane followed soon behind them, leading three huge wolfhounds tethered on silver chains, their large heads chaffing and pulling against the restraints. Their coats were dark and matted but there was no mistaking their lineage: they were bred from the same bloodstock that roamed Ragging Brows Forest. The fawning Bludroot brought up the rear along with Lord Edweard.

They were an unholy bunch. Snowdroppe was stunningly beautiful in her blood-red velvet dress, yet so deeply conniving and artfully duplicitous. She carried the fennec fox in her arms, petting it adoringly. Then there was Caedryl dressed in a severe black gown – haughty, cold and jealous – followed by the mean-hearted twins, Lapis and Muprid, with Bludroot proudly positioned as the Thane's High Shrove. Not for the first time, Tallitha speculated about the secret route that her mother must have taken between Winderling Spires and Hellstone Tors. The tunnel had to end somewhere inside the castle and begin somewhere in the heart of Winderling Spires.

Snowdroppe took her daughter's hand and led her towards the Thane. He looked as wild as ever with his tangled grey hair knotted into bunches in a mad fashion, and his steely black eyes alighting on Tallitha, magnetically drawing her in. His sharp anvil-like features portrayed his wickedness.

'I don't think Tallitha has met her great uncle, Lord Edweard,' Caedryl sneered dismissively, introducing the vain man.

He was a younger version of the Thane, with a shock of black hair tied in twisted braids.

'You're wrong,' he snapped. 'Tallitha and I became acquainted the other day. Pretty girl …' he added, for the sheer pleasure of annoying Caedryl.

Caedryl pouted and twisted away from him, smoothing down her stark black dress. Lord Frintal smirked at their competitiveness. He took pleasure in his entourage being on bad terms with one another. It kept them in their place.

'Sit here, Tallitha,' the Thane demanded, pointing to a chair at the large table. 'Now, Mistress Flight, what have you to tell us about my granddaughter's progress through The Black Pages?'

Sedentia raised her eyebrows at the grand assembly, sniffed her hankie and cleared her throat. She threw a disdainful look at Tallitha, then turned to face the Thane:

'Either her power is blocked, as she maintains,' she replied gruffly, 'or the girl is deliberately refusing to co-operate.'

Tallitha turned pink at being discussed in such an offhand manner. Snowdroppe let out a cry and sprang like a cat from her chair, pouncing on Tallitha, shrieking and dragging her from the table. The wolfhounds lunged forward on their chains at the melee that ensued, growling and snarling to join in the fray.

'Is this true?' she snapped, her eyes spitting hatred and her nails digging sharply into Tallitha's arm. 'Don't you dare disappoint me after all I've done for you! I've had to endure years of boredom at Winderling Spires – and all for this!'

Snowdroppe dragged her errant daughter behind her, darting across the room like a serpent, her long clothes flying in all directions. Lord Frintal leapt to his feet, gripped Tallitha's face in his vicious hands and stared deep into her eyes. Tallitha felt herself weakening under his mesmerising gaze.

'I haven't done anything wrong!' Tallitha cried. 'I've tried using my powers, but it's no use.'

'Bring me my One True Mirror,' the Thane demanded.

Bludroot scurried forward carrying an oval mirror and handed it to the Thane. Lord Frintal grabbed Tallitha, pulled her to him, held the mirror to her face, and gazed deep into the looking glass with her, penetrating her mind with his cold, grey eyes. Tallitha tried to resist but his will was too strong for her.

'She speaks some truth,' he said coldly, letting her go. 'Yet,' he added, 'you've been artful, my girl – you've been trying to use your powers to find Esmerelda.' He laughed. 'You could have asked, and we would have told you where she was. She lies with the hags and the thieves in the Bleak Rooms.'

The assembled members of the Swarm laughed at Esmerelda's plight.

'Please let Essie go, I beg you, Grandfather,' said Tallitha plaintively.

'Oh, so he's "Grandfather" now?' mocked Snowdroppe viciously, the veins in her neck standing proud and pumping with rage.

'Please Mother, let her go and I will work hard to do as you wish.'

'Why should I help Esmerelda? She's nothing to me' answered Snowdroppe spitefully.

Lapis and Muprid smirked behind their slender white hands whilst Bludroot and Wince hopped about, revelling in the girl's public scolding.

'She has hypnotic powers,' Tallitha replied, 'without Essie I can't find the way of the shadow-flight.'

'So what shall we do with Tallitha?' asked the Thane. 'Come, Mistress Flight, I need an answer!'

Sedentia regarded Tallitha coldly. 'If she refuses to respond to me then perhaps she should be taken to see the *other one* much earlier than we planned …' she replied mysteriously.

Tallitha looked from one member of the Swarm to another as their leary faces crowded round her.

'The Mistress Flight speaks sense. Tallitha will be taken to the Wild Imaginer to complete her journey through The Black Pages!' the Thane shouted.

Snowdroppe gasped. 'But she's too raw and inexperienced for so much power!'

'She must submit!' the Thane bellowed.

'What about Essie, Mother?' Tallitha pleaded desperately. 'Surely she can help me and y-you can watch her to make sure she doesn't do anything untoward.'

Tallitha had never seen her mother look so concerned.

'But my Lord,' said Snowdroppe artfully, 'perhaps Tallitha needs to practise before she experiences the full power of the Wild Imaginer.' Her mother bowed slightly to the Thane and continued. 'Tallitha may have a point when she says that Esmerelda can help her access the shadow-flight.'

The Thane moved aggressively in his throne and eyed Snowdroppe suspiciously.

'Then that Wycham woman will be your responsibility!' he shouted at his daughter. 'If anything should go wrong, on your pretty head be it!'

Snowdroppe arched one of her perfect black eyebrows, nodding conspiratorially at the Thane.

'Esmerelda will not trick me,' she sneered, 'first, I will test the depths of her duplicity.' She shot her eyes in Tallitha's direction as a warning. 'But, should Esmerelda prove to be innocent, then

I will allow her to prepare Tallitha for the Wild Imaginer, and perhaps give her some freedom in the castle.'

'T-Thank you Mother,' Tallitha replied meekly.

Tallitha's heart stopped thumping. Now she must warn Essie of Snowdroppe's plan and persuade her to go along with the deception.

'Once Esmerelda has unlocked Tallitha's powers and she has completed the first two tests, Quillam will take Tallitha up to Stankles Brow,' the Thane announced, clicking his fingers and nodding at Bludroot. 'Summon him now.'

Bludroot's watery eyes darted about, desperate to please his Lord. He wrung his hands and bowed, scampering from the room.

'Ah yes, Quillam,' added Snowdroppe, turning to face her daughter. A wicked smile played across her lips. 'The time has come for you to meet someone,' she said ominously. 'Your adopted brother, Quillam.'

'Speak of the devil,' Edweard grimaced, 'here he comes.'

As Tallitha turned, she saw a tall young man striding towards her across the gallery.

Apparently she had another brother, but this one had the look of a wild animal embedded in his ochre-coloured eyes. It was the mysterious youth who had led them to the Witch's Tower.

Ten

'You'll be famished after that long trek,' said Bettie, putting the kettle on, and taking a selection of cold meats and pickles from the larder. 'How come you got time off to come visitin' all the ways up 'ere?' she asked, glancing at Cissie over her shoulder.

Her sister-in-law patted the snoozing dogs, then sat at the kitchen table with her chin resting on her hand, staring vacantly ahead of her.

'I've been stayin' with our Rose for a while,' she said quietly, clearing her throat. 'Just helpin' out in the shop, bakin' and such like.'

Bettie could tell something was amiss. Cissie was avoiding eye contact. It was as if she'd slipped back to that time when she wasn't herself, after the awful tragedy. It had taken years for Cissie to recover, if indeed anyone could recover properly after such a terrible loss. Bettie knew she would have to tread

carefully. She didn't want to dredge up distressing memories for her dear sister-in-law.

'But what about Winderling Spires, won't you be missed at the big house?'

'The G-Grand M-Morrow has s-sent me away,' replied Cissie sadly, her words catching at the back of her throat. Her face crumpled and she hastily wiped a tear from her cheek.

Bettie pushed a cup of tea and a cheese sandwich across the table. 'Nay, don't get upset, there's nowt you can do about it now.'

Cissie shook her head, unable to fight back the tears and played with her food. She had no appetite. 'I know Bettie, it's not that – my loss was a long time ago,' she added softly.

'Then has it got summat to do with those Winderling bairns?'

Cissie lifted her damp, tear-stained face. 'I can't bear to lose Tallitha and Tyaas as well, not after what happened … b-before,' she cried, stumbling over her words.

'I knew it,' Bettie said flatly, folding her arms. 'Well, I promised that woman Esmerelda I wouldn't say owt, but you're family after all.' She hesitated, leaning forward and taking Cissie's hand. 'They were here, a few weeks back, before they went off to Ragging Brows Forest.'

'That awful place!' cried Cissie. 'I've had a bad feelin' gnawin' away at me. I thought they were goin' by Shivering Water. But why didn't you stop 'em, couldn't you have done owt?'

Bettie leant forward and took her sister-in-law's hand. 'If you couldn't stop 'em, how d'you think we could? They were dead set on goin'. We warned 'em about those folks goin' missin.'

Cissie gripped Bettie's hand. 'Missing? Who's gone missing?'

'Some folks a while back. Lookin' for mushrooms they were, up by the ravines. Never came out of that forest again by all accounts.'

Cissie gripped the edge of the table. 'It's worse than I feared. I have to find them!' she cried, jumping to her feet.

'Nay,' said Josh, pulling off his muddy boots and striding into the kitchen. 'That's no job for you, my lass.'

Cissie bit her lip, her eyes pleading with her brother. 'Come with me then, to see if there's any sign of them,' she asked. 'I can't just sit and do nowt. I've thought about nothing else these past weeks.'

Josh sat next to his sister while Bettie made the tea for the family, buttering warm scones and slicing the freshly baked bread. The delicious smell of the home-cooked pastry and warm loaves filled the farmhouse kitchen.

'What about the farm? I can't just leave it,' said Josh, looking at his wife for approval. 'Bettie, my love, what do you say?'

She licked her sticky fingers covered in strawberry jam and gazed thoughtfully at her husband.

'I think our Cissie's right. A day or two won't 'urt and as long as you're careful. The girls can help out while you're away and –'

'Please Dad, can we come too?' asked Spooner excitedly, bounding into the kitchen and handing a basket of brown speckled eggs to her mother. 'We'll be ever so good, and we can help you with the search!'

'Hello, my chick,' said Cissie, jumping to her feet and

cuddling her pretty niece.

'Not likely! Now go and fetch that sister of yours, tea's almost ready,' scolded Bettie.

'Well Josh?' asked Cissie.

'Aye, go on then – I never could refuse you owt,' he replied.

Cissie kissed her brother on his ruddy cheek and helped Bettie lay the table.

'Thanks, our Josh,' she beamed at him. 'This means the world to me.'

'Aye lass, I know how precious those children are to you. But let's hope we don't all live to regret it.'

*

'Please let us come with you,' Lince wheedled away at her father, stroking his arm. 'We're not children anymore.'

It was a bright, sunny morning and the girls were angling to get their own way, desperate not to be left behind.

'No, your mother will have a fit. Besides, it's your day for milking and you promised to help while I'm gone. We'll tell you all about it when we get home this evenin'.'

'It's not fair, you never let us do anything exciting!' shouted Lince petulantly. 'I'm goin' to find our kid.'

Lince pulled a face at her father and ran off to find her sister.

'Those girls are growin' up fast,' said Cissie, watching her niece fly across the farmyard. 'Perhaps they could've come with us after all, to help in the search?'

'Not likely, Bettie won't hear of it. You ready?' he asked. 'We've a fair walk ahead of us, and we want to get there and back in daylight. I don't like the thought of being in that forest after dark.'

Cissie waved goodbye to Bettie, who was busy feeding the chickens, followed her brother out of the gate and up through the high sweet pastures until they reached the edge of the forest. Since childhood, Cissie had listened apprehensively while her brothers and sisters snuck into each other's bedrooms late at night and recounted haunting tales of Ragging Brows Forest. It was the dark place where the wild mushrooms grew, the Honey Fungus and the Destroying Angel and where wild beasts were said to roam at night – but she had never dared to venture there before: she'd never had a reason to, until now.

As the day wore on, it became clear to Cissie just what an enormous task they had embarked upon. There was no sign that Tallitha and the others had ever been in the woods – it was like looking for a needle in a haystack. The old forest was a gloomy place, and Cissie's stomach churned as they ventured further into the dark wood.

'Whereabouts are we?' asked Cissie, sounding breathless. 'This forest is a mean, dark place even in the middle of the day.'

Josh stopped by a fallen log, wiped the sweat from his brow and passed Cissie a drink of water.

'We're at the eastern edge, well away from the ravines at Snipes Edge,' said her brother staring warily about him.

Cissie parted the tangled creepers and stared ahead into

the puddles of greyish light. Twisted, gnarled tree trunks, dark overhanging branches and thickets of wild brambles hindered their way, obliterating most of the meagre sunlight that had attempted to force its way through the heavy foliage.

'Do you think they came this far?' asked Cissie desperately. The dismal atmosphere created by the greenish light was oppressive, and she felt queasy with the thought that her dear children had ventured into the heart of the dark wood. 'I'd hoped that studious boy, Benedict, would have had the gumption to leave a note or a sign.'

Josh sighed, running his fingers through his sweat-ridden hair. 'I don't know, lass. What did you think we'd find?' he said, rubbing the cuff of his shirt over his brow. 'It's a long time since they were here and their tracks will be cold by now.'

'I'm not sure,' she said despondently. 'I'd hoped we'd find a sign, but I can see now what a huge task this is, being in this desperate, dismal place.'

Cissie slumped heavily onto a broken log and poked the ground with a stick. The forest was an overgrown jungle of twisting creepers, ivy and brambles forming impassable clumps of woody undergrowth, clawing and twisting up the tall trees all the way to the top of the forest canopy. In the patchy light and heavy silence, Cissie's heart pounded with the thought of the children wandering around lost and frightened in the gloomy forest after dark.

'Perhaps we should call it a day,' suggested Josh. 'We can try again tomorrow if you've a mind to, but we must have a proper plan. This aimless scouting about isn't getting us anywhere.'

Cissie nodded. She knew her brother was right. So they began retracing their steps through the wet bracken. The dim path was obscured by brambles and strewn with straggling branches that clung to their clothes and snagged at their hair. Dense overhanging foliage, long tough grasses and patches of wild flowers edged the route, with bluebells erupting amongst the glades in swathes of pretty purples and blues.

But as Cissie peered ahead through the trees she saw a flash of golden-yellow, a streak of bright colour, darting amongst the branches. Was it a trick of the light? No, there it was again!

Someone was running away from them into the heart of the forest.

'Quick, Josh!' she shouted. 'There's someone running over there!'

The farmer darted through the soggy bracken, leaping over fallen trees and zigzagging like a deer through the forest far ahead of Cissie. She tried to keep up with him but he was much too fast for her. Then she heard him bellowing, his voice sounding sharp and angry.

'Come here at once! Stop running, I tell you! When I catch you, I'll ...'

Then Cissie heard a number of heavy thuds as bodies tumbled headlong into the undergrowth. When she finally caught up with him, Josh was sitting on the ground panting heavily with both hands gripping his two struggling daughters. The girls were dishevelled and red in the face.

'Spooner! Lince!' shouted Cissie. 'What are you doing here? Your mother will be mad with worry!'

The girls looked exasperated. Lince pulled a green woolly hat over her fair hair, covering the flash of golden colour that had given her away.

'Leave me be, Dad!' shouted Lince indignantly, pulling away from Josh's grasp.

'What do you mean by goin' against me?' he said, staring hard at both his girls in turn.

'You should've let us come in the first place, when Spoons asked you. Me and our kid, we're good at tracking – we practically live in this forest. I've got my knife and Spoons has her longbow, and we know how to use them,' she insisted, twirling her knife in the air to make a point.

'What! Don't tell your mam, she'll say it's my fault, letting you roam about these wild, desolate places.'

'But Dad, we can take care of ourselves!' shouted Spooner. 'You have to let us grow up sometime.'

'But not right now, eh?' he said. 'We'll have hell to pay when your mother finds out.'

Josh sighed, dusted down his clothes and peered through the trees. 'We must get out of here,' he said, looking nervously into the darkness. 'Let's be rid of this rum place.'

'But what about the Skink?' asked Spooner, watching their reaction. 'She knows all about Tallitha and the others …'

'What Skink?' cried Cissie. 'What did she say?'

Lince leant against a tree and her sister crouched next to

her, tying the laces on her strong leather boots. Cissie could see that her nieces were at home in the remote, hostile environment: like two woodland elves, they blended right into the strange, haunting forest.

'Not much, you disturbed her,' Lince replied, 'she ran over there – as soon as you started makin' all that noise.'

She pointed towards the thickly packed woody darkness.

'We were chasing after her when *you* caught us,' added Spooner, looking askance at her father.

Josh blushed slightly and began kicking the earth. 'She must've said summat, lass.'

He looked taken aback, and slightly overawed by his daughters' newly found independence.

'She said a woman and some children had been up to the Skink village. They'd left for the caves with two Skinks, but the Skinks ... one was called Rooster.'

'Ruker, she was called Ruker,' interrupted Spooner, her short dark hair sticking up in messy clumps.

'Yeah, Ruker – well, she came back without them.'

Cissie turned pale and grabbed Josh's arm. 'We have to find that Skink!'

'But how will we do that?' he asked, sounding exasperated with the madcap plan.

'Leave her a message, a forest sign,' explained Lince. 'She's bound to return at some point after we've left.'

'But will it work?' asked Josh gruffly.

'Got a better idea?' Spooner added.

Lince scored one of the silver birch trees in three places, peeling back the slivers of bark in long strips. She inserted a whittled stick behind the bark and twisted the hanging strips into a series of knots. Josh watched in amazement at his daughter's mysterious skills.

'How will the Skink know what that means?' he asked, scratching his head.

Lince gave him a dirty look. 'She's a Skink, of course. She knows the same as I do. Come on,' she said forcefully, 'we'll meet her here tomorrow. And that means *all* of us – we're coming too this time.'

*

'I won't have it! Tell 'em Josh, they're not goin' back into that awful forest – not now, not ever!' cried Bettie, waving her hand in the direction of her sullen daughters.

Spooner and Lince sat awkwardly by the fire as their mother paced the kitchen, glowering and having one of her regular motherly fits.

'Mam, we know what we're doin',' said Lince, bored by her mother's scolding. 'We've been goin' to the forest for years, and we know how to take care of ourselves. Whenever there's any sign of danger we climb the trees, just like the Skinks.'

Bettie moaned and sat down with a thud by the blazing hearth.

'Roamin' the countryside, off doin' whatever you like, with all

the dangers and wild animals out there – you're just children …'
she sniffed, looking at her husband for support.

'Mam, we're not little anymore.'

'No, you're not, but sometimes I wish you were. Tucked up
in bed at night time where I know you're safe …'

'My love, they do seem to have a lot of forest know-how, and
–' said her husband sheepishly.

Bettie jumped to her feet and turned her anger on her
husband.

'You keep out of this, if you're takin' their part! I blame you
anyways, allowing them to go hither and thither. They're never
at home, from dawn 'til dusk.'

Their mother was in a blither. Spooner nudged her sister
beneath the cushions. She had an idea.

'But the Skink won't come if we're not there,' she said, looking
directly at Cissie for support.

'Spoons is right,' said Lince, eyeing her mother for any chink
of weakness. 'Besides, Aunt Cissie's on our side – you think we
should come, don't you, Aunty?'

'What?' cried Bettie, 'Our Cissie, you're never goin' to agree
with them!'

'I-I don't know what to say for the best, Bettie,' replied Cissie
awkwardly. 'There's no doubt that the girls have impressed me
today with their knowledge of the forest, but I don't want you
upset with me, or with them.' She sighed, turning to the girls.
'You've put me in a right pickle,' she moaned, giving Lince a hard
stare.

Bettie stared into the fire, patting Barney's warm firm body. He rolled over, snuffled and stuck his legs into the air for his tummy to be rubbed. Their mother's face looked drawn in the firelight.

'We'll all go,' said Josh, trying to placate his wife. 'You don't have to come into the forest, my love. One of the girls can sit with you.'

'Like a nursemaid? Oh, Dad!' shouted Spooner, banging the sofa with frustration. 'That's just daft!'

Josh knitted his eyebrows into a scowl. 'That's an end to it. If we go, we all go as a *family*. One of you will stay with your mam by the entrance to the forest. I mean it!'

The girls knew by the look on their father's face that there was no point in pushing it further: that was the end of the matter. It was the only deal that was going to be struck that day.

Eleven

That night a fierce gale blew up. From out of the dark purple skies, a swirling mist gathered pace and prowled over Sweet-Side Pasture, snaking its way over Badger's Dyke and down Holly Pot Ghyll, creeping menacingly over the hills that surrounded the farm at High Bedders End. The storm howled around the walls of the isolated farmhouse, rattling the windows and making the trees moan, their branches creaking and groaning in the blustery squall.

In the warm doziness of the farmhouse kitchen, the dogs began to stir, awoken by the strong winds, raising their sleepy heads and sniffing the night air for any strange new scents.

Suddenly, Barney sprang from the warmth of the fireplace with his hackles bristling, his eyes shining and emitting a low-belly, rumbling growl. There was something abroad that night: something untoward creeping about in the farmyard, and it had put both dogs on high alert.

'What's up with them dogs?' asked Spooner sleepily, rolling over and shaking her sister.

'Go and let them out,' mumbled Lince, pulling the eiderdown over her head. 'Leave me be, I let them out the last time they made a fuss.'

Spooner yawned, clambered out of the warmth of the big double bed, and wandered half-asleep downstairs into the shadows of the darkened kitchen. The last of the glowing embers smouldered in the grate and intermittent beams of moonlight danced on the tiled floor as Spooner walked across the kitchen to comfort the worried animals. But the dogs were unusually distressed, whining and scratching at the underside of the backdoor. Then Sticker reared back, his lip curled, and he snarled at something outside in the darkness.

'What's up boy?' the girl asked fearfully. 'Come away from there. Stop it now.'

As she crouched down to settle the dogs, there was a sudden clattering noise outside. Spooner leapt to her feet and saw a hooded figure dart momentarily in front of the kitchen window. In a flash she had flattened herself against the wall and slid noiselessly to the floor.

'Shh, stay quiet boys!' she whispered nervously as she knelt in the shadows.

Sticker whined and scratched, desperately forcing the tip of his nose under the door and clawing frantically at the mat. Spooner's heart thumped in her chest as she pulled a resistant Barney towards her for protection.

'Stop it, Sticker,' she whispered in the dog's ear: 'stay, boy.'

But the big dog continued to bear his teeth and snarl, his lips quivering with alarm. There was something on the other side of the door trying to get in. Spooner crawled to the hearth and grabbed the poker then she crept under the table, avoiding the patches of moonlight streaking through the kitchen window, and lunged for the back door. In one quick movement she wrenched the door open.

Nothing stirred apart from the wind whistling through the trees, whipping up the dirt in the farmyard and blowing a whirlpool of scattered leaves through the open door. Tentatively, Spooner inched forward and peeked outside. That night, huge terrifying clouds as big as mountains, sped across the sky and blotted out the moonlight. The sinister presence bore down on the farmhouse as something unspeakably evil gathered speed, and slithered like a serpent towards the back door. Spooner's felt the unwanted presence slip around her legs, licking upwards as she stood frozen with fear. The dogs sensed the invisible malevolence and retreated, cowering to the floor, whining and slinking back into the shadows.

'W-Who's t-there?' Spooner asked nervously, staring out into the blackest of all nights. 'I-I know there's s-someone th-there. C-Come out and s-show yourself!'

She held the poker over her head, ready to strike, when a strong gust of wind blew in her face, forcing her backwards and making her stumble. The moon suddenly revealed itself from a trail of blue-black clouds and knife-like shadows zigzagged haphazardly across the small patch of garden, intermittently obscuring her view of the scattered outbuildings.

Then, from out of the darkness, two elongated shapes emerged from the old barn. The pointed shadows stretched across the ground, jagged against the moonlight.

Spooner steadied her nerves and stepped bravely into the windswept farmyard.

'Show yourself at once!' she cried.

In an instant the shadows grew bigger, stretching to the tops of the tallest trees before flinging themselves down onto the lonely farmhouse, enveloping the buildings in a rush of swirling darkness. Spooner shivered, tightly closed her eyes and steeled herself against the encroaching fiendish presence when a rush of evil swooped past her, touching her with icy fingers, trespassing into the farmhouse, seeking something out.

'W-What do you want with us?' she whispered, her eyes watering with fear.

The sound of wicked laughter licked past her and she caught a glimpse of a hooded face, whispering in a strange language: '*Lucier nerva vex, lucier nerva vex ...*'

Then the malevolent presence vanished. In a heartbeat the shadow-shapes shrunk to the ground and disappeared into the dark night. In their wake they left a solitary figure lurking by the outbuildings.

'Who are you?' she cried, raising the poker.

Her hand shook with fear as she stepped further into the dark night. All at once the dogs' courage returned as they raced passed Spooner and leapt on the cloaked intruder, pulling the body to the ground. There was a scuffle in the dirt as the prostrate figure wrestled with the snarling animals.

'Call the dogs off! It's only me!' shouted a strangely familiar voice.

Spooner ran towards the heap on the ground, dragging the dogs away.

'Okay boys, heel! What's your business here?' she shouted, holding the poker ready to strike the huddled body in an instant.

Then the figure rolled over in the dirt and slowly drew back the black hood.

'Well I never!' said Spooner, stepping backwards.

The face staring back at her was Benedict's.

'Y-You said to call in, on m-my way b-back,' Benedict stuttered at the astonished girl.

'What you doin' back here all alone? Where're the others?' she asked, looking frantically about the empty farmyard.

But Benedict continued to gawp at her. He seemed stunned and lost for words. Perhaps he too had been scared by the ominous shadows.

'Was there someone with you? I thought I saw someone else out here in the darkness,' she faltered, staring fearfully into the night as the shadows seemed to encroach once more and cluster all around her. 'I-I've never seen a night so dark,' she stammered.

Spooner kept one eye on Benedict as she turned towards the old barn, but the farmyard was empty.

'It's just little old me, it must have been the dark night playing tricks on you,' said Benedict, dusting down his dirty clothes and pulling himself to his feet. 'Aren't you going to invite me in? Then I can tell you all about what happened to us, out there.' He gesticulated vaguely towards the mountains in the distance.

Spooner regarded the intruder. She was unsettled about the whole encounter. He had given her quite a shock, appearing out of nowhere at the dead of night. It was the darkest night she had ever seen, if truth be told.

"Course, I'll get me Dad. If I'd known it was you, I'd have called the dogs off earlier,' she answered, giving him a sidelong glance.

What an odd thing to do, thought Spooner, *to turn up in the middle of the night and skulk around in the farmyard. Why didn't he just knock at the kitchen door?*

But Josh and Bettie had already heard the rumpus and were standing on the doorstep with their mouths open, staring foolishly at their daughter and the dusty, bedraggled boy.

'Get our Cissie!' cried Josh to Spooner, patting Benedict on the back and ushering him inside the warm kitchen. 'Well you're a sight for sore eyes. Where're the others?' he asked, staring out into the darkness.

Benedict regarded the farmer sheepishly. He lifted his shaky hand towards the mountains and turned away, his eyes brimming with tears.

'Nay lad, don't get upset,' he said, trying to console the boy.

'Those dogs were frit to death, howlin' their heads off, they were,' said Bettie, pulling a shawl around her shoulders. "Tis a sign of ill fortune when dogs howl at night – a bad omen and no mistake.'

The farmer narrowed his eyes at his superstitious wife, but it was rare she got the signs wrong.

'Perhaps they're trying to tell us summat,' she added, raising an eyebrow in Benedict's direction.

'Warm yourself up by the range. My sister will be glad to see you,' said the farmer.

Josh lifted the curtain and peered through the kitchen window, perturbed by the black night skies and the unearthly milk-white mists rising from the ground. He had never seen the like before: never as thick, and never as black.

'On my life, 'tis a dirty old night out there.' He turned to look at Benedict. 'I 'ope you ain't brought this with you,' he said, half-jokingly, 'looks like a bucketful of bad luck.' But the boy didn't respond. 'I'll just check on the animals,' the farmer added, casting his eyes over the nervous boy.

Josh wanted to make certain that no one else was skulking around. He checked on the animals, but apart from the dogs who were still a bit skittish, nothing else seemed amiss apart from the dark night itself. He lit his pipe and stared up at the heavy, purple skies. Out there, alone with the blustery wind, the black sky seemed to envelope him – to creep all around him like a sinister presence.

'Get a grip, man,' he mumbled.

Josh shuddered, unnerved by the peculiarity of the night, before he turned on his heel and walked quickly back inside the kitchen, firmly fastening the back door.

Benedict stood by the fire, rubbing his hands together,

regarding the assembled Wakenshaws with some reserve. His mother's plan had worked after all. His secret was safe. The Queen had been right. The family knew nothing about his real identity or about what had happened to the others who were now imprisoned in Hellstone Tors. Bettie brought him a bowl of soup and bread as Josh stoked up the fire.

'Benedict!' cried Cissie as she rushed into the kitchen, fastening her dressing gown. 'But where have you come from? What's happened to the young'uns?' she shouted, peeking behind the sofa in case Tallitha and Tyaas were hiding from her, playing one of their pranks.

Benedict turned his face away with a sharp intake of breath.

'What is it my lad? You have to tell me.'

'They were ...' he faltered, 'taken.'

'Oh my word, I knew it!' cried Cissie, hugging the boy to her side. 'Get him a strong drink, Bettie. He's had some kind of shock. Look, he's shakin'!'

Benedict buried his head in Cissie's arms to hide the despicable lie that was written all over his face. He had to compose himself or they would uncover the deception. He must remember everything his mother had told him. Queen Asphodel had instructed him to look forlorn and desperate. She had made him rehearse his lines and to practice his part until he was word-perfect. Benedict's task was to deceive the family and to persuade them to go further into the forest, much further than they'd ever been before: deep into its heart, right up to the ravines.

Snipes Edge was the most desperate of places in Ragging Brows Forest: desolate ravines where the wild mushrooms grew in abundance. Benedict knew the plan off by heart. One of the Groats had been instructed to leave a response on Spooner's tree-sign to entice the family up to the ravines. Benedict had only to persuade the family to follow him to Snipes Edge for Asphodel's wicked plan to fall into place.

'Come now, drink this,' said Cissie softly, comforting the boy and lifting the glass to his trembling lips. ''Tis a shot of Bettie's elderberry wine.'

Benedict lifted his head and sipped the drink, fluttering his moist eyelashes and gazing pathetically at the assembled party.

'I t-tried my best t-to help them,' he cried, grabbing Cissie's hand, 'b-but I failed.'

''Course you did, my dear,' Cissie replied, stroking the boy's damp hair.

'But it was all in vain once the Murk Mowl had them in their clutches.'

'Oh my word,' cried Cissie, flopping back on the sofa, reaching out for her sister-in-law's hand. 'H-He means the *Dooerlins*.' The colour drained from her face. *Not again, please not this again.*

'What did you call 'em?' asked Bettie, sounding horrified. 'Murk something? Nay lad, we know them heartless critters as the Dooerlins in these parts.'

She sat next to her sister to comfort the bedraggled boy.

'Oh Josh, what'll we do? Those children and that poor woman Esmerelda, lost out there!'

'What's goin' on?' asked Lince, yawning and shuffling into the kitchen, her feet coming out of her slippers. Then she caught sight of Benedict.

'What you doin' here?' she cried.

'Shh, he's all tuckered out,' replied her mother. 'He turned up, out of the blue; well, out of the night – and a wicked night it is out there,' she said, gesticulating towards the howling gale.

They listened to the wind buffeting the farmhouse as Bettie stroked the dogs and tried her best to settle them.

'There boys, settle down now.' She turned to her husband, her face etched with worry. 'I don't know what's got into these dogs, they're frit to death.'

Josh walked to the window and peered out into the hideous darkness. He drew the curtains tight over the window, turned and shook his head.

'I ain't never seen a night so queer,' he said, looking baffled. 'Carry on lad, what 'appened next?' he asked.

Benedict lowered his head into his hands. The women fussed over him.

'Come lad, you 'ave to tell us sometime,' said Bettie.

Minutes passed. Benedict buried his head in Cissie's arms and a plaintive note came into his weak voice.

'We … we got separated in the c-caves. The Skinks … I was with them. We went one way and Tallitha and the others were snatched in the skirmish.'

Cissie gasped and put her hand over her mouth.

'But where were they taken?' asked Spooner.

Benedict shook his head and presented his most sorrowful face to the assembled party. 'The Skinks know more than me,' he bleated. 'They showed me the way here so I could make my way back to Winderling Spires, to warn the Grand Morrow. B-But they're going back to the caves, to find my cousins.'

He lifted his head as the tears trickled down his distraught face.

Cissie stood up and marched over to her brother.
'That's settled then,' she announced, looking gravely at the others. 'Tomorrow we're goin' to find those Skinks!'

Twelve

'Come on, Bettie my love, the forest is a way off yet. Sit here with Lince and sun yourself, take a breather. You're always sayin' you need a bit of peace and quiet.'

Bettie flopped down on the grassy bank, fanning herself in the morning sunshine. Her long hair had come loose. She was flustered and fussing about the journey ahead.

'I'll get no peace while you're in that dreadful place. I won't rest 'til I see you walking back down yonder path. I've a funny feeling in the pit of my stomach. I've had it all morning. I do wish you wouldn't go.'

But Josh was in no mood for another discussion about the dangers that awaited them.

'It's settled, you know we have to go, but we'll be back as soon as we can.'

He patted Bettie's hand and kissed her cheek, turned and

began scrambling up the hillside with Benedict and Spooner running after him.

'I'll watch out for any danger,' said Cissie, embracing her sister-in-law. 'Look after your mum,' she added to a sullen Lince, who had lost the penny-toss on who should stay behind with their mother.

The girl shrugged her shoulders moodily and began whittling away at a piece of wood.

But Cissie had a deep sense of foreboding too. She had slept badly, tossing and turning, dreaming of becoming entangled in the grasping branches that snagged at her clothes and dragged her further into the heart of the forest's steely darkness. She woke the next morning, nervous and out of sorts.

Deep in her own troubled thoughts, she followed Josh up the steep hillside, climbing over the jagged rocks as, once again, the menacing forest began to blot out the morning sunlight, rising above her like a seeping shadow against the skyline. Before her was the dark entrance to the forest with its hungry mouth – it seemed to be waiting for them, eager to welcome its prey. As Cissie clambered over mossy logs and twisted roots into the eerie stillness of the old wood she was plagued by a gnawing sense of uneasiness. The sunlight ebbed away with every step, retreating until Cissie was surrounded by flickering shadows. They made her heart leap with dread. Branches creaked underfoot, and strange butterflies, blue-black and purple-grey, fluttered around her.

'Look everyone! There's a message,' said Spooner excitedly,

racing towards the silver birch and peeling back the bark on the tree-sign.

Benedict hovered on the edge of the group, sneaking furtive glances into the depths of the forest as the others gathered round the tree.

'What does it say?' asked Cissie, peering over Spooner's shoulder.

The girl raised her eyebrow. 'Aunt Cissie, there aren't any words written down, just secret signs,' Spooner explained enigmatically. 'Signs that only some of us can read.'

Spooner stared at the twisted bark, inspecting the detail on the inserts of twig and leaves that had been placed in the tree-sign since yesterday.

'Well?' asked Josh sharply. 'Does it make any sense or not? I expect we've come on another wild goose chase.'

Spooner flashed her father a disdainful look. 'Shh, wait a moment, can't you?' She rubbed her fingers carefully over the bark and twigs, interpreting the reply. 'We have to go further into the forest, up to the ravines,' she said. 'The Skinks will meet us there.'

'Not on your life! There's no way I'm goin' up to Snipes Edge. Who knows what we'll find,' said Josh, looking over his shoulder into the gloomy mass of pine trees. 'Besides, that's where those folks went missin'.'

Cissie raised her eyebrows at her brother. 'What else does it say, my dear?' she asked her niece.

'That they know where Tallitha and Tyaas are.'

'Well that's it. I'm going, even if you're not,' Cissie replied firmly.

'I'll come too,' said Spooner.

'Nobody's goin' in there,' said Josh anxiously grabbing his daughter's hand and pulling her back the way they had come.

Spooner yanked her arm away from her father. 'Get off me, Dad, I'll do as I please!'

'You can't come if your dad won't allow it,' said Cissie, 'but he can't stop me. Benedict, are you coming with me?'

'Nay, our Cissie, you can't mean to go to the ravines! That place has a terrible reputation – people go missin''

'Come with me then, and Spooner too. There's safety in numbers, and Spooner can take care of herself.'

Josh looked from Cissie to Spooner and over to Benedict. Both his sister and daughter were determined to have their own way.

'What do you say, my lad? Will the Skinks help us find Tallitha and the others?' said Josh, his face torn with indecision.

Benedict scraped his feet in the mound of leaves and pushed back his floppy hair. It fell back down again. He looked at the farmer from under his dark, heavy fringe with a shifty sort of look.

'I'm fairly sure the Skinks will have the answer. It isn't that far to the ravines from here.'

'Are you sure, lad? Seems a long way to go to meet 'em, if you ask me.'

'The Skinks brought me down this path yesterday. They

must have left the sign for you,' he explained slyly, enticing them further into the trap.

'Come on Dad, we'll be in and out in no time,' said Spooner, taking his hand and yanking him towards the path, 'if you stop wasting time.'

'But what if something happens? What about your mam?'

'Mam will be fine. Stop mithering Dad – you do fuss!' said Spooner.

Spooner was excited: she was about to get her wish! They were going to explore the heart of the forest, right up to the mysterious place where the curious mushrooms grew at Snipes Edge. Her sister would be green with envy when she got back!

Benedict beckoned to the others to follow him.

'It's this way,' he said pointing towards the path that wound deep into the forest. 'Here,' he said, holding out his hand to Cissie, 'let me help you over these logs.'

Josh raised his arms in defeat. 'Have it your own way,' he said, shaking his head and following Benedict and the others down the path.

Something felt odd to him, going all the way in to Snipes Edge to meet the Skinks, but the others would have their way. Maybe he *was* being overly fussy, like Spooner had said. After all, the Skinks had left them a message. As he followed the others down the path he kept reassuring himself that everything would be fine.

So the party trekked through the dense undergrowth, much further than Benedict had first led them to believe. The once-luscious foliage curled into a canopy of drab, overhanging creepers; purple acrid-smelling plants lined the route, spitting their sour aroma over the dank earth. With each step Josh became more troubled. Unearthly noises rippled through the trees – the sound of unfamiliar birds calling out to each other high above them and wild animals screeching in the undergrowth.

'This forest is changing before our eyes,' called Josh nervously to the others. 'Are you sure this is the way?' he asked Benedict.

Cissie's insides were awash with trepidation. 'He's right, Benedict, where are we?'

The boy turned with an exasperated look on his face. 'Don't fret,' he replied, 'I know what I'm doing.'

So the group of explorers ignored their instincts, swallowing their fears as they tramped further into the dark twisted forest. They climbed over blackened tree roots, passing heavily-pungent flowers and pushing their way through the clinging undergrowth until they were lost in the tangle of spiky twigs and overhanging branches, caught like struggling flies in the forest's dark web. Eventually Josh could stomach it no longer as the overpowering gloom dripped down through the criss-crossed branches.

'I thought you said it wasn't far!' he cried, his voice rising with fear.

He was panicked by the ever-fading light.

'It isn't much further. Come on, nearly there,' replied Benedict, sneaking a sidelong glance at the exhausted farmer and his frantic sister.

Lead them further into the forest, Benedict: just a little further, step by step … His mother's words pounded in his ears. *Right up to the bad place, to the ravines at Snipes Edge …*

'Come on, nearly there,' he repeated, encouraging them. 'I remember this path from yesterday, the Skinks brought me this way,' he said.

'We're coming, lad!' cried Cissie, 'but hold up a minute, 'til I get my breath.'

Cissie stopped and leant heavily against a fallen tree, gasping for air in the suffocating atmosphere. Benedict slyly watched the old woman struggle through the tangled undergrowth.

'Here, let me help you,' he offered. 'Take my hand and come with me.'

'Thank you Benedict,' she said, smiling at the boy.

That's right my pet, lead them to where the wild mushrooms grow; to where the clumps of Destroying Angel lie in the bitter earth; to where it's ever-dark and cold as the grave. I will hold off the Black Hounds until you're there. My creatures will obey me. Take them right up to the Edge, remember. Then I will set the beasts free.

Benedict bit his lip and shuddered. He didn't want to think about what would happen to these kind people who had given him shelter. *Stop it! Stop thinking about that,* he said over and over in his mind. He had to obey his mother, or else she would punish him dreadfully.

But the Queen's heartless words came back to him: *Lead them into the trap, my pet. Leave them at the head of the ravines and slip away. I'll be waiting for you in the forest.*

Benedict parted the tall ferns to reveal a glade leading up to a rocky incline with the tall trees surrounding the infernal ravine.

'Nearly there. Snipes Edge is just over that rocky incline,' said Benedict finally, beginning to hang behind the others.

'I hope so, lad,' said Josh, staring anxiously ahead of them and moving quickly through the tall ferns. 'I haven't the stomach for much more of this miserable forest, the stench is summat awful,' he complained, putting his hand over his nose.

The others passed through the ferns, one by one, taking in the eerie atmosphere. Greenish light percolated down through the tree canopy and the air was damp and fetid, redolent of the smell of decaying vegetation percolating up from the well of the ravine.

'Look Dad, we're here!' shouted Spooner, climbing on to the rocky ledge and leaning out over the terrifying drop. 'It's such a long way down.'

She gazed into the abyss and then up to the sky, where the greenish light ebbed through the branches of the tall pine trees that rimmed the ravines at Snipes Edge.

Cissie and Josh clambered up the rocky incline and held onto the branches, leaning forward and staring way below into the cavernous black hole.

'It's cold and forbidding up here,' whispered Cissie fretfully to her brother, 'but we're in the right place – you can see the mushrooms growing over there.' She pointed to the Honey

Fungus clustering round the base of a gnarled tree stump.

'Look at these beauties!' cried Spooner, pointing to a patch of fungi.

'Keep away from them!' Josh warned. 'They're Death Caps, and they're deadly poisonous.'

Tumbling way below them, the deep ravines cascaded in layers of jagged slate into a cauldron of swirling vapours rising up from the smoggy depths. Plumes of violet-coloured mushrooms oozed out of the rocks like pustulating sores, giving off a sickly, rotting smell like the smell of death itself. Cissie turned quickly away and put her hand over her nose.

'I don't fancy hanging round here,' she said to her brother anxiously. 'The air is putrid.'

'How long should we wait for those Skinks?' asked the farmer nervously, turning to Benedict.

But the boy was nowhere to be seen. Josh clambered back down the rocky incline, but Benedict had vanished. It was as if the boy had been swallowed up by the mist.

'Where is he? I thought he was with you,' called Josh apprehensively to his daughter.

She followed her father down the rocks.

'I don't know Dad, he was here a second ago.'

Spooner tuned to look for the boy, but the patch of ground where Benedict had been standing was eerily vacant.

'I don't like it,' said Josh quietly, 'there's something amiss.'

Curls of misty white vapour swam over the earth. It was in that moment that Spooner remembered her fear from the previous night, when the thick darkness had swept round their farmhouse and Benedict had appeared, like a ghostly apparition, from out of the strange night. She had been certain that there was someone or something with him, but the boy had denied it. Perhaps he had lied to her. She shivered and rubbed her cold body.

'Benedict!' shouted Cissie. 'Where are you? Come out now, this is no time for daft pranks. Always messin' around ... he'll be hiding somewhere,' she said nervously, though somehow she didn't believe it.

The seconds passed by and Benedict still did not return. Josh searched the undergrowth by the edge of the glade to see if the boy was hiding. But there was no sign of him.

'D-Do you think he's left us all alone on purpose?' asked Spooner hesitantly.

'I never did trust him,' sighed Josh. 'Always summat about him, shifty-like.'

'Don't say that,' whispered Cissie as her eyes travelled nervously over the inhospitable terrain.

Snipes Edge was indeed a desolate, ghoulish place. The meagre sunlight ebbed down through the criss-crossed branches, landing in pale streaks above the ravine. But the light was greenish-yellow: a sickly, swirling fog that provided an ideal feasting place for grotesque hovering insects. The heady smell of the exotic plants and pungent toadstools hung menacingly in the damp air. Cissie wrung her hands and stared out over the glade in desperation. She felt sick from the acidic, rotting smell and the gnawing realisation that Benedict had enticed them to the Edge for some underhanded reason. In her heart, Cissie knew that whatever it was, a bad thing was about to happen. Pinpricking fear began to tingle up her spine.

'I'm sorry, brother,' she whispered nervously, 'I fear that boy has left us here on purpose – but for what, I dread to think.'

'Perhaps it's a trick of some sort,' he said fearfully, his eyes darting towards the undergrowth.

Then, out of the darkness Spooner heard a noise coming towards them through the dense wall of pine trees. She couldn't make it out at first. *Thud, thud, thud* – the sound reverberated across the forest floor.

'What's that?' she asked fearfully. 'I-I heard something, over there.'

She pointed into the gloomy hinterland of the forest.

'It sounds like pounding feet,' whispered Cissie, staring at Spooner's terrified face.

The terrible noise was the relentless pad-pad-padding of the wild dogs' paws thumping heartlessly through the bracken, crunching on the fallen leaves and racing towards their prey

Spooner clutched her father's arm.

'I-Is it a trap, Dad?' she asked. 'Has Benedict tricked us?'

'Aye my lass, I fear we've been deceived by that treacherous lad.'

'Oh, heavens!' cried Cissie desperately. 'Josh, what shall we do?'

The hapless travellers stood on the rocky slopes of the

ravines waiting for the first sighting of whatever was tracking them – *seeking* them – out in the darkness. The farmer stared desperately before him, wiping the trickling sweat from his brow. His family was in dire peril and there was nothing he could do to save them. The colour drained from his face and his heart thumped from the grinding fear rising nauseatingly from the pit of his stomach.

Then, out of the gloom he heard the low growls of the beasts. The sounds rumbled over the forest floor, winding swiftly through the undergrowth until, all at once, the terrible gut-wrenching howling started. The Black Hounds were pounding through the undergrowth making their way inevitably towards them.

'May the good spirits protect us,' were the only words that Cissie could muster.

Thirteen

Cissie felt her insides turn to stone as terror seized her whole body. She held her niece's trembling hand and squeezed it tight. Spooner was rooted to the spot, scared to take a breath lest the rising fear catch in her throat and cause her to choke. The awful pounding of the hounds' paws had stopped some feet away, somewhere just out of sight. She watched the bank of ferns surrounding the glade for any sudden movement; any twitching that would herald the dogs' approach. Dusk had silently descended over Snipes Edge like a dismal shroud.

'What's happening, Dad?' asked Spooner, her eyes watering with fear.

Josh stood motionless, staring into the gloomy night. He had already scanned the glade for any means of escape, but there was no way out. Behind them was the sheer drop of the ravine and in front of them the hounds were waiting, salivating.

Josh was poised for the moment when the fern tendrils would start to quiver and the loathsome creatures would finally slink into view. He stared into the shadowy bracken: deep, deep into the haunting, foggy twilight ... waiting. Then out of the gloom he saw them. Seven, eight pairs of evil yellow eyes piercing the darkness.

They were completely surrounded by the Black Hounds.

Cissie made a desperate sound, and grabbed hold of Spooner as the loathsome pack edged out of the undergrowth, revealing their ravaged bodies and dirt-black matted fur, growling and snarling. The hounds slunk across the earth in pack formation, alert to every movement of their leader, waiting for the signal to attack. The grisly ringleader was the biggest, most vicious-looking creature Josh had ever seen. The hideous beast licked his ferocious jaws, snarled, barred its fangs and bided its time.

'What'll we do?' cried Cissie desperately, clinging on to her brother.

The three lonely figures huddled together on the rocky incline and waited. Cissie knew it was her fault that they were in such a mess. If she hadn't insisted they come looking for the children and if Benedict hadn't turned up in the middle of the night with betrayal in his heart ... She couldn't understand why he had done this to them. Cissie couldn't fathom the boy or his motives, to abandon them here, to meet this gruesome end

In the madness of the moment Josh decided that there was only one solution. He hastily grabbed his loved ones, pulling them back towards the edge of the ravine. They stumbled desperately over the uneven rocks, crying out in abject terror. He knew their deaths would be quicker and less painful by jumping into the ravine, rather than being torn to pieces by the vicious bloodthirsty hounds. He would jump first and pull them down onto his breast. At least they would die together. Their end would be over in a matter of seconds.

But the beasts were in no hurry to attack. Their prey was cornered, and was theirs for the taking. There was no escape from Snipes Edge when the Black Hounds were on the rampage. The hounds' yellow eyes glinted savagely and their fat tongues lolled at the side of their blood-red jaws, salivating at the thought of the tasty feast that awaited them.

Then the huge wolfhound, the fiend covered in scars and bite marks, scratched at the ground, lifted his dreadful jaws and howled. A terrifying, blood-curdling sound filled the glade. Now the pack was ready to strike.

'Dad!' Spooner screamed.

Her cries of anguish reverberated through the forest.

Josh didn't flinch. He grabbed hold of their clammy hands and prepared to take a huge step backwards over the abyss. As Cissie and Spooner realised what was about to happen they stared frantically into Josh's face. The next step would hurl all three of them to their deaths.

'No, Dad!' shouted Spooner, desperation written all over her face.

Josh opened his mouth, tears rolling down his cheeks at the thought of what he was about to do.

I-I'm sorry lass,' he stuttered.

Then, out of nowhere, came a cry from above whooshing over the ravines, gruff and raw like the wind through the forest:

'Quickly, grab them!'

From out of the midst of the tall pine trees, Ruker flew through the air and lunged for the girl, while Neeps and Spelk grabbed the others and carried them high into the dusky night, rising swiftly over the ravines and up into the trees over Ragging Brows Forest. The Black Hounds howled ferociously, leaping frantically into the air with wild abandon as their supper vanished before their eyes. One rangy creature sprang a little too far, wriggled desperately in the air to save his hide, yelped pathetically and clattered helter-skelter down the rock face, into the jaws of the ravine.

'It's the Skinks!' shouted Spooner breathlessly.

She beamed at Ruker as they sailed through the forest twilight, skimming the tall pine trees. The cool night air rushed past them as they climbed ever higher into the tree canopy. The Skinks were the rulers of the forest: nimbly alighting on the tree platforms, effortlessly taking command of the tethered ropes and leaping into the air, making their way swiftly and expertly through the trees, taking Spooner and the others far away from the mouths of the marauding beasts.

Cissie buried her head in the Skink's body and sobbed with relief. She kept tight hold of the one called Spelk, a blonde-haired creature who shouted instructions to the others whilst flying with incredible ease across the night sky. The farmer didn't care that he was far above the ravines, ripping through the forest with a Skink called Neeps. He was grinning from ear to ear. He was alive! They were all alive! It was a miracle!

'Stop here!' shouted Spelk to the others, jumping nimbly onto the wooden platform. 'This will do, my friend,' she said to Cissie, laughing at the woman's astonished face and bringing her to a sudden halt.

Ruker and Neeps alighted on the platform close behind her.

'Josh! Spooner!' cried Cissie, clutching her brother. 'I thought we were done for!'

Josh wrapped his daughter in his arms and kissed his sister fondly.

'Follow me,' announced Spelk, 'there's much to discuss.'

*

Spelk's tree house was warm and cosy like all the dwellings in Hanging Tree Islands. Supper was bubbling away on the stove while Lem, a young male Skink, chopped the vegetables and stirred the pot, welcoming the flabbergasted trio into the wonders of the treetop world.

'I can't believe what just happened,' said Spooner breathlessly, her eyes shining with excitement, 'and that we're all the way up here. Lince will be so jealous when I tell her.'

'Your mam will be beside herself with worry, so stop showing off. I only hope she's had the sense to go home.'

'Our kid will be bored by now and will have wandered off with Mam in tow. You said to go back to the farm if we weren't back by dusk,' said Spooner.

Despite her excitement, Spooner felt a twinge of guilt imagining her mother's misery as dusk approached.

'Just think on, my girl. We nearly ended up as wolf-fodder down there.'

'Sorry Dad,' she said sheepishly.

Josh knitted his eyebrows as he remembered how close they had come to death. Then he turned to the Skinks:

'You saved our lives and we're forever grateful to you. How did you know we were down there?'

'We've been watching Benedict for days,' said Ruker, her face clouding over with the thought of their betrayer. 'He's been roaming the forest with the heartless Queen.'

'A Queen!' exclaimed Spooner, excitedly. 'Who's she?'

She was agog at the thought of an evil Queen in Ragging Brows Forest.

'Queen Asphodel, the ruler of the Dark Reaches,' Ruker replied, turning to face Cissie. 'She's Benedict's mother.'

Cissie threw up her hands in horror.

'Well I never! Then Benedict betrayed Tallitha and Tyaas too, the wicked boy!' she cried, her face puckering with anger.

'He betrayed all of us in the caves, just as he left you to meet your grisly end at Snipes Edge,' said Ruker. 'He's been under the Queen's control all along. It was a set-up from beginning to end. He'll always do her bidding and that of her wicked sister.'

Cissie stared at Ruker. 'Sister?' she asked looking puzzled, her face darkening.

'You know her as Lady Snowdroppe,' she replied.

Cissie's eyes sparked with hatred and she gripped her chair. It was all starting to fall into place.

'Snowdroppe!' she cried, rising to her feet and pacing the room. 'Then she's responsible for this treachery, and doubtless for Asenathe goin' missin' too! That vain woman was never kind to them bairns,' she said finally. 'She has no love in her heart for any child.'

'But what happened to you?' asked Josh.

Ruker recounted how she had met Tallitha and the others in Ragging Brows Forest.

'Then we were captured by the Murk Mowl, and handed over to the Groats and Queen Asphodel,' Ruker replied.

'The Dooerlins,' Cissie cried mournfully. 'I've kept those children safe from those devilish creatures all these years ... and now they've been taken!'

'But what do they want with Tallitha and Tyaas?' Spooner asked. 'What's this all been for? Why lead them all the way to Breedoor?'

'It don't make no sense,' said Josh. 'Her own children an' all ... what's this Snowdroppe to do with the castle?'

Cissie shook her head. 'There's dark mischief afoot and it has something to do with the Morrow secrets. The old family's been riven with danger and intrigue ever since the time of Edwyn Morrow.'

'The Shroves are in on it, I know that much,' said Ruker

'Marlin!' cried Cissie. 'I knew it! Both him and Grintley attacked me when the children went missin'. Then they told the Grand Morrow that I'd helped the children escape and she banished me from Winderling Spires.'

'They're all in on it,' said Ruker bitterly.

The Skink recounted all that had happened to them on their journey under the Out-Of-The-Way Mountains, while Lem served a supper of delicious forest fare: wild rabbit stew, root vegetables and, to follow, a blackberry pie with fresh cream. The farmer licked his plate clean and finished off second helpings.

'When did you last see them?' asked Spooner.

'We had to leave them at Melted Water,' Ruker replied. 'They were headed for Hellstone Tors. But I promised Tallitha I would come and find her, and that time is now.'

'That's foolish talk,' said Spelk. 'You'll never get into the Tors. You're a Skink and will be captured in an instant. No, we need a better plan than that.'

'But I promised her,' insisted Ruker. 'She's in trouble. I had a dream about Tallitha trapped in that dreadful castle. She was all alone, crying out for me.'

'We have to find them,' pleaded Cissie.

'Unless you have a well thought out plan, you're sure to get caught,' urged Spelk.

'She's right,' said Neeps

Ruker paced the floor. 'Well, anyone got any bright ideas?'

'The clues to what happened in the past lie in Winderling

Spires,' said Cissie. 'We have to get into that house and spy on the Shroves as they've spied on us all these years. But it'll be difficult: they're wily creatures, and Marlin knows the house inside out, much better than me.'

'Count me in!' cried Ruker. 'I've been waiting to get my own back on that rattlesnake Benedict.'

'Me too,' added Neeps grinning, 'sounds like quite an adventure.'

'Certainly does, but how do we get into the house?' asked Ruker.

Cissie sighed. 'It won't be easy.'

'That old place is bound to have a tunnel or two,' suggested Ruker.

Cissie's face brightened. 'Well, there's the tunnel that leads to the mausoleum, the one Tallitha used.'

'Then we'll have to follow the same route,' said Ruker, 'but in the dead of night.'

Spooner was agog at all the talk of tunnels and mausoleums, weird old houses and wicked Queens. The thought of breaking into Winderling Spires at night was an adventure too good to miss.

'I can help too!' she added cheerfully.

'I've heard that before,' said her father. 'We've all had enough adventure for now.'

'But Dad, me and our kid could be so useful.'

'That's enough! I don't think I can bear to let you out of my sight after what just happened.'

Cissie sighed and shook her head. 'There's a problem,' she said, biting her lip. 'Tyaas has the key to the tunnel gate. I left it unlocked but the Shroves may have meddled and locked it again.'

'Is there anyone who could help us to get inside the Spires? We need someone on the lookout for us who can get us another key just in case,' said Neeps.

'There's Mary Brindle, Snowdroppe's ladies' maid. She's my 'alf cousin and she don't like her mistress one jot. But how can I get word to her so she can check the tunnel?'

Spooner's face lit up. 'I could do it!' she said excitedly. 'I could visit Aunt Rose and slip a note to Mary.'

'No! I won't hear of it,' exclaimed Josh.

'Well, what other ideas do you have?' asked Spooner, observing her father's troubled expression.

'I'm afraid she has a point,' added Ruker. 'If you'll just agree to her suggestion ...'

Josh wagged his finger at Spooner. Her face brightened with excitement. She knew she'd got her way and was going to be part of the adventure.

'The only way I'll agree to any of this my girl, is if you go visitin' your Aunt Rose with your mam. She'll need to keep an eye on you,' said Josh emphatically.

'And our Lince, she'll have to come too. It's not fair, Dad, she's missed out on all this fun and she'll only sneak out and follow us if you don't allow it.'

Josh threw up his hands in defeat. His girls were beyond

him. They were too old to be kept indoors, yet too young to be wandering about getting into all kinds of scrapes. What Spooner thought of as fun and adventure, he considered deadly dangerous.

'Well, that's all you're doing, and your mam will 'ave to agree first …'

Spooner's face lit up. They would wheedle away at her. Their mam was no match for her and their kid.

'It may work,' said Ruker thoughtfully. 'Neeps, what do you think?'

'Try and hold me back,' said Neeps. 'Just tell me where to go and who to fight. I'm with you all the way until we get Tallitha and Tyaas back home.'

'And Esmerelda,' added Cissie, 'we mustn't forget all about her.'

Fourteen

In the late evening, after Embellsed had departed, Tallitha drew her brother next to her. She told him about her plan to free Essie and what had occurred in the gallery. The boy's mouth fell open as he listened intently to his sister.

'What did you say?' he asked, spluttering at the news.

'He's our adopted brother, and he's a foundling,' replied Tallitha, 'so he isn't related to us at all, but it was a shock nevertheless.'

'What's a foundling?' asked the bewildered boy, trying to absorb yet more unwelcome information about his complicated family.

'Someone abandoned as a baby. Apparently he was found out there somewhere,' she said, gesticulating towards the wild northern terrain.

'But who is he?'

'I don't know, and I doubt he does. Mother found him and brought him to Hellstone Tors.'

'That's a bit unlike her,' replied Tyaas. Their mother was not renowned for her compassionate nature. 'When was that?'

'Before she married father. He's been her adopted son ever since, a bit like a stray kitten or a wolf cub, more like. There's something wild and untamed about him,' she added.

'How do you mean?' asked Tyaas apprehensively.

'His yellow eyes unsettle me. They have the look of the hunter in them.'

'Damn him! He knew who we were all along. He's hiding something,' said Tyaas.

'Definitely,' replied Tallitha, 'but the odd thing is, we were bound to find out about him eventually.'

'He wanted to check us out first, to keep us guessing.'

'The Swarm consider him as an outsider. It's the way they look at him,' she said. 'He's not one of them, but then I'm not sure who he *is*.'

'Do you think we're in for any more shocks? It's all a bit much, if you ask me.'

'Nothing would surprise me,' she sighed and stared out of the window. 'Not a day goes by that I don't regret leaving Winderling Spires, and now I have to meet the Wild Imaginer.'

'Who's that?' he gasped.

'I have a nasty feeling it's someone much worse than the dreadful governess,' she replied apprehensively.

Tallitha explained all about the tests she had to do from The Black Pages.

Yet the thought of travelling alone to Stankles Brow with the mysterious Quillam filled her with a sense of excitement and foreboding. After all it was an adventure, and it meant she could leave the confines of the castle. But she didn't know whether she could trust Quillam. And what did the Wild Imaginer have in store for her?

Tyaas broke her train of thought: 'Can't I come too?' he asked.

Tallitha shook her head. 'They won't let you. They'll keep you here in case I make a run for it.'

Tyaas's face clouded over. 'I never get any fun,' he complained. 'It'll be boring here without you.'

'Don't worry, I have a plan, but it will be dangerous. It involves you and Essie. You must break into the Witch's Tower and steal the pact.'

Tyaas brightened up. 'Then we'll have to find where Essie is being held to warn her about Mother,' added Tyaas.

'I've tried making contact with her, but nothing seems to work,' replied Tallitha despondently.

Tyaas sat with his head in his hands, thinking. This wasn't something he did very often but he was certain that his sister just needed a good nudge in the right direction.

'What about that gemstone the Thane gave you?' he asked.

Tallitha rummaged in her dressing table and handed the stone to her brother. He held it up to the candlelight, and it sparkled in a rainbow of shimmering lights. Tyaas suddenly began twirling the stone and muttering in Ennish.

Tallitha's mouth dropped open and she giggled.

'Since when have you been into all this? Are you serious?'

'If it means we can warn Essie, I don't care,' he replied, blushing.

'Tyaas, you do surprise me,' she said, looking quizzically at her brother, 'but okay, have a go.'

'It's quite heavy,' he said, as he dangled it before Tallitha's eyes. 'Now concentrate and look at me. *Canya-fe, canya-fe,*' he began chanting.

His sister fell about laughing.

'Oh Tyaas, you are funny, I can't take you seriously,' she giggled. 'When did you hear those words?'

'I've been w-watching you,' he stammered.

'When was that?'

'I watched Essie hypnotising you, when you thought I was asleep. Now do you want to try this or not?' he answered, his voice becoming tetchy.

'I can't look at you while we're doing it, you'll make me laugh,' she sniggered.

Nevertheless, Tallitha composed herself. She blew out the candles, drew the heavy curtains, making the room as dark as possible to obscure Tyaas's intent face.

'Close your eyes,' said her brother. 'Try to imagine Essie's bewitching eyes, the pungent smell, the way she led you to the shadow-flight. I want you to focus all your power on finding her.'

Tallitha did as she was asked. The room was still, and the silence made Tallitha feel drowsy. She let her body and mind completely relax. Breathing deeply, she remembered the first time Essie had hypnotised her in the Great Room; encircling her, wrapping her long scarves around her face, her smouldering eyes boring into her and Esmerelda's lilting Ennish words:

'Snenathe ne certhe merl can an le ner
Cerna la bernatha ne tor na lam, berche berche ne cer
Snenathe ne certhe merl can an le ner.'

Tallitha remembered Esmerelda's repetitive humming and the sweet heady scent as she began to slip under the old spell, making her drift away.

'Open your eyes and watch the shimmering pendant,' Tyaas insisted.

He dangled the gemstone before Tallitha's eyes. It was as if Esmerelda was twisting the amulet before her, moving it backwards and forwards.

'Focus on finding Essie,' urged Tyaas.

The flashing lights danced together like a dazzle of precious stones: diamond, ruby, topaz, emerald and sapphire slices of shimmering colour spun over the walls, throwing out a thousand sparkles that bounced off the ceiling and spun dizzyingly across the room, mesmerising Tallitha. She felt her body sliding, pop-popping through the middle plane, and *whoosh!* – Tyaas's charms had worked.

In an instant Tallitha slipped into the infinite space that stretched before her. Her weightless body whipped up the tunnel with the silver cord floating behind her. She had entered the shadow-flight and she tumbled – *whoosh!* – out on the other side into the soft grey light.

*

In the depths of the dungeon, Esmerelda had fashioned her days by making friends with the other prisoners and piecing together the dark history of the castle that now imprisoned her. She came to know Cremola Burn and Leticia Trume, the women who the Cave-Shroves had spoken about on Raw-Ripple Island. Cremola was a dark-haired beauty despite her time in captivity, and Leticia, the older of the two women, took it upon herself to watch over the younger prisoners. They became Esmerelda's confidants and the three women became expert in the to-ings and fro-ings of the guards. When the Groats were at their sleepiest, just after dinner, it was then that the women whispered to one another.

Esmerelda slowly learned about Asenathe's downfall, that she had indeed fallen for the Thane's son, Arden, but that after his death she had been drugged with a powerful potion concocted by the Neopholytite, who had used her as bait to lure Tallitha to Hellstone Tors. Esmerelda could not forgive herself for having missed the vital clues. Tallitha had tried to warn her, to tell her that Asenathe appeared both as a young girl and as an older woman, but she hadn't listened to her. Nothing would have deterred Esmerelda from her obsession with finding her cousin.

On that afternoon, Esmerelda lay dozing on her straw mattress. She dreamt that Tallitha was in the corner of her cell, and that the girl was beckoning to her. Tallitha's distant voice vibrated in the netherworld and slowly infiltrated Esmerelda's sleepy state. She felt a tingling sensation, like fingers running over her entire body and she woke with a start. There before her was the blurred outline of Tallitha, it wasn't a dream at all.

'*Essie, Essie,*' Tallitha murmured.

'You mustn't stay here,' Esmerelda replied urgently, rising and running towards her. 'It's too dangerous, the Groats may hear us talking.'

Esmerelda hurriedly peered out of the grate in her cell.

'*But I must warn you,*' Tallitha replied, looking about her. There was nowhere safe in the cell. '*Come with me to the middle plane.*'

'My powers are weakened here,' replied Esmerelda, 'I'm not sure I can access them.'

'*Then let me take you with me, relax and breathe deeply and we'll say the words together.*'

Esmerelda nodded and they spoke the Ennish words. '*Snenathe ne certhe merl can an le ner,*' they whispered over and over again until the spell took hold.

In an instant Esmerelda felt herself slipping away from her body. She joined hands with Tallitha, and they edged through the spirit passageway and out into the foggy light.

'*I've waited for you every day,*' cried Esmerelda. '*My powers are not as strong as yours, and this prison has dulled them further.*'

Tallitha's hazy outline shuddered. *'I'm here now,'* she said gently, taking Esmerelda's hand. *'Tomorrow they will release you, but you will only remain free on certain conditions ...'*

But Esmerelda wasn't listening ...

'I'll make them pay for what they've done to us,' she hissed.

The anger in her voice vibrated through the middle plane.

'No Essie, you must listen to me! The only way to defeat the Swarm is to break the Morrow pact.'

'But how can we do that?' Esmerelda asked.

'There's a way, I'm certain of it, but first I must develop my special powers. I've persuaded the Thane you're the only one who can help me access the shadow-flight – that's my first test.'

'What if their power is too strong and they possess you? Take you over completely!' Essie warned.

'That's why you must help me. Tomorrow Snowdroppe will test you in some way, to see whether you can be trusted. Somehow, you must outwit her.'

'Very well, I will curb my desire for revenge – but only for now. Leticia and Cremola know the ways of the dark sisters. They will help me.'

'I'm to be tested by the Wild Imaginer at Stankles Brow, but first you must help me to progress through The Black Pages.'

'Whatever happens you will come back stronger. We must discover the way to break the pact ...'

Together they whispered the Ennish words once more then Tallitha felt the flood of Esmerelda's warm embrace before her cousin drifted away.

Then Tallitha was bumping down the tunnel, lights flashing before her eyes. There was an enormous *whooshing* sound, then a *thud* and a tremendous *thump*, and Tallitha woke with a start. The air rushed back into her lungs with huge searing gulps.

Tyaas was shaking her awake.

'You did well, Tyaas,' she moaned. 'I found her.'

The boy's eyes shone eagerly.

'But she wants revenge against the Swarm. Let's hope she'll bide her time.' Tallitha rubbed her aching head. 'While I'm at Stankles Brow, you and Essie have an important task to perform.'

'Will it be fun?'

'It will be deadly dangerous.'

'Great!' he cried excitedly. 'Tell me what you want me to do.'

'You must break into the Neopholytite's tower and discover whatever you can about the Morrow pact.'

'Is that all?' said Tyaas sarcastically, pulling a face at his sister.

But secretly he was overjoyed. At last he had an adventure of his very own.

Fifteen

'Don't stand there hopping about like a complete imbecile, bring me that woman Esmerelda Patch!' Snowdroppe shouted, standing with her hands on her hips and towering over the unfortunate Bludroot. Her eyes flashed venomously.

The Shrove whimpered, spun round on his heels and sped off down the corridor. Snowdroppe groaned and paced the floor clutching her stomach. Her face had a sour look, and was the shade of sickly green. The tight pain in her belly was due to the weryke curse she was carrying inside her. The curse would do its worst on Esmerelda Patch as it fizzed and curdled in her gut, it would winkle out all that woman's falsehoods.

'Hurry up, damn you!' she shouted after the scurrying Shrove.

Snowdroppe had spent the morning conferring with the Neopholytite, who had created an especially nasty treat from her arsenal of curses, just for Esmerelda. The witch had sat hunched in her winged armchair, wringing her wrinkled hands in anticipation of Snowdroppe's evil request.

'Delicious, quite delicious,' she crooned, wagging her crooked finger. 'It has to be a dark, potent weryke to ferret out all her lies, even the smallest ones. Now, let me see ...'

The Neopholytite closed her dead black eyes for several blissful minutes as she chanted to herself, chuckling nastily and cogitating on the problem.

'Do hurry up, I haven't got all day,' grumbled Snowdroppe, pacing backwards and forwards across the gloomy interior of the hideous Bone Room.

She couldn't abide her grandmother's infernal tower. It gave her the shivers with its perpetual darkness, bloody drapes and wild, beady-eyed birds caw-cawing away at her.

The Neopholytite suddenly snapped open her eyes. They swam like bottomless black pools in her pale, shrivelled face.

'Yes! I have just the one!' she cried at last. 'This weryke is an old and beautiful curse. It will test her lying mouth,' she croaked. 'It will flush out all her horrid little lies.'

'Make it quick, can't you? I hate this bit,' Snowdroppe complained, her face twisting into a frown. 'It's so uncomfortable!'

'Ready, my pet?' said her grandmother. 'Then let us begin. *Calamistra, navar shenine malancthon deit,*' she chanted.

The Neopholytite put the palms of her hands together and blew softly between her two gnarled thumbs, slowly opening the

189

back of her hands to release an inky trail of bluish-black smoke that snaked its way towards Snowdroppe. The smoke wound round and round in a snail shell pattern, forming itself into a spinning cloud that hung ominously in the air. Snowdroppe gathered all her strength, opened her mouth and snapped like a ravenous dog, gobbling up the weryke in one foul bite. Her beautiful face turned pale, she screwed up her eyes and let out a huge resounding belch.

'Eurgh, that was disgusting,' Snowdroppe moaned.

The witch cackled wickedly and her ashen face lit up at the sound of the satisfying belch.

'Wonderful! That delectable little weryke will keep until later. It will nestle obligingly in your gut,' the Neopholytite chortled, 'but remember: the curse only lasts until your next meal. Forget that rule and eat too soon, and it will turn its venomous power on its host,' she explained, wagging her finger at her impatient granddaughter.

Snowdroppe grasped her belly and her mouth quivered.

'It's impossible to forget it,' she snapped, 'with this foul curse sitting heavily in my stomach. It's giving me atrocious wind,' she cried, and another series of enormous belches erupted from her dainty mouth.

'Be off with you! And remember, I want to hear every gory detail of Esmerelda's pain. Sweet weryke, do your worst!' cackled the Neopholytite. 'I also want to meet my grandchildren, especially the girl.'

'Of course, Grandmother,' Snowdroppe replied, 'but not until she has been to Stankles Brow.'

Snowdroppe picked up her skirts, belched once more and hurried from the dismal tower.

The witch was certain that Tallitha had somehow penetrated her lair. She wanted to see this interesting child for herself.

*

In the cold bowels of Hellstone Tors, way down in the underbelly of the enormous castle where the black water dripped into putrid puddles and the verminous rats lived in their scores, the women of the Bleak Rooms were wise to the ways of the witch and were determined to arm Esmerelda against her forthcoming trial. Cremola Burn and Leticia Trume had experienced the enchantments of the Neopholytite and the cruelty of the dark sisters at first hand, so they prepared an ancient remedy and a word-spell antidote to protect Esmerelda against the force of the savage weryke.

'What're you two doing?' Esmerelda asked, peering over Cremola's shoulder.

The women were huddled over a table in the central dungeon. Cremola Burn hastily turned and put her finger to their lips.

'Shh, Essie! You must be quiet or the guards may hear us.'

'We've made you a weryke-balm pie, full of our magic,' Cremola announced excitedly, her eyes sparkling with delight.

Leticia lifted a slice of the heavy uninviting pie to

Esmerelda's mouth. 'Now take a bite. It will lessen the effect of Snowdroppe's weryke curse.'

The leaf pie was filled with a greenish-brown stodge, rough hedgerow plants, rolled herbs and slivers of fungus.

'But it looks disgusting,' Esmerelda replied, forcing herself to take a nibble.

'More!' insisted Leticia, encouraging Esmerelda to take mouthful after disgusting mouthful of the strange pie.

Leticia, the eldest amongst them, cherished her companions as if they were her own daughters, and had taken care of them in the prison. But her years of imprisonment had begun to take their toll. She looked worn out and ever more frail of late.

'I know it doesn't taste good my dear, but close your eyes, chew and swallow.'

The women badgered Esmerelda until she had eaten half of the revolting pie. Cremola advised her friend to be on her guard, knowing that Snowdroppe's weryke curse would burrow away at her, working its evil to prise out all her secret thoughts.

'We know that Snowdroppe's weryke will be a truth spell, but we don't know which one she will use from the witch's arsenal.' She drew Esmerelda close to her. 'It will suddenly attack you out of nowhere, and even with this magic pie inside you and the word-spell it will be a painful ordeal.'

'Hush, Cremola,' said Leticia, 'you mustn't say another word or the special warding-off properties of the weryke-balm pie will be ruined.'

'What does she mean?' asked Esmerelda, who was rubbing her aching stomach.

She was full to bursting with the revolting concoction.

'You must keep saying this word-spell antidote over to yourself, as it will arm you against the curse. Say these words: "*malancthon vita melta*",' Leticia instructed.

'And take some of the leftover pie to Tallitha. She will have need of it when she travels to Stankles Brow. It will protect her,' Cremola added.

'*Malancthon vita melta*,' repeated Esmerelda as she folded the remainder of the dry flaky pie in her handkerchief.

'I'll come back for you, never fear,' she whispered as she hugged Cremola and Leticia farewell.

Then a Groat guard opened the gate and poked his head into the dungeon.

'Come with me,' he hollered. 'Be quick about it, the High Shrove is waiting.'

Esmerelda looked at her friends one last time and began the ascent up the cold stone steps. Standing above her Bludroot was frantically hopping about, agitated to return at once to the impatient Snowdroppe

*

The Groat bundled Esmerelda through the dark passageways and up to Snowdroppe's palace, passing through the arch of stone ravens into a fabulous courtyard with a scented lavender fountain that led up to a resplendent oval sitting room. The room was surrounded by ornate balconies overlooking a rocky precipice with the roar of the ocean far beneath them.

Snowdroppe stood with her hands covering her stomach. Her beautiful face was distorted with pain from the nasty weryke that curdled away in her belly. She fed her yapping fennec fox from a plate of perfectly prepared morsels that rested on a pedestal.

'Stiggy's hungry. Aren't you, my pet?' she purred, knowing that the fox was gobbling up much better food than Esmerelda had eaten for days.

But Snowdroppe's cruelty had no effect on Esmerelda. The last thing on her mind was food of any kind. Her belly was full to bursting with too many helpings of the weryke-balm pie.

'You're filthy,' said Snowdroppe, rising and flicking dirt from her clothes. 'Has the accommodation not been to your standard?' she teased viciously.

Esmerelda's steely face stared straight ahead of her. She clenched her teeth, determined to ignore Snowdroppe's wicked taunts. She rehearsed the words of the antidote, alert to the weryke from whichever part of the room it would assault her.

'You know why you're here,' Snowdroppe snapped, still clutching her stomach. 'If you pass the truth trial you will have some freedom in Hellstone Tors. I may even allow you to have a luxurious bubble-bath. But if you don't, then I'm afraid it's back to the Bleak Rooms with you.' She laughed wickedly. 'Bludroot, take Stiggy and leave us.'

Snowdroppe decided to taunt her prey first.

'Before I begin the test,' she announced, 'I want to know why you have poisoned Tallitha against me.'

Esmerelda was taken aback and remained silent. She prepared herself for the onslaught of the weryke, her eyes scanning the room for any sign of the evil curse.

'Refusal to answer is tantamount to lying' shouted Snowdroppe, 'and will deserve the same punishment! What special gift does Tallitha have? Is she deliberately preventing her progression through The Black Pages? Out with it!' she cried, firing questions at Esmerelda.

The muscles in Snowdroppe's fine neck throbbed with rage. 'Answer me!' she screamed, spittle flying from her red lips like spurting acid.

But Esmerelda remained resolute. Snowdroppe's eyes flashed with wicked delight as she moved in to release the weryke.

'Have it your way! This will hurt, but it will drag the truth out of you.'

Snowdroppe began to chant in a strange tongue:

'*Calamistra, navar shenine malancthon deit.*'

She pursed her beautiful red lips and a trail of bluish-black smoke curled out of her mouth, forming into a vaporous cloud that gathered momentum and streaked like an arrow across the room. Before Esmerelda could prevent it, the weryke darted into her mouth and down her throat in one enormous surge. She choked and spluttered.

'That will make you talk!' shouted Snowdroppe nastily.

Esmerelda's eyes rolled back in her head and she clutched her neck, crying out in pain as the inky weryke slipped down her throat and started to invade every part of her body. The weryke twisted and turned, slicing and jabbing away inside her. But despite the pain, Esmerelda knew she must remain conscious. She repeated the word-spell over and over to herself: '*Malancthon vita melta, malancthon vita melta.*' The searing intensity was only just bearable.

'Please, Snowdroppe!' Esmerelda cried, clutching her stomach and grimacing with every cut. 'Release me from this curse, I beg you!'

'You mean nothing to me! You always despised me at Winderling Spires! You made that abundantly clear. Well, this will teach you!'

Through the pain Esmerelda could hear Snowdroppe's shrieking. She clapped her hands with malicious delight as Esmerelda fell to the floor, curling into a ball and writhing in agony. When the weryke had done its worst, it spun from Esmerelda's mouth in a blue fog and disappeared out of the window with a squeaking sound like a huge balloon losing air.

Snowdroppe lifted Esmerelda's head by her hair and looked into her drowsy eyes.

'Let me be,' pleaded Esmerelda. 'No more of that weryke. I will do whatever you say.'

'Excellent!' Snowdroppe cried. 'You don't know how long I have waited for those words to fall from your lips.'

'I will repeat the question,' Snowdroppe snarled, pacing

around Esmerelda. 'Why have you poisoned Tallitha against me?'

Esmerelda uncurled her body and lifted her ashen face to Snowdroppe. 'Tallitha is young and has never been away from home before. She needs time to adjust to the ways of Hellstone Tors,' muttered Esmerelda.

Snowdroppe recoiled at Esmerelda's response. She had expected a litany of abuse to spew forth from her captive's mouth but instead here was the voice of reason. She stood with her hands on her hips and looked perplexed.

'What did you say?' she shouted, spit flying from her mouth.

She would have liked nothing better than to fling Esmerelda back into the Bleak Rooms, or worse, let Hellstone Tors have her soul – to take her to its heartless core, to the Darkling Stairs, where a worse fate would greet her.

Snowdroppe rounded on Esmerelda. She would try another tack.

'Then tell me, what talents does Tallitha's have?'

'She has many, she's a s-special g-girl,' Esmerelda stuttered.

Snowdroppe spun round and stared at the woman lying prostrate on her floor. Part of her was disappointed by Esmerelda's compliance but she knew the weryke could not lie. The curse was too potent.

'In what way is she so special?' demanded Snowdroppe.

Esmerelda slumped forward.

'Wake up and answer me,' she demanded, pulling Esmerelda up by her hair. 'I must know everything!'

'I feel ill,' she moaned.

'What can Tallitha do?' screeched Snowdroppe into Esmerelda's pale face.

'Please believe me,' she gasped, 'I don't know the full e-extent of her powers.' Esmerelda wretched like an animal.

Snowdroppe pulled a disgusted face and stepped out of the way. She wanted rid of the woman if she was going to vomit all over her beautiful rugs.

'Is she deliberately blocking her journey through The Black Pages?'

Esmerelda gagged and held a hand over her mouth.

'Sometimes Tallitha doesn't understand the extent of her powers. B-But I have helped her access the shadow-flight before and I can help her now, if you want me to.'

Snowdroppe eyed Esmerelda suspiciously. She didn't trust her. She would have her watched at all times in case she tried any of her tricks.

'Then if you do as I say I will allow you to help Tallitha with The Black Pages,' replied Snowdroppe. 'But one false step, and I will take you to the Darkling Stairs myself.' She came very close to Esmerelda and whispered in her ear: 'Then Hellstone Tors will have its way with you. It will eat you alive.'

Snowdroppe clicked her fingers and Bludroot, who had been eavesdropping, hurried into the oval room.

'You can go to your cousin, Asenathe,' she snapped. 'But don't rejoice too much,' she added nastily, 'she won't know you.' She turned to the Shrove. 'Take this woman to the Lady

Asenathe's palace. Give her a change of clothes and make her wash, she smells bad.'

Beneath her tousled hair, a faint smile fleeted momentarily across Esmerelda's pale lips.

The weryke-balm pie and Leticia's word-spell had worked their magic. This time she had fooled the wicked Snowdroppe, well and good.

Long may it last, she hoped.

Sixteen

Esmerelda stepped over the threshold of Asenathe's palace and walked down the silent, empty passageways. All the rooms had a melancholy air: they looked abandoned and forlorn, with every piece of furniture covered in dustsheets.

'I thought my cousin would be here to welcome me,' said Esmerelda, following the Shrove up the gloomy staircase.

'She'll be sleepin',' the miserable creature replied.

'But it's the middle of the day.'

'She's always sleepin, that one,' said the Shrove.

Bludroot bustled down the next landing and showed Esmerelda to her apartment. She was excited to see Asenathe once again, but when she returned downstairs, bathed and refreshed, there was still no one to greet her. The dismal palace was shrouded in a deathly stillness. No one stirred in any of the grand reception rooms.

Eventually, after exploring a number of staircases and corridors, she located her cousin's chamber on the fifth floor. The curtains were drawn in the darkened room and Asenathe lay sleeping soundly in a large, messy bed. The blankets were strewn across the floor and the windows had long been unopened. The room smelled stuffy and medicinal – of a long protracted illness.

'Asenathe, wake up! It's me, Essie!' she cried, rushing to the bed and shaking her cousin.

Asenathe's eyes fluttered momentarily, but she could not keep them open.

'Who's there?' she moaned. 'Leave me be, I must sleep.'

Esmerelda leant over, listened to her cousin's laboured breathing and smelled her warm breath. There was a whiff of the noxious Berrow plant lingering on her lips. Asenathe had been heavily drugged with a sleeping potion.

'Please wake up, Attie,' said Esmerelda, using her cousin's childhood name.

The old name, used once again after so long, caught in the back of Esmerelda's throat. She stroked her cousin's face, now much changed with the intervening years, kissed her cheek and tried to wake her once more. But Asenathe only moaned, her eyelids fluttered and she curled into a ball, pulling the blankets over her head and falling back into a deep sleep. Esmerelda whispered her name again and again but it was useless. Her cousin was unreachable.

On the bedroom cabinet was a glass stained with a dark brown liquid. When Esmerelda sniffed the rim, the pungent smell of the bitter herb stung her nostrils. She reared back in disgust.

Then Esmerelda heard the sound of footsteps and someone calling to her from below.

''Ello, is anyone about? I've been telled to come and fetch thee,' the voice shrieked up the stairwell.

When Esmerelda reached the hallway, one of the Shroves was waiting for her, glowering from the bottom of the steps. He was a shabby creature with greasy hair and a twisted mouth.

'I'm Embellsed, m'Lady,' he said and bowed obsequiously. 'I'm to take thee to the Mistress Flight in the Withered Tower at once.'

Esmerelda followed the Shrove along the chilly hallways, through the labyrinthine corridors of Hellstone Tors and up the treacherous staircase into the tower. Tallitha was waiting patiently for the arrival of her cousin, standing beside the pinched-faced governess who sourly greeted Esmerelda. The Wheen-Cat circled with her tail swishing and her green eyes flashing furiously as she hissed a catty welcome to Esmerelda. Tallitha did not run to greet Esmerelda – she knew better than to show any affection in front of her governess.

The older women eyed one another with deep suspicion: the stout, hatchet-faced Sedentia, and the gypsy-like Esmerelda, both attempting to gauge the extent of the other's powers and to see which would win if it came to a real test of their strength.

'Through here,' she barked, pointing into the Book Room.

As they stepped inside the sound of the chattering Nooklies met their ears and the sulphurous aroma hung in the air.

'According to Tallitha,' Sedentia announced sarcastically, sitting down with a thud into the squashy armchair, 'you're the only one who can propel her to the shadow-flight and prepare her for the Wild Imaginer.'

'I will do whatever I can to help,' Esmerelda answered, inclining her head towards the governess.

'Tallitha must progress through The Black Pages. So far she has proved an awkward student. Either she is unwilling or unable to access the shadow-flight. So your job is to unleash her power. I'll be watching every move, so don't think you can trick me,' she snapped.

She gave Esmerelda a cold, hard stare and pushed The Black Pages into her hands. Sedentia pointed to the first chapter.

'Tallitha must access and control her shadow-flight. Do you think she will be able to do it?' she asked, snapping her eyes at Esmerelda.

'Do you mind? I *am* still here,' said Tallitha.

'With practice,' answered Esmerelda, smiling secretly. 'What else must she do?'

'Travel through four of the elemental tests in The Black Pages. The first is the shadow-flight – moving her spirit-self to another location. Then she must learn how to control the shadow-flight so she can travel through time.'

'What's the next test?' asked Esmerelda.

'She must learn how to read minds, but she will go the Wild Imaginer for the last two tests.'

Tallitha gasped. It was all becoming a little scary.

'What's the last test?' Tallitha asked cautiously.

Sedentia pursed her lips. 'The last test is not so easy.' She hesitated and stared at the girl. 'You must commune with the dead.'

'With the dead? But that's horrible!' Tallitha cried.

'It's difficult to perform. The Wild Imaginer can teach you,' replied the governess.

The girl's face had turned ashen.

'Come, let's not dawdle about,' Sedentia added brusquely, her teeth protruding as she sucked on a minty sweet. 'Tallitha's first task is to travel by shadow-flight to the location of the Wild Imaginer up on Stankles Brow. Then she must report what she has seen.'

Esmerelda stepped towards Tallitha.

'Are you ready?'

'Yes, Essie,' she replied.

Esmerelda lifted the amulet from beneath her shirt, wafted it in the air and the sweet familiar smell trickled from the pendant, pervading the room. She began to speak the haunting words of the old Ennish chant that she had first uttered in the great room in Winderling Spires.

> 'Snenathe ne certhe merl can an le ner
> Cerna la bernatha ne tor na lam, berche berche ne cer
> Snenathe ne certhe merl can an le ner.'

Tallitha's eyelids fluttered and her thoughts fragmented

into disconnected images. She felt her body start to stretch and drift away, her dream-self floating from her still body. It was the old feeling of being dragged, then *pop, pop* and *whoosh! –* the familiar slipping sensation enveloped her, pulling her through the narrow passageway and up into the soft grey light. The silver cord trailed limply behind her as she stepped towards the tunnel, then it suddenly whipped her upwards in an exhilarating spiral, releasing her spinning into the sunlit clouds.

Cool air rushed past her face with tremendous force as she darted like an arrow across the bright heavens. Tallitha was free from the confines of the gloomy castle, the shadowy darkness and the hateful Morrow Swarm. The shadow-flight whisked her far away from Hellstone Tors, up into the wild blue sky over rough churning seas, beyond the cliffs and out over the wilderness of Breedoor. Far below, the mountainous terrain became a patchwork of dark forests, swampland and rivers, like a painted map spread out in greens, blues and browns as far as she could see.

Instinctively, Tallitha sensed that she had reached her destination, and the shadow-flight began to slow down. Then there was a sudden snag against her body and with a final jerk she was dragged down into the heart of the forest and snatched into the cluster of tall, sharp pine trees that covered the hillside. The force of the descent took her breath away as Tallitha fell through the trees, her arms flailing about, wildly grasping at the disappearing branches to slow her tumble earthwards. At the final second, plummeting fast, there was a sudden snag and another jerk and Tallitha stopped, hovering a small distance above the forest floor.

Soft puddles of sunlight filtered down through the canopy and landed in intermittent golden patches on the ground. The dappled light guided her as she wound cautiously in and out of the trees, tripping past trunks and branches until she spied a cave crowned with a fine stone raven. A fire burned before the entrance that was covered with a forest curtain woven from leaves and swathes of moss. It was no ordinary cave. This was Stankles Brow.

Below her four wolfish heads reared up, growling and slavering, their yellow eyes searching the trees for any sign of an intruder. The leader of the pack, a raggedy grey hound, leapt at once into the air, and with the others following behind began pounding across the earth, their growls turning suddenly into a hideous howling that seared through the forest. Tallitha's heart pounded as she retreated further up into the canopy, watching as the curtain overhanging the cave quickly parted and the gnarled face of a Shrove appeared through the gap.

''Ere, stop tha' noise,' squawked the bad-tempered Shrove.

Three other shrovish specimens pushed past the first Shrove and hobbled out into the forest, scanning the terrain with their beady eyes.

'What is it, Warbeetles – is anyone there?' called a grey, frizzy-haired Shrove.

To Tallitha's astonishment, the creatures were all female Shroves. She had never seen them before. They were slightly smaller than their male counterparts, with frizzled unkempt hair, bright eyes, hooked noses and pointed hairy ears. They stood with their hands on their hips, staring out into the darkest patches of the forest.

'There's nowt that I can see, Sourdunk,' answered Warbeetles.

'Those hounds don't make that sort o' fuss for nowt,' Sourdunk replied. 'Come away in and we'll tell the Imaginer'.

So this was Stankles Brow, thought Tallitha, taking in her sinister surroundings in order to report the details to Sedentia.

Below her, the hounds were circling and growling, churning up the ground with their paws and snapping their hideous jaws, hoping to locate their next meal. Suddenly the pack leader leapt into the air and sunk its claws into the tree trunk. It slithered back down to earth to the sound of tearing bark. The others followed their leader, growling, leaping and snarling, trying to locate the invisible intruder. They couldn't see her, but they could smell her.

Tallitha flew up into the cover of the highest branches, her stomach fluttering uncontrollably, and she repeated the Ennish chant over to herself. Suddenly she felt a snag and a jerk, a familiar pop-popping, and she was whisked up into the air and away into the shadow-flight, through the tunnel and back to Essie. She slipped back into her still, numb body with a thud and gulped, taking huge mouthfuls of air into her lungs.

'Well, what did you see?' asked Sedentia stroking the black fur of the Wheen-Cat. Slynose intermittently hissed at Esmerelda.

Tallitha blinked at the two women as they peered at her expectantly.

'It was beautiful. I-I saw mountains and dark forests,' replied Tallitha, catching her breath.

Her governess's whiskery chin came too close, and a waft of mint and tea emanated from the pouting woman.

'What else did you see?' she asked. 'I need more details, to prove you were there.'

'In the heart of the forest I saw a cave covered with a woven curtain made from the forest itself and crowned with a stone raven. There were wolfhounds roaming outside, and a horde of female Shroves.'

'Enough. That will do, I am satisfied,' she said, curtly.

Sedentia snatched The Black Pages from Esmerelda, turning to the second chapter.

'Now onwards to our next test,' she said bewitchingly. She eyed Tallitha suspiciously. 'Now, don't pretend,' she barked. 'I know you were able to see Asenathe at different times.'

'But I don't know how I did that,' Tallitha replied, turning her perplexed face to Esmerelda.

'Colours and lights,' said Esmerelda.

Sedentia nodded her agreement. 'You must learn how to control the power, pinpointing the exact location at the right time. Here, take The Black Pages and study the second chapter. Focus on the colours above all else, then choose one colour and use it as a guide.'

'What do you mean?' asked Tallitha.

'The colours will speak to you, if you let them. It is a singular gift – if you have it, of course. Otherwise it will take hours of practice.'

'Do you know the time-spanning recitation?' Sedentia asked, pushing her vexed face into Esmerelda's. 'Well?' she barked.

Esmerelda pulled away. 'Of course I do, but it's a powerful spell and I've never used it on Tallitha before,' she said.

'Well, now's the time, get on with it.'

'Where do you want Tallitha to travel to?' asked Esmerelda cautiously.

The governess pursed her lips and chuckled.

'To a place and a time that she must see for herself,' she said menacingly. Sedentia took Tallitha's face between her fingertips and stared into her eyes. 'Tallitha, you must learn how to span time and locate a certain day in the history of the Morrow family.'

Sedentia Flight wrinkled her nose and began to laugh uncontrollably.

'What are you proposing?' Esmerelda asked, guardedly.

Sedentia ignored Esmerelda and turned to Tallitha.

'Your task is to travel to Winderling Spires. Back in time to when the Grand Morrow tried to find her missing daughter, when something even more sinister occurred.'

'No, not that!' shouted Esmerelda, 'You must choose another time for the test.'

Slynose hissed as Esmerelda raised her voice at the governess. Her mouth arched into a vicious snarl and she bared her sharp white teeth, spitting viciously.

'Do you refuse?' cried Sedentia.

Esmerelda's face crumpled and she let out a small cry.

'But Tallitha doesn't know about ... what happened, back then.'

Sedentia laughed wickedly.

'Of course she doesn't, but she soon will!' Sedentia stamped on the floor. 'The Lady Snowdroppe has insisted that we use this event as the time-span test!'

'What is it, Essie?' asked Tallitha, her eyes searching her cousin's face.

Esmerelda's face blanched. 'It seems you must see for y-yourself,' she stuttered, squeezing Tallitha's hand. 'Try not to be too unsettled by what you encounter.'

Tallitha studied the pages and was drawn to an illustration of a golden crown. She concentrated, and a fuzzy golden glow started to surround her.

'You must look for a golden light in the time-travel,' said Esmerelda, observing the glow that had developed around Tallitha's head.

Esmerelda spoke the word-spell of a strange incantation and her voice sounded like a hundred tinkling bells.

'You must repeat these words after me and learn the time-span rhyme. Are you ready?' asked Esmerelda.

'But I can't speak in tinkling bells,' Tallitha answered.

'Don't worry, it's an old spell and the bell-words will stick to your tongue like confetti,' Esmerelda explained.

Tallitha closed her eyes and waited for the time-span rhyme to begin.

'*Lythin weche, lythin weche wetherwynde, ower wetherwynde, tore weche,*' Esmerelda whispered as the bell words formed into tiny bright shapes.

They tripped from her tongue like molten fireflies darting in all directions until the room was filled with silver lights.

'Open your mouth, Tallitha, and let the Wetherwynde Spell in,' urged Sedentia.

Tallitha parted her lips and the fireflies invaded her mouth, nestling in clumps on her tongue. As they melted, a sugary taste erupted in her mouth like popping candy and her whole body tingled with the time-span spell. She repeated the words of the molten wetherwynde and the sound of tinkling bells fell from her lips.

'*Lythin weche, lythin weche wetherwynde, ower wetherwynde, tore weche.*'

The bell-words bounced from Tallitha's mouth and surrounded her whole body like a golden coat of armour. Then, in a rush of lights like a firework exploding into a thousand colours, her spirit fled from her body, bursting into the foggy light and up into the tunnel.

This time the shadow-flight took a different form. An array of images flashed before Tallitha's eyes like a pack of spinning playing cards. First, Tallitha saw Marlin and Grintley whispering together in the sun parlour; then she saw the sisters, Sybilla and Edwina, dining on their balcony in the Crewel Tower; the next image was of Cissie shopping in Wycham village, and of Tyaas playing a game in their old tree house. Tallitha repeated the words of the time-span rhyme to pinpoint the exact place and time of her journey: '*Lythin weche, lythin weche wetherwynde, ower wetherwynde, tore weche,*' she whispered Finally she located the trail of golden light that surrounded Winderling Spires. Tallitha's spirit-self tumbled headfirst into the swirling colours. Then she was spinning headlong into a kaleidoscopic whirlpool of dazzling lights. She took a deep breath, dived into the pool and erupted out on the other side. Now she was a part of the scene itself – she had entered another place in time.

Tallitha flew towards the enormous house, over the mausoleum and across the gardens, past the greenhouses and high up into the bewitching towers of Winderling Spires. The telltale golden light shimmered way below her, drawing Tallitha instinctively towards a turret window, high up in an unfamiliar part of the house. Tallitha flew downwards, peered inside, slipped the latch and edged over the windowsill. But the image inside was grainy, like peering through muslin. In the strange place, where time had spun her backwards, Tallitha was invisible – she could see and hear the others in the room but they couldn't see her.

A much younger Agatha Morrow stood before Tallitha in her study, perusing her spell books and mixing a potion. The room was filled with strange artefacts, bones and skulls, mounds of purple and silver ash in pewter bowls, bottles of potions and an array of stuffed animals in glass cases that stared vacantly with their glass eyes. Then the image flipped forward. Tallitha watched as a tousled-haired child ran laughing through the main hall of Winderling Spires with Cissie in tow, playfully scolding and chasing the child into the garden. Then the image flipped forward once more. Her Great Aunt Agatha was in her study once more, but her face was grave. Her hands gripped the spell book and she cried out the words of an Ennish spell:

'*Indomilla vex ceraneste majestice, Indomilla vex ceraneste majestice!* – Come to me, Kastra! Help me find my daughter and wreak revenge on the Morrow Swarm!'

Tallitha watched as a sapphire light tried to enter the study. She saw a figure clawing its way through the light – but something was wrong. A heavy web was forming like a skin across the room, preventing Kastra from entering. She tried to break through the threads but it was useless.

'Don't fail me, Kastra! I have used a dark spell to bring you here,' Agatha cried. 'The spell will make Winderling Spires vulnerable to the other witches ...'

But the shimmering blue light ebbed and faded. Agatha's face clouded, and Tallitha watched as the study filled with a crimson-orange flame that licked about the room, devouring a hole in the web. Agatha Morrow shrieked and stumbled, cowering in terror.

'Get away from here!' she cried.

A fiery figure slipped through the hole in the web like a slithering snake. Her hair was the colour of leaping flames and her eyes a burning orange; her clothes were made of dancing flames and her face shimmered bronze-gold. Her whole body shook with a terrible frenzy.

'Kastra has stolen the Morrow child, but she was ours! She should have been mine!' the flaming figure screamed and shuddered. 'Do you know who I am?' she cried menacingly.

Agatha lowered her eyes and nodded. 'T-The Grand Witch, Selvistra,' she mumbled.

'Indeed, I am Selvistra Loons from the Larva Coven, and I have come to stake my claim on a Winderling child in return for our loss. The spell you have cast demands it. So tonight … beware the Dooerlins!' she laughed.

The Grand Witch hovered menacingly in the hexing-space, slicing and savaging the web with molten fire as Agatha fell into a stupor. The image flipped forward once more as Tallitha watched the Dooerlins steal into Winderling Spires at dead of night. In a gruesome huddle they crept through the Spires and snatched the dark-haired child from a small attic bedroom. The sleeping child was hurriedly bundled into a blanket, and disappeared into the night.

Then Tallitha was alone in a bright space. The images clicked backwards one by one and finally vanished. She repeated the Wetherwynde Spell and the air filled with the sound of tinkling bells, the shimmering confetti spinning around her as she slipped back into her body with a thump. The two women were waiting for her.

'I saw a child and a flaming enchantress,' Tallitha muttered, 'and the Dooerlins were there!' She had turned quite pale. 'B-But she's a witch,' she cried, gripping Esmerelda's hand. 'My Great Aunt Agatha is a witch!'

Sedentia clapped her hands with glee.

'Excellent, my work is done! You can be dispatched to the Wild Imaginer.'

'Aunt Agatha does have c-certain powers,' Esmerelda replied haltingly.

'That's not what you told me before!' Tallitha exclaimed, as Esmerelda blushed. 'What about the other sisters?' she asked: 'are they witches too?'

'They may be,' Esmerelda answered feebly.

Tallitha didn't know whether to laugh or cry. The Morrow family was riven by so many dark secrets – secrets known by some members of the family and carefully hidden from the rest.

'Where was the child taken?' she asked Esmerelda.

'No one knows the answer to that question.'

'Where did the child come from?'

'From Wycham village,' Emerelda answered quietly.

'So you see, Tallitha, all is not as you thought it was,' Sedentia added nastily. 'Your precious Esmerelda has kept secrets from you. Remember, *all* the Morrow family are blessed with extra special talents: the Grand Morrow and her sisters are not so innocent after all!'

'B-But what does it mean? What happened to the child? Who was the Grand Witch?' Tallitha asked, looking from her governess to Esmerelda, but they both remained silent.

Sedentia laughed wickedly and moved towards the window, turning her back for a few seconds. Esmerelda hurriedly snuck the parcel of weryke-balm pie into Tallitha's hand and winked at her.

This will protect you, she mouthed.

Tallitha nodded and crammed the pie into her pocket.

'This is your destiny, your bloodline,' said Sedentia, turning to face the girl. 'I will report your progress to your mother. You've reached the next level and you're ready to meet the Wild Imaginer. Remember all the chants and spells you have heard and practice them,' she instructed.

The Wheen-Cat circled around the governess's legs and Sedentia picked up the dark animal, petting her fondly. Slynose buried her nose in Sedentia's neck, rubbing her head against the governess's ear and mewing all the while, *whispering something ...*

'They're all witches!' Tallitha kept repeating incredulously to Esmerelda, 'Great Aunt Agatha, your mother and my grandmother – they're all witches! I can't believe it!'

Seventeen

That morning the castle had been washed with a sprinkling of fine rain as Tallitha and Tyaas stood in the walled gardens accompanied by Sedentia and the slippery-bodied Wheen-Cat.

'Which direction are we going in?' asked Tallitha, but Sedentia was too preoccupied to answer, peering anxiously across the courtyard for Quillam.

Tallitha tugged at her governess's robes. 'How long will it take to get to Stankles Brow?'

The governess turned abruptly and pointed over the battlements.

'It's way over there, to the Northern Territories, through Hegglefoot and Cinder Edge. Perhaps three or four days by foot, maybe more, depending on the weather.'

'What will happen when I get there?' asked Tallitha apprehensively.

'You'll find out in good time,' Sedentia answered gruffly.

'But who is the Wild Imaginer?'

A faint smile crossed the governess's lips.

'The Wild Imaginer is steeped in dark powers that are much stronger than mine, taught to her by a powerful Grand Witch and handed down through the generations. Hopefully Esmerelda Patch will have done her best to make you ready to meet her challenges.'

Slynose circled the governess, mewing and making a fuss. Sedentia picked up the black cat, nuzzling her fur, whispering in her ear. The Wheen-Cat turned her head and focussed all her attention on Tallitha.

It was unnerving how that cat stared at her, thought Tallitha.

Then, from out of the castle, the tall youth came striding across the grassy bank.

'Come, Quillam is here,' Sedentia announced.

Tallitha noticed that Quillam's clothes were like a second skin: taut against his muscular body, they were the colour of the earth – a deep walnut-brown – and his sleek, black hair was tied into a glossy ponytail. Quillam moved across the ground like an animal, his steely ochre eyes glinting as he quickly scanned the assembled party.

'You took your time,' grumbled Sedentia. 'Here's some food in case Tallitha can't stomach your foraging.' She thrust a package into Quillam's hand. 'You're well able to catch your own supper, but remember to cook it first – Tallitha is a lady and will not eat raw meat.'

'Have you arranged for the Groveller to meet us?' he asked, tucking the package into his bag.

'At the appointed place,' the governess replied, 'he will provide safe passage through Hegglefoot and up to Stankles Brow.'

Quillam stared at Tallitha but did not speak. He looked untamed in the bright morning sunlight. His slanted yellow eyes and sharp features resembled a hunter's.

'Come, I'll unlock the north gate,' announced the governess.

Tallitha bent down, pushed the key to the apartment into Tyaas's hand, and murmured in his ear.

'You know what you must do whilst I'm away. Find Essie and be careful.'

Tallitha felt in her pocket for the weryke-balm pie. She would eat it later to ward off any bad magic.

Tyaas watched as Tallitha slipped out of sight and away to Stankles Brow. He was sad at their parting, but also excited at the prospect of exploring the castle on his own – Essie would only slow him down. He had seen the entranceway to the Darkling Stairs and was more determined than ever to get inside the Witch's Tower. With a sorrowful backward glance as his sister disappeared from view, he sauntered back towards the castle to plan his next move.

Sedentia led Tallitha and Quillam down the steep hillside to the lower levels of the hanging gardens, with Slynose swirling round at her heels. She opened the gate and pointed down through a dark opening in the castle wall.

'The Wild Imaginer is waiting for you,' she said ominously to Tallitha.

With that, she watched them disappear down the stone staircase. Sedentia picked up the Wheen-Cat and spoke softly to her.

'Now follow them, my pretty one. Make sure they go to Hegglefoot and meet with the Groveller. Watch them, my darling – smell the dark aroma of the Morrow stain and follow its scent,' she urged.

Slynose rubbed her head against Sedentia's cheek and sprang nimbly from her arms, slinking along the ground after Quillam and Tallitha and stalking them down the dark steps.

*

Down and down they scrambled, along the crooked path that overhung the perilous cliffs. Way below the sea churned and dashed against the rocky shoreline and the salty air stung Tallitha's cheeks. Without a backward glance, Quillam started down another steep winding path to the seashore.

'Why didn't you tell us you were our adopted brother? You lied to us!' she shouted, clambering down the rocky pathway.

Quillam ignored the girl and clambered down the cliff face, scattering loose rocks beneath him.

'Hey! I'm talking to you!' she shouted, racing up behind him.

As she approached he turned savagely, grabbing hold of her arm and dragging her further down the craggy hillside into a cave.

222

'Ouch, that hurts!' she cried, struggling to get free.

His wolfish face came right up to hers. His breath was hot on her face and she could see the bright amber flecks in his ochre-coloured eyes.

'Be quiet!' he said harshly. 'Their spies are all around us.'

'Get off me!' she cried, pushing him away.

'Stop shouting!' he snapped, his white teeth glinting.

Tallitha pulled her jacket back into shape and scowled at the youth.

'Where do you come from?' she shouted.

A shadow passed over Quillam's face and he turned away. He crept to the entrance of the cave and peered outside, scanning the rugged hillside back up to the castle. There was no one around that he could see, but that didn't mean they weren't being followed. The rocky terrain was full of crevasses where a Shrove could easily hide and spy on them. Yet, unbeknown to Quillam, the crafty Wheen-Cat was doing just that, sneaking down the rocky incline, hiding in the caves and following the pair. She had carefully stored Tallitha's smell into her cat-memory and was following the girl's scent as it wafted up the hillside on the breeze.

'We can talk later,' he said. 'Then we'll make camp and head for the Grovellers' village.'

'What do we want with them?' asked Tallitha abruptly.

'Everything is not what it seems out here,' he answered mysteriously.

With that he began crunching down the steep incline, intermittently looking over his shoulder to make certain Tallitha was keeping pace with him. The path twisted and turned until it reached the sand dunes that disappeared into the hazy distance. Tallitha's feet sank into the soft sand as she dragged each foot out, stumbling after Quillam who was racing along the beach.

'Over here!' he shouted, pointing towards a maze of rock pools that glistened in the heat of the day.

All the while, Slynose kept her distance, stalking them over the rocks and leaping over the sand dunes when they weren't looking, her paws sinking into the soft sand.

The seascape was wonderful: a new world that Tallitha had never experienced before. She picked up a handful of shells and threw them out over the incoming waves, watching them sink into the sea before being washed back to shore again. She ran to Quillam's side, laughing and breathing in the fresh sea air.

'I never want to go back to that hateful castle!' she called out into the wind. 'I'm free!' She twirled round with a huge smile on her face. Tallitha stared out to the sea across the waves as far as her eyes could see. 'What's out there?' she asked, pointing way into the west and shading her eyes from the sunlight dazzling on the water.

'Beautiful islands and faraway places full of amazing adventures,' he replied wistfully.

'Have you been across the sea?' she asked.

'Not yet, but I mean to one day.'

Tallitha dangled her feet into a sparkling rock pool as Quillam began searching for muscles, prawns and crabs, fishing them out with his bare hands and storing them in a jar for supper.

'Tell me about the Wild Imaginer?' she asked.

Quillam squinted at Tallitha in the sunshine.

'You have to do the tests, that's all I know,' he answered sullenly.

'But I don't want to join their hateful brood,' she answered.

'You have no choice. You're the next in line. Lord Frintal has decided.'

'Can't he un-decide? There has to be a way out,' she said, twisting her hair in and out of her fingers and splashing her feet angrily in the pool. She remained undeterred. 'There's always a way out of everything, if you try hard enough.'

Quillam watched her keenly out of the corner of his eye. She was an unusual girl. Perhaps there was just a chance she could succeed in her quest.

'The only way is to break the Morrow pact,' he said gravely.

Tallitha studied Quillam in the bright sunshine. There was something about this youth, the turn of his mouth and the way he moved his hands when he spoke that she couldn't quite put her finger on, but it was familiar nonetheless.

'Then tell me how to break it?' she asked.

Tallitha wasn't about to tell him what she'd found out from the silver-haired spirit. She wanted to know what he knew. She could play his games of secrecy too.

Quillam regarded her keenly. 'First, you have to get inside the Witch's Tower without being caught and then locate the pact.' He leaned forward, watching the rippling water, and becoming awkwardly quiet for a few moments.

Tallitha stared into the distance. Tyaas and Esmerelda had a dangerous task ahead of them.

'And the pact? Is it a riddle?'

He shrugged and looked out to sea. He was exasperating. If he knew anything, he wasn't about to tell her. She tried a different approach.

'How do you fit into all this, with our mother?'

'I don't,' he answered darkly.

He gazed down into the rock pool, watching intently for the zigzagging eels to appear from under the rocks.

'Then where do you come from?' she asked.

He looked uncomfortable. 'I don't know,' he replied.

'What do you mean, "you don't know"?' asked Tallitha.

A look of sadness flitted across the face.

'I remember being in the forest and then Hellstone Tors.'

'But whose child are you?'

His face darkened. 'That's why I sought you out,' he said, watching her. 'I want you find out where I come from.'

'Why me?' she asked incredulously. 'What can I do?'

Quillam smiled, eyeing her curiously: the way her dark hair fell in messy strands and her eyes stared straight at him, fearless and determined …

'Because you can see things that others can't.'

'How do you know that?' she asked abruptly.

As fast as lightning Quillam reached down into the water, cupped a struggling eel in both his hands and dropped it into the jar with a huge plop. He avoided eye contact, tightly turning the lid on the struggling creature.

'Well?'

'I saw you go into a trance and heard you say some stuff. You were sort of glowing'.

'You followed me into the governess's tower!' she exclaimed.

'Yep, I climbed up the walls to the highest bookshelves and watched. You were easy to spy on!' he replied, grinning.

Tallitha folded her arms in disgust. He was no better than a nasty Shrove, creeping about and spying on her. But Quillam didn't care a fig about what she thought of him. He carried on fishing for their supper while the Wheen-Cat prowled along the rocks and swished her tail.

'Do you have any idea about how to break the pact?' she asked.

'You have to do these tests. Then you'll be a match for the Swarm – play them at their own game.'

'What about Mother?'

'Only then will you be able to outmanoeuvre Snowdroppe and the rest of them.'

Tallitha eyed him keenly. 'But she's your mother too,' she said. 'Don't you care for her?'

'Do you?' he asked fiercely.

'She's not easy to love,' replied Tallitha, resigned to their mother's spiteful nature.

'Perhaps when you can see the past and the future, you can find out about the pact and how to break it,' he answered.

'I have dabbled with that already,' she said thoughtfully,

'but I need to learn how to control the power so that it will take me where I want to go.'

'You could find out where I was born,' he suggested, giving her a sidelong glance.

She didn't reply but bit her lip. 'It's so risky. What if I become one of them?'

The youth roughly took her face in his hands and stared into her eyes. He was deadly serious.

'Look, we have an agreement of sorts,' he continued through gritted teeth. 'I need you to find out about my past, and you need me to help you to escape your future. Besides, there's no one else who will help you.'

Perhaps he was right. She pulled her face away from him.

'But what if I become one of them?'

'You can protect yourself.'

'How will I do that?' she asked incredulously.

'You'll find a way,' he said mysteriously, his yellow-flecked eyes narrowing at her. 'Come on, we have a long trek before nightfall.'

They carried on up the next hill with the Wheen-Cat sneaking behind them, sniffing out Tallitha's unmistakable scent. For the girl had the Morrow stain upon her.

*

Tallitha was distracted. Perhaps Quillam was trying to trick her into discovering his past before delivering her into the hands of the Swarm? It was difficult for her to trust anyone after Benedict's betrayal. As Tallitha followed Quillam over the next blustery headland and further into the wilderness of Breedoor, she thought about what the youth had said. Perhaps she could outwit the Swarm. After all, she *had* hoodwinked Sedentia and had met the silver-haired spirit.

Gradually the sandy pathways transformed into overgrown trails and the dunes gave way to undulating hills, where curtains of mossy tendrils hung limply down from the trees. The ground was damp, squelchy and covered with leaves the colour of nutmeg and cinnamon. They climbed over hills and trudged through rugged, unrelenting landscapes and as their path climbed ever upwards the weather turned bitter, becoming tinged with a touch of frost. Just ahead, Tallitha could see a film of mist seeping from the earth, whilst all around her the trees were bare like blackened bones reaching up into the threatening sky.

'What is this dismal place?' she called out to the youth.

'This is Sunkwells Bottom,' replied Quillam. 'It gets chilly out here at night on the approach to Hegglefoot.'

Tallitha shuddered and wrapped her scarf around her neck, pulling up her collar for extra warmth. But it wasn't just the cold weather that had made her shiver: the further she travelled inland from the beautiful seashore, the more she felt troubled by the mysterious northern lands. The air was damp and clawing, like breathing in wet cotton wool and the stark terrain had an unsettling effect on her.

'I've been here before,' she said flatly.

Quillam's eyes flashed at her. 'When was that?' he asked incredulously.

'It was part of the first test from The Black Pages. I don't mean on foot.'

'Oh,' he replied, 'then you've seen the Wild Imaginer's cave?'

'I've seen the wolfhounds circling in front of it,' she whispered. 'It didn't look very inviting.'

'It isn't,' he replied and marched onward.

He must have been there before, Tallitha thought.

As the evening wore on, the fog began to rise out of the earth, covering the ground with a carpet of thick, swirling mist. The cries of the seabirds had been replaced by the plaintive screeching of the forest animals calling out to one another through the foggy light. Quillam set about making camp in the hollow of a large oak. The inside was dry, and the youth foraged for makeshift bedding, expertly lighting a fire by rubbing twigs together and blowing the embryonic flames into being. Then he set about cleaning the fish and crustaceans from the rock pools.

'Here, help me fillet,' he demanded, throwing her a knife. 'You can peel the vegetables you have in your food parcel. Onions and carrots will make a good fish supper.'

Tallitha watched the youth while he showed her how to gut fish and make a stew.

'I thought you'd be out catching animals and skinning them, the way that old bag Sedentia was talking,' she laughed.

'It wouldn't be the first time.'

Tallitha gave him a disgusted look and continued.

'This reminds me of the time I spent with Ruker,' Tallitha said wistfully.

'Who's that?' asked Quillam, looking at her quizzically and stirring the pot.

'A Skink who rescued us in Ragging Brows forest then travelled with us into Breedoor. Ruker said she'd rescue me, if she didn't hear from me.'

'A Skink wouldn't come into Hellstone Tors – it's too dangerous,' said Quillam. 'She'd better try some other way, if she dare.'

Tallitha's face reddened and she looked away. The other night she had seen Ruker in a dream, a premonition of sorts: the Skink had reached out to her, and Tallitha felt certain that Ruker knew she was in danger. The dream had played on her mind unlike other fleeting dreams.

'Ruker won't fail me,' replied Tallitha defensively. 'She'll come back to find me, someday. I know she will.'

Eighteen

That night the wind blew fiercely out in the wilderness of Breedoor on the approach to Cinder Edge and Hegglefoot, whipping through the undulating hills and howling through the tall spiky trees. Tallitha slept fitfully, curled up in her bed of fallen leaves within the hollow of the old tree, wrapped in a woollen blanket with Quillam sleeping at her side. But her sleep was troubled by fractured dreams that slipped into ghoulish nightmares, leading her into hoary dreamscapes where the hideous Dooerlins roamed Winderling Spires; where ghostly spectres appeared out of nowhere, dragging her up sinister staircases into dark, eerie tower rooms – to the top of the Darkling Stairs!

Nearby, the stalking Wheen-Cat kept her spiralling green eyes on the sleeping pair – dozing on and off throughout the blustery night, hunting her shrew supper with vigour, but keeping one eye on Tallitha all the while.

In the depths of sleep, Tallitha heard a noise and woke with a start. Looming over her was the round, weather-beaten face of a fat Groveller.

'Quillam!' she screamed, clutching the blanket to her chest and shaking the youth.

He sat bolt upright, automatically reaching for his dagger in his sleepy state.

'What now?' he cried. 'You've been moaning in your sleep, tossing and turning and keeping me awake all night.' He yawned, scratched his head and caught the stranger's eye. 'Morning,' he said brightly to the grinning Groveller.

'You ready?' the huge-framed man asked, stamping his feet in the blistering cold. 'It's a sharp wind we've got for our journey.'

Overnight the snow had fallen, leaving a blanket of crisp silvery frost over the forest floor. Tallitha's breath came in steamy puffs of icy mist. She hurriedly dragged another jumper from her bag and pulled a woollen hat over her head.

'Got any food in that bag?' asked the youth.

The Groveller threw Quillam a loaf of bread.

'Come on Tallitha, we've still got a fair trek ahead of us,' said Quillam between mouthfulls.

'But where are we going?' she asked, scrabbling across the ground to keep up with the pair who were striding off into the trees. 'Don't I get any breakfast?'

'To Grovell-by-the-Water,' answered Quillam, throwing her a chunk of bread.

'Suggit's the name, by the way, and foragin's the game,' the huge Groveller announced cheerfully over his shoulder.

He had a way of walking that resembled his ponderous nature: plodding and cumbersome.

Tallitha ran her eyes disparagingly over the Groveller's hairy face and raced up behind Quillam, cupping her hand and whispering in his ear:

'But the Grovellers were horrid to me when we arrived in Hellstone Tors.'

Quillam laughed a loud belly laugh in Tallitha's face.

''Course they were. They thought you were all stuck up and hoity-toity – didn't you, Suggit?'

'Not me, Sir – it was the missus and her sisters. They can be downright mean and ornery when they've a mind to,' he tutted.

'Why do we need Mr Suggit to guide us?' Tallitha asked Quillam, turning up her nose at the Groveller. 'I thought you knew the way to Stankles Brow.'

She was unimpressed with their lumbering guide.

'Eh, miss? No formalities out 'ere. Suggit – just plain Suggit will do. I'm your safe passage across country. Round 'ere, there's much to be a-feared of. 'Tis a rum old place is Hegglefoot – weather's always changin', strange folks on the move out 'ere – and I'll get a few shillings for my trouble from thems at Hellstone Tors.'

'The Grovellers know the lie of the land through Hegglefoot,' the youth added, slapping the Groveller on the back. 'He will see us through the marshland, won't you, Suggit?'

'Aye, and away from any nasty sorts.'

Now, what does he mean by that? thought Tallitha.

But she was in no mood to enquire. She was more interested in Quillam, who had perked up since the large Groveller had joined their party. He was like a different person, animated and talkative, often sharing jokes and asides with Suggit that she didn't understand.

The Groveller chipped in:

'Tonight we'll stay in my village – onwards and upwards!' he called, cheerily marching up the steep bank and disappearing over the brow of the hill.

Tallitha was fed up. Breakfast had been unsatisfactory, she was tired and now they had this fat oaf for company. But as they reached the brow of the next hill the terrain changed dramatically. The landscape was riddled with deep potholes and water-filled gullies, and the ground was turning soggy underfoot. The weather was fickle on the top of the hills, just as Suggit had predicted, and soon a chilly mist seeped out from the dank earth. It twirled in ghostly tendrils through the blackened trees and blotted out their footpath, covering the land in a milky white murkiness. Dead ahead, a tunnel of tree trunks erupted out of the ground, forming a dark canopy over their pathway. It was deathly quiet save for a few solitary birds calling mournfully through the foggy grey light.

The Wheen-Cat slunk along the road behind them, a moment out of sight, swishing her long black tail and watching as the three travellers disappeared under the boughs of the overhanging trees. Slynose had come to the end of her journey. She had fulfilled her task. Tallitha had been safely delivered into the hands of the Groveller, and would soon be at Stankles Brow where the Wild Imaginer waited for her. Besides the Wheen-Cat never ventured into the wet soggy marshlands. She despised the thick mud that clung disgustingly to her beautiful black paws.

Slynose could sense that the shifting-spell was wearing thin. Her time as a cattish creature was ticking away, and she could feel her female form jarring away inside her, rubbing against her bones, waiting to break free. The Wheen-Cat licked her paws for the last time and slunk to the side of the road, shuddered, rolled into a black ball of fur, arched her skinny back, and in one deft movement Caedryl sprang, dark and funereal, from out of the Wheen-Cat's body. She shook herself all over like some sleep-awoken beast, smoothed down her sleek black hair, straightened her clothes and followed the snaky path all the way back to Sedentia and Hellstone Tors.

*

'It's so cold out here,' complained Tallitha, trudging through the furrows of deep snow. 'My feet are like blocks of ice.'

She stamped her feet and rubbed her hands together, pulling her scarf tightly over her mouth. Her woollen gloves were encrusted with beads of sparkling ice.

'It's always cold on the top o' these exposed hills. The weather's brutal in Breedoor and can change speedier than a stoat racin' after its dinner. That's why you need the likes of me to keep you from fallin' down a pothole or gettin' lost in the mire,' answered the cheery Suggit.

By the time they reached the Groveller village, they had tramped for many miles. Tallitha was exhausted, unable to keep pace with the others as they clambered over the desolate hills. Soon the chimney tops of the cottages in Grovell-by-the-Water appeared above the mist. The hamlet lived up to its soggy name. It was marooned in a cosy dip lodged between two hills, and had about twenty dwellings laid out to the west of the bleak marshland that stretched miserably into the distance.

'You're back then, Suggit,' a voice erupted from the mist. 'You took your time. Got any good pickin's?' hollered Rye, Suggit's esteemed wife.

As the mist cleared, Tallitha recognised the gruesome Groveller from the courtyard at Hellstone Tors.

'Aye lass, I 'ave,' shouted Suggit, patting his knapsack. 'Four fat rabbits and a brace o' squirrels. The varmints just need skinnin' and they'll make for some tasty stews,' he replied with a jolly chuckle.

At this news, the redoubtable Mrs Suggit beamed a toothless welcome at her husband and continued sucking on her clay pipe. As Tallitha clambered down the hill, Rye eyed the girl with suspicion, jerking her chin in her son's direction.

''Ere, them folks from the Tors have arrived,' she hollered, scratching her broken fingernails across her blotchy face. 'Get inside, our Archie, there's a good lad, and put the kettle on.'

The grubby boy ran into the kitchen, called out to his sister and began boiling the water for the tea. A small girl appeared from the washhouse to greet them, took Tallitha gently by the hand and ushered her inside the warm cottage. Tallitha immediately slumped into a big, cosy armchair, closed her eyes and fell into a deep sleep beside the crackling fire. After the freezing cold of Breedoor, the soothing warmth of the kitchen was a blissful relief. She dreamt of the Skinks creeping down the dark corridors in Winderling Spires with Cissie by their side. They were spying on the Shroves, following them down the larder steps and into the deep brown earth …

''Ello there, young miss, you been sleepin' for a long while,' said one of the Grovellers, giving Tallitha a good shake. 'Wake up and 'ave some supper. We've made braised rabbit stew and baked spuds,' the Groveller announced, handing her a bowl of steaming meat and vegetables.

Tallitha yawned and opened her sleepy eyes, taking in the cheery scene in the Groveller kitchen. Quillam sat at a card table, playing a game of dominoes with Archie, while the small girl called Tootle, dressed in patched dungarees, eagerly watched from a high stool, cheering her brother on. Three Groveller women, two of them fat and the other one skinny – Rye, Lutch and Buckle – sat hunched together on a lumpy sofa puffing on their clay pipes, chatting about this and that, while the four men supped their ale around the big kitchen table.

'There's been strange goings-on through Hegglefoot,' announced one of the women. 'That bloke Gimble from Much Grovell told me yesterday – after rabbits, he was.'

'More odd than usual?' asked Suggit, quaffing his pint.

'It'll be them witches at their tricks again,' proclaimed Rye, nudging the other women.

She had a face like a box of broken spanners – but then again, none of the Grovellers could boast good looks.

'I saw them in their fancy wagon settin' up camp at Stankles Brow,' replied Buckle, the thin Groveller, coughing and spitting into the grate. 'Spied on 'em, I did.'

Her spit flew through the air like a revolving missile, and landed with a splat by Tallitha's feet. The girl quickly averted her eyes. She didn't want the Grovellers to associate her with the "posh ones" from Hellstone Tors – she was different from them. Besides, she had to get along with the Grovellers now she was a guest in their home. Tallitha held her breath and listened to every word.

'What were they about?' asked Suggit, drawing more ale from the barrel.

'I didn't stay long, didn't want to get caught starin' at Grand Witches, and they 'ad their wolves with 'em. But I saw summat odd,' she added, nodding and keeping the others in suspense.

'What? Don't keep us waitin',' demanded Rye. 'We always tell you stuff.'

Rye raised her eyebrow at Lutch, her chubby sister, and the two Grovellers elbowed Buckle in the ribs to get on with her tale.

'Yes, I'm gettin' to it – them witches were hob-nobbin' with the *Dooerlins*,' she whispered, 'in broad daylight too.'

'Never!' cried Rye and Lutch together.

''Tis rum doings when those mean devils poke up their heads from the bowels of the earth,' added Suggit.

'Aye, and talk with the witches,' added Rye sagely.

The men clustered together over their pints, murmuring about what they had heard. Try as she might, Tallitha could not hear what they were saying, what with Lutch's incessant chatting and the commotion made by the children constantly running through the kitchen. Only the words 'unheard of', 'sorcery' and 'evil doings' percolated over the noise in the room.

Tallitha's attention drifted towards Quillam. He was a different person in the Groveller's company, laughing with Archie and Tootle and happily joking with the gregarious Lutch. She was a stout, jolly sort with a shock of brown hair and a flattish, frying pan-shaped face.

'You be careful my lad, when you're out there, what with the witches and Dooerlins roaming the Brow,' she warned.

'Ah, Ma,' he joshed, 'I can take care of myself.'

Quillam caught Tallitha staring him.

'Everyone calls her Ma,' he explained, his face reddening.

'Not everyone, just my bairns,' she chuckled, giving Quillam an affectionate hug. 'I looked after this tyke when he was a nipper,' she explained, 'he came to me as a bairn straight out of the wilderness of Hegglefoot – like a wood elf, he was. We found him wanderin' outside our back door one fine mornin', wild as a wolf cub, mucky as a pup, jabbering away in gobbledygook, and hardly a stitch on him.'

The assembled party laughed heartily, remembering the infant Quillam's peculiar half-naked introduction to their village.

Tallitha did not take her eyes from the youth's face. Quillam's cheeks burned hot and he turned away. So he had lied to her after all.

*

Early the next morning, after a hearty Groveller breakfast of poached duck eggs and squirrel sausage, they departed, following the lumbering Suggit out of the hamlet and meandering across the bleak marshland into the foggy grey light. They tramped for miles, zigzagging over the hillocks of tough grass that indicated a safe pathway through the hostile marshlands. Above them lay a rinsed-out winter sky, cold and ice-grey, blocking out any glimmer of sunlight. As they climbed the next hill, the weather swiftly changed into a bitter, ferocious wind that bit like a knife through their outer garments. Tallitha's feet ached and her eyes watered with the relentless cold and blustery winds.

'Hold on, you two!' she called out to the others who were striding way ahead of her. 'Where are we? How much further is it?' she cried, her small voice vanishing into the squally wind.

Suggit regarded the terrain and the lie of the land to get a fix on their position.

'We're entering Lethland,' he called, shouting above the weather. 'This country around 'ere is known as Hegglefoot, where the Whivelstone stands proud. Beyond through that forest yonder is Stankles Brow,' he said, raising his hand towards the north.

Tallitha's eyes followed to where Suggit was pointing. The wind howled fiercely, blowing her scarf across her face, but in the distance she could see a stone monument sticking out of the high ground with a mound at its base.

'What's the Whivelstone?' she asked, forging ahead through the battering gale to keep up with Suggit and Quillam.

'It marks an old battle site,' he replied, 'and the gateway to the Northern Wolds – bandit country.'

'What happened out there?' Tallitha asked.

Quillam and the Groveller exchanged knowing glances.

'Later,' the Groveller hollered into the wind. 'This gale is takin' my breath away – we need to keep our strength for walkin'. Come on!' he shouted.

Suggit lowered his head and stamped up the pathway, into the blistering headwind. The three traversed the ravaged countryside, pitted with knolls and craggy outcrops, whilst fleeting pointed shadows and jumpy blackened shapes followed in their footsteps, a few steps to the left and a few steps to the right. The Black Sprites of the Northern Wolds had come to spy on the wayfarers, biding their time and keeping out of sight.

As evening approached the wind abated and the Groveller led them to a sheltered hollow in the foothills of the mountains. Quillam set about making a fire and Suggit skinned two squirrels for supper and roasted them over the flames, fat spitting into the dark sky as the Groveller turned the carcasses round on a stake, basting them with pepper and salty oil. Both Quillam and Suggit lashed into the sticky meat, sucking on the bones, grease dripping from their fingers, eating every last piece of flesh and certain parts of the animals that Tallitha didn't want to think about. She turned her nose up when they offered her a haunch of tender squirrel meat, preferring to eat the dried food from her bag of provisions.

'What about the battle at Whivelstone? Tallitha asked inquisitively.

'It was long ago,' replied Suggit, wriggling his ample bottom into a comfy spot against the boulder.

The Groveller drew several deep puffs on his pipe, and the sweet acrid smell of smouldering tobacco wafted into the night air, billowing blue smoke all about him.

'The battle was hard fought between the old tribes from the Northern Wolds, and Edwyn Morrow's followers.'

Tallitha wrapped herself in her blanket to keep warm against the chilly night. How did the Groveller know all this? She hugged her knees waiting for him to smoke his pipe and continue.

'The story goes that Edwyn Morrow and his entourage escaped from Wycham Elva with the help of a powerful sorceress – a Grand Witch called Kastra.'

'Kastra – but I've heard her name before!' replied Tallitha excitedly.

'Aye, but the Grand Witch Kastra made Edwyn pay dearly for her magical powers when she cast her spell over the Morrow pact.'

Tallitha's eyes glistened in the firelight as she slugged back a tumbler of apple gin. It tasted bitter on her tongue but it warmed her body against the seeping cold.

'What did he have to do?'

'Kastra wanted something precious for her trouble, for having to leave her old home in Wycham Elva.'

Tallitha gasped. 'Where did she live?' she asked, guessing the answer.

'In Winderling Spires,' replied Suggit, 'in one of the old wings. But she came and went at will, travelling across the lands round 'ere, practising her bewitchin' and learnin' new spells.' He puffed on his pipe and wriggled his behind to find a more comfortable spot. 'But what she agreed to do for Edwyn Morrow meant she could never return while the pact was in place.'

So there had always been witches in Winderling Spires. Tallitha felt the skin on her hand begin to prickle and she scratched at the stain. Perhaps the sorceress had lived in the Raven's Wing?

'B-But what did Edwyn give up?' she asked hesitantly.

'The Morrow child,' Suggit replied.

'The Morrow child!' Tallitha gasped.

It had to be the child the silver-haired spirit had told her about.

'Aye, Miss, he was a hard-hearted man and a coward. He exchanged his first-born child for Kastra's magic web of protection and his freedom.'

'But that was his own child!' Tallitha cried.

'Oh, that Edwyn was a nasty one. Once he'd secured his freedom, he turned against the sorceress, Kastra, in favour of a Grand Witch called Selvistra and together they captured the castle at Hellstone Tors. He tried to use Selvistra to trick Kastra and get his child back but she didn't succeed. It was a rum business. Witches hate being tricked more than anythin', especially by their own kind.'

So that's how it all happened, thought Tallitha.

'Did he ever get his child back?' she asked.

Suggit shook his head. 'Nay, that child was long gone. Anyway, those two Grand Witches were sworn enemies from that day forward and the sorceress Kastra swore to avenge the trickery that had been played upon her. She joined forces with one of the northern tribes, called the Black Sprites, who weren't happy at being expelled from Breedoor or the loss of Hellstone Tors. There was a fierce battle up at Whivelstone Craggs but the sorceress Kastra lost to Edwyn's Witch, the evil Selvistra Loons.'

Tallitha realised that she must be the flame-haired witch she had seen in the time-travel test.

'But what happened to the child?' she asked.

Tallitha had to pinch herself. She couldn't believe she had finally started to unearth the mystery surrounding the pact.

'We heard that Edwyn's child was secreted away to be taught the dark arts by Kastra Micrentor, the sorceress …'

'Kastra Micrentor!' Tallitha cried. 'But that's the name of the cabinet in the Neopholytite's tower! How did Edwyn get hold of it?'

'Selvistra captured it during the battle at Whivelstone. Once Edwyn had the pact safely stored in the Bone Room, Kastra couldn't destroy it or wreak her revenge on the Swarm.'

Slowly, elements of the mystery were falling into place.

'Then Edwyn's Witch must have been extremely powerful,' said Tallitha.

'Aye, they're all powerful, them Grand Witches from the Larva Coven,' said Suggit gravely. 'But Kastra and Selvistra's enmity lasts to this day. Edwyn paid Selvistra in precious stones to do battle with her witch-sister Kastra Micrentor and the Black Sprites. Then after the battle, rumour has it that Selvistra stayed for a while in Hellstone Tors to teach her spells to his remaining daughters.'

Tallitha's mind was racing. Selvistra must have taught the Morrow Swarm all her spells, and they were eventually passed down to the Neopholytite along with Micrentor's Cabinet. She had to find out about what happened to the Morrow child.

'Quillam, are you listening to this incredible story?'

Throughout the tale, the youth had been quiet, staring into the fire. He looked up from the flames, his ochre eyes flashing in the darkness.

'I heard,' he answered flatly.

'Tell me more about Kastra Micrentor and the Grand Witches,' asked Tallitha, excitedly. It was almost too much to take in.

'It's just as I've said,' Suggit replied, looking nervously about him.

'But there must be more!' demanded Tallitha.

Suggit sighed.

'She wants to know about the different kinds of witches,' said Quillam, whittling a stick.

'Oh, right you are,' he said, and cleared his throat. 'Well, there are witches like the Neopholytite who have special powers, but they 'ave their limitations. Then there are the Grand Witches whose power is terrifying and eternal.'

Tallitha was hanging on his every word.

'Please go on,' she said.

'Once Edwyn had betrayed Kastra, she swore to break the Morrow pact, but the spells that Selvistra laid were too powerful and Kastra couldn't enter the castle. Selvistra surrounded Hellstone with a dark brew of witchery – and more besides, I've 'eard tell.'

Tallitha knew he meant the beast's skeleton. The power of the Bone Room that surrounded the Neopholytite must protect the Swarm too.

'Where's Selvistra now?' she asked

The Groveller shrugged. 'Ain't 'eard about that one for years. But some say she's still about up on the northern shores, plyin' her wickedness.'

Tallitha felt unnerved by the Grand Witch Selvistra Loons.

'What about the Morrow pact?' she asked.

'That cursed pact has been responsible for a trough of wickedness.'

'How can it be broken?' asked Tallitha, twirling her hair in and out of her fingers. She watched as the flickering flame danced in Quillam's ochre eyes. 'You know, don't you?' she asked the youth.

'I only know a little,' he replied hesitantly, twisting his dagger into the earth. 'I've heard that someone from outside the Swarm must break the pact. They must enter Hellstone Tors of their own free will and destroy the Morrow pact.'

Break the pact for her … of your own free will. Tallitha's stomach lurched as she remembered the haunting words of the silver-haired spirit. She felt the tingling sensation running across the palm of her hand as she realised that she was the one who had to enter the castle and break the pact. Perhaps everything that Suggit had told her was the reason her family was so peculiar, and why her mother couldn't love her children properly. These were the consequences of the hideous pact that had spanned the generations, and had warped them all.

'B-But how do you know all this?' Tallitha asked, turning to Suggit.

'We Grovellers used to be part of the northern tribes, though we're much more civilised than them folks – decent-like. We left the northern lands and settled in the villages by the Tors, for work mostly, and the tale has been passed down through the generations.'

'Quillam, did you know about this too?'

The youth averted his eyes from Tallitha.

''Course, everyone knows bits and pieces of the old story.'

'B-But when I asked you about the pact, you told me you didn't know,' she faltered, looking hurt.

Quillam hadn't told her everything after all.

After a few campfire tales, and a tot or two of apple gin, the Groveller's head began to droop and his eyes grew heavy. Finally he slumped against the boulder and in no time began to snore.

Tallitha pounced on Quillam, her eyes burning with rage.

'You lied to me about your past!' She spat out the words, crouching on all fours like a tiger. 'You didn't tell me about the battle, about all those witches and the Morrow child and you knew everything all along!'

Quillam's yellow eyes glazed over with annoyance.

'Woah there, calm down! You don't own me – I can tell you what I please,' he replied, rebuffing her.

'Why didn't you tell me the truth?'

'I didn't lie, I just omitted a few details,' he snapped moodily. His face contorted and his next words were delivered with venom. 'Just like when Snowdroppe dragged me away from my home,' he hissed. 'I didn't ask to be taken to Hellstone Tors, to be sucked into that unholy mob. I was quite happy out here with the Grovellers.'

Tallitha swayed back on her haunches and regarded the youth.

'Mother kidnapped you?' she asked, twisting her hair in and out of her fingers. Their mother's cruelty never ceased to amaze her.

'That's about right,' he sighed. 'Lapis and Muprid were out riding with their governess near to the village. They found me playing, and although they were only young themselves they took a fancy to me, said they wanted a pet and wanted to take me back to the castle.'

Tallitha was horrified.

'What about Buckle?' she asked, feeling ashamed at her outburst. 'Didn't she mind?'

'She couldn't go against the Swarm. The Grovellers depend on Hellstone Tors for their bread and butter. Anyway, Snowdroppe decided that I was an interesting distraction for some unknown reason, and informed Buckle she was keeping me as her own.'

'But that's awful!' cried Tallitha.

'She took me the same day.'

'I-I'm sorry,' answered Tallitha, 'I-I didn't realise.'

Quillam shrugged but his face burned. 'It's all in the past. I come back to Grovell-by-the-Water whenever I can. But what happened to me back then means I'm always on my guard with people I don't know – I don't trust them. That's why I don't have to tell you everything whenever you ask me,' he snapped bitterly.

Tallitha blushed.

'What about the Morrow child that Edwyn gave up?' she asked. 'Was she ever found?'

He shrugged his shoulders. 'Maybe she's out there somewhere,' he said. Then he turned to her and added sarcastically: 'Perhaps when you've practiced with the Wild Imaginer, you'll be able to make contact with her.'

'But that child must be dead by now,' she said sadly.

Quillam face formed into a sardonic smile.

'I thought one of the tests was communing with dead people,' he said.

Tallitha shuddered at the prospect.

Quillam flashed his ochre-coloured eyes, and grabbed Tallitha roughly by the throat.

'Concentrate on the living! Don't you understand? I want to know the truth – about how I came to be wandering around

Hegglefoot as a child!' he shouted, glaring at Tallitha. 'That's where you come in – you have to help me find out about my past!'

Nineteen

In the intervening days Esmerelda observed Croop arriving each evening with a cloudy aromatic drink and a selection of fancy sweets for her cousin. On the third occasion after the Shrove departed, Esmerelda hurriedly poured the drink away and hurled the sweets into the sea from her casement window. Slowly, Asenathe resurfaced from her stupefied state. She began to remember events and to smile at Esmerelda with some recognition. She was still disorientated, but over time she returned to her old self, her sweet nature coming back to the fore despite her poisonous years in the company of the Morrow Swarm. But Asenathe's recovery had its painful moments. She came to realise how much Caedryl had been influenced by the Morrow Swarm, and that she had lost her dear Arden forever. Reuniting with Essie was both a joy and a sorrow. Asenathe felt guilty for the years they had been apart, especially once she knew how much Essie had sacrificed to find her.

'We mustn't let the Swarm know you're free of the drug – then you can still observe them at close quarters,' said Esmerelda

'I will be able to deceive them. I know their ways,' replied Asenathe sadly.

'You will have to pretend in front of Caedryl too – Attie, she can't be trusted,' Esmerelda added.

'I understand. It won't be difficult,' she replied. 'Caedryl seems to have little time for me these days. It breaks my heart to see how she's changed.'

Asenathe stared out of the window towards the dark mountains where her imagination took her far beyond their peaks to her old home of Wycham Elva.

'What about Mother? Has she forgiven me?' she asked, her eyes blurring with tears.

'She misses you dreadfully and blames herself. She's always been angrier with me than with you. But in the end, all will be well,' Esmerelda replied.

'But will it? I worry so for Caedryl. She has become one the Swarm now. When I was well, I could shield her from their influence but since her father died I have become powerless,' she cried. 'She's become so strange and distant, I hardly recognise her.'

Esmerelda had no comfort to offer Asenathe concerning her wicked daughter – she had witnessed the girl's cruel streak at first hand. Caedryl's desire for power had poisoned her, and Esmerelda knew there was little they could do to change her.

Asenathe revealed how the Morrow Swarm had planned

Tallitha's deception from the beginning, and that she had been used as bait to entice the girl to Hellstone Tors. She wept at her part in the deceit and at the threats that had been made to her should she not comply with their wishes. But Esmerelda was certain there was more to unearth about Asenathe's past in Hellstone Tors. When she was certain that her cousin's strength had regained, she turned to the questions that had been plaguing her for some time.

'I don't understand how you became one of them?' she asked, perplexed by her cousin's ability to live with the hateful brood.

Asenathe's face puckered and she blushed slightly.

'I've never been as strong as you, and Arden protected me for many years,' Asenathe replied.

'But you aren't a direct descendant of Edwyn Morrow's,' she added.

Asenathe coloured. 'There's something you should know.' She turned to Esmerelda and bit her lip. 'My father, Machin Dreer, was one of the Swarm.'

'Did you know that when we were young?' Esmerelda asked, dismayed by her cousin's ability to keep such a secret from her.

Asenathe nodded and replied meekly: 'Partly. I searched Mother's papers and found evidence that he had flown to Hellstone Tors, but I didn't realise then what the Swarm was.' She blushed. 'It seemed so exciting to look for him, and Snowdroppe told me where he'd be –'

Esmerelda interrupted her.

'Snowdroppe! She's the one who told us about your betrothal

to Cornelius Pew, and then encouraged you to flee to Hellstone Tors!' she exclaimed, her face clouding over. 'Did you ever find him?'

'He had died by the time I reached the castle,' Asenathe answered sadly.

So there *were* things that Essie didn't know about her beloved cousin.

Asenathe could see she had offended Esmerelda by not telling her the truth.

'My Arden was a good man, the only good man here. If it hadn't been for him I would have tried to escape, maybe to wreak my revenge on the Neopholytite, but I was too scared and the Swarm threatened me. Then my Caedryl came along,' she explained, her eyes filling with tears, 'and Arden warned me about the Darkling Stairs.' She suddenly gripped her cousin's arm. 'The terrible steps that lead to the Neopholytite's tower.'

Esmerelda was struggling to absorb the information. She felt wounded by Asenathe's subterfuge, but there was nothing she could do – it was all in the past. Their time was now and they had to break the pact.

'Is it possible to climb into the Witch's Tower without being caught?' asked Esmerelda.

Asenathe shook her head. 'People have tried over the years, but many have been lost, never to return.'

'I've heard the terrible stories. Leticia's sister Alyss was given to Queen Asphodel as a child along with Leticia. Alyss was a curious girl and wanted to see the witch. But it all went horribly wrong on the Darkling Stairs. Alyss was caught by the Night Slopers and handed over to the Neopholytite. She kept the girl, like all the other poor souls in the witch's soul-catcher. Leticia, who was too old for the Neopholytite's purposes, was condemned to the Bleak Rooms.'

'We must find out what's in that pact in order to destroy it,' replied Esmerelda determinedly. 'And Attie, this time you must help me to trick them all. You have to be strong. What did you have to swear to uphold the pact?'

Attie's face crumpled. 'That's the problem – I've tried to remember what I said when I was sworn, but it's as if my mind has been completely wiped clean.'

'Then we have to get inside the Witch's Tower and find out what the pact says for ourselves,' replied Esmerelda.

'But how can we do that? The Darkling Stairs are much too dangerous and there's no other way in. We'll get caught,' Asenathe replied.

'Remember when we were young, playing in the Spider's Turret, and we used our fledgling powers to try and find the child?'

Asenathe nodded. 'It didn't work though,' she mused sadly.

'We were young and inexperienced, and no match for the Dooerlins.'

'We'll never get through the witch's armour of spells. The skeleton that protects her is from the battle at Whivelstone and is steeped in sorcery.'

'I've been mulling over an idea. Tonight we will make contact with Tallitha. Our combined power may just get us inside the tower.'

'What about the boy, Tyaas – should we involve him?'

'Leave him be, we don't want to draw attention to ourselves. Besides, he's safer where he is.'

'After all these years, I can't believe that we will work together to bring down the Swarm.' Asenathe beamed at her cousin, and clutched her hand. 'Ready?'

'No time like the present, Attie – lead on,' replied Esmerelda.

The two women began climbing up the rear staircase to a secluded turret room at the top of Asenathe's tower.

*

Tyaas was determined to embark upon his very own adventure. In his mind's eye he had imagined entering the Neopholytite's tower, bravely overpowering the witch, and discovering the Morrow pact for himself. After Embellsed had departed for the night, Tyaas unlocked the door and slipped out of the apartment onto the shadowy landing.

But as usual, Tyaas hadn't quite thought through all the details of his adventure. There was no Quillam to guide him through the castle and he was caught off guard by the sheer enormity of Hellstone Tors, especially at the dead of night. Then there were the wolfhounds: somehow in his excitement to begin his quest he had forgotten all about them. But he soon heard them bounding along the lower landings, on the scent for any creature that dared to roam the castle after midnight.

Tyaas stood still in the darkness with the sweat running down his back. He would have to take the route Quillam had shown them.

In a flash he darted into the recess, pressed the panel and disappeared into the cavity. It was pitch-black in the wall-tunnels and although Tyaas tried to follow Quillam's original route by crawling about on his hands and knees, he came to a dead end. Now what was he going to do? He had no matches and he couldn't see a thing.

The boy was stumped. He sat on the floor with his head in his hands. Now he was well and truly stuck. He couldn't go any further that night – it was too dark to find the way forward – and he couldn't leave the safety of the cavity or the hounds would be upon him. There was nothing for it: he would have to sit it out until the morning. By then the wolfhounds would have finished their nightly patrol, and hopefully there would be some chinks of light so that he could see what he was doing. Tyaas curled into a ball, rested his head on a dusty beam and fell asleep.

Unfortunately, he also hadn't planned for the early stirrings of the Shrove-Marker. When Embellsed entered the northern tower the next morning he was flummoxed. The boy wasn't in his bed. Just like his wayward sister! The Shrove stood, scratching his head and turning this way and that.

'Where are you?' he cried, roughly pulling back the bedclothes. 'Damnable child! You'd better come out and let me see thee,' he called to Tyaas. 'I want none of your foolish pranks this mornin".'

The apartment was eerily silent. The Shrove panicked. He peered under the bed, flung back the doors of the wardrobe and ambled into the untidy dressing room. But the boy had vanished. Embellsed's stomach lurched and he felt terribly queasy. All his worries about the missing key came flooding back and he hopped about in a blither.

'What am I to do?' he jabbered like an imbecile. 'If they 'ave that key, I'm done for.'

A trickle of cold fear started at the top of his spine and ran all the way down his skinny back. Now he'd be for it. He would lose his position and be consigned to the lower SShroveling ranks forever, unless ... unless he said the boy was ill. That was it! He would have to pretend that Tyaas had a fever, something nasty and catching, until he could lay his hands on the young whippersnapper. The Shrove frantically rolled up a thick blanket and positioned it in Tyaas's bed to make it look like the boy was sleeping. He stood back to observe his handiwork and made a pathetic mewing noise before racing out of the apartment to begin scouring the castle for the errant boy.

*

'Stop!' Snowdroppe shouted at the Shrove. 'What are you doing on this corridor without your charge? Where's Tyaas?'

Embellsed froze. He had been frantic with worry and had

foolishly decided on a shortcut instead of using the late stairs. Now what was he to do? He hopped about and turned to meet Snow-droppe's withering gaze.

'Well?' she shouted angrily 'Tyaas is supposed to be with me this morning.' She petted Stiggy and regarded the Shrove with suspicion. 'Do you expect me to wait all day?'

'May it please you, m'Lady,' he said, fawning. 'I-I was in such a rush – just on me way to the apothecary, to see Smithers …'

'Smithers! What for?' she asked crossly.

'The young master has a bit of a fever this mornin',' the Shrove lied, wringing his hands.

'Then I shall see to him,' she announced, turning and making her way to the northern tower.

The Shrove stood shaking in abject misery and confusion. What was he to do? He slavered, blinked, then scampered after the haughty woman.

'Beg your pardon, ahem, s-sorry m'Lady,' he mumbled, coming up behind her. 'His ailment might be catchin'.'

'What did you say? Does he have spots?' she asked, frowning at the hapless creature.

'S-Some red ones with a yellowish pus, but I didn't get too close,' he cowered obsequiously. 'I thought Smithers could prepare a salve for the boy.'

Snowdroppe wrinkled her pretty nose in distaste. 'Very well, quick about it then,' she announced, changing her mind and sauntering back to her palace. 'Keep me posted about any developments.'

Embellsed watched as Snowdroppe disappeared down the

corridor. Then his whole body quivered from head to toe. He had done it now! He had lied to *one o' them!* Now what would he do? All that would be left of him would be mincemeat and bone if they found out he had deceived a member of the Swarm. In a terrible sweat he scrambled headlong up the late stairs and raced along the winding corridor, nearly tripping over his feet as he burst into Tyaas's apartment. The door banged shut behind him and Embellsed stopped dead.

'In a bit of a hurry, aren't we?' Wince announced, turning his bug-eyes on the quivering Embellsed.

Wince was sitting cross-legged in the young master's armchair. He looked like he owned the place. Embellsed's mouth dropped open but he couldn't get a word out.

'Err, I-I-I –,' he bleated, slavering and wringing his hands.

'Where's my whennymeg?' Wince bellowed impatiently. 'I've been waitin' all this time and thinkin' to myself: *that miserable Shrove is tryin' to wriggle out of our bargain.* So I came up here this mornin' to find you and have it out – an' well, I found this pretty state of affairs.'

Wince rose, scuttled towards the bed and dramatically threw back the blankets.

'I-I c-can explain,' moaned Embellsed desperately. 'It's all to do with the missin' key, and now that dreadful boy must 'ave it and he's gone! I must find 'im before *they* do.'

It was all too much for Embellsed. He was beside himself with anguish and fell upon Wince, clutching desperately at him and begging the Shrove to help him out of his dreadful predicament. Wince grabbed Embellsed by the collar and lifted up his distraught face, spit flying from his mouth.

'I must have jewels!' he shouted malevolently. 'Pretty jewels, for all my trouble. You must steal some gorgeous gemstones from Bludroot's storeroom! There's rubies and topaz stones – I know 'cause he told me!'

'Oh my life!' the miserable Embellsed cried out.

The thought of creeping into Bludroot's lair and stealing from the High Shrove made him sick with fear. It was a horrible mess and he was stuck in the middle between the vicious Lady Snowdroppe, the missing boy and the obnoxious, sneaky Wince. It was a terrible to-do and in the horror of the moment the wretched Embellsed could only think of one possible means of escape. But he would have to do it quickly before he lost his nerve.

'I will do as you ask,' he muttered, 'but please, come with me and help me find the missin' boy, else I'll never get near Bludroot's storeroom. They'll toast my gizzards!'

'Jewels, I want jewels!' Wince cried, pouncing on Embellsed, his crooked eyes bulging with burning avarice.

'I-I u-understand,' Embellsed stuttered with trepidation.

Wince smoothed down his ruffled hair and composed his angry countenance.

'Out of my way, you bumblin' fool,' Wince said sharply.

He pushed the trembling Shrove to one side and marched down the winding corridor to the top of the lath steps.

'After you, of course,' murmured Embellsed.

'Well, where shall we start?' Wince demanded as he edged down the precarious steps.

But they were the last words he uttered. Embellsed reached over the Shrove's shoulder, pretending to whisper in his ear and in one deft movement he tipped the unsuspecting Wince off the late stairs. The Shrove turned to take a final look at his assailant, his wretched face stunned with the awful realisation that certain death awaited him, and with a whimper he tumbled headfirst from the lath steps and bounced off the walls of the long shaft – *thump, thud, thump!* – landing in a grizzly grey heap at the bottom.

Twenty

The enormity of Embellsed's hideous crime hit him square in the face like a hammer-blow. His stomach lurched and he clutched at his thumping heart as wave after wave of fear and gut-wrenching panic flooded over him with nauseating regularity. He had murdered one of his own – it was unheard of in Shrove legend. His frail body shivered uncontrollably.

'Oh my, oh my!' he bleated, wringing his sweaty hands.

But he couldn't think about it all now. He would drive himself crazy with worry, and he had to find that boy before his deception was discovered by the Lady Snowdroppe.

He grizzled away to himself, bemoaning his fate and wringing his hands in despair. It was all Tyaas's fault and that wayward girl's for stealing the key in the first place. The Shrove flattened his trembling body against the dusty wall of the shaft, desperate to hide his guilt-ridden face from any prying eyes that might be scanning the late stairs from below. In one movement he leapt from the top of the lath steps and fled down the corridor as though the Neopholytite herself was after him with a boiling curse. He scurried along the landing like a Shrove possessed, past Quillam's hidden recess, treading an almost parallel path to the one that Tyaas was taking on the other side of the wall – had he but known it.

*

When morning came, a chink of sunlight burrowed its way into the darkened cavity, piercing Tyaas's slumbers. The boy awoke, rubbed his eyes and stared about the dusty space. Before him, Quillam's armoury of knives and climbing equipment lined the walls. Tyaas took a backpack, a length of rope and a knife, drank some lukewarm water from a flask, and pushed matches and candles into his pockets. Now he was ready for his adventure.

On the other side of the wall he could hear distant footsteps racing along the landing. Tyaas waited until the sounds had faded before hitching the backpack over his shoulder and following the path that Quillam had shown them. He climbed down ropes and up ladders, squirmed under smelly floorboards, and finally pulled his tired body up into the dusty shaft next to the Witch's Tower. There before him, sitting snug at the bottom of the shaft behind the crumbling brickwork, was the entrance to the Darkling Stairs. But Tyaas wasn't scared – he was excited.

He removed his shoes, pressed his ear to the door and eased the handle, turning it without a sound. Tyaas tiptoed inside the eerie space like an agile cat on tender paws.

The hallway was as dark as he had imagined. He crouched by the door and waited until his eyes grew accustomed to the gloomy interior. The shaft above him was illuminated by a sulphurous yellow light that hung ominously in the air, souring the atmosphere with a bitter odour that clung to the back of his throat. A wide black painted staircase adorned with raven-head carvings stood before him, leading up to the Neopholytite's tower. But Tyaas had devised a plan to avoid setting foot on the dangerous stairs. Once he got his bearings he tiptoed across the floor and clambered up the wooden stair post in three quick movements without touching the black staircase – he suspected that any pressure on the treads would alert the secretive Night Slopers. Tyaas was a lithe, fearless boy, and he perched himself firmly on the handrail, taking easy fluid steps and using the rough outline of the brickwork as handholds, edging soundlessly to the top of the Darkling Stairs like a crab up the slanted wooden rail.

All the while, snug beneath the stair treads, tucked into the warm tight spaces, a host of Night Slopers slumbered on in their cattish way, their tails swishing in the darkness as they dreamt of chasing their prey in the Witch's Tower. But the Night Slopers were unaware that their territory was being invaded by the inquisitive boy. Between the stair treads, their grey-black fur poked out like antennae, alert to any untoward movement on the Darkling Stairs.

The handrail came to an abrupt end where it met the big newel post at the head of the Stairs. Tyaas slid noiselessly down the wall and sat in the crook between the handrail and the post, surveying the arched entrance to the witch's lair. Yellow sulphurous smoke curled out of the Witch's Tower, wound its way past the boy and snaked down the stairs in wispy tendrils. Tyaas peered into the gloom to get a better view of the Neopholytite's inner lair, its skeletal shape bathed in candlelight and reflected against the mirrored walls. Then he slunk further behind the newel post, wrapped his legs over the balustrade and hid in the cramped space. He bided his time.

Eventually his patience was rewarded. One of the Groat guards ambled into the corridor, stretched his limbs and hollered down to the bottom of the stairs.

'You ready?' he barked, peering down into the eerie sulphurous light.

'All's well, let me up,' came the reply from below.

The fat Groat pressed a lever in the wall and the stairs shuddered and altered shape. The Groat at the bottom waited for the shuddering motion to stop before climbing upwards onto the angular stair treads, taking two steps at a time. Tyaas smiled to himself – he had discovered the way to avoid the Night Slopers. It just needed someone to climb to the top and make the stairs safe for everyone else. The Groats grunted at one another and changed guard duty. The new guard pressed the lever after his mate had left, and the stairs resumed their previous position.

When all was clear, Tyaas crept to the archway of the Neopholytite's lair and gazed at the cathedral-like space: the huge skeleton of the dead beast enveloping the room with its grizzly ribcage and the bleached bones running vertically down the walls. It was like being inside an enormous dead whale, thought Tyaas, and it smelled about as bad – of pungent decay and bitter herbs. He took a step nearer to the witch's lair and peered round the edge of the arch.

The Neopholytite's tower was empty apart from two sleepy Groats lounging against a column and several black birds of prey flying around the room, landing in the bone-rafters and caw-cawing to each other. The witch had planted a number of spirit traps about the room and clusteres made from rowan sticks with long strands of black hair wrapped in cobwebs. Micrentor's Cabinet was enticingly close and Tyaas was desperate to creep into the Bone Room, take a peek inside and maybe even steal the Morrow pact! His heart pounded with excitement. To his knowledge, no one else had ever managed to get this far inside the Neopholytite's lair without being captured. His eyes were glued to the cabinet and the several small drawers, one of which was partly open. The cabinet was so temptingly close … Perhaps he could make a dash for it? For a heart-stopping second, he almost ran across the Bone Room and into the Neopholytite's lair. But he knew it was just a flight of fancy – the Groats would catch him in an instant.

In that final moment before turning to leave, something bright and shiny caught his eye. The witch bottles glimmered prettily, the dancing candlelight refracting through the crimson glass in the darkened space. One of the bottles was positioned on top of the stone lintel that adjoined the archway just above his head. *I must have a souvenir from the witch's Bone Room*, Tyaas decided in a flash. In the next instant he had scaled the wall, lifting the crimson witch bottle in one deft movement, and tucking the precious cargo into his bag. *It might come in handy*, he thought as he edged gracefully down the wall.

Though he did not know it, Tyaas had captured a great prize. Inside the witch bottle, precious elements of the Neopholytite lay twisted, bound together to forge her spell. Strands of the witch's long grey hair and clippings of her nails were wrapped together in a silken parcel, lodged with a curse tablet and sealed with dark red wax. This was the witch's protection against magical attack, and now Tyaas had the key to unpicking her power in his knapsack.

Tyaas stole back to the head of Darkling Stairs, taking one final look at the witch's lair before pressing the wall panel and bolting out of the tower through the dusty wall cavities and back to the safety of his apartment. Or so he thought.

*

Embellsed was waiting for him. In the intervening hours the Shrove had agonised over his plight, but had hatched a cunning plan.

The Shrove pounced on the boy as he entered the room.

'So, Master Tyaas, and what 'ave you been up to?' he barked, hopping up and down like a mad thing. 'Give me that key, you young whippersnapper!'

Tyaas was taken by surprise. He fumbled in his pocket and the Shrove snatched the key out of his hand.

'I was j-just exploring,' he mumbled. 'Please don't tell Mother.'

This was just what Embellsed had counted on. He eyed the boy keenly, sniffing his dirty clothes. He smelt of cobwebs, dust and sulphur. The boy had been to the dark secret places!

'Your mother has been askin' for thee,' the artful Shrove replied.

Tyaas cut his eyes at the Shrove. 'What did you say to her?'

'I telled 'er you was ill, spotty and grotty, and she didn't like the sound of that. I covered up for thee and you'd best know how to be grateful.'

But Tyaas wasn't stupid – the Shrove needed his silence for a reason. He knew that Embellsed would be finished if the Swarm discovered he had neglected his duties and had let him wander the castle alone. He *was* the Shrove-Marker, after all. So Tyaas was quite happy to go along with the deception – it suited him fine. *Odd how things turn out*, thought the boy.

''Ere, look sharp.' The wily toad sidled up to the boy. 'You must take this medicine that the apothecary has prepared for thee.'

It was green and tasted vile but Tyaas swallowed it nonetheless. He wiped his mouth with the back of his hand and turned to face the Shrove. Tyaas had been hatching a plan of his own and he knew that his idea was worth a try at least – nothing ventured, nothing gained. He braced himself.

'I want you to take me to Asenathe's tower,' Tyaas demanded.

'None of your nonsense, to bed with thee,' snapped the Shrove.

Tyaas was on sticky ground. If he pushed it too far the Shrove might turn nasty and refuse. But something in Embellsed's haggard countenance encouraged Tyaas to pursue his goal. Perhaps the boy sensed the fear that plagued the Shrove for the vile crime he had just committed. Emboldened, Tyaas continued.

'Don't you have more to lose than me?' he asked, cocking his head to one side and eyeballing the Shrove. 'If Mother finds out about my escapade she'll be cross with me and may lock me up for a day or two, but if she discovers that you let me wander the castle alone, what will happen to you? You may lose your position, or worse!'

Embellsed's hands were clammy and his brow was sweaty. He mopped his forehead and hopped from one foot to the other. Did the boy know about Wince? Had Tyaas witnessed something out there in the castle? He was in another messy pickle – he had better do as the boy wanted.

'Well?' asked Tyaas.

The Shrove looked like he might be sick. He had turned a washed-out shade of grey.

'I'll take thee, b-but not now, later.'

'When?' Tyaas demanded. He didn't trust the old weasel.

'Tonight, I'll get the key,' moaned the Shrove, as yet another onerous task was laid before him. 'But you'll have to climb the late stairs with me to avoid them hounds.'

With that, the Shrove turned on his heel and darted out of the apartment.

Tyaas sat down with a thud. He couldn't believe it! His plan had worked!

Then he felt in his bag, and his fingers touched the cool exterior of the witch bottle.

*

'Hold onto the walls and don't look down,' mumbled the Shrove desperately.

Tyaas climbed down the lath steps following the path of the old Shrove, precariously balanced in the darkness. Embellsed was frantic, holding out his hand and guiding the lad down each step. What if the boy should stumble? What if he too should die? But that crime did not bear thinking about.

'Nearly there,' said the Shrove nervously. 'Now along this corridor, and be quick about it. This is hound territory after the bewitchin' hour.'

Before them stood the grand entranceway to Asenathe's palace, carved with grotesque arachnids and nests of spiderlings. Embellsed waited until the Groats had sauntered off for a sly drink, then he dragged Tyaas up the steps, turned the key in the huge door and pushed the boy into the dark hallway.

'I'll be back to collect you before the cock crows,' said Embellsed, hastily looking over his shoulder and retreating back into the castle.

Now Tyaas was alone. He lit a candle and began exploring

Asenathe's palace. He wandered up staircases and down corridors until he eventually found Asenathe and Esmerelda in a small turret room. He could hear them talking, and softly turned the door handle.

At his entrance their faces were a fright. He was the last person they expected to interrupt them in their nocturnal activity.

'Oh it's Tyaas! He's here too,' said Essie, sounding relieved.

She was talking to a shadowy figure.

By the window stood a grainy image of Tallitha, grey and flimsy against the candlelight. The women had been communicating with her, trying to use their combined power to enter the Witch's Tower, but the old spells that protected the Neopholytite were too strong.

'Tallitha!' Tyaas called excitedly. 'Where are you?'

'*I can't say, it will break the shadow-flight,*' Tallitha's image replied.

'What are you doing here?' asked Asenathe, coming towards Tyaas. 'How did you find us?'

'That's a long story,' Tyaas replied, 'but I've just climbed up to the entrance of the Witch's Tower – up the Darkling Stairs!'

Asenathe grasped Esmerelda's hand. 'So there is a way in after all!' she cried, beaming.

'*So we're all agreed,*' said Tallitha, '*I will continue my search for Kastra and discover all I can about how to break the pact. Only then will I return in secret.*'

The image shuddered and moved towards Tyaas.

'*Are you okay with that?*' she asked her brother. '*Perhaps they will make you take my place, but I will return in time to save you, I promise.*'

Tyaas nodded and smiled at his sister.

With that, she blew a kiss to them all and disappeared into the night.

Twenty-One

'**A**re you two sure you know what you're doin'?' asked Bettie, sitting in her sister-in-law Rose's cosy kitchen.

Her daughters were finishing off a hearty breakfast of bacon, sausage and fried eggs, whilst Rose poured cups of tea and Cissie dried the pots.

Lince wolfed down rashers of bacon, thickly sandwiched between two pieces of buttery toast while Spooner dunked bread into her gooey egg yolk and sighed despairingly at her mother.

''Course Mam, stop fussin'. We're goin' to the servants' entrance to ask for Mary Brindle.'

'She's Miss Brindle to you, my girl,' her mother said tartly. 'Then what?'

'We'll invite her for tea at Aunt Rose's tomorrow after she finishes at the Spires. It's not difficult!' insisted Lince.

But Bettie wasn't convinced and her furrowed countenance

said it all. After the terrible night she had spent waiting for her daughter and husband to return, certain she would never see them again, she was not so sure about the expedition. She tenderly ran her fingers through Spooner's unruly mop of dark hair. Her daughter shrugged her mother's hand away.

'Do stop it Mam, I'm trying to eat my breakfast!'

Bettie turned to Cissie, her face pleading with her sister-in-law for reassurance.

'They'll be fine as long as they keep to the plan and don't draw attention to themselves,' said Cissie, drinking a cup of tea. 'You might 'ave to wait a while though,' she added to the girls. 'One of the servants will 'ave to find Mary in the Spires, and she might be anywhere.'

Bettie bit her lip and continued to voice her concerns. The girls would be cross with her for wittering on, but that old house was a conundrum and the thought of it always made her feel unsettled.

'I know I said this earlier but don't, whatever you do, go inside,' she urged, nodding at Rose to take her side. 'And don't talk to them 'orrible Shroves.'

'Ooh, they're an odd lot, always connivin' and thinkin' they rule the roost,' replied Rose.

Rose, one of the local shopkeepers, was a little older than her sister Cissie and renowned for her delicious pastries and cakes. The villagers were never out of the shop on Rose's baking days.

'I don't like the thought of you in that weird house – never liked it since I was a bairn. It's a spooky old mansion full of strange, hoity-toity folk with peculiar ways. They're just not normal, if you ask me,' Bettie complained, helping her sister-in-law to grease the baking trays and line the cake tins.

'Aye, your mother's right enough. Take that Sybilla – always off doin' peculiar things at the undertakers. Her and her black-headed pins. She gives me t'shivers, wanderin' round the village like a ragamuffin, chantin' and talkin' away to herself,' Rose added.

Bettie and Rose nodded disapprovingly, acknowledging their agreement on the matter. Bettie pulled out a chair, sat down and tried once more to get her daughters to pay attention.

'Don't talk to no one in that house apart from Miss Brindle, d'you hear?' their mother stressed, giving Cissie a sideways look. 'They're all weird, if you ask me.'

'Yes Mam, we heard you,' the girls said in unison, bored by their mother's fussing.

'Come on Spooner, let's be off.'

Lince scraped her chair across the floor and grabbed her jacket. She couldn't bear to listen to her mother's woes – besides, the girls had other plans afoot. They kissed their mother and aunts goodbye, slipped out of the cottage and across the village green, shouting "hallos" to Hattie and Maisie Minkle, running over the small bridge and past the houses that straddled the edge of Wycham village.

Cissie stood at the kitchen window, parted the net curtains and watched the girls as they skipped down the road, chatting and laughing together without a care in the world. Hanging at the edge of the window, underneath the nets, two green witch bottles hung side by side. Relics of their grandmother's time – her magic methods to ward off the evil ones, thought Cissie, biting down hard on her lip. In a wink of an eye she chinked the bottles together for good luck and repeated an old Wycham saying under her breath.

'They will be okay, won't they?' asked Bettie anxiously.

''Course they will, my dear. They only have to ask for Mary,' she said, turning and giving Bettie a warm hug.

But Cissie's tummy did a little flip – a flutter of concern. Those girls had become a law unto themselves. Could they be trusted to stick to the plan? Cissie reassured herself that as long as they kept well away from the Shroves, they would be fine.

'Come on, let's start baking. I'm looking forward to trying out these new recipes,' said Cissie, trying to divert Bettie's attention with practical tasks.

'Mrs Bumtage gave me this recipe – now where is it? Ah yes …   Sherry Raisin Bread: chopped almonds, rye flour and this,' Rose giggled, pouring three glasses of her best sherry.

'Good health!' she announced, chinking glasses with Cissie and Bettie.

'Bottoms up!' cried Cissie, and the women fell about chuckling, sipping their sherry and descending into hoots of merriment.

They fastened their aprons, took the flour barrels down from the shelves, and within a few minutes they were weighing out the butter, raisins and yeast whilst laughing at Rose, who had managed to get flour all over her rosy cheeks.

*

It was a bright sunny day and the girls were in high spirits, overexcited because they had hatched a plan of their own. This was their opportunity to sneak into Winderling Spires and explore the strange rooms and mysterious floors for themselves. It had all started that night at the farm, when Tallitha had visited on her way to Ragging Brows Forest and they had quizzed her about living in such a grand house with its reputation for so many peculiar goings-on. Tallitha had whispered to them about Asenathe, about finding the book with her name in it, about the sinister Shroves, all the locked rooms and abandoned wings. From that day on, Spooner and Lince had been desperate to explore the creepy old house and to see Marlin and the weird sisters for themselves. They giggled conspiratorially to each other as they snuck round the back lanes, avoiding the main thoroughfare up to the house. It was impossible to do anything in Wycham village without the neighbours tittle-tattling, unless you knew your way through the winding snickets, where no one ventured apart from a farmer or two.

'Look, there it is – all dark and sinister!' Lince said bewitchingly to her sister and made a ghostly noise: 'Woo-oo-oo-oo! Come on, this way!'

Spooner laughed, putting her arm through her sister's as they began the walk up to the grand house, whispering about what they would do once they got inside. They sneaked down a back ginnel that wound its way through the countryside between a high hawthorn hedge on one side and a coppice on the other. The path led to the outlying meadows that surrounded the southern slopes of the Spires and to a gap in the wall.

'Are you ready?' asked Lince with sparkling eyes, full of excitement at the adventure that lay ahead.

'You bet!' answered her sister.

The girls stood by the southern perimeter wall and planned their tactics, watching the house all the while for any sign of movement or a glimpse of an interesting Shrove. There it stood: the mysterious Winderling Spires, looming over the countryside with its imposing Gothic towers, ancient wings and ominous stone gargoyles. The house was surrounded by acres of well-tended gardens, and populated by the hard-working Skinks going about their husbandry tasks – and a couple of Skinks that Spooner had got to know quite well. She scanned the gardens, but couldn't see any sign of Ruker or Neeps.

'Where's that Skink, Ruker?' asked Lince. 'I want to see her too.'

'Aunt Cissie has arranged to meet both her and Neeps by the treehouses once we get Mary Brindle in on the plan.'

'I don't see why they can't just sneak into the house,' said Lince

'If Cissie gets spotted there'll be trouble. Besides, they plan to set up camp and hide inside the Spires for a few days to spy on the Shroves.'

'What fun,' said Lince excitedly, 'Come on, I can't wait to get inside that creepy old house.'

The servants' entrance was located down a flight of steps at the rear of the West Wing. When the door finally opened, a young kitchen maid stared at the two girls, looking them up and down with a saucy stare.

'Who did you say you was lookin' for?' she asked, peering down her nose at the two village girls standing before her.

They were all hoity-toity and above themselves in this house, even the lowest ranking servants, thought Spooner.

'Miss Brindle, she's a relation of ours.'

Spooner wasn't going to give the uppity madam any more information. The maid pulled a face as though she had been sucking on a lemon.

'Who should I say's calling?' she said tartly, folding her arms.

Lince pulled a face and was about to give the maid a mouthful when her sister stepped in.

'Spooner and –'

'I'll deal with this, Sophie,' said an older woman, coming to the door and edging the maid out of the way.

'Well, I never,' said Mrs Armitage. 'Come in, my dears. I was just about to have tea. Sophie, get the kettle on and bring a selection of fruit tarts from the cold store. I expect these girls would like a freshly baked tart, wouldn't you now?'

The kitchen maid gave the housekeeper a put-upon look, tutted at the unfairness of her miserable existence and hurried back towards the kitchen, grumbling under her breath. The housekeeper ushered the girls into the passageway and closed the door behind them.

'You must remember me? I used to play with you when you were little girls. Your Aunt Cissie used to bring you up to the Spires to show you off. How is the poor woman, by the way?' she said, making a grand pretence of concern.

'Just the same,' said Lince, trying to avoid the subject of her aunt whilst attempting to fathom who the chatty woman was.

'Thanks, we'd love a cuppa – wouldn't we, Lince?' Spooner replied, nudging her sister hard in the ribs.

Now they were inside the spooky old house they could have a good nose about – even find a Shrove or two to spy on.

Mrs Armitage bustled ahead of them, marching down the stone-flagged passageway, past the storerooms and up into the first of the steaming sculleries, through the cold larders, bakeries and pickling rooms, and into the grandest kitchen they had ever seen. Lince could not believe the abundance of ripe plums, downy blueberries, plump raspberries and golden pears piled high on long kitchen tables, with the kitchen staff busy peeling, chopping and sieving all the fruits ready for bottling. The smell of luscious summer fruits, bubbling and splattering away in big copper pans, their heavenly scents rising in clouds of steam over the kitchen and oozing enticingly down the sides of the sticky jam jars, invaded Lince's senses and made her mouth water.

'In here, girls – you make yourselves comfortable. I was just ordering the groceries for next week, but that can wait,' said Mrs

Armitage, showing them into her parlour. 'Now tell me what, brings you up to the Spires?'

Spooner decided she would tell the older woman the truth – about the invitation at least.

'We came to ask Mary – I mean, Miss Brindle – to tea tomorrow, at our aunt Alice's.'

Mrs Armitage smiled sweetly at the shabby girls sitting awkwardly in front of her. She was onto a good bit of gossip with these two. Now she would find out all about Cissie Wakenshaw's disgrace, and what easier way than to wheedle it out of her nieces trapped in her parlour? The kitchen maid knocked twice and brought in an enormous tea tray, which she wobbled nervously, chinking the china teacups much to Mrs Armitage's annoyance.

'M-mmm,' the housekeeper said dismissively. 'I think we'll have a better selection of tarts than that! What do you say, girls?' She waved Sophie away. 'Go on, stop gawping girl, and get back to the bake house – blueberry and apricot tarts is what's wanted, and don't forget the whipped cream!'

Mrs Armitage presented a kind face to her guests whilst continuing her insidious interrogation. Spooner and Lince tried their best to avoid her prying questions and waited for maid to return with more fruit pies. It was hard work sidestepping the dogged housekeeper.

'Now tell me, how is dear Cissie? Has she recovered from her dreadful ordeal?'

Spooner averted her eyes from the prying woman, staring round the cosy parlour, and left the conversation to her sister.

'She's doin' fine,' Lince replied. She wasn't about to start gossiping with Mrs Armitage.

'Oh, that's not what the maids have been telling me. They're quite worried,' she replied, blithering on regardless.

Something of interest caught Spooner's attention. She made a deft eye movement towards the open cupboard, that only Lince could decipher. They contained all the floor plans of Winderling Spires.

There was a knock and the door opened.

''Ere you are, Mrs Armitage,' said the flushed maid, bobbing her knee and placing a plate of glazed fruit tarts in front of the irritable housekeeper.

'Have a tart – go on, have two,' insisted Mrs Armitage. 'Just baked this morning,' she said biting into a delicious blueberry tart and licking her fingers one by one. 'Off with you, Sophie, there's more to do than stand here all day like cheese at fourpence!' she shrieked at the flustered maid, who hurried out of the parlour clutching her cap.

'But she must have had a shock, what with the Grand Morrow sending her off like that?'

Mrs Armitage tutted sympathetically and her face took on a pained expression. Her objective was to encourage the girls to reveal the worst of their aunt's sins.

'She's not said owt,' replied Lince, munching on a strawberry tart.

'Must be odd for Cissie not to be part of the Spires anymore,' the housekeeper sighed. 'Dreadful business all round, I'd say. But how has she coped?'

Mrs Armitage replenished the girls' teacups whilst clicking her tongue at Cissie's plight. Lince shrugged dismissively and slurped her tea, whilst Spooner crammed another juicy tart in her mouth.

'Not sure,' was all Spooner said, crumbs falling all over Mrs Armitage's nice clean floor.

The housekeeper's face darkened at the mishap. She was about to complain but changed her tack.

'Oh, never mind that, dear. Now, what were you about to tell me?'

'Not much to say,' replied Lince, desperately looking at her sister to help her out of the predicament.

Mrs Armitage was frustrated with the monosyllabic pair and was about to ask yet another question when there was a knock at her door.

'What is it now?' she snapped.

A flustered Sophie entered and dipped her knee ever so slightly.

'S-Sorry Mrs Armitage, but them mistresses upstairs,' she said, gesticulating upwards and pushing her greasy hair off her forehead. 'They want to know when t'tarts will be ready.'

'Bother them all with their wants,' she hissed. 'Who do you mean, girl?'

'The sisters up in't tower – they've sent their Shrove down with a big tray. He's hangin' round and won't be budged till he has the tarts and I don't know which ones you want to give 'im,' she said, giving the girls a sidelong glance.

Mrs Armitage sighed and slapped her knees with annoyance.

'There's always something to do in this great monument of a bothersome house. Never a minute's peace: staff complaining, the cook on the rampage, all the meals to plan and them upstairs with their demands!' she groused as she shuffled crossly to the door.

She stood in the glass-fronted passageway and remonstrated with Florré, who was determined not to be fobbed off by the housekeeper. The girls could hear their raised voices shouting about fruit tarts and pies. In time the housekeeper returned.

'Sorry girls, but I'll have to go with that miserable old Shrove to the bakery. His mistresses want a selection of tarts and I can't be doing with him picking about, making a mess. There'll be none left once he gets his greedy good-for-nothing face in the trough.' She turned to leave but then changed her mind. 'Oh, and another thing – Mary's out just now but I'll make sure she gets the message. What time was the invitation for?'

'About five-ish, me mam said,' replied Lince.

'Very well, you finish your tea and stay here 'til I get back. Then we can finish our nice little chat.'

With that the housekeeper bustled out of the parlour in a pickle of a mood. Spooner and Lince raised their eyes at one another, waited for a second, and then raced over to the floor plans. They opened the cupboard doors as wide as possible and gazed at the complicated drawings of each mysterious floor.

Now this was their golden opportunity to explore Winderling Spires.

Twenty-Two

After they had studied the floor plans, which made little sense to them, the girls tiptoed towards the door of Mrs Armitage's parlour.

'Nick a couple of tarts for later, our kid,' said Spooner. 'I'll have a plum one this time.'

Lince pocketed some of the juiciest tarts and wrapped them in a napkin as Spooner carefully opened the door.

'Come on, there's no one about,' she whispered. 'All the servants are 'aving a bit of a skive, seeing as that housekeeper's not 'ere.'

The girls crept out of the parlour and down the glass corridor, following in the footsteps of Tallitha and Tyaas.

'What about 'im?' whispered Lince, pointing at a plump lad who was dozing with his feet on the kitchen range.

Spooner put her finger to her lips and beckoned to her sister to follow. They moved like silent mice past the chubby kitchen boy, out along the cold dark passageway and up a flight of stone steps to a darkened doorway.

'This must be the entrance to where the posh folk live,' explained Lince, cocking her ear and listening at the door.

Then they heard a grandfather clock strike the hour.

'You go first,' said Lince, holding tightly onto her sister's jacket and breathing right down her neck.

'Get off, you're strangling me!'

Spooner flinched and gave her sister a warning flash with her eyes.

'Sorry, but it's dead creepy down here.'

Spooner gently turned the handle and peeked round the edge of the door. They were standing at the servant's entrance leading to the grand hallway of Winderling Spires. The grandfather clock tick-tocked melodically in the echoing timeless space as the smell of beeswax polish and scented lavender wafted towards them.

'What do we do now?' whispered Lince, straining to see past her sister's head.

Spooner took hold of Lince's hand and darted across the hallway, hiding beneath the oak staircase. It was dark and spidery, filled with discarded walking boots and old gardening coats.

'We have to get to the third floor, further if we can – that's where Tallitha's room is,' whispered Spooner. 'Come on, let's make a dash for it.'

She checked that the hallway was empty. Then, in a flash,

she dragged her sister behind her up the main staircase, taking two steps at a time. The girls raced up the stairs, breathless and amazed, glancing warily above them at the heavy wooden bannister that wound its way to the top of the old house, peering at the ornate wooden carvings and weird gargoyles that jutted out at intervals from the high ceilings. It all went by in terrifying blur as they raced up the next staircase, hardly stopping for a second.

'Down here,' mumbled Spooner as she fled headlong down a mirrored landing and dived into a recess on the second floor.

'Oh, let me catch my breath!' wailed Lince, falling heavily against the wall. 'Where're we goin' now? What if we get caught?'

'Shh – stop moaning! Come on, we're going up there,' her sister said, pointing to a staircase at the far end of the passageway. 'I thought you wanted to explore as much as me?'

Lince had thought so too, but now she was actually inside the strange old house the gloomy atmosphere on the upper floors unnerved her. It was so quiet and other-worldly. The house was lost to a time gone by, with sinister landings and creepy staircases. She expected something ghoulish to leap out at any moment.

Spooner led her up the next flight of stairs and sped down another long corridor. Lince felt quite dizzy at the end of it. She stood breathless next to Spooner, who by now had her ear pressed up against a half-open door.

'Listen,' Spooner whispered, 'I can hear someone talking, just in there.'

Inside, two Shroves were gabbling to one another … in SShroveling! Spooner gesticulated madly to her sister and they hovered outside the door, listening to the soft lilting sounds:

'*Leth se tendlem, caniis deth neller,*' one Shrove spoke to the other.

'*Nester se hemtell deth tendlem …*' the second Shrove replied in a wheezing tone.

Spooner stared through the crack in the door, and watched as the two creatures disappeared up a staircase situated in the corner of the large suite.

'Let's follow them and see where they go,' Spooner announced excitedly.

Lince bit her lip.

'It's too dangerous. What if they see us?'

'Come on, they're so wizened and peculiar, just as Tallitha said they would be. I want to find out what they're up to.'

'I'll wait down here then,' answered Lince nervously. 'You go if you want to.'

'It's not like you to be so chicken,' replied her sister.

With that she was off.

Lince didn't like the old house. She crouched behind a large sofa and waited, watching the light catch the shimmering glass baubles and crystal chandeliers. A familiar smell pervaded the room – flowery and a little sharp – but Lince couldn't quite place it. The room was so grand and beautifully dressed: full of pearl-grey satin, hand-woven carpets, lilac velvets, and rich damask curtains embroidered with delicate white flower patterns that trailed along the floor beneath the long windows. As she peered towards the furthest window she saw a grand piano in one corner, just where Spooner had disappeared up the enclosed staircase. Beside the piano, covering the small tables and the windowsill were many bowls of snowdrops. That was the smell she had recognised. *A bit odd to have snowdrops at this time of year*, she thought to herself.

The minutes ticked by and still her sister hadn't returned. Now her legs had gone to sleep. Lince stretched her legs, spreading them out over the edge of the marble fireplace, carelessly knocking the fire tongs with her feet. In a split second Lince darted forwards, trying to avert disaster, but the fire tongs fell on the hearth with a terrible clatter. She jumped up and stared at the sitting room door, holding her breath, waiting for someone to enter. There was a noise on the stairs and Spooner barged through the door. Her eyes were out on stalks.

'Run for your life!' she shouted as she flew across the room like a scalded cat.

Spooner lunged for her sister, dragging her from the room, down the next staircase and the next before disappearing into a darkened recess, shaking and breathless.

'What's the matter?' asked Lince.

Spooner's face had turned quite pale.

'Witches!' was the only word she uttered.

Lince gasped and put her hand over her mouth.

'What do you mean? What happened?' she whispered hoarsely.

'I'll tell you later. It was terrible!' she cried. 'We've got to get out of this spooky house!' Spooner's eyes shone with terror. 'Come on, let's make for the next staircase.'

But getting out of the house wasn't that easy. First they saw a Shrove ambling along the corridor carrying a tea tray. Then just below them, two of the servants began sweeping the stairs.

'What'll we do?' murmured Lince. 'We'll get caught and we'll be for it! What if those witches cast a spell on us?'

'Shh! Keep still and wait in there,' answered her sister, pushing her into an empty room.

Spooner crept along the landing, peered over the bannister and surveyed the grand hallway. Down below, the front door stood enticingly ajar, just beckoning at them to make their escape, but the servants stood between Spooner and hallway. They were taking an age brushing the stairs. Spooner crept back to her sister.

'We'll wait for a few minutes,' she said breathlessly, 'then we'll make a dash for the front door. I don't care if we're seen – we have to get out of this terrible house.'

'Oh no, we'll never make it!' Lince wailed.

'We're going!' replied Spooner.

The sisters crept onto the landing and listened. All was silent, apart from the melodic tick-tocking of the grandfather clock. Spooner poked her head over the banister. The hallway was now quite empty.

'Now, run for it!' she whispered hoarsely to Lince, grabbing her hand and flying down the stairs.

They raced for their lives, running across the hallway and out of the house, into the sunshine and as far away from Winderling Spires as their legs could carry them.

*

Mary Brindle sat primly in Rose's best sitting room wearing her fine new summer bonnet, sipping tea and eating a dainty sandwich. She had the look of someone who still had the coat hanger in her dress – straight-backed and a little formal – but she was a kindly woman nonetheless.

'Lovely ham, Rose,' she said, dabbing her lips.

'I got it from the butcher this morning,' replied Rose a little awkwardly.

The peculiar events of the last few days and what Mary Brindle would make of them were playing on her mind. What if she wouldn't go along with the plan? Then what would they do?

Mary Brindle hadn't been invited to tea at her cousin's house for quite some time, and was curious to know the reason for her visit. She guessed that her cousins had something interesting to ask her, something that they wanted her to do.

'Mrs Armitage was wondering what happened to the girls,' said Mary hesitantly, watching for any reaction from the two women. 'The kitchen maid, Sophie Hitchins, saw them flying down the drive like a pair of mad things – she couldn't shut up about it all evening.'

Cissie and Bettie exchanged awkward glances. Those girls

could not be trusted to do even a simple errand without getting into bother.

'I told them not to step foot inside that house,' exclaimed Bettie, 'but they never listen to a word I tell them.'

'Old Armitage probably wanted all the gossip about Tallitha's disappearance,' she said, turning to Cissie. 'She never misses a trick, that woman. She can be a bit nosy.'

The women sat like stuffed birds, their eyes darting from one to the other, exchanging village gossip and pleasantries, waiting to see who was going to break the silence about the real reason for the visit. It was Cissie who couldn't stand it any longer. She pursed her lips and cleared her throat.

'I'm not goin' to beat about the bush any longer, our Mary – we need your help. It's about the trouble up at the house with Tallitha and Tyaas, but it also involves their mother, the Lady Snowdroppe, as well.'

Mary Brindle raised her eyebrows and sat forward. She was now listening intently to every word her cousin uttered.

*

'What they sayin'?' asked Lince, nudging her sister out of the way. 'I want to hear an' all.' She pressed her head against the wooden balustrades on the staircase.

Spooner budged up, and the pair crouched on the top step as they tried to overhear the conversation being held downstairs. Lince was still reeling from Spooner's account of her ghastly experience in the Spires. After she had left her sister, Spooner had followed the Shroves but had been unable to keep up with them as they scampered off down one of the shadowy corridors. She was at a loss as to what to do next, and had just decided to return to her sister when she came across something far more sinister.

At the end of the corridor she discovered a doorway covered by a heavy curtain. She couldn't resist peeping through the draped velvet. Spooner told Lince that the room was dark and spooky, filled with stuffed birds and potions. Then she had heard whispering in a strange language. That's when she saw the two witches, those two old Morrow sisters, sitting huddled together in the darkened room chanting and moving a crystal ball about on a table that was strewn with weird cards. Lince wasn't absolutely convinced that Spooner had it right about the sisters being witches, but the story was creepy nonetheless.

'What did Cissie just say?' asked Lince.

'Shh, I can hardly hear,' insisted Spooner digging her sister in the ribs.

'I will help you – but it will be dangerous ...'

'Those girls are ...'

'Tomorrow evening then, late on ...'

'The Shroves will ...'

'What they saying now?'

'They mentioned us,' said Spooner irritably. 'Quick, they're coming!'

The girls darted further up the stairs and hid behind a chest on the landing.

'Thanks, Mary. Until tomorrow then,' said Cissie and kissed her cousin on the cheek.

She stood at the bottom of the staircase with her hands on her hip.

'You two can come down now,' she shouted upstairs to her nieces.

'Damn, now we're for it,' Lince swore under her breath.

The girls shuffled into the sitting room, only to be greeted by their three female relatives standing stiffly with their arms folded.

'Well, you may as well tell us what happened,' snapped Cissie. 'We know you left the Spires in a hurry – one of the kitchen maids spotted you running down the drive.'

The girls exchanged glances. Damn that gossipy maid!

'Come on, out with it,' insisted their mother.

The girls stood awkwardly together – one twiddling with her hair, the other going pink.

'Well?' asked Cissie.

'Our Spooner says she saw two witches in that house.'

Spooner kicked her sister on the ankle, but it was too late. Their mother's jaw had dropped.

'I knew it! Didn't I say they were up to no good in that sinister old house?'

'Witches?' asked Cissie. 'What do you mean, witches? What on earth were they doing?'

But the information didn't come as a complete surprise to Cissie. At the back of her mind, there had always been a niggling suspicion about the Morrow sisters, all three of them.

Bettie stomped towards her girls and gripped Spooner's face in her hand.

'I told you not to go inside, didn't I?'

'Yes, Mam,' she replied sheepishly.

'Go on then, what did you see?' asked Rose.

'The old sisters were behaving weirdly. I saw them with my own eyes chanting in a funny language in a dark room, playing with crystals and séance cards.'

'Did you now …?' Cissie replied.

She stared out of the window and bit down hard on her lip.

Twenty-Three

That night, dark clouds obscured the moon and the air was chilly and damp. Owls hooted and dog-foxes barked their nightly calls as Cissie lifted the latch of the cottage door and set foot out into the starless night. Swathes of fog hovered in milk-white patches rising from the fields surrounding Wycham village, cloaking the earth in an ethereal grey blanket. Cissie hurriedly pulled a scarf over her head and hastened down the lane, looking this way and that, relieved that the moon's brightness had been masked, concealing her nocturnal activities from the eyes of her prying neighbours.

Leaving the village by the muddy back lane, she took one of the winding snickets that led up to the Spires and entered the grounds through a gap in the perimeter wall. Cissie felt a rush of excitement as she tramped across the lower meadows and made her way towards the tree houses where the gardening Skinks slept. Soon she would be inside her beloved Winderling Spires –

oh, how she had missed its all-encompassing brooding presence and its dark comforting spaces in the intervening weeks!

Ruker and Neeps were waiting for Cissie as arranged, crouching at the foot of their tree house. Together, all three slipped past the rows of greenhouses and out through the grounds, swallowed up in an instant by the ghostly mists that clung heavily around the Spires that night. The ancient graveyard sat like a festering carbuncle on the perimeter of the grounds, and at its northern edge, the family mausoleum sprang out of the earth like a phantom in the foggy night.

'Shine the lantern over here,' demanded Neeps, yanking hard on the rusty door.

The entrance to the crypt was caked in mud and the door creaked ominously on its rusty hinges as they dragged it open across the rough stony earth. They stepped over the threshold and lifted their lanterns to survey the inside of the dismal tomb. Shadows leapt menacingly from behind the coffins and scaled the walls of the ghoulish crypt, licking the domed ceiling with a grizzly fervour. All at once Cissie shivered – a cold presence slipped like an icy hand across her face and her skin turned instantly to goose-flesh. She repeated an old Wycham blessing to ward off evil spirits, and stared wide-eyed into the gloomy recesses of the cold mausoleum. There before her lay the silent, mouldering generations of the Morrow clan: the large family crest forged in brass on each coffin, stacked on top of one another in their icy tombs, locked for eternity in the dismal sepulchre.

Ruker broke the icy spell that had gripped them all.

'We all know the plan,' she said, trying to rally their spirits. 'We make our way through to the end of the tunnel where Mary will be waiting to meet us. If she isn't there, or the door is locked, we're to wait until she arrives.'

The others nodded apprehensively in the flickering candlelight and edged past the rows of neglected tombs. As Cissie's eyes wandered over the dusty caskets, perched lonely and unloved on their stone plinths, she remembered family stories in which these long dead individuals had featured. She noticed the coffin of Septimia Morrow – the seventh daughter of a seventh daughter – and as such endowed with a sinister reputation, even for a family as strange as the Morrow clan. Septimia had bewitching powers, so they said, and could summon the dead. She could see things from beyond the grave, and her untimely death had been shrouded in mystery. In the ghoulish atmosphere of the sinister crypt, Cissie shivered and wondered whether the old tales that circulated in Wycham village had some truth to them after all and the Morrow sisters *had* inherited Septimia's strange gifts. The sisters were odd, there was no doubt about that.

Neeps broke her train of thought.

'Who are all these weird folk?' he asked, wiping a dirty brass inscription to reveal the name of the dead person encased inside. 'Grimphen Uriah Morrow – now there's a cheery name,' he said, shivering at the thought.

'They're all members of the Morrow family, even this little bairn,' Cissie said sadly, lightly running her fingers over a child-sized coffin, once white as snow but now turned a sepulchral ash-grey in the intervening years. For a moment she stood and stared at the blurred inscription. 'Well I never!' she suddenly cried. 'It's the tomb of little Arabella – a dear child, so it was said – such a sorrowful time for the family. Shine the light over here, Ruker, so I can read the words.'

'We must be on our way,' Ruker replied, trying to hasten Cissie through the eerie mausoleum.

'I won't be a minute,' explained Cissie, bending to read the inscription and brushing away the years of grime that had created a film over the brass plaque.

She pondered the words on the inscription. There was something amiss: the age of the child was missing, and so was the family crest.

'It doesn't make sense,' she said, trying to piece together the family history. 'Perhaps they buried the child in haste.'

But Cissie could see from Ruker's expression that she was keen to get moving.

'I'm coming,' she said, trotting behind them through the arch and into the chilly tunnel.

The biting chilliness hit them immediately as they stepped down inside the dark underground passageway. Cissie placed her handkerchief over her nose to block out the vile stench of rotting vegetation, but the desperate sounds of scurrying vermin scratching their nails and squeaking in the darkness could not be masked.

'Take care underfoot,' said Ruker, 'it's slippery – here, hold on to me.' She reached out her hand to steady Cissie.

As they lifted their lanterns to guide their passage through the gloomy tunnel, the mossy grey-green walls and dripping ceiling stared back at them, oozing droplets of copper-coloured water that seeped through the arched brickwork overhead. Neeps led the way, his lantern illuminating the slimy, putrid colours that streamed down the stained walls, and disturbing a group of silky black rodents nestling in a crevice at the foot of the wall.

'Eugh, rats,' whispered Cissie. 'This place is worse than I imagined.'

'Ignore them,' said Ruker, stepping over the scurrying rodents. 'Come on, not much further.'

Neeps reached the end of the tunnel and pulled on the heavy gate. It began to creak open with the unnerving sound of scraping metal on stone, grating eerily in the stillness.

'Shh! – open the gate carefully, you're makin' a right old din in there,' whispered Mary hoarsely from the boiler room as her anxious face began to appear through the gap. 'At last – I thought you'd never get here.'

Once on the other side, Cissie hugged Mary and the two began to talk in hushed tones. Mary eyed the Skinks with some suspicion. Cissie caught her haughty stare.

'These are my friends, Ruker and Neeps – the ones who saved my life in Ragging Brows Forest,' Cissie explained, hoping that Mary's frostiness would abate. But it didn't.

Mary Brindle had an acute sense of the correct order of

things, particularly where servants were concerned, and her pecking order did not include gardeners being allowed inside the big house. She sniffed disapprovingly, gave the Skinks a sideways look and nodded begrudgingly at them.

'How do?' she uttered through pursed lips. 'I've checked – everyone's asleep and I haven't seen any Shroves. Follow me, and we'll make our way up to the fifth floor to Asenathe and Esmerelda's Great Room.'

Cissie took hold of Mary's arm. 'Much too dangerous,' she said. 'I've thought of a better place to hide, where no one ever goes these days.'

The others listened intently.

'Is it safe and secluded?' asked Neeps.

'Aye, it's certainly remote, but it's tricky to reach,' replied Cissie mysteriously.

'Sounds ideal – where is it?' asked Mary. She had no idea where Cissie meant.

'Best not tell, then they can't prise it out of you. We'll need supplies though.'

'Don't worry about that, I've got it sorted. Been squirreling away bits and pieces, and I'll be able to get fresh bread to you each day.'

'Leave the food in Esmerelda's room late on when everyone's asleep, and we'll pick it up from there.'

Mary handed them packages of supplies for the night.

'These should keep you fed and watered for now.'

'Follow me,' said Cissie. 'Blow out your lanterns. I should be able to feel my way in the dark from here. Now, all hold hands.'

She led them in a raggedy snail trail out of the boiler room and through the deep chilly cellars, past the racks of dusty wine bottles and soap-scented laundry rooms, feeling her way along the pitted walls as she counted off the doors and inched through the passageways in the dead flat darkness.

'Up here,' she whispered, gesticulating to the others and climbing up a series of steps leading past the cold sculleries.

Cissie stopped by the door to the big kitchen and listened. It was late and no one stirred on the other side of the door. She turned the handle and stepped inside. Moonlight bounced off the brightly scrubbed pans, lighting their way past the benches set out with eggs, fruit and vegetables for the next day's menus. She led them out into the passageway and up to the servants' staircase. Cissie carefully opened the door to the grand hallway, and the intruders stepped into the majestic space.

Tall flickering lanterns burned on the large oak sideboard, making pools of light in the entrance hall and throwing dancing patterns up the walls of the cavernous hallway. Ruker and Neeps stared warily overhead at the enormity of the grand house as it disappeared up into the ravaging darkness. They crept behind the two women, stealing silently up the staircases, on the lookout for any sudden movement. The Skinks could not believe their eyes as the grandeur of Winderling Spires meandered on and on ahead of them.

'Can you believe this place?' murmured Neeps, staring wide-eyed at the huge paintings and fabulous chandeliers.

Ruker shook her head and directed her comments in Mary Brindle's direction.

'Seems to me that some folks have way too much whilst others have nothing, scratching a living as gardeners.'

'Shh, be quiet, can't you?' Mary replied tartly. 'Someone will hear you.'

The raggedy gang crept up ornately carved staircases and along twisting corridors, passing room after room until Cissie bade Mary farewell somewhere on the fourth floor. The ladies' maid nodded disparagingly at the Skinks, and disappeared off into the shadows.

In the ominous darkness they kept close together, inching forward, alert to any sound in the gloomy expanse of the house. The dark recesses on every corridor unnerved the Skinks, and Ruker kept her hand permanently locked around the sheath of her dagger, waiting for someone to leap out at them in the leaden darkness. Eventually Cissie beckoned eagerly to them, and opened a small door leading to an enclosed staircase. She shone her lantern upwards, put her finger to her lips and proceeded to climb up the slatted wooden treads. Up and up she went, pausing every once in a while to get her breath or sitting down on the stairs to take a rest.

The Skinks lost count of the flights they trudged up – maybe seven floors, maybe eight – before Cissie, who by this point was hot and bothered, stopped and leant heavily against the wall. Her breathing came in rapid gulps as she placed the lantern on the floor and mopped her brow.

'Here we are at last,' she panted. 'Thought I wasn't going to make it. It's been many years since I came up here.'

She smiled mysteriously in the lamplight and pressed her foot on the weathered skirting board. A small door suddenly clicked open. Ruker peered inside a cramped space between the wood panelling and the outer wall of the big house.

'Where on earth are we?' she asked. 'Hold that lantern higher.'

Neeps shone the lantern into the dusty corners of the dark cavity.

'This hasn't been opened for a long time,' Cissie replied between breaths.

She put her whole weight against the hatch door and it suddenly sprang open. A huge draught of cold night air blew through the opening and into their faces. Cissie bent on hands and knees and squeezed her body through the gap.

'Come on,' she whispered, disappearing into the windy, black night.

Ruker poked her head out into the damp night air and gripped hold of the doorframe as the wind buffeted her face.

'We're nearly as high as Hanging Tree Islands,' she said merrily to Neeps.

They found themselves on the highest, windiest parapet of Winderling Spires, out on a wide castellated ledge overlooking a sheer drop. Far below, the moonlit gardens spread out into the dark shadows that crept all the way to the mausoleum and the outskirts of the grounds.

'Where're we headed?' Ruker asked, crawling along the parapet.

'To that turret over there,' said Cissie breathlessly, pressing her body against the parapet wall to shield against the strong gusts of wind.

She pointed towards the far corner of the house, to where a black turret leapt out of the main building and pierced the night sky.

'Shine some light, Neeps, there's a good chap,' said Ruker, attempting to get a better view of their surroundings.

Neeps lifted the lantern and surveyed their lofty surroundings where the roofs of the Spires met the castellated parapet. Enormous grey-winged hawk moths fluttered restlessly towards the light, banging into the lantern and bouncing off into the night, leaving a dusty trail behind them. The beam of light flashed along the roofline past grotesque gargoyles to where a beautiful Gothic turret spiralled from the corner of the house like a dark twisted tree.

'Creepy,' said Neeps peering at the Gothic edifice. 'Who lives in there?'

'It's empty,' Cissie replied. 'It's another of Esmerelda and Asenathe's secret hidey-holes.'

The turret was resplendent. Its twisted stone columns and beautiful stained glass windows twinkled in the lamplight, flashing purple, crimson and azure colours into the night. From each corner of the turret, four ornately cast metal spiders sprang from their nest, brandishing their legs in the darkness. Just then the moon appeared from behind the clouds, revealing a beautiful spider's web in twisted metal sitting proudly on top of the Gothic turret.

'Wow, that's some hidey-hole,' announced Ruker.

'But will we be safe in there?' asked Neeps.

'Oh yes,' Cissie replied. 'You see, there's no way into the Spider's Turret from the inside of Winderling Spires, but you can get into the house from the Spider's Turret.'

'How's that?' asked Ruker.

'There's a trapdoor inside.'

'But who built it? Doesn't the family know of its existence?'

'The old sisters may have known, but doubtless they will have forgotten all about it by now. As to the Shroves, Miss Asenathe tried to keep the building work a secret. The carpenters were commissioned to develop a unique trapdoor that only worked one way.' Cissie sighed, remembering the times the girls used to play in the Spider's Turret. 'But after Asenathe went missing and Essie returned home, she never came up here again,' she said sadly. 'Her heart had gone out of it.'

'How do we get inside?' asked Ruker

'Through an entrance round the back.'

'What's it like inside? Neeps asked.

'A bit dark and spooky,' she replied.

'Here', said Ruker as she fastened a rope round Cissie's middle with a double knot. 'Just to be on the safe side,' she grinned. 'Hey, Neeps, hold the lantern to guide us?'

Neeps led the way, treading nimbly over the broken edges

of the old valley gutter, gripping hold of the spiked horns of the overhanging gargoyles and creeping towards the Spider's Turret in the moon-soaked night.

Twenty-Four

'It won't budge,' said Ruker, straining hard against the door at the rear of the Spider's Turret.

'That's because it's locked,' explained Cissie, thrusting a key into the Skink's hand. 'There were only three keys made, one for each of the girls and one for me – not that they let me use it much. Kept me at bay, that's for sure.'

'Why's that?' asked Neeps, shining the light on the old window.

'It was their secret place, and they were wary about letting me in. It was a game,' she explained. 'I had to say a password and sometimes they'd giggle and say I'd got it wrong. "Go away Cissie," they'd shout, "we'll be down for tea later".'

Cissie bent down and inserted the ornate key in the rusty lock.

'There's a knack to this locking device, if I remember correctly.'

She pulled the door firmly towards her and turned the key clockwise. It turned with a resounding thud. Then there came a shudder and a squeaking noise as the rear window suddenly jumped open.

'Is this the way in?' Ruker asked, slightly baffled, peering through the window down into the dark room.

'It's a false entrance,' Cissie explained. 'Neeps, give me a lift up over the window ledge, there's a good lad – I won't manage otherwise.'

The Skink bent down so that Cissie could clamber over his shoulder. Unfortunately, he tipped her up a little too quickly and she bundled headfirst over the windowsill, landing with a soft thud on a bed down below.

'Ouch!' she cried. 'That drop was further than I remember.'

'You okay?' asked Ruker breathlessly, rolling head-over-heels next to Cissie.

Then Neeps tumbled over the ledge and the three of them lay in a heap on the mattress. They were on a large bed covered in a purple velvet quilt. The big squidgy cushions piled up in the middle had softened their fall. Cissie clambered over the others, stepped onto a wooden ledge, secured the window and drew the curtains.

'You can light the lantern now,' she said to Neeps.

As the light flickered across the Spider's Turret, the peculiar little room took shape before their eyes. The walls were lined with irregular shelves and alcoves, nooks and crannies containing a vast array of gloomy paraphernalia – the funeral ornaments

of the dead: brooches, rings and death lockets, mourning fans and funeral vessels adorned with tiny portraits of the dearly departed.

'This is all a bit weird,' mumbled Neeps, inspecting a specimen jar in the candlelight.

It glistened as the light refracted through the glass and into the viscous amber liquid, landing on the embalmed body parts from long dead insects.

'This looks a bit ghoulish, if you ask me,' agreed Ruker, studying a mound of black feathers and jars of pickled fungus.

Cissie chuckled and shook her head.

'Well, you know what youngsters are like. The girls had a bit of a phase and were obsessed by spooky things, but the whole thing was harmless. They just liked playin' at makin' daft old spells and make-believe.'

'I'm not so sure about that. This room seems to be set up for sorcery of some description,' replied Ruker.

She kicked the corner of a rug that was sticking up to reveal a black pentagram painted on the wooden floor.

Cissie bent down to take a closer look.

'Oh my!' she gasped. 'I never knew that was there,' she answered, biting her lip. 'They must 'ave covered it up when I came up here.'

The Skinks were right – there was something eerie about the room.

'It means the girls were dabbling in magic,' said Ruker. 'I wonder what they discovered up here.'

The Skink picked up a death mask from the alcove. It was a sombre replica of a woman's face forged at the time of her death, painted in alabaster-white and set with closed eyes and dead white lips. Cissie lifted the lantern and shone the light all around the room. As it flickered across the walls, a long line of similar death masks were revealed along the top shelves – artefacts of the dead and the wherewithal to summon them back from the grave. There were funeral posies and wreaths, death amulets, rat skulls and rune tablets, tarot cards, a rabbit's foot and an Ouija board.

'B-But what were they doin'? I thought they were just messin' about …' she said grimly, her voice trailing off.

All three of them began searching the alcoves, digging amongst the tiny animal skulls and funeral bells, looking for clues as to what the girls had got up to inside the Spider's Turret. At the bottom of the shelves was a cupboard with books and papers inside. Ruker took out a small book and began flicking through the pages.

'This is more serious than playing games,' she added, handing the book to Cissie. 'It seems they were dabbling in the occult, if this book is anything to go by. It has incantations to wake the dead and scripts in a funny language.'

'Oh my,' said Cissie softly.

She screwed up her eyes in the meagre light. There were death spells and pages of necromancy tables indicating the best times of the year to summon the dead, with the names of famous mediums and spirit seekers written down on one side of the page.

'Some of this writing …' she murmured. 'Oh, it's so difficult to make it out in this light.' She paused, lifting the book closer to the lantern. 'It's in that strange Ennish tongue and the writing is in a beautiful italic script.'

Ruker turned the book this way and that, but she could make neither head nor tail of the words.

'Who do you think wrote it?' Ruker asked.

Cissie peered closer. It was a beautifully bound volume but the handwriting didn't look familiar at all. The lettering consisted of complicated flourishes and curls. It was a mature hand – it was a lady's hand. At the back of the volume was a leather pocket containing a number of loose-leaf pages. These were copies, made from the incantations in the main volume by a more juvenile hand.

'Not sure I like what I see,' Cissie announced. 'These incantations are written in Asenathe's hand,' she said, staring at the Skinks. 'The girls must have been copying the spells from this old book, but heaven knows where they got it from! Wrap it up quickly and put it back on the shelf, it gives me the creeps,' she said, pushing the volume into Ruker's hand.

'This turret will do us though, even if it is a bit weird,' said Neeps staring about him.

'I suppose it will have to do for now,' Cissie replied, 'but I have grave misgivings about what we've found in here. Those girls shouldn't 'ave been allowed to get into such mischief. Had I but known, I would have put a stop to it.' She hesitated and bit her lip. 'But the whole family, and particularly those sisters, were always strange.'

Neeps stretched out his tired body across the bed.

'I'm bushed,' said the Skink, yawning and closing his eyes.

'By the way,' said Ruker, 'where's the trapdoor into the main house?'

'We're lying on it,' replied Cissie. 'The contraption is under this bed.'

Cissie covered Neeps with a patchwork quilt. He had already rolled into a ball, and was breathing deeply.

'We'll take a good look around in the morning. We can make a plan once we see what's through the trapdoor and find our bearings in the old house. Goodnight Cissie,' said Ruker, yawning and wrapping herself up too. 'I'm afraid I'm beat as well, it's been a long and exciting day.'

Cissie blew out the lantern, wrapped herself in a blanket and closed her eyes. But the eerie turret had made her unsettled and had put her nerves on edge. The sweet sanctuary of sleep evaded her. She lay in the darkness remembering the times she had struggled up to the turret to find the girls larking around in their secret room. Each time she had to play their game and repeat the password – and more times than not, they had kept her out. Ruker was right: Esmerelda and Asenathe must have been up to some strange things in the turret, delving into the black arts and other things that didn't bear thinking about. She should have guessed what they were up to, what with their family history, but she hadn't wanted to think ill of her chicks. Besides, they were just young girls.

The hours wore on and still Cissie could not rest, unable to rid herself of the feeling of dread. Eventually she opened the curtain to allow the light to shine through the window. The moonlight danced across the room and played patterns on the glass cabinet. Through the pane Cissie's eyes suddenly alighted on a toy boat with a sail, discoloured and frail with age. The boat was painted in red and blue and she knew that the name of *Danny* was picked out in dark blue lettering across the hull. Why hadn't she noticed the toy boat before? It was there in full view amongst the remnants of the girls' lost childhood. She sat straight up in bed as if she had seen a ghost. In a way she had. Her heart was thumping out of her chest.

'It can't be,' she cried softly, staring at the forlorn little boat abandoned in the dusty cabinet.

In a spilt-second the gut-wrenching memories came tumbling back, one after another, unbidden and painful like a blade to her breast. Danny must have lent his little boat to the girls before they went missing. She let out a small cry like a wounded animal, pulling the quilt up to her chin, her eyes shining in the darkness.

'Danny, my little one,' she cried.

It hurt her to say his name after all this time. But he was lost to her forever. She wept, tears running down her cheeks and soaking into the quilt.

'Cissie, you okay?' asked Ruker half-asleep.

'Just a bad dream,' she whispered. 'You go back to sleep.'

Cissie wiped her face, crept from under the quilt and lifted the fragile boat from its resting place. She caressed the name on the hull, cuddled it to her chest and mumbled the child's name over and over to herself:

'Danny, my Danny ...'

At some point, still clutching the precious boat, her heart broken with the memories of her lost child, Cissie drifted off into a troubled sleep.

Twenty-Five

'Marlin, come here at once!' the Grand Morrow shouted. 'Stop skulking about.'

She peered over her spectacles into the shadows of her grand sitting room. Agatha knew that the Shrove was lurking just out of sight. He always seemed to be watching her these days.

Agatha Morrow sat at her desk surrounded by stacks of books and faded documents, pensively studying the well-thumbed pages and making notes in her black spidery handwriting. She was overwrought and her expression had taken on a worn, crumpled look since the day of the children's disappearance.

The Shrove crept from behind the bureau and slithered noiselessly to his mistress's side. Agatha shot him a withering glance and continued to pore over her documents.

'Have my sisters been downstairs lately?' she asked, without looking up from her books.

The Shrove hopped about whilst surreptitiously peeking at the Grand Morrow's notes.

'I 'aven't seen them for some days, m'Lady. Shall I help you with that?' he snivelled, edging closer and glancing over her shoulder.

'No! Thank you,' Agatha replied. She quickly covered the notes she had made with her hand. 'You can put those books away,' she added, pointing to the pile on the floor.

The Shrove bowed obsequiously and did as he was asked. What was the Grand Morrow up to, he thought, ferreting about in her old books? She hadn't touched her sewing for days. Marlin suspected something was afoot.

Agatha repositioned her spectacles and continued perusing the pile of old volumes. She was overwhelmed by the enormity of her task and was concerned that the book she was looking for had somehow been mislaid – it was a small volume after all, and could have dropped down the back of the bookcase.

The Shrove relished the old woman's distress and chuckled inwardly to himself. There was much she didn't know and so much that he did. The wicked thought felt delicious to the mean old Shrove. Marlin had been charged with keeping a close eye on the Grand Morrow, even more so than usual. He had to report any developments or changes in her behaviour to Bludroot, and ultimately to the Thane of Breedoor. Marlin observed her keenly.

'Is that all m'Lady?' he asked, rubbing his hands together.

Agatha was distracted. She stared fretfully towards the gloomy mountains in the distance, her lip trembling and shooed the Shrove out of the room – she must get rid of him. She would send him on an errand.

'Ask Mrs Armitage to serve tea in the Library.'

The Shrove bowed and scuttled from the room.

Agatha Morrow was in a quandary. It had been many years since she had consulted the ancient books, and even longer since she had used any of their rituals or spells. If she couldn't locate the book there was only one course of action left to her. She would have to eat copious amounts of humble pie in front of her sisters – well, Edwina Mouldson, to be precise. She had exhausted all avenues and now desperately needed her sisters' help.

The Grand Morrow's world had become an unhappy, solitary place without the proximity of those she loved. Tallitha and young Tyaas had been missing for weeks, with no word from any quarter. She had hoped that Esmerelda or that young fellow Benedict would get a message to her, but the long, empty days without any news had been unbearable. The tears trickled down her cheeks, falling with a soft splash onto the pages of the ancient scripts. She brushed them hastily away, her breath catching in the back of her throat, and she stared once more at the mountains that divided Wycham Elva from the lands of Breedoor in the hope that a solution would present itself. But nothing did.

Of course it was all her fault. If she hadn't been so determined to settle Asenathe with Cornelius Pew, a much older but safer match, then this sorry state of affairs could have been avoided. She had been trying to protect Asenathe from a fate similar to her own – from a marriage to a man like the evil Machin Dreer, who had deceived her most dreadfully. Agatha shuddered at the memory of her inauspicious match. The man had been a devil! But she hadn't envisaged in her wildest dreams that her daughter and niece would run away. She had been a misguided old fool playing with the lives of others, and there wasn't a day that she didn't regret it.

Over the years that the Grand Morrow had ruled Wycham Elva, she had used all her power to protect her lands against the forces that lurked in Breedoor and to ward off the evil eye of the Swarm. But her potency did not reach beyond the boundary of Wycham Elva, where the land curled towards the dark mountains, and the ominous spells of the Swarm ran wild. She had waited much too long for Tallitha and Tyaas to return of their own accord. Now she would have to find them for herself.

Agatha rose, leaving her books and papers strewn across the desk, and made her way through the sitting room, down the long corridors, past the sewing rooms and tapestry looms, up a winding staircase and into her sunny dressing room. She looked at herself in the mirror and sighed: a severe old woman stared back, sombrely dressed, with piles of grey hair tied loosely on the top of her head. Agatha pinched some colour back into her lumpy cheeks and locked the doors leading from her apartment to her dressing room and bedroom. She brushed down her dress and steeled herself for the meeting to come.

Tucked behind the four-poster bed, hidden beneath the hanging wall tapestry was a wooden partition. It was the entrance to an old staircase that hadn't been used for many years. The

Grand Morrow squeezed her body behind the ornate headboard, lifted the tapestry and pressed the lever on the secret panel. It opened with a creak. Agatha stepped over the skirting board into the musty darkness and began the long ascent to the Crewel Tower. The time had come to meet with her sisters and persuade them to join in her plans.

It had been many years since Agatha had trudged up the wooden stairs. She held onto the bannister and a lump came into her throat. When they were children, the three girls had trodden the hidden passageway every day, their laughter ringing out as they played hide-and-seek or snuck into each other's apartments late at night to delight in midnight feasts and spooky stories. Her younger sisters had looked up to her in those days, had hung on her every word, but now they kept their distance. Age had made her into a proud, stern woman and had hardened her heart. Agatha's eyes glistened at the memory of such happy times playing with her sweet dear sisters. Their joy had been a lifetime ago – since then, she had embarked on a disastrous course of events that had ultimately led to Asenathe's disappearance and had caused her estrangement from Edwina and Sybilla.

On each turn of the staircase Agatha stooped to peer out of the lattice windows, glimpsing the dark mountains through the dirty windowpanes. She stared at the The-Out-Of-The-Way Mountains and pondered at the task that lay ahead of her. Beyond their snowy peaks was the infamous castle at Hellstone Tors, where she suspected her beloved children were being imprisoned. She had let them all down with her headstrong ways.

As Agatha rounded the next bend, she noticed something lying in the dust in the corner of the stairs. There in a heap of litter was a soft grey rabbit, its floppy ears twisted and moth-eaten. The rabbit lay forlorn and abandoned, its legs hanging limply down over the worn stair tread. Agatha picked up the soft toy, brushed away the dirt and held it next to her heart, fondling its shabby ears. Tibby was the rabbit's name – dearest Tibby, her beloved rabbit. She had forgotten all about the toy's existence, blotted it out as she had also blotted out her love for her sisters. It was all too painful. Agatha wiped away a tear and continued up the dark, dusty steps, holding Tibby tightly in her hand and dreading the event to come.

At the top of the staircase Agatha composed herself and pushed open the door. The beautiful sitting room was just as she remembered it, with its fabulous balcony and passageways leading to secret rooms and hidden vaults. Her sisters froze as Agatha stepped towards them.

'Good gracious!' shouted Edwina. 'What are you doing up here?'

Agatha had rehearsed what she intended to say. She must be at her most charming to win her sisters over.

'Can't I visit my little sisters?' she asked tentatively, sad that her presence had elicited such a reaction.

Sybilla's mouth hung open like a dead codfish while Edwina continued to gawp at Agatha.

'Well, are you going to invite me to sit down? I'm quite exhausted after that arduous climb. No wonder I hardly ever see you downstairs,' she jested, but her joke fell flat.

Edwina pointed imperiously to the armchair and sat down on the sofa opposite her eldest sister, her back straight and her nose in the air. Sybilla continued to gawp as Edwina rang for their Shrove.

'Florré, you'd better bring the tea,' was all that Edwina could muster. 'Sybilla dear, do close your mouth.'

The Shrove was flummoxed. He hovered anxiously, trying to overhear the reason for the Grand Morrow's visit.

'Florré!' snapped Edwina, staring at the bumbling Shrove. 'Tea! At once!'

The Shrove bobbed his head and scurried out of the room.

Sybilla snapped her mouth shut and joined Edwina. They sat like two stuffed birds, staring in amazement at their elder sister.

'This will be about that granddaughter of yours,' said Sybilla nervously as she played with her black-headed pins.

'That girl has put us to a great deal of trouble, going off like that,' replied Edwina tartly. 'However, as I recall, she went off with your daughter, Esmerelda!' She flung the words at her sister.

Sybilla flushed pink and remonstrated with Edwina, mouthing words behind her hand. Edwina sat po-faced and rigid with righteousness.

'Now sisters, I haven't climbed all those stairs to hear you quarrel,' said Agatha softly, stroking the ears of her soft toy.

Sybilla's eyes lit up.

'Goodness! Is that your old rabbit? She does bring back fond memories, doesn't she dear?' she smiled sweetly at Edwina.

Her sister sat stiffly with her arms folded in a huff on the sofa.

Agatha tried once again. 'I've come to discuss our missing children,' she said, her eyes perusing the stony faces of her two younger sisters.

'Do you mean all the missing children?' asked Sybilla, searching Agatha's face.

'Well, do you Agatha?' asked Edwina with emphasis.

'I-I want them all home in Winderling Spires,' she replied sadly. 'Every last one of them.'

Edwina Mouldson stared coldly at Agatha, taking in her eldest sister's jaded demeanour.

'But what can we do beyond the boundary of Wycham Elva?' Sybilla asked meekly. 'At least here we're safe from the Dooerlins.'

Edwina pouted. 'Unless of course, you inadvertently let them in, like the last time,' she replied forcefully, spitting the words in Agatha's direction.

Sybilla and Agatha exchanged knowing glances, remembering the night when the Dooerlins had stolen into Winderling Spires and the dark deed had been committed.

'Well?' asked Edwina, 'what do you propose?'

'Since that last dreadful episode I have used my spells to keep Wycham Elva and Winderling Spires safe from the Dooerlins, warding off the evil eye of the Swarm. But it's time for more than talismans and charms.' She sighed. 'It wasn't my fault all those years ago when the spell went wrong … It was a terrible error.'

Edwina watched her elder sister suspiciously. 'You're feeling guilty about the loss of Asenathe,' she snapped. 'You shouldn't have arranged that ridiculous marriage to Cornelius Pew – he was old enough to be her father!'

'I know that now, but at the time I had my reasons!'

'Pah!' Edwina interjected.

'I was determined to save her from my fate,' Agatha murmured sadly. 'But we must do our absolute best to free our children – to summon help – from a particular q-quarter,' she added enigmatically.

Edwina raised an eyebrow at her sister. 'It's been many years since you tried that route, and you failed miserably the first time,' she said tartly.

'She didn't mean to fail, dear,' said Sybilla, trying to smooth Edwina's ruffled feathers.

'When Asenathe went missing I offered to help you, but you would do it your own way and you were weakened.' Edwina sniffed with pompous indignation.

'I should have listened to you. I admit that now, but time has moved on, as has the course of recent events.'

It was like an exciting tennis match. Sybilla's head bobbed from one sister to the other, watching them in the desperate hope that Agatha and Edwina might be a little more sisterly to one another, just like the old days.

Agatha cleared her throat. 'Can we put that behind us? I want all three of us to combine our powers.'

'What exactly do you mean?' asked Edwina, suspiciously.

'I've searched high and low for that old spell book but it's vanished – and as you rightly say, I've tried that route before. So, my dear, I want you to use your powers as a medium,' said Agatha.

'That sounds exciting, dear,' Sybilla suggested, turning to see if Edwina felt similarly.

But Edwina sat like a stuffed dummy. Sybilla, on the other hand, was all of a flutter at the thought of a rapprochement between her sisters. She might be able to use her old spells again and practise with her black-headed pins. It had been so long since those glorious bewitching days when Winderling Spires had been brimming with spells and sorcery. But Agatha's terrible mishap with the Fire Witch had put an end to that.

'Exciting? What nonsense!' interrupted Edwina, putting a dampener on proceedings. 'Have you forgotten what happened the last time?' Her eyes flickered antagonistically in Agatha's direction.

'We lost the sweet child,' said Sybilla softly. 'The one who was taken from us at the dead of night.'

'Exactly!' said Edwina stiffly. 'Agatha's powers were weakened by calling on the Grand Witches, and the Dooerlins found a chink in her armour of spells. They forced their way into the Spires and stole the child,' snapped Edwina.

'But if we work together it will be different this time,' Agatha replied in a consolatory manner. 'I agree, calling on Kastra was a mistake – I thought she would help me.'

'Maybe she wasn't powerful enough,' said Sybilla.

'Or she tricked you! The Grand Witches always want something in return,' Edwina replied.

'We must do something,' Agatha pleaded.

'She's right, Edwina' said Sybilla, 'or the family will die out. There will be no one left to protect the Spires. Then the Morrow Swarm will invade Wycham Elva and all will be lost!' She cried out at the dreadful thought, lent forward and took her elder sister's hand. 'I will help you, dear,' she said sweetly.

Sybilla looked beseechingly at Edwina.

'But it's dangerous,' Edwina replied, softening. 'We might lose everything – gambling with our powers in the netherworld will be deadly dangerous. In any event, the children may return in time and Essie always comes back eventually.'

'I'm not prepared to take that risk – I have waited too long for my Asenathe. I can't make the same mistake with Tallitha and Tyaas. Surely we have to try – will you help me?' she begged Edwina.

At that moment Florré entered with a tea tray and bumbled towards the table.

'You've forgotten the tarts,' said Edwina abruptly and shooed the Shrove away.

Florré's ears were twitching, on the alert for any snippets of information.

The Shrove grumbled away to himself about ... "no one asked for any tarts before," ... and ambled out of the door, leaving it slightly ajar as he slunk to the floor. He pressed his ear to the gap to overhear what the sisters were planning. The words that met his ears caused him to salivate. The three sisters were reuniting after all this time. He must alert Marlin at once! There was much for the Shroves to do.

'Well?' asked Agatha. 'Success depends upon your help, Edwina. Remember the power of the three: *trethorin nallin cempothra.*' Agatha spoke softly in Ennish, holding Edwina's gaze. 'You have the power to contact the dead-ones.'

The Grand Morrow lowered her eyes, hoping that her silky-tongued flattery would win her sister over. Edwina finished her tea and straightened down her dress.

'We need your talents as a medium to contact Septimia Morrow,' Agatha pleaded.

'Ooh, yes,' sighed Sybilla. 'If anyone can help us, Septimia will. You're the best dark mediator there is, Edwina.'

Sybilla hugged her knees with the anticipation of contacting their long dead relative.

Edwina looked like the cat that had got the cream and had a tasty mouse to look forward to for supper. She had waited years for this moment.

'So will you forgive me, dear sister? Shall we three join together and make contact with Septimia Morrow? She's the one who will be able to tell us how to destroy the pact.'

Agatha's eyes searched her sister's face and she pressed the small grey rabbit against her chest. Perhaps it was the memory of those bygone days, or the victorious sensation of having won, but Edwina softened.

'Yes,' she said solemnly, 'I will commune with the seventh child of the seventh child – *trethorin nallin cempothra,*' she whispered. 'We will join forces to get all our children home.'

The power of the three gifted sisters, together again at last!

'Come – we will inspect our old hexing space,' said Edwina, beckoning to her sisters to follow her.

Agatha's face relaxed and she sighed with relief, smiled warmly at her sisters and kissed the soft grey rabbit on its floppy head.

Twenty-Six

Florré had his instructions from Marlin and he relished them. He waited until the foolish sister, Sybilla Patch, was alone before he played his wicked hand.

'When shall I bring t'tea this afternoon?' he asked, hobbling next to his mistress. 'I only ask, m'Lady, because yesterday when I came back to lay out the strawberry tarts you was all missin'.'

Sybilla turned pink and began fiddling with her black pins. 'W-We were b-busy and we lost track of time. I was with my s-sisters, we were –'

'Oh m'Lady, all the sisters, back together again,' said the wily Shrove with a crooked smile.

Sybilla brightened, her eyes glowing with pleasure as she recalled the happy reunion of the Morrow sisters.

'Why yes, Florré, the Grand Morrow and Edwina they … w-we all h-had tea together in the Fedora Wing.'

Of course the cunning Shrove knew that his mistress was not telling him the truth, but he bent a little closer.

'That's a bit of good news, m' Lady,' the Shrove said beguilingly. Florré enjoyed playing Sybilla's little game. 'I always hoped you would resolve your differences, if you don't mind me being so bold as to comment.'

Sybilla flushed and fiddled with her pins, confused and happy all at the same time.

Now Florré had his opportunity. He reached inside his jacket pocket and carefully placed four black boxes onto Sybilla's table.

'I thought you might like these, m'Lady. They came my way last week when I was 'elpin' the undertaker with a special job, and I know how partial you are to these fine things.'

Sybilla's cheeks glowed pink, her eyes brightened and she quickly opened all the boxes. She gasped with delight and clapped her hands.

'Oh Florré, my special pins, and bodkins, little needles – my beauties!' she moaned, closing her eyes and clutching a box to her chest.

Florré had produced not only the wonderful black-headed pins, but ebony-encrusted darning needles and jet-inlaid bodkins. Sybilla crooned over her treasures, bewitched by their utter gorgeousness. The Shrove had softened her up, and now he moved in for the kill.

'M'Lady, shall I pour you a cup of tea whilst you tell me all about your interestin' visit with your sisters?' Florré whispered like a slippery eel, setting out the teacup.

'Thank you, yes of course, Florré. Oh, they are lovely, so pretty. How did you get these bodkins?' Sybilla asked, inspecting her new needles. She gazed with fondness at her dear Shrove. Her sisters were much too suspicious. Florré was such a sweet-natured creature.

'You're such a loyal, kind Shrove to bring me these death trinkets,' she crooned, stroking the silver bodkins. 'Just a little milk and two sugars please ...'

*

Deep under Mrs Armitage's pantry in the semi-darkness of their Shrove burrow, Marlin and Grintley were hunched on the cold earth floor, salivating as they listened intently to Florré, who rubbed his hands together and hopped about as he spoke of all that he had learned in the Crewel Tower.

'I knew them sisters were plannin' summat,' he grizzled. 'That thin cranky one, the Lady Edwina, spoke them old words in Ennish and then they all began to look a bit too friendly-like, chattin'. It fair put my teeth on edge to witness it.' He shook himself all over like a damp dog, shivering and moaning.

Grintley's shrivelled face formed into a nasty sneer. 'But those three 'aven't been on good terms for years,' he bleated, licking his feverish lips. 'They despise each other.'

'Just my thinkin',' muttered Florré. 'So later I duped that foolish one with a few trinkets and she let the cat out of the bag.' The other Shroves were hanging on his every word.

'Get on with it!' shouted Marlin.

'They're plotting to break the pact!'

Florré was especially pleased with himself.

Marlin frowned and rubbed his whiskery chin. 'Pass the berry juice, Florré, I need to think,' he demanded, taking a glug of the thick blackcurrant brew and wiping his feverish lips.

'Damn and blast the Grand Morrow! I should 'ave seen this comin', what with her rummagin' through her old books, and she 'asn't been at her sewing for days. She sent me on a wild goose chase, gettin' the tea that she never drank. She went up to the Crewel Tower when my back was turned.'

'What does it mean?' asked Grintley.

'She's been frettin' about those blitherin' children, but more to the point she 'asn't visited her sisters in the Crewel Tower for many a year. What else did you 'ear?' he asked, pointing his vexed face next to Florré.

'They spoke of one of the long dead-uns,' answered Florré, nodding sagely.

'Which old crone was that?' Marlin snarled. 'There are many of them in t'family.'

Florré scratched his head and pondered for a while. 'Erm, I just cannot think of t'name,' he uttered feebly.

'Come on, it's not that difficult,' Marlin said impatiently. 'Was it Fedora, the first Grand Morrow?'

'Nay, that dun't ring any bells,' answered the forgetful Shrove.

'What about Clarissa, or Hortense?' he asked sharply.

'Come on numpty, or I'll lamp thee one with my fist to jar your ailing memory.'

Marlin raised his hand to the cowering Shrove. Florré reared back and hissed at Marlin.

'Give us a chance, can't you?' Florré bleated.

He hopped about, all of a twitter. Then his eyes lit up.

'I've got it!' he cried. 'Septimia was 'er name. I 'eard it right. They're goin' to make contact with that dead-one to find out about how to destroy the pact.'

Marlin looked as though he had just sucked on a lemon.

'I'll be damned,' he cursed. 'We must watch those old crones carefully. 'Tis a rum day when they start being friendly and take to each other's company.'

'What shall we do now?' asked Florré anxiously.

'We'll do what we do best,' snarled Marlin. 'Hide behind doors, listen in to their conversations, eavesdrop on the sisters; and when we know what's afoot, I'll go to Hellstone Tors and report to Bludroot.'

The two Shroves nodded their agreement at Marlin. Then Grintley and Florré skittled off to spy on the sisters who were having breakfast together in Agatha's morning room.

Marlin snacked on some leftover meat, chewing on a knucklebone, sucking on the gristle, and biding his time. He licked his greasy fingers one by one and plotted his next move. The crafty old Shrove muttered away as a kernel of an idea began to take shape in his devious mind. *That's it – of course!* He knew where the three sisters would congregate at the dead of night to carry out their nefarious deeds.

'Yes, yes, I've got it!' he weaselled away, pleased with his artfulness. 'Now that's just the place they would choose to make contact with the dead-ones.'

*

'Did it work?' Edwina asked sharply, gazing down at Agatha's mud-splattered boots and then up at Sybilla's pink, flustered face.

The two sisters bustled into the Crewel Tower and hurriedly closed the door behind them. They were breathless and overexcited.

'Marlin and the others should be freezing their boots off as we speak,' Agatha announced cheerfully. 'We laid out the séance table next to Septimia's tomb just as you instructed.'

'We foxed them well and good, didn't we Agatha?' Sybilla chuckled, gazing fondly at her sister. Then her face clouded over. 'But don't we trust our dear Shroves anymore?' she asked, her expression becoming fretful.

Agatha raised an eyebrow at Edwina. The two sisters knew exactly what the other was thinking. The Shroves were definitely up to something. Agatha had often had her doubts about Marlin's loyalty, particularly since he failed to track Tallitha and Tyaas when they escaped from Winderling Spires, but she had put them to the back of her mind. Sybilla was a dear sweet soul and Agatha didn't want her upset – after all, the Shroves had always served the family and she had no concrete proof of their duplicity … well, not as yet.

'It's just a game, Sybilla dear, to keep them from following us,' explained Agatha. 'They may not agree with our way of making contact with the dead,' she added.

Sybilla's face softened and she smiled at both her sisters. 'To distract them?' she asked.

Her sisters nodded and Sybilla relaxed. She was feeling chirpier than she had for years. It was wonderful having all her sisters back on good terms and she didn't want to think ill of the Shroves. She felt a warm glow inside her – it was like being children again.

'Are you ready Sybilla?' asked Edwina. 'It's been some time since we tried this.'

'Oh yes, dear! I'm quite excited about working with my poppets again,' exclaimed Sybilla.

Her cheeks flushed with anticipation as she fiddled absent-mindedly with her black-headed pins and thought longingly about her collection of individually-sewn grave dolls. Sybilla's dark talent was her ability to make rag dolls exactly in the image of their dead female ancestors. The dolls were woven from the intricate needlepoint and the samplers that each Morrow woman had sewn in her lifetime were used as a bridge between this world and the next.

'What shall I do?' asked Agatha.

'Watch out for the ruby glow. The guiding light will appear along one of our corridors indicating which path we must follow,' answered Edwina.

The sitting room in the Crewel Tower was designed like a

spider's web, with eight corridors leading to spinning rooms, archives, manuscript vaults and rooms that Agatha had never visited before. Sybilla placed seven black candles around the table, and the sisters sat together in the flickering light. Edwina took a large book from her shelves, chose a passage and began to speak the words of the incantation:

'*Lamenta ne, clethora mellesta, lamenta ne,*' she exclaimed. '*Sepora nan tulleth, lamenta ne, clethora mellesta, lamenta ne.*'

The candlelight was suddenly extinguished. Only one lone candle remained lit, guttering ominously against the draught.

'It's so cold,' shuddered Agatha, staring about her into the shadows.

She felt something moving silently between them. Edwina repeated the incantation as a dark presence swirled like a fog past their faces. The spectre had snuck in from one of the corridors and repeated the words of the incantation in a haunting voice:

'*Lamenta ne, clethora mellesta, lamenta ne,*
sepora nan tulleth, lamenta ne,
clethora mellesta, lamenta ne.'

'Who's that?' asked Agatha, sounding terrified.

'Shh, it's only our guiding spirit,' warned Sybilla. 'Don't disturb her.'

'It is time, sister,' instructed Edwina, rising from the table.

She took hold of Sybilla's outstretched hands and they crossed their arms like children at the start of a spinning game.

The sisters turned slowly at first, then gained momentum, spinning round and round, leaning backwards and counting off the corridors as they twirled upwards.

'*Ine, duce, tre, me, linka, sept, na, seva, devana, venta,*' they chanted together in harmony. '*Ine, duce, tre, me, linka, sept, na, seva, devana, venta.*'

Their voices quickened as they continued the mesmeric chanting, spinning faster and faster until all that Agatha could see was a whirlpool of colour as her sisters pirouetted before her. Then Edwina and Sybilla rose up into the dome of the Crewel Tower like a spinning top made of fantastic kaleidoscopic colours.

One of the corridors hummed with an undulating ruby-red glow, lighting the way.

'It's worked – the corridor is alight with colour!' Agatha announced excitedly. 'Edwina, Sybilla, you've done it!'

Edwina repeated the incantation and the sisters' frenetic spinning began to slow down until they landed lightly on the floor, gasping for breath. Sybilla clapped her hands with glee at the sight of the ruby glow.

'That was such fun,' said Edwina, smoothing down her hair and clothes. 'Sybilla, don't forget the sewing box and the little portraits.'

Sybilla's clothes were all over the place. Her skirt had billowed up and her face was the colour of scarlet red apples. She picked up a rose-patterned sewing box, rummaged about to check the contents were all correct and smiled endearingly at her sister.

'Yes, all here, Edwina. Shall we be off?'

'I have the other special accoutrements,' she said mysteriously, patting her canvas bag.

'What have you got in there?' asked Agatha.

But Edwina just smiled enigmatically.

'This way,' she said, following the ruby glow that danced enticingly down the dark corridor.

*

Marlin was perished. His creaky joints had gone stiff with the freezing cold. He had been lying in the same position in a vacant, dusty coffin space since the daylight had begun to fade, waiting for the sisters to arrive. His arm had gone to sleep and he was beginning to fret.

'Grintley, Florré, are you there?' he called out into the gloomy crypt. 'There's summat up – one of you go and see where those blasted sisters have got to.'

Florré struggled out of his narrow space. He was covered from head to foot in spider's webs and dust.

'Grintley's 'avin a bit of a doze. I'll go up t'tower and find out what's 'appenin.'

'Be sharp about it. I'm starvin' and clammered with t'cold in this awful tomb,' Marlin moaned, shivering.

Florré scuttled from the mausoleum, back along the smelly, dank tunnel and into the soapy washrooms of the old house. He too was stiff with the cold that had soaked into his old bones. As he snuck into the big kitchen, his eyes alighted on a flagon of elderberry wine and a plate of steaming pasties that stood enticingly on the dresser. The cosy warmth of the kitchen range was sorely tempting. He would just take a nip or two of the sweet wine to revive him. After the first draught of the soothing wine, swiftly followed by one of the cook's delicious meat pasties, the Shrove began to feel drowsy.

The comfy armchair beckoned and Florré's eyelids drooped with tiredness. He would just sit down and close his eyes for twenty winks – after all, what harm could it do? Florré licked his lips, curled his spindly legs underneath him, tucked his hands beneath his head and fell into a deep sleep. He dreamt of his soft burrow deep in the tunnels of Winderling Spires, of pretty trinkets, and …

'You lazy tripe-hound!' shouted a furious Marlin, banging the armchair. 'I've been waitin' on ye for ages, stuck in that freezin' tomb, and here I find ye asleep with an empty noggin of wine by tha' miserable side!'

Florré woke with a terrible fright and a thumping headache. Where was he? There was so much shouting and hollering, and Marlin was hopping about like a Shrove possessed.

'I'm frizzled to death an' all! Did ye not think of us when you filled your face with hot pasties, lyin' in that horrible tomb with only the Morrow ghouls for company?' yelled Grintley.

'Oh m-my,' stammered Florré, 'I-I must have fallen asleep, I-I didn't mean to. What time is it?' he stammered.

'Everyone's in bed! It's near to midnight – 'ave you not found those sisters yet?'

'I'm goin' now Marlin, don't you fret,' said an apologetic Florré as he fell off his chair, landed with a bump on the floor, rolled over and skittled nervously out of the kitchen door.

'Hurry up, you eejit,' hissed Marlin angrily. 'Now we'll be 'avin' a bit of a sit and a sup whilst you're about it.'

Florré rubbed his eyes, skated frantically across the stone flagged hallway and made his way up to the Crewel Tower. He hauled his exhausted body up the staircase and knocked on the sisters' door, but all was silent. He hovered, rubbing his hands in the eerie chilliness of the night. Gingerly, he opened the door and stepped inside the circular tower room – everything was in total darkness. Florré had a quick look around, as much as he dared to, and decided that the sisters must have gone to bed – after all, it was close to midnight. He scampered back to the kitchen like a rat out of a trap and reported his news to a bad-tempered Marlin.

'Are you sure, you numbskull? You look 'alf-asleep to me,' Marlin sneered, munching on another juicy meat pie.

'I tell thee the tower was pitch-black, they always go to their beds early.'

Marlin was in a foul mood with the lazy Florré.

'I'm going to sleep meself!' he shouted angrily. 'We'll try again tomorrow. You have to overhear every word those sisters say, do you 'ear me?' He flung the words at the hapless Shrove. Marlin yawned, his mouth stretching open wide to reveal his wiggling tonsils. Then he gave Florré a nasty clout on his ear and snuck away to his comfy lair.

347

Twenty-Seven

'Come on, it's this way,' urged Sybilla excitedly. She raced along the narrow passageway, tripping past the ruby glow, then down a series of steep steps stencilled with silver lettering, and into a dark panelled corridor.

Agatha had never been to this part of Winderling Spires in her life – she hadn't even known of its existence. But the old house was renowned for its spooky twists and mysterious turns, and there were many rooms she had never visited. The corridor was like a dingy rabbit warren full of nooks and dark crannies stretching out into the dead-flat darkness. Round the corner, a dim light showed up a number of painted doors.

'You've gone too far!' shouted Edwina. 'This door here has the sign upon it.'

She turned the handle and stepped into a tall brightly-mirrored closet.

'Have I, dear? Oh yes, here we are,' said Sybilla, cheerily poking her nose into the shimmering space.

The mirrored walls repeated their reflection into hundreds of images.

The sisters squeezed into the closet. Edwina closed the door and turned the key. Agatha could not imagine what would happen next.

'Close your eyes,' instructed Sybilla, 'then you won't feel too sick.'

'Sick?' Agatha cried. 'Whatever do you mean?'

The next moment Agatha felt her feet give way as the closet plummeted down through the Spires, hurtling past floor after floor, veering off to the left then to the right with an alarming rickety-rackety noise and a dreadful sea-sickening motion. Agatha felt terribly queasy, her stomach lurching nauseatingly from the rapid descent, and she clung onto Edwina to get her balance. Her sisters looked equally shaken from the see-sawing motion. Then suddenly the closet miraculously began to slow down and landed softly with a gentle thud.

'Goodness,' remarked Edwina, 'that was more unnerving than I remember.'

'It was desperately exciting!' cried Sybilla, staring bright-eyed all around her.

But Agatha's face had turned a sickly green colour.

'I told you to close your eyes, dear,' said Sybilla.

'Isn't there an easier way to get here?' asked Agatha, pinning up her tousled hair and following Edwina out of the door. 'Down a staircase, perhaps?' she added sarcastically.

Edwina turned to face her elder sister in dismay. 'The route to the spirit-room is different every time, identified by our only guide and the ruby glow,' she explained, looking askance at Agatha. 'You see, sister, you don't know as much as you always think you do.'

'So it would seem,' replied Agatha, looking warily about her. 'Where are we now?'

'Well, the thing is dear, that we don't really know. Somewhere in the heart of Winderling Spires, we think, where the spirit incantation has taken us,' said Sybilla.

'We are, Agatha, where we are meant to be,' Edwina added pompously.

The ruby glow continued bobbing along the skirting board, and the sisters followed the light until they reached an oval door that was surrounded by ornate raven carvings. In the centre was an iron door handle carved with the skull of a bird.

'Here we are, at the Dead Room,' explained Sybilla excitedly. 'Say the words, Edwina!'

Edwina Mouldson pulled herself up straight, closed her eyes and breathed deeply. She spoke the words in a shrill tone.

'*Trethorin nallin cempothra, trethorin nallin cempothra!*' she chanted, '*Trethorin nallin cempothra, trethorin nallin cempothra!*'

In the stillness of the corridor the dark presence whipped past them. Edwina knocked three times and the oval door creaked open.

'Step inside, sisters,' Edwina announced as she passed over the threshold.

She lit the four ruby wall lanterns and as they spluttered into life the room took shape. It was painted in black, lined with old cabinets of curiosity and several mirrors draped with black crepe. It was an odd-shaped room, like being inside a pea-pod.

'My tiny ones!' cried Sybilla excitedly, spying her collection of grave dolls. 'Oh, I have missed you, my darlings!'

Sybilla was the arch-seamstress of the Morrow clan and the keeper of the potent grave dolls. She hurried towards the glass cabinets and inspected the rows of cloth dolls sitting forlornly, tumbled against one another on the dusty shelves. She counted them carefully, each one representing one of the dead Morrow women.

'They're all here!' she shouted excitedly to Edwina.

Each grave doll was dressed in several pieces of embroidery, hand-sewn into dresses and skirts. They had stark embroidered faces, with painted crimson lips that had lost their sheen over the years and waxy, flat dead eyes. Each doll's hair had been cut from their namesake's head at the time of death and stitched into place in a raggedy fashion, sticking out at odd angles or hanging down over their faces.

'Here's Hortense – her dead face is so sweet,' crooned Sybilla, taking a brown-haired doll from the cupboard and clutching it to her chest. 'And here's Laurabelle, she's my favourite.'

Sybilla was in raptures reuniting with her dollies.

'Find the replica of Septimia Morrow and place her on

the table,' instructed Edwina. She began rummaging in the embroidery box and retrieved the sampler and a portrait of Septimia Morrow with long black hair. The portrait had a severe expression and Septimia was dressed in a dark silk gown. Edwina draped black lace over the portrait and placed it on the table.

'Here she is,' Sybilla purred. 'A little faded, aren't you?' She rested the floppy doll against the portrait of Septimia Morrow.

The doll's head drooped to one side and her black hair fell forward, partly obscuring the deadpan face.

Edwina placed Belladonna and Green Spotted Lepiota into a bowl and added a purple liquid from one of the cabinets brimming with bewitching potions. The concoction fizzled and bubbled, releasing its heady perfume into the pea-pod room. Then she lit the three black candles and placed them on the circular table.

'Septimia's stitching is one of the oldest samplers that we possess,' Sybilla purred, turning over the ancient embroidery in her hand.

Agatha watched as her sisters laid out the Dead Room to summon Septimia from the other side. Sybilla placed the letters of the alphabet around the edge of the table and an upside-down crystal glass in the centre. Edwina caught Agatha staring at her.

'This Dead Room contains the power to summon those who have departed from this life. There are many ways to summon the dead, but this is my method – we must each touch the portrait and then repeat the words embroidered on Septimia's sampler.'

'Does it hurt to be brought back from the dead?' asked Agatha.

It was always something she had wanted to ask her sister.

'How does she know, dear? She isn't dead,' said Sybilla, giggling.

Edwina shushed Sybilla, who had become giddy with excitement.

'I have been told it's a traumatic, harrowing experience,' replied Edwina.

'What do you feel when the spirit takes you over?' asked Agatha.

'It's like dreaming someone else's dreams,' answered Edwina. 'Septimia's spirit will take control of my voice and will relay her responses through me,' she answered, closing her eyes. 'She may also speak through the Ouija cards. Ready?'

They each touched the portrait and repeated the words on the sampler to summon Septimia's spirit from the other side:

Danitha mallecur na tresta,
Septimia transcenda, danitha mallecur na tresta,
Septimia transcenda.

Death defy and death decay, come to us we fear no ill, from o'er the grave, from the dank, dark tomb, tell me your secrets, bring them to me, I call upon you, Septimia Morrow, to span the death divide.

'Keep saying the words. I can't feel her presence yet,' Edwina spoke softly.

'Perhaps she's being awkward?' Agatha suggested.

Her sisters gave her an acid look.

'It's a harrowing process, being summoned from the other side,' answered Edwina.

Sybilla was impatient to begin.

'She's much too dead!' she shouted. 'She needs some encouragement!'

With a malicious glint in her eyes, she pulled one of her black-headed pins from her cardigan and stuck it into the replica of Septimia Morrow.

'That should wake her up!'

The doll stiffened, jerked her head upward and a wailing, ear-piercing cry filled the pea-pod room.

'Again, repeat the words, sisters!' cried Edwina. 'There is contact, she is out there! I can feel her spirit-presence vibrating across the great divide.'

Edwina closed her eyes and shivered, her face taking on a blue-white pallor.

The candles dimmed to a spluttering glow as the deadly draught of ghostliness seeped from every corner of the room, curling from behind the cupboards, snaking up through the floorboards and twirling round the pea-pod room like misty breath on a frosty morning. The atmosphere became deathly cold and dark. The sisters' breath turned to crystal-mist as they blew on their hands to ward off the icy blasts. Edwina reached for the glass – her fingers were white to the bone like frozen twigs.

'Keep her warm,' Agatha insisted, wrapping the shivering Edwina in a blanket. 'She must concentrate.'

In the misty darkness of the pea-pod room the three sisters hollered out their ancient chant to welcome the dead soul of Septimia Morrow, the seventh daughter of a seventh daughter, from across the veiled divide.

*

Septimia Morrow unfurled her ghostly form and moaned in her dead, dark slumber. She had been awoken by the sisters' urgent summons calling out to her across the milky white expanse: the veiled space that separated the living from the dead. The shrill voices hearkened to her and sliced through the darkness like a twirling arrow, lancing the astral plane at full speed and puncturing her sombre dead tranquillity. Soon she would be sucked from her dead-space into the frantic realm of the living, squeezing through the gap in the rippling veil and spinning out of control like loose thread on a spinning reel. Septimia ran her hand over the two sleeping forms next to her and bade them farewell. Siskin and a pale child raised their heavy heads and watched helplessly as Septimia cried out in pain.

Something sharp and stinging had pierced her body, spinning her round, stabbing like a dagger into her frail form, dragging her ephemeral being from its resting place and flinging her headlong towards the outer reaches of the shadow world. Septimia wailed like a banshee as her ghostly shadow-form shot past the shoals of watching apparitions. Septimia was being taken beyond the death-realm to meet the descendants of the Morrow clan.

*

'I'm so cold,' moaned Edwina, her grey face etched with the effort of dragging Septimia from her deathly rest.

'More blankets, sister,' insisted Sybilla, whose nose had turned quite blue.

Agatha leapt up and dragged a bundle of blankets from one of the cupboards, wrapping up their cold bodies. Edwina's eyes were jet-black and her face was frozen, white and trembling.

'The glass ...' muttered Edwina, placing a shaky finger on its rim.

The sisters followed suit and placed their icy fingers on the glass, peering nervously about the room for the first sighting of Septimia's ghoulish presence. The room was still and dark. Then a faint rapping noise came from under the table and the alphabet cards began to glow in the darkness like miniature beacons. Without warning, the crystal glass slipped across the table making a noise like broken nails down a blackboard.

'What's she saying, dear?' asked Sybilla, trying to keep her finger on the darting glass.

'She is spelling out her name,' answered Edwina, reading out the letters: 'S-E-P-T-I-M-I-A.'

'I can feel her frenzied spirit, like a coil twisting about my heart,' she moaned.

Her body twitched uncontrollably.

From the dark recesses of the pea-pod room, a creamy white ghostly mist began to fill the space, pervading the atmosphere with the foul stench of death. The glass whipped across the table and Edwina's eyes were glued to its darting movements.

'Septimia is in the room,' she whispered hoarsely.

She bent towards the table, removed her finger from the glass and emitted a growling sound from her throat.

'What's happening?' cried Agatha, but Sybilla was frozen in horror.

Edwina's face was distorted and her breath came in rasping bursts. She panted like a desperate animal, then jerked her head upwards. Her face was strained and harrowed by Septimia's sudden invasion. Edwina's eyes clouded over and she began to speak in a hollow disembodied sound. It was the voice of the long dead Septimia Morrow.

'*I have been sleeping and you have woken me,*' she moaned.

The sisters stared at each other in the darkness. Sybilla nudged Agatha into speech.

'We m-must break the pact of E-Edwyn Morrow,' Agatha stammered.

The ghostly grey mist whipped around the room. The presence of Septimia Morrow made the sisters tingle with dread.

'*Why do you summon me?*' the spirit asked, speaking through Edwina.

Edwina's face was blank. Her eyes were dead and black, staring straight ahead of her.

'To help us free our children from the Swarm, and bring them home to Winderling Spires,' answered Agatha.

'*That cursed pact for which I forfeited my life and that of dear Siskin's too …*' Edwina uttered chillingly in Septimia's voice.

The room again became silent and dark.

'Edwina, what's happening?' Sybilla pleaded.

Her sister's life seemed to have drained from her body. Her face was deathly pale and her eyes stared ahead like empty dark pools.

'What shall we do?' Sybilla cried. 'Edwina is fading from us.'

'We must wait until she returns,' replied Agatha. 'Septimia is communicating with her.'

The sisters waited until the candles glowed once more. Edwina's eyes snapped open, and her pale lips quivered as she spoke in Septimia's voice:

'*The pact can only be destroyed in the Witch's Tower.*' Edwina gripped the table. '*The pact is protected by a three-fold hexing spell – an old curse, one of the darkest spells of them all.*'

'What kind of spell is that?' asked Sybilla desperately.

'Shh, I don't know,' insisted Agatha, 'let her explain it to us.'

'*First, you must destroy a hair or lash, take a nail or a tooth, take skin or blood from she who now weaves her evil threads of bloody darkness.'*

Her dead black eyes moved like jelly.

'*Then fling the accursed pact into the witch's whirlpool,*' added Edwina, '*along with a piece of the witch.*'

The room grew brighter for a moment. Edwina gripped the table and she spoke the final element of the thrice-fold spell.

'*Finally, when the Morrow child renounces the blood-soaked words of Edwyn Morrow, then, and only then, will the dark pact be broken.*'

The room grew silent, a huge gulp of ghostliness shot from Edwina's mouth and she slumped forward across the table, knocking the candles and scattering black wax across the cards. The icy mist gathered in a cloud, then evaporated as Septimia's spirit was sucked back in a huge rush into the netherworld. The candlelight sprung forth from the lanterns, and the pea-pod room grew warm.

'That was terrifying,' said Agatha, shaking.

'Wake up, Edwina, she's gone now,' said Sybilla.

Edwina's face was streaked with tears and her hair stuck out at odd angles.

'What did Septimia say?' asked Edwina, lifting her ashen face.

'She told us a complicated hexing-riddle,' replied Sybilla. 'We must decipher it to break the pact, but it makes no sense to me, dear.'

'It is many riddles within a riddle,' added Agatha. 'She spoke of her untimely death and that of Siskin Morrow.'

Edwina sighed. 'They died trying to save the Morrow child and were murdered.'

'How do you know, dear?' asked Sybilla.

'When I was in the trance, she showed me terrible things,' Edwina added, her eyes staring blankly ahead of her.

'Where do we find "the blood-soaked words"?' asked Sybilla.

'What do we do with "the hair" or "the blood"? Whose "bloody darkness" did she speak of?' Agatha asked, desperately.

It was a dark conundrum.

'But even if we decipher it, we can't travel to Hellstone Tors,' added Sybilla.

'No, I'm afraid we'd never manage the caves,' Agatha replied, biting her lip, 'but somehow we have to get this information to Tallitha and the others.'

Edwina's face had contorted with the aftershock of keeping the dead spirit inside her. She gasped for breath and then spoke slowly.

'Someone has to steal a hair or nail from the witch in the dark tower. She's the one who now weaves her "bloody darkness". Then the Morrow child must renounce the "blood-soaked words" and the pact will be broken.'

'But how do you know all this?' asked Sybilla nervously, twiddling her pins

'Septimia took me to another place and showed me many things. Up into a dark tower room in Hellstone Tors, where I saw a veiled face. It was the face of the witch who now weaves her threads of bloody darkness. She's the one who keeps the pact in a wooden cabinet. We must get word to Tallitha about the three-fold hexing-spell – then she must arm herself with all the resources at her disposal to break the hideous Morrow pact.'

Twenty-Eight

'Be careful,' Cissie whispered, staring anxiously through the open trapdoor. 'You must be on the alert for those Shroves – they can be anywhere at any time.'

The Skinks slowly edged down the ladder and peered into the gloomy corridor.

'It's all clear, you can come down now,' answered Neeps, holding the ladder steady.

Cissie followed them down the ladder, closed the trapdoor behind her and joined the Skinks on the shadowy landing.

'I'll take a look down here,' said Neeps, trotting off down the corridor to explore the upper landings.

'Where are we?' asked Ruker, lighting a candle.

Before them a series of doorways lined the walls and a faint light trickled in from a window at the far end of the corridor. They were at the very top of Winderling Spires amongst the countless storerooms and attics.

'I don't know this part of the house at all,' answered Cissie, brushing herself down, 'but I can tell that we're in the old eaves.'

'But I thought you'd always lived here?' added Ruker, sounding mystified.

'Not when I was younger – besides, it's a rum old place with many floors and wings. I haven't been allowed to explore all over the old house. The Grand Morrow likes it that way.'

'Over here you two, I've found another step ladder,' called Neeps, disappearing through a hole in the floor.

He balanced halfway down the ladder and held out his hand for Cissie.

'Oh, I don't like this,' she wailed, staring down at the dizzying drop to the next floor. 'The ladder's a bit rickety.'

As she began climbing down the ladder juddered precariously to one side.

'Ruker!' she called out.

'I've got you,' the Skink replied, grabbing Cissie by the arm. 'Neeps – go and check out the next floor before we blunder into someone.'

Neeps nodded and scooted down the ladder, disappearing off into the distance.

Once Cissie had got her breath, she clambered back up to join Ruker. She sat on the floor with her legs dangling down, staring down at the shadowy floor in the distance.

'You seem a bit preoccupied,' said Ruker. 'Anything wrong?'

Cissie's usually cheerful face looked drawn and tired.

'I didn't sleep well. That Spider's Turret has a peculiar atmosphere, it was a mistake goin' there,' she said fretfully. 'If you must know, I-I felt haunted by the past,' she whispered sadly.

'What upset you?'

She hesitated. Ruker could tell something was amiss.

'Last night when you were asleep, I s-saw something,' she stammered. 'It brought back the past,' she sighed.

'What is it, Cissie? You look so sad.'

Cissie took a small red and blue boat from her pocket. She ran her finger over the hull and bit her lip.

'Many years ago I lost my child and this was his toy boat,' she sobbed 'I'm sorry – it's brought back so many upsetting memories.'

'I'm sorry, I didn't k-know you had a c-child,' Ruker stumbled over her words.

Cissie's eyes brimmed with tears and she hastily wiped them away. 'Please, let's forget about it, I shouldn't have said anything. I never speak of it any more, and there's nothing you can do about it.'

Ruker didn't know what else to say. The silence between them hung heavily.

'All clear,' called Neeps standing at the bottom of the ladder. 'There're a couple of empty rooms – seems no one has been inside them for years. We can hide out there until we decide what to do next.'

The eaves rooms in Winderling Spires occupied most of the

enormous attic space and some of the floor beneath. They had been left empty for many years apart from a few servants, who lived over the East Wing, and were now used as storage rooms, piled high with old furniture and boxes. Neeps had found an ideal spot behind a tallboy and a wardrobe in one of the rooms to plan their entry into the main house.

'Mary will have left the food in the Great Room by now,' said Cissie, pulling herself up on tiptoe to look out of the dirty window. 'Now then, I'm trying to work out where we are.' She rubbed one of the windowpanes and peered through the grime. 'There's the path down to the village,' she said, craning her neck to get a better view. 'So the front of the house is over there, which means – yes, I think we're somewhere above Asenathe's room.'

'Sure?' asked Neeps.

'Well, I'm not absolutely certain,' she added, 'but we should go down the next staircase. We can get our bearings when we finally locate the Great Room. Then when the light is fading we can start spying on the Shroves – see what the pesky creatures are plotting.'

'We should split up after we've eaten,' suggested Ruker, 'that way there's a better chance that the others can carry on if one of us gets spotted.'

'We should decide on a place to meet up,' added Neeps.

'We'll meet back in Asenathe's room,' suggested Cissie.

The others nodded.

'In that case I'd better explain the layout of this old house – at least the parts I know as best I can ...'

She began describing the layout of Winderling Spires, working her way through the floors she was familiar with: the colours of the passageways, the wings that were occupied, like the Crewel Tower, and the ones that were not, the spidery stairways and the raven-carved doorways, so that the Skinks could get a sense of the enormous house. It took a long time, and it tested Cissie's memory. By the end of it the Skinks were thoroughly bamboozled.

*

Finding the entrance to the Great Room was relatively easy once Cissie had crept down the next staircase, and was able to orientate herself in the big house. They ate the bread and cheese left by Mary, and dozed on the circular bed until the light began to fade. It had been decided that Cissie, who understood the house better than the Skinks, should take the main reception rooms and the servant's floors below stairs; Ruker and Neeps were to concentrate on the wings and the upper floors as best they could.

Cissie began rummaging in the back of the girls' wardrobes. She was determined to find a sensible outfit for the task ahead. She was looking for a pair of breeches, a jacket and a stout pair of boots that would enable her to get about the old house and hide more easily if necessary. At the back of Esmerelda's dressing room she found a selection of wigs and she chose a short brown hair piece to cover her own greying locks. She added make-up, touching up her cheeks with rouge, and donned a pair of strong leather gloves. Once she was satisfied with the result she went back into the Great Room and woke the Skinks.

'How do I look?' she asked twirling round.

'Different. Slimmer,' said Ruker. 'You should dress like that more often, much more practical.'

'We'll use the enclosed staircase,' she said, pointing to a small corridor. 'That's our safest bet.'

'After you,' Ruker replied with a dramatic flourish.

Cissie smiled, eased the small wooden door open and stepped down into the dusty silence.

*

Agatha Morrow's grand sitting room was bathed in the dying embers of the warm evening glow as Cissie stood in the outer recess of the Fedora Wing, pressing her ear against the door and listening intently for any noise. She had snuck down the last staircase and stolen along one of the smaller passageways at the back of the house, making sure her foray into one of the busiest thoroughfares in the Spires was timed to coincide with the servants' tea-time. By her reckoning they would all be down in the servant's quarters savouring Edna Dibbens's delicious meat pies and sweet pastries. The cook was a stickler for the servants' mealtimes – Cissie knew she could set her watch by her.

The sitting room was silent. Cissie braced herself, repeated an old Wycham saying for good luck, and carefully turned the door handle. It squeaked ever so slightly. Cautiously, she stepped into the familiar room and breathed in the scent of fresh lavender and beeswax. The shadowy old room was just as she remembered it, but over by the window the Grand Morrow's desk was strewn with books and there were reams of papers haphazardly scattered all over the floor.

'That's odd,' thought Cissie, picking her way through the mess and bending down to pick up one of Agatha Morrow's letters.

She knew she shouldn't, but she couldn't help herself. She began reading the letter. It wasn't terribly interesting – just a note to her sisters about household matters. Cissie had never seen the Grand Morrow's handwriting before, but the black spidery writing was oddly familiar, scratchy and faint. Cissie stared again at the italic script and a shiver passed over her. It was the same hand that had written the original dark incantations in the Spider's Turret.

'Oh my goodness,' she uttered under her breath. 'Then it is true, she is a witch!'

She crumpled the letter to her chest. She couldn't breathe. For a split-second Cissie stood frozen to the spot, unsure of what to do or where to go. The revelation had spooked her, making her think about Danny's disappearance once more. The rumours that had circulated around Wycham village, about the Morrow sisters and the sinister old house, were not nonsense after all. She had to get out of there and decide what to do next. In an instant she darted across the sitting room, sped through Agatha's interconnecting sewing rooms, past the looms and tailor's dummies, and out into the shadowy morning room which had dispensed with its usefulness for the day.

Breathless and scared, she crouched by the side of the oak dresser, tried to quieten her rapid heartbeat and waited, pondering all that she had discovered and what it could mean. It had troubled her. She decided to sit it out and wait until the servants had finished their chores. In time, the evening sun began to sink low in the sky and the shadows lengthened, creeping like spiky fingers across the wooden floor until the whole room was in the grip of a haunting darkness.

Cissie knew that the Shroves could be lurking anywhere in the big house. She decided that her next move would be to explore the servants' quarters using Mrs Armitage's entrance behind the old grandfather clock. *Tick-tock, tick-tock* – the old clock beat out its hollow rhythm as Cissie crept towards the door, hurriedly opened it and stepped into the cold darkness at the top of the narrow servants' staircase. She inched her way down the stone steps in the pitch-darkness, feeling the wall with her fingertips, then along the familiar passageway until she hovered nervously behind the kitchen door. Inside she could hear raised voices. It was the usual hubbub and chatter that took place in the busy kitchen. Oddly, they were still at their chores even though the hour was getting late. Cissie pressed her ear to the door and listened.

'Sophie! Where are you, you lazy good-for-nothing?' bellowed the flustered cook. 'Bring me the big pie dish from the larder and the damsons. Mary's just been down, and Lady hoity-toity Snowdroppe wants a hot plum pudding for her husband's supper at this god-forsaken hour!'

'Right you are,' shouted the kitchen maid, drying her hands and flying from the sink.

'As if he wasn't stout enough with all the food he puts away – and apparently Madam is off out!' moaned the cook, fed up with her lot.

Edna Dibbens was exhausted, desperate to go to her room, put her feet up and have a good strong cup of tea.

As the implication of the cook's words sank in, Cissie's stomach lurched. That evil Snowdroppe had returned to Winderling Spires! But how could it be? How had she done it?

'Barney!' hollered the irascible cook. 'Get off your fat bottom and start stoning those plums, do you hear me?'

A chair roughly scraped across the tiled floor, feet began racing this way and that and the poor kitchen boy swung into action.

Now Cissie was in a right pickle.

She would have to sit it out until they had stoned all the plums, weighed the flour, made the pastry and had the hot plum pudding ready for the Lady Snowdroppe's portly husband.

*

High up above her, as the night settled in good and dark, Ruker and Neeps realised that they were hopelessly lost in the terrible maze of a rambling house, wandering aimlessly back along a corridor that they had already been down.

'Which way now?' asked Neeps, scratching his head and staring down the dark corridor.

'It's a mystery. This house is a jumble of passageways – we keep going over the same ground,' she replied.

'What'll we do?'

Ruker stared over the high stairwell, at a loss to know where they were.

'I've had enough. Let's find Cissie,' she urged. 'We'll go down the next staircase we come to and head for the big kitchens.'

'But I thought we were meeting back in Asenathe's room?' replied Neeps. 'What if we stumble upon a Shrove or two?'

'That's the idea,' Ruker added, smirking viciously. She relished the thought of grabbing the weaselly Marlin by the throat and wringing his scrawny neck. 'Anyway, I have a funny feeling that something's not quite right.'

So the Skinks crept through the ghostly Spires, managing to avoid the Shroves and keeping out of sight of the yawning servants, who were heading wearily for their beds. As Ruker leapt into door recesses and hid behind corners to avoid the oncoming servants, she thought the adventure was reminiscent of outwitting the Black Hounds in Ragging Brows Forest – listening, hiding, waiting, then rushing for the next safe spot. Eventually, run ragged with anxiety, they located Mrs Armitage's doorway and came upon Cissie crouching in the darkness, her frightened eyes peering out at them, shining bright with fear

'Only us,' said Neeps hoarsely, winking at her terrified face.

'Oh my,' she sighed, grabbing at her heart. 'You didn't 'alf give me a jolt.'

'What's happening in there?' asked Ruker.

Cissie put her finger to her lips and pressed her ear to the door. The noises had finally ceased. She beckoned to the others and they crept into the kitchen, slunk over the tiled floor and hid by the side of the huge ovens. The cluster of long knives and the shelves of copper pots shone in the light that filtered in from the housekeeper's corridor. They crept underneath the big kitchen table and waited. It was then that they heard the noises: the sounds of scampering feet running across a stone floor, and the sound of someone dragging a heavy load. It was coming from the large pantry and the door was slightly ajar.

Cissie and the Skinks sat huddled together hidden by the folds of the tablecloth. They didn't dare move a muscle. Then Ruker mouthed the word 'Shroves' in the darkness. She could smell them – their greasy hair and their tainted, unwashed clothes wafting out across the kitchen. The cunning creatures were up to no good, ferreting about in the large pantry. Ruker tapped the side of her nose and then, like a stalking cat, she slipped from beneath the table and slunk on all fours towards to the pantry door. Inside, she heard the sound of a door creaking open and feet scampering away into the distance.

Ruker held her breath and peered through the crack in the door. Then she saw him. It was the back of a Shrove disappearing through the trapdoor and down under the house. *What are those creatures up to?* When she was certain the Shrove was out of hearing, she waved to the others who crept up next to her and together they snuck into the pantry.

'We have to follow that Shrove,' she whispered. 'He's just disappeared down there,' she explained, pointing down into the black hole.

'What, you want us to go down there?' asked Cissie, sounding horrified. She stared warily down into the unwelcoming bowels of the steely-black tunnel. 'I never knew such a dreadful place existed, and in our best pantry too!'

'Shh!' Ruker hissed. 'We came to spy on them, so let's do it.'

They edged down the stone steps one by one, into the earthy darkness of the Shroves' burrow, holding on to each other's trembling hands. The fetid smell of unwashed bodies and rank food filled the Shroves' lair spreading out before them with its piles of junk and mess.

'It's one of their stinking burrows,' Cissie whispered, tightening her grip on Ruker's hand.

'It don't half smell rotten,' said Neeps, wafting his hand in front of his face and peering into one of the smelly Shrove holes.

It was filled with bundles of rags and cluttered with stashes of old food.

Further down the tunnel a faint light glimmered in the distance. It flickered in and out of the dead flat darkness just enough for them to use the light as a guide. Ruker beckoned to the others and they sneaked out of the main burrow and stood at the entrance to the tunnel. It smelt of stale air and echoed with the drip-dropping of water. Then the sound of voices and the gabbling sound of Shroveling came back up the tunnel to greet them.

'Now, what are those mean critters up to?' asked Ruker, screwing up her eyes.

'Beats me. Where does this tunnel lead to?' asked Neeps.

'It's so cold and inhospitable,' Cissie added. 'Why would any soul want to come down 'ere?'

'Let's just go a little further to get a better view,' urged Ruker, taking Cissie's hand and leading her step by careful step into the darkness.

' B-But what if they catch us?' asked Cissie.

'We'll be as quiet as mice,' answered Neeps with his hand poised on his dagger.

The three wary explorers crept down the tunnel and snuck behind an outcrop of jagged black rock. There before them, they could see the hunched bodies of the Shroves against the glimmering light. Marlin and Florré hovered, conferring with one another and wringing their hands as Snowdroppe suddenly appeared from out of the darkness. She stood outlined by the light, shuddered violently in a most unsettling way and then disappeared like a lightning bolt down the tunnel and out of sight.

Cissie, Ruker and Neeps stood and gawped at each other.

'So that's how she does it,' whispered Cissie eventually, amazed at what she had just witnessed.

'She uses sorcery. She just vanished in a puff of smoke,' added Ruker.

'We mustn't linger,' replied Neeps, making his way back towards the burrow. 'Those Shroves will be back up here in an instant.'

'You're right, but we'll return when the coast is clear,' said Ruker following Neeps.

The others stared at her bright, excited face.

'What for?' asked Cissie, searching the Skink's expression for an explanation.

'Because, my friends, we're following that sorceress, the evil Snowdroppe, all the way into Hellstone Tors.'

Twenty-Nine

The fantastic tales that Suggit had told Tallitha went round and round in her head. She tried to make sense of it all. Witches! Grand Witches! Then there was the Larva Coven, the Morrow child, trickery, old battles and the enmity between Kastra Micrentor and Selvistra Loons. The evil Selvistra Loons! Tallitha was scared of her and what she might do to her, most of all.

'You still with us, miss?' Suggit asked. 'You look like you're miles away.'

'S-Sorry, I was daydreaming,' she replied.

'Anyways, buck up, 'cause we're 'ere,' he said.

Suggit beckoned to Tallitha to come closer as he parted the dense overhanging branches. Through the heavy foliage, the forest glade at Stankles Brow came into view.

'There's the cave – the Wild Imaginer will be waiting for you. Quillam will accompany you from here. I'd best be off.' He turned to the youth. 'You can find your own way back?'

Quillam nodded. 'Sure, I remember the way,' he replied. 'It's been a while since I was up here, so thanks for guiding us over the marshland.'

The two friends said farewell and hugged each other.

As Tallitha peered through the trees and Suggit slunk back through the forest, the wild dogs sensed their presence, lifted their ragged heads and began growling and pounding across the earth towards them. The Shroves, Sourdunk and Warbeetles, threw back the curtain that covered the cave and called for the dogs to round up Tallitha and Quillam. The animals snarled, raced towards the visitors and began nipping viciously at their heels.

'We've been waitin' on you two,' hollered Warbeetles, pushing Tallitha and Quillam through the woven curtain.

Tallitha stumbled inside and gasped. The cave was unlike any place that she had ever seen before. The walls were covered with fine tapestries, the furniture was dark and sumptuous, upholstered in deep green and purple velvets, and there was a huge fire roaring in the grate.

'Down those steps in front of you,' ordered Sourdunk, 'the Wild Imaginer is waitin'. You come with me,' she said, turning to Quillam.

Tallitha threw a nervous glance in the youth's direction.

'C-Can't he come with me?' she asked hesitantly.

'Nay, you 'ave to meet the Imaginer alone. Quillam may join you later,' replied Sourdunk. 'The steps go down over five floors.

At the bottom there's a passageway – walk to the end and the Wild Imaginer will be there to meet you.'

The interior of the Wild Imaginer's dwelling was a resplendent underground palace with a number of ornate doorways leading from the winding staircase. On each landing, paintings lined the walls and beautiful chandeliers lit the long corridors as Shroves scurried about fetching this and carrying that. Once she was certain the Shroves had gone about their business, Tallitha crouched in a small recess, reached inside her bag and began to inspect the less than fresh weryke-balm pie. It tasted disgusting but she ate every mouthful, hoping that the pie would ward off some of whatever nastiness awaited her.

At the bottom of the winding staircase, a grand hallway spread out in front of her festooned with mirrors and ornate cabinets. A red carpet lined the flagstones and at the end of the corridor, long crimson velvet curtains covered the entrance to an archway crowned with the heads of fine stone ravens. Tallitha hesitated as two skinny hands with the appearance of scrawny birds' feet hurriedly parted the curtains. The fingernails were blood-red. In an instant the curtains were flung apart and Queen Asphodel stood at the opening, her long bean-pole body covered in a black lace gown, with the wild ocelots roaming at her feet.

'You!' Tallitha cried. 'What are you doing here?'

'Why Tallitha, aren't you pleased to see me?' Asphodel replied, moving towards her. 'Come, we have much to do.'

' B-But … I don't understand, where's the Wild Imaginer?'

Asphodel threw back her head and peals of laughter filled the underground passageways.

'I am the Wild Imaginer, Tallitha. I am the one who is steeped in the bitter magic of the past, schooled in the arcane ways by the Grand Witches of the Larva Coven.'

Tallitha didn't want any part of Asphodel's dark magic. She hesitated and took a step backwards, but Asphodel came towards her, almost skimming across the red carpet.

'Don't try and resist me. The magic is there inside you, just waiting to be activated. You are a Morrow woman, after all.' She pressed one of her sharp nails into Tallitha's breastbone. 'Magic is in your bloodline,' she added, smiling wickedly.

The nail pierced her breast like a bee sting.

'Ouch, you're hurting me,' Tallitha cried and pulled away.

Asphodel pushed her face right next to Tallitha's.

'Come with me,' she demanded, clicking her fingers. 'The Black Pages only ignite what is already inside us, lying dormant.'

The Queen led Tallitha into a beautiful room the size of the Great Room at Winderling Spires. Squawking birds of prey were tethered to their poles and caged on tall plinths, and the wild ocelots scurried about Asphodel's feet wherever she went, watching the Queen's every move. Tallitha could see that the animals and the birds obeyed the Queen. Asphodel murmured to the wildcats and they yawned and stretched out by her feet. Velvets and silk tapestries covered the walls of the cave and a clutch of pure golden stalagmites and stalactites covered with rubies, emeralds and sapphires stood behind the Queen's throne.

Asphodel caught Tallitha staring at the precious stones.

'These beauties are but mere trinkets. My real treasures are stored elsewhere, deep where no one can steal them from me,' she hissed.

The sweet smell of vanilla and burnt orange wafted across the room as Asphodel walked past Tallitha, clicked her fingers and pointed towards an ebony partition.

'Your little friend is here,' she announced.

Then Tallitha saw him. He turned to greet her, his face blushing slightly and his hair falling into his eyes. It was Benedict.

'Get away from me!' Tallitha cried. 'I can't bear to look at you!'

Benedict coloured and pouted sullenly at his mother.

'I did say she might be a little cross,' the Queen replied, turning to her son. 'Stay with us, Benedict, and observe as Tallitha attempts her next challenge.'

Tallitha couldn't bear to look at her betrayer.

'But first a little test of my own.'

The Queen spoke in Ennish: '*Calindra sestra, melanthan, calindra sestra, melanthan.*' I am looking deep inside you, Tallitha. You cannot resist me – tell me, what is in your heart?'

Tallitha could feel the weryke-balm pie in her stomach, churning and curdling, warding off the spell of the enchantress. Tallitha spoke haltingly but firm:

'I am but a girl from Wycham Elva, come here at the Swarm's request.'

'Then you are ready,' the Queen replied, satisfied by Tallitha's answer.

She beckoned to Benedict to come closer.

'Very well,' said Asphodel, 'we shall begin with the art of mind reading.'

The Queen clicked her fingers and Sourdunk appeared from the back of the room.

'Bring Quillam to me,' she demanded and the Shrove scuttled off. 'Take The Black Pages and turn to the third chapter,' she said, handing the book to Tallitha.

'B-But how did you get this book?' asked Tallitha, her eyes scanning the Queen's severe face.

The Queen threw her a dismissive look.

'The Black Pages are mine, lent only to your governess for the first of our tests.'

The Queen hovered close to Tallitha, and a smell of pungent fruit filled the air.

'Remember, you will never be able to read the mind of one of the Swarm's unless they allow you to, and it will take practice to read the mind of someone who isn't present, so we will begin with the simplest level – Quillam is a good subject,' she announced regarding the youth as he entered the room. 'Focus on the colours, Tallitha, then one colour will became more dominant than all the rest.'

Tallitha stared at the fabulous colours as they seeped from the pages, spreading like waves across the room. The wonderful blues, deep meridian, cobalt and azure swept across the floor in rivers of bright blue liquid, erupting with starbursts of colour.

'Say the words from the chapter, Tallitha,' the Queen ordered.

Tallitha looked down at The Black Pages and read the Ennish words. All the while she could feel the weryke-balm pie like a lead weight in her stomach warding off any attempt by the dark sorcery to completely overpower her.

'*Neamptha la nerva sempte mellefitious,*' Tallitha repeated, closing her eyes. '*Neamptha la nerva sempte mellefitious.*'

Quillam stood before her, his ochre-coloured eyes shining.

'Tell me, what is in Quillam's mind?' demanded Asphodel. She turned to the youth. 'You must think of something that Tallitha doesn't know.'

As the fabulous blue colours and the Ennish words from The Black Pages began to take their hold, Tallitha had the curious sensation that she had experienced the feeling of mind-reading before. It was akin to the heightened awareness she sometimes had with Cissie and her brother when she felt she knew what they were thinking. In the past she had attributed this to the fact that she knew them both so well, but now she realised it was a special gift.

'Concentrate and say the words,' commanded Asphodel.

Tallitha repeated the phrase: '*Neamptha la nerva sempte mellefitious.*' She stared into Quillam's stunningly yellow-flecked eyes and then *whoosh!* – she was slipping away, like the sensation of diving into a deep pool. She was swimming, dipping down, diving and gliding underwater, delving into the crevasses of his mind and coming to the surface with glimmers of his thoughts. Tallitha spoke Quillam's thoughts out loud.

'*Alyss Trume, Mattie Burn, Elsie Wood and Grace Eversedge*

are the women trapped in the soul-catcher in the Neopholytite's tower ...'

'Enough!' shouted the Queen. 'Those names are not be spoken here!' She flashed her coal-black eyes at the youth.

'*Some of these lost souls were captured by the Dooerlins,*' was the last of Quillam's thoughts Tallitha was able to read, but this time she didn't speak the words out loud.

A crooked smile played across Quillam's lips – enough to let Tallitha know he hated Queen Asphodel as much as she did.

Suddenly Tallitha felt the diving sensation take hold of her again for a fleeting moment. More thoughts came to her mind, but they weren't Quillam's – Benedict was letting her read his mind!

'*Release me from the Queen! I'm sorry for betraying you, Tallitha, I had no choice. I knew no better then, please forgive me. I'll do whatever you ask.*'

Tallitha's eyes flickered for a moment over Benedict's sorrowful face. She eyed the boy with suspicion and yet he seemed so lost and vulnerable. He blushed slightly and Tallitha turned away. She couldn't think about Benedict now. How could she ever trust him again?

'Now on to the final test: communing with the dead-ones,' the Queen announced.

She clicked her fingers and Sourdunk appeared.

'Have you prepared the Dead Room?' she asked.

'Yes, m'Lady, 'tis all ready for you.'

The Shrove led the way upstairs to a mysterious darkened room laid out for the séance.

'Sit there,' the Queen instructed Tallitha. 'Benedict and Quillam, you sit on either side of her.'

The table was covered with letters so that the spirits could speak using the glass as it spun round the table. In the centre there was a pile of bloodstones and the carved ebony head of a raven that Tallitha coveted. She ran her fingers over the bird's skull.

'These artefacts are the insignia of the Swarm,' said Asphodel. 'They will help you locate our dead-ones. Reach out and find Tollister and Brimwell Morrow, the great-great grandparents of the Thane.'

Tallitha remembered their creepy portraits hanging in Hellstone Tors.

'Say the litany of the dead after me: *Death defy and death decay, come to us we fear no ill, from o'er the grave, from the dank, dark tomb, tell me your secrets, bring them alive, I call upon you, Tollister and Brimwell Morrow, to span the death divide.*'

Tallitha nervously repeated the words of the death litany.

The room grew colder and wisps of milky white mist curled across the floor.

Tallitha felt an ice-cold hand brush against her face and suddenly the glass started to spin across the table ...

*

'Quillam, wake up,' Tallitha whispered, shaking the youth.

He stirred and propped himself up on his arm.

'What now?' he yawned.

'You fell asleep. That miserable Shrove, Sourdunk, has gone.' Tallitha's face looked drawn and tired. 'You have to get me out of here. I'm not doing any more of those dreadful tests – I've learnt all I need to know from that heartless Queen.'

Quillam could see that the girl was determined – she was plucky and she had spirit.

'Where do you want to go?' he asked, searching her face.

Tallitha sat in bed, hugging her knees. Her eyes were shining with excitement.

'Back home to Winderling Spires to see my Great Aunt Agatha – I'm sure those sisters know more than they ever let on. Now they must tell me how to break the pact.'

'That will spoil the Swarm's dark plan,' he mused. 'They'll be furious. They'll have to get someone else to take your place as the thirteenth member.'

'I don't care about that,' Tallitha said, frowning.

'But haven't you forgotten about your brother and Esmerelda?'

Tallitha twisted her hair in and out of her fingers.

'I-I've spoken to them already. They know that I intend to escape.'

'They may pick Tyaas instead of you,' he added.

Tallitha bit her lip. That thought had already occurred to her.

'It's a risk, of course, but I'll return to Hellstone before the ceremony happens and pretend to hand myself over. By then I will have discovered how to break the pact,' she answered determinedly.

Quillam gave her a curious look.

'If you're sure, I will take you. But I want you to promise me something first …'

She smiled. 'That I'll find out where you're from – I promise I'll do whatever I can to help you,' she replied softly in the darkness. 'But the only way home is back through the caves, through the territories of the Groats and the hideous Murk Mowl,' she said apprehensively. 'We'll have to go past Old Yawning Edges and Sour Pits.'

'Sounds like an adventure to me,' he replied.

'There's one more thing,' she whispered. 'I have to find the Grand Witch Kastra. She's the one who took the Morrow child.'

'Then first we must head out into Breedoor for the Northern Wolds.'

'Perhaps Kastra will know a different underground route to Winderling Spires,' Tallitha added.

'From what I hear, she knows all about the land of Breedoor and its mysteries,' he replied.

'But how will we get out of here?' Tallitha asked.

'Leave that to me,' Quillam replied mysteriously.

'But what about those hounds?'

'We're not going that way,' he replied, packing his belongings. 'Ready?' he asked.

'What? Do you mean right now?'

'No time like the present,' the youth replied. 'Let's get out of this hellhole. It will be a pleasure to lead Queen Asphodel on a right merry dance.'

'But which way are we going?' she asked, her eyes widening in the candlelight.

'I know a way, never fear. It will bring us out way beyond Stankles Brow to the edge of the Northern Wolds.'

'You've thought of everything,' she replied, grinning at him.

'You forget, I've been here before, and I always make it my business to find an escape route. I dislike Queen Asphodel as much as you do.'

'Won't the route be guarded?' she asked.

'It's much too dangerous, too steep and full of potholes. They wouldn't imagine we'd try and escape that way. Besides, I slipped a sleeping potion into the guard's food earlier,' he said, listening at the door.

Tallitha smiled at Quillam's ingenuity.

'How did you know I'd want to escape – and tonight?'

'I've known from the first time I met you. You told me, if you remember. So I decided to be ready the moment you gave me the word. Somehow I thought it would be soon.'

'There's one more thing,' Tallitha took hold of Quillam's arm. 'You must help me get rid of the Morrow stain.'

'Kastra will know what to do – after all, she's one of the Grand Witches,' he answered.

'How many Grand Witches are there?' she asked, intrigued by the mysterious Larva Coven.

'There are many Grand Witches,' he replied mysteriously. 'Kastra Micrentor, Selvistra Loons, Alwynne Moor and Deddendra Close are the witches I've heard tell of – descendants of the infamous coven.'

'Are they so terribly wicked and dangerous?' Tallitha asked.

'You must be on your guard with them all, but Selvistra and Deddendra are the worst – vengeful and mean.'

Tallitha bit her lip. She didn't like the sound of either of them.

'Come on,' he urged.

Tallitha picked up her bag and followed Quillam out of their room and past the snoring Groat. They crept down a long cold passageway, turned the next corner and Quillam lifted the edge of a heavy wall tapestry to reveal a layer of shiny bare rock.

'Through here,' he whispered.

He squeezed his body between two abutting black rocks, holding out his hand to guide Tallitha through the slanted gap. In the dark space Quillam lit the lantern, secured a rope at the head of the shaft and shone the light down into the deep, dark pothole so Tallitha could memorise the twists and turns of the journey ahead of them.

'It's a long way down into the Bitter Caves,' he warned. 'Watch out for the jagged rocks. When you feel them, we'll be making a sharp turn to the right and through a winding tunnel.'

He doused the light and they began their long, tricky descent into the pitch-black darkness. Icy water dripped through the rock fissures and trickled over their fingers as they clambered down the coal-black shaft. Tallitha recognised the familiar sharp bitter smell of the dank caves hitting the back of her throat in icy gulps. In that instant she felt a sudden tingle inside her as the thrill of adventure stirred in her stomach. This was it! She was on the move again. She had come so far, and yet there was still so much to do. She had to find the Grand Witch Kastra, discover the secrets of the Morrow pact from the old sisters and, against all the odds, defy the Swarm and break the hideous pact once and for all. But for now she felt exhilarated and alive. She was escaping into a new and exciting world, further into the mysterious lands of Breedoor, into the vast wastes of the Northern Wolds, and perhaps even beyond.

Who could tell what fantastic adventures lay ahead of her? She revelled in the thought of the secrets that were still to unfold.

'We're here,' Quillam called out, breaking her train of thought.

As he approached the deep winding tunnel Quillam lit the lantern, and as the candlelight flickered and struck the dark, grey-green walls Tallitha smiled excitedly to herself.

In that moment, she realised she couldn't wait for the next stage of her adventure to begin. She was back in the labyrinth of twisting tunnels that lay buried beneath the Out-Of-The-Way Mountains, on her way to certain danger, magic and freedom.

'Wait for me,' she called eagerly to Quillam and bravely clambered down into the deepening darkness.

Thirty

Unbeknown to Tallitha and Quillam, they were heading into an even more treacherous netherworld: a subterranean maze of intricate layers, the next more dangerous than the last. The perilous caves under Stankles Brow were a muddle of slippery tunnels and narrow potholes laid with Queen Asphodel's tricks and traps. Snared with cobwebs, trailing from the rocks like feelers in the dark, the webs quivered as Tallitha brushed past them on her tricky descent and as the trembling motion whipped through the tunnels, moving from web to shimmering web they eventually reached Asphodel's bedchamber and shuddered across the hangings on her four-poster bed.

The Queen rolled over in her sleep and stirred from a troubled dream, awoken by the vibrations. Immediately her black eyes shot open and she sat bolt upright.

'Sourdunk!' she hollered, leaping from her bed.

The Shrove ambled into the Queen's bedchamber from the nooky recess outside her door.

'What's amiss, m'Lady?' she replied.

'The girl's escaped! Call the guards! Benedict!' She hollered. 'Wake up and help us catch them!' she shouted, peering into the boy's chamber.

Benedict awoke and reluctantly joined his mother.

'Find out which tunnel they have taken from Stankles Brow!' she shouted, grabbing her robe. 'The foolish girl has gone down into the Bitter Caves with that interloper Quillam. Do you hear me, Benedict!' she yelled.

'Yes Mother, I'm on my way now,' he answered meekly.

'We must catch her before she goes down into the Leaden Riddles – my magic is useless there. Get word to the Murk Mowl – they must search every crevasse and bring her back. But remember,' she added, 'Tallitha must remain unharmed, we have plans for that girl in the Swarm, but as to the betrayer, Quillam – kill him!' she raged, her eyes shining with hatred.

*

As Tallitha alighted onto the damp floor of the deep winding tunnel, the Murk Mowl were already on the move, tracking them through the twists and turns of the Bitter Caves.

Their oily, translucent skin, marked with battle scars, glistened menacingly in the torchlight, and their hideous bizarre metal piercings glinted and jangled as they marched. Their bug-eyes bulged with bloodlust as they sniffed the sweet scent of the girl. They drooled at the thought of the tender youth – his flesh soon to be encased in a Murk turrow.

In the damp, dank passageways, many pairs of hideous Murkish eyes seared through the pitch-black tunnels, searching the Bitter Caves for the youth and the girl, savouring the moment when they would catch them.

'Quillam,' Tallitha whispered urgently, moving closer to him. 'Did you hear that noise?'

She pointed down the deep tunnel winding far away into the dripping darkness.

The youth raised the lantern and peered into the murky passageway. Water seeped down the green encrusted surfaces as though the walls were weeping blackened tears.

'Yes,' he murmured warily, 'but didn't the noise come from over there?' he replied, pointing in the opposite direction.

The desperation in his voice made Tallitha sick with fear.

'I don't know where it came from now,' she whispered. 'These caves are full of terrifying echoes and unearthly moans ...'

Their lantern shone across the tunnel to a mass of boulders slaked in mud and grime where rivulets ran between the rocks. 'What's down there?' she asked.

The distant sound of water gushed away beneath them.

'The Leaden Riddles,' Quillam answered gravely. 'A honeycomb of underground streams and shafts –'

His voice suddenly trailed away as the sound of pounding feet reverberated through the caverns.

Tallitha reared back and put her hand over her mouth – the lingering stench of stale sweat and stinking Murkish breath wafted towards them.

They stared at each other, their eyes shining with fear.

'It's the Murk Mowl,' she whispered, the words catching in her throat. 'They're after us!'

'Come on!' shouted Quillam. 'We have to get out of here!'

He grabbed her hand and pulled her after him round the next bend in the tunnel.

The meagre light from their lantern provided only scant visibility. They stumbled onwards, lost in the labyrinth, feeling their way, running their hands along the cave walls oozing with water and tripping over the protruding rocks. Then they heard the clatter of swords against the rock face and the gut-curdling screams of the Mowl in full battle mode.

Suddenly, in the distance, a light flashed in the pitch-blackness.

'Look!' cried Tallitha, coming to a complete halt.

Then there was another flash, and then another!

They were surrounded. They inched backwards, away from the bouncing beams of light as the shadows lengthened and the flickering from the Murk Mowls' torches leapt like twisted fingers along the cave walls, getting ever closer.

Tallitha's heart was pounding.

'What'll we do now?' she asked.

But Quillam was transfixed, frozen to the spot. He seemed to be waiting for the moment when the hideous pack would catch them, their translucent clawing hands reaching out and seizing them in the darkness. *What is he waiting for?* Tallitha thought. She could bear it no longer. The Mowl were getting closer … they had to do something, and quickly.

'Maybe there's a way out,' she said urgently, holding the lantern and peering down into a dark fissure. 'There's a stream down there. We could follow its path.'

She beckoned to Quillam to take a look.

'Not into the Leaden Riddles,' he replied. 'It's too risky, we don't know what's down there.'

Quillam knew if they caught him, he wouldn't survive. The Queen would have given the order for him to be killed. But the alternative was a terrible gamble. The Leaden Riddles were treacherous, the habitat of many a strange creature. He peered anxiously into the coal-black fissure – if he stayed and fought, at least Tallitha would survive, but down there they both might perish.

The light from the Mowls' torches flamed and guttered behind them, gleaming along the green and red streaks in the tunnel walls.

Quillam turned to face their hunters.

The Murk Mowl shrieked behind them, clattering their swords.

There was nothing for it.

'We've no choice! I won't let the Murk Mowl capture me and kill you!' she said forcefully.

'Not down there!' he shouted.

But it was too late. Tallitha darted through the gap, seizing Quillam's arm and dragging him after her. For a second the lantern shone across the deep cavern where a waterfall plummeted into a turbulent stream.

'Jump!' Tallitha shouted, dropping the lantern.

Quillam grabbed Tallitha's hand and they leapt from the ledge into the rushing waters.

Down and down they tumbled into the realm of absolute darkness and into the world of the Leaden Riddles.

Tallitha screamed, then the breath went out of her as the force of the waterfall overpowered her, submerging her in a deluge of raging water. They were cascading down a sheer rock face covered in water.

Quillam landed awkwardly, the impact knocking the breath out him and spinning him downwards. Then he was sliding and tumbling in and out of the raging waterfall, following Tallitha's zigzagging path. He struck a boulder that knocked him sideways, back into the torrents and bumping into Tallitha who spun in the opposite direction.

'Quillam!' she screamed, before tumbling into the roaring stream.

Then Quillam was falling head over heels, down into the watery depths.

The force pulled him down into the rapids – hurtling him along, bumping him into rocks, and bouncing off the side of the cavern wall. He struggled to right himself and lunged out for the rock face speeding past him, before clinging onto a boulder at the water's edge. He burst up to the surface and took a huge gulp of air. The pain smashed through his lungs.

'Tallitha!' he shouted, searching madly for her.

There was a moment or two of silence – then she bobbed up next to him.

'I'm here!' she replied, grabbing at him and spluttering.

They clung to the boulders, gasping for air, bedraggled and desperate to fill their lungs as the water raced past them. Somehow they had made it to the bottom of the shaft, bruised and battered but without serious injury. Quillam hauled himself onto a ledge and pulled Tallitha out after him.

'That was the craziest thing you've ever done!' he hissed, breathless, dripping wet.

She ran her fingers through her soaking wet hair.

'We're alive aren't we? I don't think the Murk Mowl will follow us down here,' she said, hesitating, listening for the sounds of their Murkish screams. But all she heard was the fast flowing water. 'We both know they would have murdered you if we'd stayed.'

'I know but –'

'I couldn't leave you,' she whispered into the insidious darkness.

She could hear Quillam's urgent breathing.

'Okay, what'll we do now?' he asked. 'Any more bright ideas?'

She could tell he was annoyed at her.

'Follow the stream – perhaps it will lead us out of here –'

He cut her dead. 'Or take us further into the Leaden Riddles, to be lost forever.' She could almost hear his brain whirring, desperate to find an escape route. 'Okay, you win, let's follow the stream and see where it takes us.'

Quillam checked that his dagger was still in its sheath.

The water gushed below their feet, swirling round the snake-like bends of the stream, rushing downwards, echoing into the distance.

Just above the roar Tallitha heard a different sound – a distant cry, and then a screech.

'What sort of creatures live down here?' she asked nervously, keeping tight hold of Quillam and following him along the edge of the stream.

'Nasty creatures that thrive in the wet and the dark, and blindworms that won't hurt us – I'll catch some later.'

Eurgh! thought Tallitha, shivering and edging forward – *blindworms for breakfast!* Perhaps it had been rash to come into this dark place, but she hadn't thought about the consequences. She had jumped on the spur of the moment.

Then came the sound of a rapid whirring motion overhead.

'What's that?' she murmured.

Quillam listened intently. It was the sound of wings, soaring and whooshing through the air, dipping and pitching through the hollow caves and skimming above the turbulent stream.

He pulled her to him.

'Vault Glimmers! Quick!' he shouted, slipping back into the stream and dragging Tallitha down with him.

'But what are they?' she squealed.

Rising panic started in the pit of her stomach.

'Bat-like creatures – blood suckers – now dive!'

Tallitha ducked as a barrage of wings soared above her. One of the creatures glanced her a nasty blow across the side of her head, shrieking and flapping its wings, clawing and biting. Tallitha felt its sharp teeth puncture her scalp as she plunged under the water. The cold took her breath away. She could feel a sharp sting from the creature's lancing blow as she came up for air, gasping and struggling for breath. The clamour of Vault Glimmers spied her in the darkness, their blood-red eyes locating their prey and bombarding her from on high, shrieking and clawing.

They bit and scratched like vultures, their talons slashing.

'Quillam! Quillam!' she screamed, flailing her arms at the Glimmers, trying to push them away.

'Dive!' he shouted, stabbing at the swooping creatures with his dagger.

But it was pitch-black, impossible to take aim and the torrential stream kept dragging him under.

Tallitha took a huge gulp of air as the Vault Glimmers attacked her again, biting her with their pointed teeth, slashing her arms and head with their vicious claws. Blood poured from her wounds as she dived down into the surging water, desperately searching for Quillam, going round and round in circles. But she had lost all sense of direction in the dark and the cold. She couldn't find him in the swirling mass of swell and bubbles.

Tallitha could taste her own blood in the water. She felt sick and shaky from the shock of the assault. She was beginning to lose consciousness.

Quillam swam round and round, diving intermittently, desperately trying to find Tallitha under the water, down to where the cold eddies swam like eels on the bed of the stream.

But it was no use. He darted back to the surface.

'Tallitha! Tallitha! Where are you?' he shouted desperately.

But only the sound of his voice echoed back to him in the darkness.

There was no response.

*

Tallitha's strength was ebbing away. She rolled over in the water, trying to keep afloat. The current had her in its grasp. It was dragging her away, further downstream, round the hairpin bends, her hair floating behind her like a mess of tangled weeds.

'Quillam,' she called out but her voice had no strength above the noise of the rushing water.

*

Quillam could hear the Vault Glimmers screeching in the distance. He swam downstream calling out her name, again and again, but still there was no response.

'Tallitha! Tallitha!' he cried.

But there was only the noise of the raging water.

Tallitha had completely disappeared.

It was as if the Leaden Riddles had completely swallowed her up.